Robyn Lee Burrows was born and raised in the north-western New South Wales township of Bourke, but has since settled in the Gold Coast hinterland. She is a Scorpio, born with the moon in Pisces, and describes herself as independent, emotional and creative. She is married with three sons, two of whom refuse to grow up and leave home, and custodian of two cats and a dog. In her meagre portion of spare time, she enjoys watching good movies, dining out and, naturally, reading. *West of the Blue Gums* is her sixth novel, and ninth book. To find out more about Robyn and her books, feel free to visit her website at www.robynleeburrows.com.

WITHDRAWN
FROM COLLECTION
V2

AUG 1 4 2004

04 06 1 ic

WEST OF THE BLUE GUMS

ALSO BY ROBYN LEE BURROWS

Dairies & Daydreams — The Mudgeeraba Story

Bush Schools & Golden Rules

When Hope is Strong

Where the River Ends

Henry Lawson: A Stranger on the Darling

Song From the Heart

When Wattles Bloom

Love, Obsession, Secrets & Lies (co-contributor)

Tea-tree Passage

ROBYN LEE BURROWS

WEST OF THE BLUE GUMS

HarperCollins*Publishers*

Extract from 'Five Bells' by Kenneth Slessor from his
Selected Poems with permission of the publisher.

HarperCollins*Publishers*

First published in Australia in 2004
by HarperCollins*Publishers* Pty Limited
ABN 36 009 913 517
A member of the HarperCollins*Publishers* (Australia) Pty Limited Group
www.harpercollins.com.au

Copyright © Robyn Lee Burrows 2004

The right of Robyn Lee Burrows to be identified as the moral rights
author of this work has been asserted by her in accordance with
the *Copyright Amendment (Moral Rights) Act 2000* (Cth).

This book is copyright.
Apart from any fair dealing for the purposes of private study, research,
criticism or review, as permitted under the Copyright Act, no part may
be reproduced by any process without written permission.
Inquiries should be addressed to the publishers.

HarperCollins*Publishers*
25 Ryde Road, Pymble, Sydney NSW 2073, Australia
31 View Road, Glenfield, Auckland 10, New Zealand
77–85 Fulham Palace Road, London W6 8JB, United Kingdom
2 Bloor Street East, 20th floor, Toronto, Ontario M4W 1A8, Canada
10 East 53rd Street, New York NY 10022, USA

National Library of Australia Cataloguing-in-Publication data:

Burrows, Robyn, 1953– .
    West of the blue gums.
    ISBN 0 7322 6881 8.
    I. Title.
A823.3

Cover images: top Getty Images; bottom Photolibrary.com
Cover design by Christabella Designs
Typeset in 10.5/13 Sabon by HarperCollins Design Studio
Printed and bound in Australia by Griffin Press on 50gsm Bulky News

5 4 3 2 1   04 05 06 07

*In memory of Moore McLaughlin, brother of
my great-grandfather. Nineteen-year-old
Moore was shepherding sheep on the bank
of Comet Creek (in the foothills of the
Carnarvon Range, near Springsure) when he
was murdered in 1862 during the aftermath
of the Cullin-la-Ringo massacres.*

AUG 1 4 2004

Song of the River
Colleen McLaughlin

I am swinging to the northward, I am curving to the
    south
I am spreading, I am splitting, running free,
I am creeping past the sandhills, going steady as the
    land fills
For all my channels lie ahead of me.

Through the grasslands and the mulga, past the
    rocks, eroded bare,
I will cover up the secrets buried deep.
For if man thinks he can beat me, I will tell him come
    and meet me,
But where and when and how my signs
    I'll keep.

Because I am Diamantina, and I rule the great
    outback,
I'm its heartbeat, I'm its keeper, it's my land.
With my channels full and flowing, and the grasses
    green and growing,
I'm the power that man must learn to understand.

I will take your heart and hold it, I will commandeer
     your soul,
If you listen to my voice and stand up tall.
If your ears can hear me singing, and your answer
     comes back ringing,
Then I'll know that you have recognised
     my call.

For this is my direction, as the sovereign of this land,
I will whisper to you the secrets of its ways.
But for you to know and share it, do not take its
     heart and tear it,
For I'll tell you now, the loser always pays.

For I am Diamantina, and the sandhills and the
     plains,
Need my water as their lifeblood — it's my land.
With my channels full and flowing, and the grasses
     green and growing,
I'm the power that you must learn to understand.

CONTENTS

PART ONE

Moving On

CHAPTER 1

'Jess, I'm home.'

The front door slams and I hear Brad's voice weaving towards me down the hallway. I shake my head, dragging myself from the past — from the might-have-beens — back to the now. A breeze sweeps past from the uncurtained window, carrying the sound of Brad's voice away yet bringing with it the sudden sweet scent of roses. Outside I can hear the late-afternoon warble of a magpie.

I'm in the kitchen at the far end of the house, staring out into the yard. For one awful moment I cannot remember how long I've been standing here, or what has brought me to this room. A drink of water perhaps, or to begin the rudimentary preparations for our meal? But although the sun, I note dully, is now low in the sky, the hands of the clock are not yet pointing to the usual time of Brad's homecoming.

Brad — my husband of four years and lover of eleven — is thirty-one, two years older than me. He's an aquatic biologist, working for the EPA — Environmental Protection Agency — in Brisbane. He studies inland water. Creeks and rivers, swamps and lagoons: any place where water lies and attracts other living things.

Over the years I've become used to the specimens and water samples he brings home, and the windowsill over the kitchen sink is usually littered with the debris of his work. The clean-freak part of me has learned to ignore this, to close my eyes to the assortment of jars and bottles, pipettes and labels. I've also learned not to examine too closely the contents of those jars and bottles — snails, shrimps, bugs or tiny fish — suspended in the regulation alcohol–water mix.

As though on cue, Brad comes up behind me now and wraps his arms around my chest. For one brief moment I stiffen, fighting against his embrace. Then I lean backwards into him. He smells faintly of aftershave and preserving fluid.

'Jess,' he begins tentatively.

I pull away from his grasp. There is a tone to his voice that demands attention.

'What's wrong?'

'Nothing! Everything's coming together for a change.'

He sweeps his hands wide, as though encompassing the whole room. A shock of fair hair flops against his forehead and I fight back an impulse to brush it away. The old Jess would have done that, unconsciously, but I find I'm not the same person I was a year ago.

'Remember the grant I applied for?' Brad is saying. 'The field trip for the bio assessment of the Diamantina River?'

Cautiously: 'Yes.'

'Well, I've been given funding for six weeks.'

Six weeks, I think. He'll be away for six weeks. Forty-two days of being by myself, thinking my endless thoughts and rehashing all those jagged memories I surely must have worn smooth by now. Forty-two sleepless nights.

'Starting ...?' I thrust my thoughts back to the conversation, vainly trying to insert enthusiasm into my voice to match his obvious excitement. But the question dies away, unfinished.

'The wet season isn't far away, another three months or so. So if I don't run with this now, it'll be ages before I get the chance to get up there.'

I stare at him, trying to make sense of the words, but they tumble together in my mind. Mentally I tally the days. *Now*. He wants to go *now*. The thought of him not being here, especially at this time of the year, is abhorrent. It means he'll be away ...

'Come with me.'

My head snaps upwards. He says the words earnestly, and the random thought in my mind is that we might be any ordinary couple discussing an upcoming holiday. He says the words and watches me, distressed, blue eyes unblinking. I shake my head, unable to form a reply.

'Jess!' There's a note of raw anguish in his voice. His mouth twists into an odd lopsided shape. He leans forward and takes my hand in his. 'Please!'

I fight back the urge to wrench my hand away and run from the room. The past sidles towards me, raw and shocking, and momentarily I find it hard to catch my breath. The memories are like an ongoing bad dream, a nightmare from which I know I'll never wake. The images stay with me every hour of every day. I shake my head again.

'I can't,' I whisper, closing my eyes against the sight of his grief-stricken face. 'It's too soon.'

Brad looks down at the floor, as though he can't bear to watch me. I can see his throat working, swallowing hard. His voice, when it comes, is measured, controlled. 'I don't have to take the grant. Just say the word, Jess, and I'll knock it back. There'll be other times.'

I try not to see the disappointment in his face. Brad's like that. He's always thinking of others, putting everyone else's needs before his own. It was one of the qualities that first attracted me to him, all those years ago.

'Of course you have to take it!'

My response is swift and automatic. There's no question of him not going. Brad has wanted this so badly. He's spent weeks preparing his submission, and the results will form part of his thesis which is due next year. I hesitate and glance towards the fridge, thinking about preparing yet another meal I don't have an appetite for. 'Six weeks,' I say faintly.

But Brad is shaking his head. 'No. I'll can the whole idea. Maybe I'll go next year when things have settled. Besides, I don't want you here alone …'

He breaks off. Mentally I supply the words he can't bear to say: on the anniversary.

'Where exactly is the Diamantina River?' I ask mechanically instead. 'Where would we be going?'

Why have I said that? *We*, not *I*. Including myself, offering him some kind of hope when in my heart I feel there is none.

'The part I'm interested in is in central Queensland. Until the last few years, there's been little research in the area.'

'Why is that?'

I'm making small talk to fill the void between us. I've become adept at this during the past year, inserting a word or phrase here and there, my mind not really paying attention to his answers. Does he realise? I wonder now. Does he know I'm acting, leading him where I think he wants to go?

'Well, the area's so remote, for one thing. And it's difficult to get funding to tie in with the rainfall. It would mean lots of small field trips so, if you came, you'd still be alone sometimes. But at least we'd be able to see a bit of each other.'

'Why couldn't I tag along on the field trips?'

He seems surprised by my question. 'No reason, I suppose. I didn't think you'd be interested, that's all.'

Within the last minute, the conversation has progressed from improbability to possibility. Suddenly I've given him reason to hope.

'Where would we stay?'

'There's accommodation on one of the local properties. It's pretty basic but ...'

My thoughts drift away, like his words, and the conversation is left unfinished. I busy myself: emptying the dishwasher, peeling potatoes for our evening meal. Brad opens a bottle of red wine — cabernet shiraz, our favourite — and pours a generous measure into two glasses.

My mind wanders unwillingly, making me examine my feelings. Why exactly don't I want to go? The past twelve months have been difficult for Brad and me, for a variety of reasons, none of which I can bear to think about right now. Suffice to say, our relationship has been tested and found wanting.

I sip my wine and share my attention between fixing the meal and half-heartedly watching a documentary on the African lion. Slicing tomatoes and cucumber for a salad, shredding lettuce. My concentration wavers. During the course of the evening we skirt around each other, and the subject of Brad's grant. *Come with me,* he had said, inviting me into his world, wanting me to become part of him again. But deep inside, within the hard dry core of me, I wonder if things can ever be the same between us. And six weeks alone with my husband seems something to be endured, not enjoyed.

Later, freshly showered, I walk naked along the darkened hallway to our room, stopping outside the closed door opposite. And although I can't bear to open the door and walk inside, I can't bear to turn away either. I stand there, caught, not knowing what to do. I feel empty and traitorous, as though by going with Brad to this faraway place — *the Diamantina* — I am deserting other responsibilities.

My breath comes in irregular waves and there's a tight feeling across my chest. I close my eyes, fighting back tears, willing myself calm. Carefully I lay my forehead against the wall and feel cool plaster on my brow. The memories, flickers of happier times, lick at my awareness. I push them away, not wanting to remember. Because remembering means pain.

There is a movement behind me. The sound of a step on the floorboards. Warm rustle of air. Brad. Instinctively I turn to him, laying my wet cheek against his shirt.

'Don't cry, Jess,' he says, stroking my hair. His voice is breaking, making small choking sounds as he speaks. 'It'll be alright. Everything will be alright. It's time, that's all. It all takes time.'

I raise my mouth, seeking warmth and familiarity. 'Kiss me,' I say, darting my tongue against his.

'Jess.'

'Shh. Don't talk. I need you. Now.'

Brad's mouth is pliable and soft. He gives a low groan and trails one teasing hand across my shoulder, over one breast. I push the hand lower, towards the dark triangle of hair. Feel his fingers parting me and I tremble, impatient, as my own hand cups his hardness.

'Now,' I say again, scarcely recognising my own voice.

'Here?'

We do it there, in the hallway. My back is pressed hard against the wall and I sense Brad's thrusts from a great distance. Despite everything, I feel isolated and detached. There seems no true spiritual connecting point between us, no one particular place where we both are at the same time. I could, I think, be having sex with a stranger.

My mind slides sideways. What do I want? What is the meaning of this frenzied frantic coupling? Am I searching for all those safe familiar emotions, wanting things to be as they had been, somewhere in the past? Inside me, grief and desire roll into an untidy blur, each indistinguishable from the other.

As though from far away, I hear Brad's exultant cry. It sounds discordant and distant, like moaning wind among pine trees. Unfulfilled I sag against the wall.

I am empty. Hollow. Devoid of feeling and somehow incomplete.

Never, ever, have I felt so alone.

For months now, I've had an ongoing dream. Once a week. Sometimes twice. Never exactly the *same* dream, but similar. Similar theme. Similar gut-wrenching fear. Similar ending. It's just the middle bit that distorts and twists, leading me down deceptive paths. And if you believe that dreams have meanings, some underlying purpose, what would you make of mine?

It's night — always night — and I'm running. Running through darkened streets in a town that is both familiar yet unknown. It is a country town, the streets set out at right angles to each other. The landscape is flat. No lights shine from windows. No dogs bark. All is quiet except for the pounding of my feet and the wheeze of my own ragged breath. And the footsteps behind . . .

There is *always* someone behind. *The hunters*, that's what I call them. They're almost silent, stealthy and menacing. How many are there? I never know. In my dream I'm too scared to turn my head and count.

So I'm running. Terrified. Muscles screaming with the effort. The footsteps come closer. Closer. A pain begins in my side but I force myself on, willing my legs that extra distance. Maybe — and it's a faint hope — I can outrun them, lose myself in the elongated shadows that spear out from the dim street lights. But I can sense their breath on my neck, and I feel the swirl of air as their arms grab towards me.

Exhausted, I come at last to a river. There is no way across, other than to swim. For one impossibly long moment I stare at the water. It swirls past, dark and oily, and I shudder. Taking a deep breath, bracing myself against the expected cold, I dive into its depths.

It is at this point I always wake. My heart's pounding. I'm breathless. Fear twists itself in knots in my belly and my skin is awash with perspiration. I sit up, holding my hands to my temples, wishing away the tension that has amassed there. Then, regaining my breath, I glance across at Brad.

The bedroom is faintly lit by the street lamp outside. He lies beside me, his chest rising and falling in the easy rhythm of sleep. His hair is tousled. His features are relaxed.

Surely, I think, I must have made some noise, cried out even.

How can he be so totally unaware?

I inherited this house from my grandparents. It's what's known as a 'worker's cottage' — the latest yuppie inner-city fashion trend. They're usually run-down and tiny, and people are now paying the most exorbitant prices for them. In typical style, there's a central hallway with rooms randomly spearing off: formal lounge, two bedrooms, bathroom, dining room.

Over the years Brad and I have spent much time, and money, restoring our home. It's bright and functional now, uncluttered and minimalist, with polished wooden floors and walls of butter gold. Two years ago we extended the rear of the house to include a new kitchen and casual family area. Now the sliding glass doors open out onto a sun-drenched deck paved with terracotta tiles, and there are planter boxes filled with brightly flowering geraniums. Further down there's a small plunge pool and a pocket-sized square of lawn, and a cascading mulberry tree that my own father picked fruit from as a child. It looks like something, I think proudly, out of a glossy home magazine.

But now, in this house, there are too many empty daylight hours to fill. There is too much energy wasted trying to find causes and reasons for what has happened. And there are too many nights spent crying, although I know tears can never erase that awful, awful pain.

It's time, I've begun thinking, that I returned to work. Back in my former everyday life I was a researcher for one of the local television companies. I'd loved the job, enjoyed searching for and piecing together bits of information for the nightly current affairs program. And I was good at it. When I left, the general manager of the station had given me a glowing reference.

Work! I think dejectedly now, caught between wanting to be needed again, depended upon, and feelings of inadequacy. The thought of getting up in the mornings and putting on corporate clothes and makeup, pretending sentiments I can never feel again, depresses me. How can I act normally in front of other people when inside my heart is splitting in two? How can I carry on as though everything is ordinary when my emotional life's in chaos?

So I shelve the idea.

Tomorrow, I think. Tomorrow I'll make a decision, change my life. Get on with living.

Always tomorrow ...

The following afternoon I arrive home from shopping, dispiritedly lugging the plastic bags filled with groceries along the hallway to the kitchen. Brad is already there, a book spread before him on the kitchen bench. The book — he shows me later — contains photographs mostly, aerial shots of large muddy water holes and dry tree-lined channels flaring out and coming back together again, meandering aimlessly across what appears to be a flat landscape.

'The Diamantina River has one main course,' he says, tracing his finger along the side of the photo of a muddy hole. 'And when it rains the water spills out into dozens, sometimes hundreds, of channels, often miles wide.'

I glance again at the photograph. From where I'm standing, it looks like filigree lace, an intricate interweaving of colours and indentations. 'What happens when it floods?' I ask.

'The countryside looks like a lake, and because the land's so flat it takes ages for the water to disperse.'

He spreads a large map of Queensland alongside, pointing to the pale blue lines of the river that weave across the paper. 'Look,' he says, an expression of excitement in his voice that I haven't heard for months. 'There are three main river systems through here — the Georgina, the Diamantina and Coopers Creek. The water from these ends up eventually in Lake Eyre.'

'In South Australia?' It's been a while since school geography lessons but there are some facts you never forget.

Staring hard at the map, I let my eyes track across the words and shadings. I look for the nearest town in what I imagine is a fairly inhospitable part of the outback. 'That's nice,' I add, stepping back and taking off my high heels. My feet are throbbing.

But Brad's head is still bent over the map. 'If we head this way,' he muses, tracing a finger along what appears to be a major highway, 'turn off here then go along this track, that'd be the quickest route.'

I come to a sudden halt, not comprehending, with my obscenely high-heeled shoes in one hand and the other on my hip. 'Quickest route?' I repeat stupidly.

'To the Diamantina. You are coming, Jess?'

'No,' I answer firmly. 'And that track you're talking about must be over two hundred kilometres long.'

'Three fifty,' he replies with a grin, giving me a look that takes me back a few years and makes me think, if I wasn't so damn exhausted, I could be persuaded to forego dinner altogether in exchange for more hedonistic pursuits.

'Don't you feel bogged down sometimes? Don't you ever want to escape?' he asks suddenly, leaning back in his chair and changing the subject.

'Escape? To where?'

Brad shrugs, runs one hand tiredly across his eyes. 'Anywhere. Away from all this. Somewhere where life is less complicated, slower.'

'Away from the memories?'

The words come unbidden but I have to ask. I need to know what drives this man.

'Yes,' he replies simply.

'I could never leave the memories behind. They're all that's left.'

I shake my head. I've never thought of escaping, haven't seriously considered the possibility of alternatives. Besides, where would we go? The outer suburbs? Some small country town? The Diamantina?

The book sits on the bench for several days. I glance at it from time to time, thinking I might scan through the text. There is, Brad has informed me, a small potted local history of the area included. 'You know,' he says casually, 'early pioneers and settlement, that sort of thing.'

He's trying to enthuse me, make me curious. Awaken those old research skills that have lain dormant for the past few years. I tentatively open the first page then push it away. No, an inner voice tells me. Don't look. Don't become involved.

Instead the name — *Diamantina* — dances through my awareness, surfacing unexpectedly at odd moments.

Diamantina. Diamantina. Diamantina.

I say it softly, linking the words, and there is a cadence, a rhythm, to the sound. It's almost musical, pleasing to the ear. What is it, I wonder, that makes some names stay in our minds? Why can't they let go and fade into memory?

Eventually, on Sunday afternoon, I take the book and sit in a chair under the mulberry tree. Above, the leaves move, propelling small patches of sun across the lawn, my hands, the cover of the book. For one brief moment I close my eyes and feel the warmth on my face. Then, taking a deep breath, I open the pages and flick through until I find the appropriate section.

'The Diamantina area around Winton,' I read aloud, 'wasn't settled until the early 1870s. One of the early pastoralists, Adam O'Loughlin, was a native of Newtownlimavady, in the county of Londonderry, Ireland ...'

CHAPTER 2

NEWTOWNLIMAVADY, IRELAND
July 1867

Adam O'Loughlin sat on the cottage step, the heat of the sun slowly warming his face as he sipped the mug of tea. In the potato field below, leaves and flowers stretched towards the sky, rippling in the breeze like a green and purple sea. He'd never seen the sea, only in books, but he imagined what it looked like. The closest he'd come was the day his father had taken him to Londonderry, eighteen miles away, and he'd gazed out across the River Foyle, wondering what it would be like to sail away on one of the tall-masted ships that had waited at the docks. How old had he been? Six? Seven? But, he thought abruptly, his mind jolting back to the present, Da had been dead from the fever these past four months. And, as the oldest male, he, Adam, was now the head of the family.

He stared morosely at the O'Loughlin fields below, feeling the burden of responsibility weigh heavily on his eighteen-year-old shoulders. The farm was a miserable patch of land really, low-lying and ill-drained, prone to moisture in the wet months. There were ten acres in total, though more than half was little better than peat bog. The cattle and sheep had long since gone, sold at a fraction of their value to pay past rents. Now there was just one pig, a runty little animal, and three acres of potatoes.

'Aye, 'tis a shame to be thinking sad thoughts on such a fine day,' said a voice at his elbow.

His mother levered herself down on the step beside him, hugging her arms around the shape of her unborn child. Adam glanced at her, then stared away, embarrassed. She'd been scarcely older than he was now when she'd married his da. Now, not yet forty years of age, she seemed like an old woman already, her hair almost white and small puckered lines fanning out from the corners of her mouth and eyes.

'How did you know what I was thinking?'

'A mother knows such things.'

He compressed his mouth, letting his gaze rove further afield. Here and there stood the occasional whitewashed cottage with thatched roof, similar to his own, surrounded by land divided into fields by dry-stone walls. Away to the left, at the top of the hill, stood the landlord's farm. The soil there was dark and sweet, and sheep — pale moving dots outlined against the lush greenness — grazed on the grass. The landlord's house sprawled across the crest of the rise, the walls unnaturally white against a newly tilled field. The central tower of the building was a dark blur against the blue of the sky. To the right, a distant line of trees marked the course of the River Roe.

'The potatoes,' said his mother, bringing his attention back to the present. 'How long do you think we'll be from digging them?'

Adam blinked and centred his attention once more on the O'Loughlin land below the house. Sometimes he imagined, if he had the time to sit and watch, he'd be able to see the new leaves grow and the petals on the flowers opening, so fast seemed the progress of the plants. And thank God, he thought. The surplus crop would be sold to pay the landlord's half-yearly rent, overdue since 'Gale Day' in May, and the remainder would fill their own barrels. The only edible potatoes still left in the house were the 'lumper' variety, not nearly as choice as the 'apples' that were now forming in the wretched soil under the waving plants.

'A few weeks,' he replied, frowning. 'Maybe a month, if we can wait that long.'

He could see two figures trudging towards them along the path that led up the side of the hill from the township below. Even from that distance he knew who they were. One was the constable, a local chap whom Adam had known most of his life. He had gone to school with the man's sons. The other — the bailiff, resplendent in his swallow-tailed frieze coat, polished shoes and dark stovepipe hat — picked his way through the puddles of water from the previous night's rain, trying not to dirty his shoes. Despite his anger, Adam stifled a laugh.

'What's so funny?' asked his mother, following his gaze.

'The bailiff trying to keep the mud from his fancy boots.'

'I don't know why he'd bother. It's the cleanest thing on the ground,' she replied dryly.

Adam watched as the two men puffed into the yard. The bailiff held a piece of paper towards Adam's mother. 'Mrs O'Loughlin, I presume.'

'What's this?' demanded Adam, intercepting it.

'Eviction notice: don't tell me you haven't been expecting it.'

Adam glanced at his mother. Her face seemed to be crumpling, folding in on itself. She closed her eyes and a single tear escaped from one closed eyelid. Her voice, when it came, sounded far away. 'What are we supposed to pay you with? Our potato crop's not ready and there's no money.'

'Tell not your complaints to he who has no pity,' mocked Adam.

'You've a month to pay up or move,' the bailiff went on, ignoring the comment, hands on his hips.

Adam took his mother's arm, squeezing it reassuringly. 'Don't worry, Mam. I'll handle this.'

'Adam! No!'

She held out her hands, protesting, but he ignored her, steering her firmly up the steps and closing the cottage door behind her before he turned to face the men. 'As you can see, my mother's not well. You'll have to deal with me.'

'And you are?' the bailiff enquired belligerently.

The question was a formality, Adam knew, one to put him off his guard. All the villagers knew each other and the constable surely would have given the man the facts during the long climb up the hill. But the question deserved an answer. 'Adam O'Loughlin, son of Hugh,' he replied patiently.

'Where's your father?'

'He's dead these past four months, as I'm sure you already know.'

'Insolent!' muttered the bailiff under his breath. Then, louder: 'Where's your brother?'

'Conor?' asked Adam, surprised. 'What do you want with him?'

'He's been seen snooping around the landlord's fields. If something goes missing, he'll be the first to be blamed.'

'And what would likely go missing up there?' taunted Adam, glancing towards the sprawling white house.

'Stock, for a start.'

'Are you calling my brother a thief?'

'I've only orders to serve this notice. It's been verified and signed by the magistrate. The landlord doesn't care if your mother is on her deathbed or your potatoes are black. He simply wants his money. You've thirty days to pay up, or else.'

'Or else what?'

The bailiff shrugged — an exaggerated lifting and settling of his shoulders that somehow seemed to belittle them all — and walked away.

The constable turned to Adam. 'Sorry, lad,' he said. 'This is not of my doing.' He gave a sympathetic nod and shifted uncomfortably from foot to foot, avoiding Adam's gaze.

Adam stared at him hard then glanced away, his eyes following the stumping gait of the bailiff as he made his way back down the path towards the village. 'You'd better go then,' he said to the man, dismissing him.

He turned and walked up the stone steps and in through the cottage door, closing it firmly in his wake. The comparative coolness of the interior enveloped him and he shivered.

'So that's it, then? This is how it's going to end.'

His mother sat in a chair beside the window. Adam could see none of her features, merely the silhouette of her face outlined against the pale blue of the sky beyond. He noted the proud tilt of her head and her upthrust chin, the way her apron swelled out with the shape of the child.

'They were asking after Conor,' he said, his voice flat.

'Conor?' Her face swung abruptly towards him and, through the gloom, he could make out the round 'O' of her mouth. 'What do they want with him?'

'The bailiff says he's been seen snooping in places he shouldn't.'

She crossed her arms over her breasts, lifting her head in a silent gesture of defeat. 'That boy'll be the death of me yet.'

'Speaking of Conor, do you know where he is? I haven't seen him for days.'

She rose silently, not answering, and took the broom from its place near the hearth. With short mechanical strokes she whisked the straw across the earthen floor, sweeping unseen dust towards the door as superstition dictated.

Anger rose up inside him, swift and strong. Bloody Conor, he thought, causing his mother distress when she needed it the least. Wasn't there enough to worry about with the thought of eviction and the prospect of yet another O'Loughlin mouth to feed? It was July already and the child was due at the end of August, mere weeks away. The potato crop would be ready for harvest and there'd not be enough hands, with his mother needing to tend to the child and Conor God-knows-where as usual.

He thought of the unborn child, Hugh O'Loughlin's last legacy before his untimely death. Tiny, defenceless thing. Never to know its father. Not asking to be born into this miserable cycle of poverty. Better if it died at birth, poor little bugger, he reasoned, then felt a sense of shame.

'Bloody Conor!' he exploded, guiding his anger towards its proper, though absent, recipient.

'Adam!' Visibly shocked, his mother leant against the broom, allowing it to support her weight as she stared at him.

'When will you stop protecting him?'

He stood for a moment, watching her. Then, as he realised an answer wasn't forthcoming, he snatched his hat from behind the door, jammed it on his head and let himself out into the sunshine.

Adam walked to the top end of Main Street. It was late afternoon and the road was deserted, not a cart or shopper in sight. Several cows stood in the shade of the chestnut tree in the centre of the market yard. Their heads turned towards him as he passed, watching silently. Above the topmost branches of the tree he could see Benevenagh Mountain in the distance, the peak hidden by cloud.

Where had it come from, the cloud? The morning had been fine and dry with no sign of rain, yet, like yesterday and the day before, already a low rumble of thunder could be heard from the hills. He swung his ear towards the sound, frowning, then impatiently pushed aside the thought and turned his attention to the reason for his walk into the village.

Where was Conor? It was true what he'd said to his mother: there had been no sign of the lad for days. Since their father's death, it seemed his sixteen-year-old brother now made his own rules, coming and going as he pleased.

The scene in the cottage earlier that morning flashed back at him. He frowned again, thinking of his mother, the way she had pushed the broom across the earthen floor of the hut at the mention of her son's name, almost violently. Was she angry at Conor, or the bailiff who had arrived on their doorstep demanding money? Or perhaps she was annoyed by the dwindling supply of potatoes in the barrel and the inevitability of yet another O'Loughlin offspring?

Adam sighed, not knowing, and took a right-hand turn into Catherine Street, heading in the direction of the river.

It was cool there, on the banks of the Roe. Dappled light fell in slabs across the grass. Water bubbled over jutting rocks, brown and foamy. Adam thought he saw the shimmer of a salmon beneath its surface, a sudden flick of scales and tail.

Distractedly he walked along the pathway. Here and there tree branches hung low across the water, the leaves almost touching. Above, he was aware of the blue flash of a kingfisher. The bridge ahead was half hidden in shadow. He leaned on the railing and stared pensively at the water rushing underneath.

In one sense he wasn't so different from the fish below. It was simply a different current pulling him, taking him in directions he'd rather not travel. Why not be a fish instead, swimming downstream to Loch Foyle? he wondered. Then he thought of the mudflats, miles hence, a breeding ground for countless species of birds, and suppressed a smile. The salmon he'd just seen, if it escaped being served on a platter at the landlord's dining table, would probably make a fine meal for some swooping gull.

He tried to project his mind forward into the future. Where would he be in ten years time? Married perhaps? Bringing another family into this miserable poverty that was Ireland? Eking out a wretched living on the land that had once belonged to his father, and his father's father before that? Surely to God, he thought, there must be more to life than growing potatoes and cutting slabs of turf from the hillsides and stacking them in the barn to dry for fuel. When there was no turf left, then what? The workhouse?

He raised his head to a sudden flare of lightning beyond the trees. The sky had become quite dark. It had turned cold, too. Adam shivered and pulled his coat tighter as he stepped from the bridge.

The path there also led along the side of the river, towards the townland of Carrick. In the field that stretched away to his right, bluebells were blooming, making a colourful carpet. Here and there, the blue was broken by gorse bushes dotted with yellow flowers. Further along the river bank stood the mill and grain store. For a moment he watched the water gushing over the wheel.

There was a movement in the field. 'Conor?' he called, straining his eyes to get a decent look. A dark figure sprinted away from him, across the grass. It was too far distant to be certain who it was, but Adam caught the gleam of light on the scales of a salmon. Poacher, he thought.

Another roar of thunder made him look back towards Benevenagh Mountain. As though in slow motion, flurries of clouds tumbled from the peak towards the valley floor, falling like a silent avalanche. The birds in the trees nearby were unusually silent. The wind had dropped, leaving the leaves limp like rags.

Adam hunched his shoulders against the cold and turned for home. There were chores waiting and he'd already wasted enough time looking for his brother. Eventually the lad would return to the cottage, lured by the promise of a full belly and a soft bed. Time enough then to read the riot act, not that Conor would take much heed.

Along the river and through the village he went. Past the cows standing in the market yard and up the muddy path towards the O'Loughlin cottage, watching all the while as the mist rolled in flurries along the ground, settling a smothering white over the damp earth. And when at last he came to his own fields, there was a white powdering on the potato plants there too, hard and cold, like frost.

'There's word in the village that two families have been evicted this week,' his mother said later as she placed the communal bowls of salt and mustard in the centre of the table, and the cup of buttermilk by each plate.

It was the usual supper: 'dip-at-the-stool'. Adam watched as the steam rose from the potatoes, their skins dark and wrinkled in the fading light. It curled, the steam, pulled upwards by some sudden draught. He thought of the fields below the cottage, the green leaves and purple flowers. 'Nothing will happen here. The luck is with us.'

His mother lit candles. She placed them alongside the potatoes and made the sign of the cross, moving her hands across her chest, her swollen belly, with sharp jerky movements. Light from the candles chased the shadows into corners. The reflection wavered along the walls like a rolling flickering wave. 'The bad luck that is not on us today may be on us tomorrow,' she pronounced darkly.

There was a place set for his brother — buttermilk and plate — although there was no sign of the lad. Adam took the topmost potato, peeled the skin back with his thumbnail and dipped it in the salt. There was a movement at the door and he glanced up, startled. It was Conor.

'Where have you been? I've needed a hand today to mend the cart wheel.'

In the candlelight, Conor was all dark eyes and mysterious smile. 'I've been out,' he replied, divulging nothing.

'Eat,' commanded their mother, pushing the bowl of steaming potatoes towards her younger son. Conor threw himself carelessly on the chair and took one, letting let it dance between his fingers. To and fro. Backwards and forwards. Barely letting the hot food touch his skin. Adam was mesmerised by the movement.

'The bailiff was here today,' he said at last.

The disdain was evident in Conor's voice. 'What did *he* want?'

Adam felt a flare of anger so intense that, for a moment, he couldn't speak.

Their mother pushed back her plate, staring directly at her younger son. Her voice was low, scarcely heard above the hissing of the fire. 'There's the rent to be paid, and the tithes, with scant potatoes left in the barrel. Praise God Almighty, we don't want to starve to death. This place is all we've got. If we lose it, we might as well lay down and die.'

Adam watched her face, the shadows from the fire playing across the contours. Worn and weary, that was how she was. He wanted to hold her, to wrap his arms around her, wanted to assure her that everything would be alright, that somehow they'd manage. But the hardened veneer of her face — and the way she'd folded her arms across her chest — had made a barricade between them, and the words died in his head, unspoken.

'Don't say that!' he replied instead, blurting the words. 'Don't *ever* say that!'

Conor laughed, a musical sound. Adam stared hard at his brother. 'For pity's sake, I can't make a go of this by myself! I need your help!'

'I'm not a farmer!' Conor dropped the potato and sprang to his feet, palms down on the table. 'And the landlord can damn well wait for his money! What else would he do with the land?'

'He wants us gone so he can turn the land over to pasture for sheep.'

'Wool for England!' snorted Conor derisively.

'That's as may be, but there's naught we can do about it. All I'm asking for is a little cooperation. We'll never get anywhere running at loggerheads with each other.'

'There's the pig,' their mother offered tentatively. 'It might fetch a few shillings at the market.'

Adam pushed aside his bowl and rose from the table, no longer hungry. The dissension rose as gorge in his throat. 'It's not fat enough! In a month or two it'll be worth more. We can hang on until then.'

A smile played oddly about Conor's mouth. 'There's no need to sell the pig. There *are* other ways.'

'Such as?'

Conor shrugged, sat back in his seat and picked up the potato again. He focused his attention on it, peeling back the skin, seeming to ignore Adam. He took one bite of the steaming flesh then replied in an off-hand manner: 'That'd be telling. The less you and Mam know, the better.'

Annoyed, Adam took his plate to the kitchen bench, not wanting to stay in the same room as his brother. As he did so, the dull gleam of scales caught his eye. He stared, almost not believing.

Two salmon lay there on a tray, limp, dark glassy eyes staring somewhere beyond the ceiling.

CHAPTER 3

After supper, Adam took a book from the cupboard. There was a choice of six, given to him several years earlier by the teacher at the local hedge school. He selected a volume of poems, most of which he already knew by heart, and settled into a chair by the fire.

Idly he flicked through the pages, but his mind wasn't on the task. His thoughts kept sliding back to the events of the morning, remembering the altercation with the bailiff. He remembered, also, looking later into the potato barrel in the kitchen and calculating the remaining supply. A week and a half's worth, maybe two at the most, if they were frugal. Then what? Sell the pig for several lousy shillings that would tide them over a few more weeks, delaying the inevitable?

The future stretched before him, a dark bottomless hole, almost beyond contemplation. Adam couldn't, no *didn't*, want to think about it. Instead he closed the book and lowered his chin onto his hand, not knowing what to do. He'd walked down to the village earlier, hearing stories similar to his own. 'The O'Malleys have been given notice, and the Shaunesseys,' one of the local farmers had said. 'At this rate there'll be no one left in the village come winter.'

Apart from the fire crackling in the hearth, and the logs shifting and settling as the minutes ticked past, the cottage was quiet. Mam had gone to bed after supper and Conor had fled into the night. Adam stared morosely at the flames flickering low. Exhausted, he laid his head against the back of his chair and closed his eyes. He felt sleep descending, a dark mass, formless and surprisingly warm. He gave himself to it, allowing it to tease him from his worries.

'Holy Mary, Mother of God!'

The cry filtered through his subconscious, merging with the remnants of some dream. Words tangled with images as his mind fought its way upwards, sluggishly, through the overlapping layers of sleep.

'Adam! Adam!'

He blinked his eyes open, not certain for a moment where he was, and turned his head towards the sound.

'Mam?'

His voice seemed slow, the words thick. His mind was cotton-wool heavy and refused to form thoughts. He closed his eyes, opened them again, thinking that this too might be part of the dream.

'Adam!' The cry came again, faint yet urgent.

The fire had long since died — there was nothing in the grate but blackened embers — and the cold bit at his feet as he lowered them to the flagstone floor.

Heart pounding, he ran to the entrance to his mother's room and pushed aside the curtain.

She was sitting up in bed, her hair wild and escaping, arms folded over the blanket around her raised knees. From the light of the lamp, he could see her pale face and the lines of pain around her mouth. Beads of sweat had gathered along her brow and they caught the light, shining like tiny prisms.

'What is it?' he asked. 'Is it the baby?'

'Aye.' She nodded and closed her eyes for a moment. Adam could see the nightdress covering her chest rising and falling, as though she fought to control her breathing. 'You'd better fetch Mrs Mullins. Tell her I'll be needing her right away.'

He stumbled along the path towards the village for the second time that day. The sky was clear, stars winking down from the blackness. Somewhere a dog howled, the mournful sound teasing at him on the breeze. A sense of desperation pushed him as he ran towards the lighted windows of the houses, boots catching on the rough stones.

He tripped once, falling so hard that he felt his shin graze beneath his trouser leg, though he was careless of any injury. His only concern was Mam, hoping she'd be alright while he was gone — blast Conor for leaving earlier — and that the child would be born safe and well. Then, in the village at last, he banged on the Mullinses' door until old Mr Mullins opened it, grumbling, 'Alright, lad. There's no need t' knock the blessed house down!'

Later, he sat on the front step of his own cottage while the midwife attended to his mother. Self-consciously he blocked his mind to the moans coming from inside, thinking instead that this was how it must have been eighteen years earlier at his own birth, his father — dead these past few months — sitting on the same step or pacing the kitchen, wondering and worrying.

His thoughts turned to the babies born after Conor. There had been five in total, none surviving more than a few months. Liam and Michael. Patrick. And twin girls, Grace and Mary. He remembered hearing the cottage filled with their pitiful cries, then silence afterwards as the tiny bodies were consigned to unmarked graves in the cemetery behind the church.

He raised his head, surveying the darkened mass that was the O'Loughlin land, wondering, yet again, at the futility of it all. Maybe when Mam gave up her childbed they'd all move on, search for something better. Surely there *had* to be something better, somewhere. Or what was the point of going on?

He laid his head on his knee. Maybe he slept — he wasn't certain — but it wasn't until dawn lit the sky that the midwife came to the door and shook her head. 'A boy,' she said brusquely, 'but he didn't even draw a breath.'

'How's Mam?'

Mrs Mullins shook her head again. 'She'll be needing a doctor.'

Conor arrived home as the doctor came out of his mother's room. 'There's little I can do,' the medico said, washing his hands at the tap. 'She needs meat to build up her strength and medicine, if she's to have a chance. But the only chemist in town has shut up shop.'

'There is no meat,' answered Adam. 'Or money. I don't know when I'll be able to pay you.'

The doctor shrugged and turned away, gathering his hat and bag. Half the townsfolk, Adam knew, owed the man for his services.

'Meat! There's plenty of salmon and trout in the landlord's streams, and more wild game in his fields than he could ever eat,' Conor said bitterly. 'But only the gentry can touch it while we must starve.'

'Don't let the wrong ears hear you say that, lad,' warned the doctor.

Conor thumped a fist against his palm. 'I don't care!' he cried, springing towards the door. 'I hate the English! We fatten pigs for their tables yet all we get is potatoes. I'll get meat for Mam, even if it kills me!'

'You can't. You'll be caught and gaoled. A criminal. What would Mam —?'

But Conor was gone, sprinting through the doorway, the door slamming in his wake.

After the doctor departed, Adam stood at the entrance to his mother's room. She lay in the bed, her body facing the wall. 'Mam?' he said.

There was no reply.

He walked to the end of the bed and lifted the rag-wrapped bundle, feeling the dead weight of the child. He peeled back the fabric and stared down at the perfectly formed features. Tiny snub nose. Eyes wide open. Arms limp.

There was a movement in the bed and Mam turned to face him, expression impassive, her eyes dark and hollow in her face. 'Do what you have to,' she whispered, her voice ragged.

He stared away, unable to meet her gaze, not knowing how to reply. What words could take away her pain, anyway? 'I'm sorry,' he said at last.

'*You're* sorry!'

'I can't change anything although I'd give anything to be able to do so.'

'Yes.'

Her voice held some kind of hopeless desperation and he wondered briefly if she was seeking reassurance. He turned from her and wrapped the body again in the rags. 'There's no money for a proper burial,' he told her. 'I'll dig a hole at the bottom of the back field.'

Outside, he blinked back angry tears as he took the shovel, spearing the tip deep into the soil. Furiously he turned over the earth, dark and peaty, and dug deeper, hoping that next season, praise God, there'd be potato plants growing again over that very place, hiding the evidence of his handiwork.

He laid the body in the hole, for a moment unable to complete the task. Miserably he stared at the sky, thinking: this is my brother, the last child of my parents. There can never be any more.

Despair churned, overtaking all rational thoughts, and he wondered how different things could have been.

If his father had lived ...

If the crop was ready now ...

If they'd had good land instead of poor ...

'If! If! If!' he muttered angrily as he threw a

spadeful of soil into the grave. If there really was a God, then surely he had deserted them.

'It's not fair!' he shouted, throwing the clods as fast as he was able, anxious to be finished and away from that miserable place.

He spent the remainder of the day attending to his mother as best he could. He brought her water and offered small morsels of potato, most of which she refused. He carried away the bloodied towels, brought her fresh ones, consigning the old to the fire. The blood frightened him: there seemed no end to it. In fact, the bleeding seemed to be worsening. Was that normal? He was loath to ask Mam, worry her unnecessarily. Was loath also to show his own masculine ignorance.

When night fell, he sat before the same fire, listening to her rasping breath in the adjoining room. He counted the seconds as they passed, not knowing what to do. If only Conor would come home. At least there would be someone else to talk to.

His mind wandered back over the years, remembering his childhood. Had anything good happened? he wondered, thinking again of his father — his body worn out by hard work and lack of food — and those dead babies and the miserable patch of poverty that surrounded them. But, he asked himself, could he really complain? In many ways, life hadn't been *that* bad. True, there had been a few winters where he'd had no shoes. But he'd never known hunger. He'd always had his parents' love and a dry bed, and a fire — like this very one — to warm himself by.

About midnight he took her water again.

'Adam,' she whispered, pushing away the glass.

Her voice was faint, barely heard, and he strained forward. In the semi-dark he reached for her hand, held it. The skin felt cold and paper-dry.

'Yes, Mam.'

'It's no use. I'm dying.'

'*No!*'

The word exploded from his mouth into the stillness of the room. He heard it reverberating around the shabby corners, the sound deafening in his ears.

'What's there to live for?' she asked in a tired voice. 'I'm weary of this life, son. There must be a better place. Your da's gone, and all those babies. There's only you and Conor left.'

'Then live for us!'

'You're almost men now. I'll only be a burden to you.'

'Never!'

'You must promise,' she went on in a whisper, as though she hadn't heard, 'to look after Conor, and that you'll both leave this place after I'm gone. There's nothing here but heartache.'

She withdrew her hand from his, tugging awkwardly at the wedding ring on her finger. 'Don't, Mam,' he said, stricken by her words, her actions.

The ring came away easily and she pressed it into his palm. It glowed dully in the half-light and he stared at it, not knowing what to say.

'Take this. And when I'm gone, sell it. It'll not raise much but it might be enough to take you away from here.'

Where was Conor? The question burned in his mind. His brother should be here to witness this, to complete their small fragmented family and to share this terrible burden. *When I'm gone* ... Mam knew she was dying, but Adam couldn't contemplate the thought. Instead he rose, fingers curling around the ring, fighting back the urge to fling it into the fire. Tears burned his eyes for the second time that day, and he blinked them away. 'Yes, Mam,' he replied mechanically, knowing those were the words she wanted to hear.

Conor walked and walked in the moonlight, a sense of rage simmering beneath his breastbone. Rage against the English landlords who conspired to take everything from them. Rage against his father who had so inconveniently and inconsiderately died, leaving them to fend for themselves. Rage against Adam and his sanctimonious ways.

Along the river bank he went, as far as the bridge. He leaned on its railing and watched the tumbling inky water. How easy, he thought, to swim away on the current, not looking back. Then he remembered his mother, and the doctor's words. Remembered why he had run from the cottage.

He stared past the path that followed the river. Further off, on the crest of a distant hill, he could see the landlord's sprawling mansion, lights blazing from what seemed like every window. But closer, the outline lit faintly by a crescent moon, stretched the landlord's fields: flat expanses of grass covering sweet-smelling soil, not the rancid poor excuse for land that was the O'Loughlin farm. Dark humps that were cattle and sheep moved silently across that same expanse. At the far end of the field, a clump of trees rose like silent sentinels, stretching branches towards the sky, moonlight sliding silver off their leaves.

Conor swung his legs easily over the fence and walked towards the trees. He knew he was trespassing but he didn't care. *Their* rules had never applied to him. Besides, what would the landlord's henchmen do if they caught him? Rough him up a little? Tell him to shove off?

Across the grass he went, the moist night air warming his face. Past the line of trees was a small cave. A mob of sheep, about a dozen or so, was gathered at the entrance. As he approached they skittered away with quick agitated steps, the bells around their necks tinkling. Taking a knife from his trouser pocket, he lunged at one of the smaller lambs. Holding the bell in one hand to silence it, he drew the knife quickly across the animal's throat. The lamb thrashed, kicking its legs ineffectually against the night air until it lay limp on the ground. Conor felt warm blood running over his palms and saw the dark ropey stream of it in the moonlight.

Hurriedly he hacked at the body. He left the bell and the severed head on the ground, as was the custom, to show that the animal had not wandered away but had been killed. Then he dragged the remainder of the carcass back through the fields, towards town. Wet grass slapped at his trouser legs. A night bird flew, protesting, into the air as he passed the clump of trees. Overhead the moon shone, pouring silver light on the landscape, lighting the way.

He stopped at the cemetery, hauled the carcass onto a flat tombstone and peeled the wool from the flesh with the blade of his knife. Blood oozed over the stone and surrounding grass, staining it dark. As he worked, Conor thought he heard noises. He turned, suddenly, several times, hoping to surprise the culprit. But he saw nothing, heard nothing, except for the rasp of leaves and the soft rustle of grass. It must be the wind, he thought, shoving the meat into a sack. On the way home, he buried the skin in a bog.

Dawn tinged the horizon pink as he hoisted the lamb onto the bench in the kitchen. 'You can't cook that in here,' said Adam, coming through the curtain from his mother's room. 'Just the smell of roasting meat will have the local constable on our doorstep.'

'It's for Mam,' he replied defiantly. 'Why should she starve while the English get fat?'

Adam ran a hand through his hair and Conor thought quite suddenly that his older brother looked pale and very tired. 'It's too late for Mam.'

A sudden fear coursed through him, a shiver of foreboding that caressed his heart for a moment then was gone. 'What do you mean?'

Adam shook his head, staring mutely at his brother.

'What do you *mean*?' asked Conor again, stupidly, his mind suddenly alert and rushing through a host of possibilities. Maybe Adam had found money somehow, sent her to hospital. Perhaps a neighbour had come by with good nourishing food and she had already left her sickbed. Or . . .

'She's dead,' Adam whispered.

The knowledge brought him to a standstill: he was too late. All night he'd focused on procuring the food, bringing it home. The meat would have made her well, stopped whatever feminine ailment it was that had been sapping her life. But he'd taken more time than he'd planned. Waited too long by the river perhaps, or spent an excessive number of minutes selecting the right sheep, when any would have done. But he'd sought lamb — tender flesh. He'd only wanted the best for his mother.

'When?' he asked dully, staring at his brother. 'When did she . . .?'

The word caught in his throat. He couldn't say it: *die*. Couldn't, couldn't, *couldn't*.

Adam glanced at the clock, frowning. 'About an hour ago.'

'And I wasn't here.'

'The last person she asked after was you. "Where's Conor?" she said.'

The thought of his mother lying dead in the room beyond made him gag and he turned away, stricken, finding it suddenly hard to breathe. He went to the front door, opened it and took in great lungfuls of air, trying to stem the nausea. It was all in vain, he thought savagely. *Everything* was in vain. No matter what happened, how hard he tried, something always conspired against him. And now Mam . . .

'She wanted us to leave,' Adam said softly, following him to the door. 'She made me promise we'd go from here and find a better life.'

'And where would that be?' Conor asked, his voice savage. The tone of it surprised him, a wash of raw emotion, and he pulled abruptly away from his brother. 'Where could we possibly find a *better life*?'

He felt a sudden need to distance himself — from his brother, the cottage and the poor, fallow fields. Needed to detach himself from the shambles of his ruined, *ruined* life. He stared at Adam for one long moment, then quickly descended the steps and walked into the dawn.

CHAPTER 4

Adam laid out his mother's body as best he could. He washed and dressed her. He brushed her hair. Then he sat the customary mug of water beside the bed.

The news soon spread and during the morning a few of the locals ambled up the hill, producing the standard clay pipes for the deceased's soul. It was a sombre, sullen day, with grey skies and low scudding clouds spitting rain. A day, Adam thought, to match his mood. To make matters worse, he was at a loss how to treat the visitors. His past experiences with death had been of hordes of bewailing mourners arriving with arms filled with food and drink. But these days none of the villagers had food to spare, and the only free drink was water.

The mourners' faces were set. Scarcely a word was said. No one seemed to have the energy for sympathy or prayers. Instead they stood around the kitchen, smoking.

'Mebbe she's better off this way,' said Mr Mullins at last, shifting uneasily on his feet. His gaze slid to the open doorway and the village beyond. 'It'll all be gone, if the landlord has his way,' he added, dispiritedly. 'How will we survive if we lose our land? That's the question.'

'What'll you and Conor do now?' someone asked Adam.

Adam shrugged, his heart heavy.

'Suppose you'll be thinking of leaving?' offered another.

Was he? Adam didn't know. All he knew was this place, Newtownlimavady, where his parents and grandparents before them had farmed the land and eked out their miserable living from the soil.

'America,' said someone else. 'That's where our futures lie. Land of plenty, that's what they say.'

'That's what *who* says?'

The man shrugged. 'Dunno. It's what I heard. Might pack up and go there meself on the strength of it, though.'

Mr Mullins took the hat around and collected the few shillings needed for the cemetery plot. The skies opened up as they buried her later, drenching those who braved the weather. Adam saw Conor standing at the back of the crowd, beneath the weeping sky, hands shoved deep in his pockets. He wanted to go to him, to wrap his arms around him and feel comfort from someone who was family. But the press of mourners around him made it impossible to move. And when he went to look for his brother later, after the ceremony was dispensed with, Conor was nowhere to be found.

*   *   *

All night Adam expected his brother to put in an appearance. His ears strained for some sound of the lad, slam of door or footstep on the path, but he waited in vain. Without company, the cottage seemed cold and empty. Adam hadn't the heart to light a fire and his appetite had deserted him. Mam's room waited behind the drawn curtain and he couldn't bear to push it aside and walk in, knowing she was no longer there.

Instead he sat at the kitchen table, head resting on the rough timber surface. Mam's words swam in and out of his tired mind, demanding attention.

You must promise that you and Conor will leave this place after I'm gone.

The words of the villager: *Suppose you'll be thinking of leaving. America. Land of plenty.*

America! It seemed so far away. *Was* so far away. He took his father's old atlas from the bookcase and opened it, tracing his fingers across the grey expanse of the Atlantic Ocean. It was mere inches on paper, but weeks away in reality. How could he afford the fare and, if the choice was his, could he bear to leave? And would Conor want to go?

His hand, sliding into his pocket, encountered Mam's ring. With everything that had been happening, he'd forgotten its existence. Now he brought it out, examined it. Turned it this way and that, watching as the light reflected back dully from its surface. At best it might bring a few pounds, probably not even enough for a single passage. Maybe he should simply send Conor. Get him away from here, give the boy a chance.

Conor! He walked to the doorway of the room he

shared with the lad. Neat. Tidy. Not a thing out of place. Now, in the cold light of another day, his brother's undisturbed bed seemed like a reproach of sorts.

A policeman came to the door mid-morning. 'I'm looking for Conor O'Loughlin,' he said to Adam.

'He isn't here.'

'That's a likely story.'

Adam motioned towards the interior of the house. 'You're welcome to look, since you think I'm lying. But you'll find no sign of him.'

'Where is he then?'

Adam shrugged. 'I don't know.'

The policeman scratched his chin, looking thoughtful. 'How old is the lad?'

'Sixteen.'

'And he's wandering the countryside?'

'Conor lives by his own rules.'

'So I've been told.'

'What's that supposed to mean?'

'He's killed one of the landlord's sheep.'

'Who says?'

The policeman turned away. 'It doesn't matter who says,' he called over his shoulder. 'But if the landlord catches him there'll be hell to pay.'

Conor walked up the hill to the landlord's house. Up the white gravel road, in broad daylight, he went, up past the clump of trees and the cave entrance where he'd killed the lamb. There was no sign of the animal's head — obviously someone had removed it.

Brazen: that was what Mam would have called him. Brazen and brash, and too bold for his own good to be even contemplating this visit. But Mam was buried in the boggy ground and he had to do this for his own, and Adam's, future.

He'd been thinking about what Adam had said about leaving Newtownlimavady. At first the idea had been shocking, and the mere suggestion had outraged him. Yet, as the hours passed, he'd had time to dwell on the idea of forging a new life away from the constraints of the old. Gradually the notion had become oddly appealing, stirring an unexpected rush of anticipation.

There was nothing here, he had to admit. No possibility of eventual wealth. No expectation of even a moderate income. Nothing but grinding miserable poverty and the immediate prospect of losing the O'Loughlin land.

And if they left?

He let his mind wander, exploring possibilities. They could go anywhere, he and Adam. Board a ship and see where it took them. Exotic faraway places, islands lapped by azure seas: he could picture himself lying on a beach, surrounded by pretty girls. Then he laughed at his outrageous imagination.

The laughter, once begun, brought him perilously close to tears. He thought of the funeral and remembered how his mother's plain coffin had been lowered into the ground, clods of damp earth falling from shovels onto its hard surface. The echo of the sound — that awful thudding — was something he found impossible to erase from his mind. He couldn't seem to picture her there, his mother, in a box under that same damp earth. No air. No light. No life.

There was a stinging sensation at the back of his eyes and the scene before him — hill and underbrush, and sunlight glaring back from the white gravel road — blurred into a mish-mash of assorted colours. Inwardly he cursed his own emotions. He had held it all in check at the funeral, stood back, not allowing anyone to see his pain. And he would do the same now. Control: that was what it was all about. Hiding the way you felt, suppressing those raw hideous emotions into some inner core. There would be time for tears later, when the business at hand had been completed. With a sigh he brought his mind back to the present as he trudged up the last of the hill.

He knocked loudly at the landlord's front door and was admitted by a maid wearing a white apron. She was young — about Adam's age, he guessed. He awarded her a broad wink as he demanded to see her master. In return, she gave a self-conscious smile and her face turned a shade of pink at his impudence.

The landlord kept him waiting half an hour. To deflect his anger, Conor strolled around the room to which he'd been admitted. He stared long and hard at the portraits that lined the walls, and the ornate furniture arranged strategically around the fireplace. The price of one fancy chair, he thought bitterly, could keep a local family in potatoes for a year.

Finally, a voice behind him made him turn. 'I see you're admiring my house.'

'*Admiring*? I hardly think so.'

'What then?'

The man had an amused indulgent smile on his face and Conor longed to smack it away. Consciously he caught his hands behind his back, restraining himself. 'I was thinking how pompous all this looks — for a farmhouse.'

'*Farmhouse*! Why you —'

The man caught his wrist, twisting it painfully. Conor grimaced, but went on. 'Well, a pretend farmhouse, really, because you let us all farm your land. You're not even a real farmer!'

The man let him go with a small shove and Conor staggered backwards. 'I'm the landlord and don't you forget that! What's your name?'

He raised himself straight and tall, as Mam had always taught him. 'Conor O'Loughlin.'

'Well, Conor O'Loughlin, I suppose you'd better state your business and be gone, before I have my men throw you out for insolence.'

'News tends to travel fast in these parts,' Conor went on, ignoring the man, 'so I suppose you've heard that my mother's dead. My brother and I are responsible for the land now.'

'Is that so?' The landlord formed his hands into a steeple, pressing the tip of his topmost finger against his chin. 'Then I presume you've come to tell me you're leaving, before I ask my men to assist you. It'd be so much better if you went of your own accord.'

'Better for whom?' asked Conor sarcastically.

'You, naturally. It'd save you the embarrassment of being evicted.'

Conor crossed his arms over his chest and stared

at the man. Two could play at this silly game of parry and thrust, and he planned to make the first lunge. 'On the contrary,' he said amiably, 'I've come to pay my dues. I know they're rather late but you'll find I've recompensed you thoroughly.'

The landlord's facade slipped alarmingly, just as Conor had intended. 'Your dues!' he spluttered, taking one step backwards.

'Yes,' replied Conor easily, putting his hand into his pocket as though to withdraw the cash. 'I managed to scrape up the money. I have friends.'

'Friends!' The landlord's face had turned a bright shade of puce and he seemed to be having trouble drawing breath.

Conor allowed himself a casual smile. 'Come, now. Surely you didn't think you could part my brother and me from our land that easily.' His hand had stopped, deep in his pocket, and he watched the man's gaze follow it there. 'But before I pay you, I should tell you there is another alternative.'

'There is?' The landlord spun the words out slowly, meaningfully, pausing deliberately before continuing. 'Now, what could that be?'

'You want our land, miserable though it is, for pasture. Fattening lambs for England, never mind that the Irish starve.'

'Impertinence will get you nowhere.'

'We could strike a deal,' replied Conor, ignoring him.

The man gave a derisive snort. 'Your land's worthless.'

'To me, maybe, but not to you.'

The landlord slid his hands into his own pockets and swayed backwards, rocking on the heels of his boots. 'You're a cheeky young fellow, O'Loughlin. So just what *do* you think your land's worth?'

'The cost of boat tickets, for my brother and me.'

'How much?'

'Ten pounds each.'

'Ten pounds!'

Might as well push for a little more, thought Conor, enjoying the exchange. 'Plus five pounds for the cost of food for the voyage.'

The man regarded him, a frown creasing his forehead. 'If I give you the money do I have your word you'll go?' he said at last.

'Yes.'

The landlord went to a nearby desk and withdrew a small tin. Casually he counted out twenty-five pounds. Conor watched as the notes made a small pile on the desk. He'd never seen so much money before, though the older man obviously had no regard for the cash.

The landlord picked up the notes and held them towards him, just out of reach. 'I want you out of the cottage by tomorrow lunchtime.'

'I can arrange that,' answered Conor easily.

The money, somehow, was in his hand and the man stepped back, a sly smirk turning the corners of his mouth upwards. Obviously he thought the arrangement a good one. 'There's the money then, and good riddance to you.'

'Thank you.'

Conor gave the man a cheeky grin and walked

ahead of him towards the front door. Now that the deal was finalised, he was anxious to be gone.

'By the way, there's a small matter of a sheep killed in the western field,' said the man as Conor reached the front step. 'You don't happen to know anything about it?'

But Conor was gone, running down the steps into pale sunshine, the money tucked securely in his pocket.

He paused at last by a clump of elm, a fair distance from the house, surrounded by a waving, nodding sea of bluebells. A sense of victory bubbled in his chest and he laughed aloud. The sound of it flew upwards, towards the sky, joined the song of birds.

The ploy had worked well. Fancy the landlord believing he'd had the money to pay the overdue rent! It just went to show what a small amount of pretence could achieve. Now, in his possession he held more money than he had thought possible. He slipped his hand into his pocket, withdrew the notes and stared at them. Flimsy pieces of paper, he thought, suddenly morose. Perhaps they had been won too easily.

He wondered what would happen if he threw them into the air, let the wind catch them and take them wherever it desired. Imagined them dancing capriciously above the tree line, just out of his reach. His grip on them tightened and he thought again of his mother. Slowly he hunkered down on the ground, hugging his arms around his knees.

There, in the meadow and surrounded by nodding heads of bluebells, he gave himself at last to racking sobs that left him exhausted and empty. He cried for his mother, for the children he might one day sire and who would never know her face. He cried for all the injustices he'd witnessed in the past few days. And most of all, he cried for all the lives cut short: his mother and tiny nameless brother, his father and all those other long-dead siblings. No matter what happened in the future, no matter what fortune, either good or bad, awaited himself and Adam, this money, however gained, had the power to change their lives irrevocably. Nothing, ever, would be the same again.

Adam woke to find his brother standing at the foot of his bed. It was almost dawn, the sky paling with the first faint flush of light. He could see Conor's shape outlined against the window and the metallic sky.

'We have to leave,' Adam said, instantly alert. 'They know you killed the sheep. The police have been here.'

Conor shifted, crossing his arms. 'No one saw me. They *think* they know, that's all.'

'They'll put you in gaol.'

'They have to catch me first.'

Adam heard his own quick intake of breath. Part of him wanted to shake the lad, to jolt some sense into him. 'Conor, be practical!'

'I am. That's why I'm agreeing with you.'

'Agreeing to what?'

'About leaving. We'll go to Londonderry and get a passage out of here.'

Adam swung his legs over the side of the bed. 'We can't afford it.'

Conor gave a chuckle. 'Of course we can. Trust me. Pack a bag and I'll meet you up in the wood. At noon.'

He was, Adam knew, referring to the small woodland that lay above the house. There, beyond the trees, lay an alternative path to town and, beyond that, the main road that led to the city.

'Noon,' he agreed as Conor slipped from the room. There was no other choice, not really. 'I'll be there.'

The hours seemed interminable. As the minutes ticked slowly by, a feeling of nervous apprehension flared in Adam's belly. How could Conor afford tickets for any sea journey? Where had the money come from?

Trust me, Conor had said, but Adam found it hard to do so, suspecting there must be some illegal method by which the boy had acquired the cash. Or perhaps there was no cash, the thought occurred to him suddenly. Conor might have some wild idea of stowing away aboard ship.

Pressing the thoughts aside, he scoured the contents of the cottage. Rickety furniture. Few meagre possessions. Nothing salvageable. Worthless really. Instead he took the battered suitcase from Mam's bedroom and packed his clothing and the few books. Then he tested its weight, swinging it from one hand to the other.

He ate his final meal in the cottage. The last of the potatoes were sprouting shoots and spongy inside.

Tasteless, he thought, pushing aside the pot of mustard. Towards the allotted meeting time with Conor, through the kitchen window he saw the bailiff at the base of the hill with his entourage of men, heading towards him. They were carrying crowbars and rope. The O'Loughlin cottage, he knew, would be destroyed like so many others in the village where the rents had not been paid. Pulled down. Set alight, rendering it uninhabitable. Obliterating any sign that Adam's family had ever lived there.

There was nothing left for him here — Adam knew that now. He had no other choice but to meet Conor and flee the town. Resignedly he let the curtain fall back into place and took his bag from the kitchen table. Then he let himself out the back door and headed towards the small wood as Conor had instructed.

It felt odd to be leaving. Seemed odd, too, to be setting off for some unknown destination. Maybe, he thought, he was only taking the shell of him, and the core, the essence of his being, would always stay here, in the place of his birth. He shifted the suitcase to his other hand, placing one foot in front of the other. Part of him wanted to look back, one last time. The other didn't want to at all.

As he came to the shadows of the trees, Conor stepped forward. 'Adam,' he said. 'You came.'

'Did you think I wouldn't?'

Conor shrugged. 'Maybe. Maybe not.'

Adam wasn't in the mood for Conor's word games. 'Let's go,' he said, stepping further into the shadows. There, in the dappled light, he could make out the path that would take them from all this. And now, more than ever, he wanted to be gone.

'*No!* Just wait a minute.'

Conor said the word with such force that Adam turned, puzzled. His brother was pointing down the hill, towards the men. 'Look,' he said.

Reluctantly Adam let his eyes follow Conor's hand. The bailiff's entourage was halfway up the hill towards the cottage. Adam saw them struggle up the slope with their tools of destruction.

'Don't you see it?' asked Conor, annoyed.

As Adam watched, the men tried to run. Towards the cottage they went, discarding shovels and rope. Something was wrong, he thought, letting his gaze travel back up the hill. He stiffened, peered forward. There, from the thatched hut of the cottage roof, issued a spiral of smoke. It was thin and dark, barely visible. Then, as he watched, he saw a spark among the thatch, then another. A bright flare, and the roof seemed suddenly like a shimmering mass, all light and glitter.

Conor was laughing now, a full-bodied chuckle. Adam stared between his brother and the fire, realisation dawning. 'How did you do that?'

'Never mind,' replied Conor, picking up Adam's bag. 'They were only going to tear the place down anyway. I simply beat them to it. Now, as you said before, *let's go*. We've a way to travel before nightfall and we'll not get there by standing like some homesick ninnies, staring.'

A grim silence seemed to have overtaken the local village as they passed through. There were no children playing in the streets or women gossiping at front gates. Only the occasional twitch of a curtain betrayed the presence of people. As they neared the church, the priest paused on the steps and raised his hand in a silent farewell.

'We'll be off then,' nodded Adam, feeling that some statement was in order. He stared over the low stone wall towards the graveyard, towards the place they had buried Mam only days earlier, letting the memories flood him, knowing they would have to sustain him for a long time to come. No one will see me go, he thought, the realisation sudden in his mind. There's no one to care.

At the edge of town he turned to Conor. 'There isn't enough money for one fare, let alone two.'

Conor grinned. 'I have money.'

Suspiciously: 'Where did you get it?'

Conor stopped, the grin replaced by a frown. 'You think I stole it?'

Adam dropped his bag onto the grassy verge of the road and rubbed his hand across his eyes. 'In truth, I don't know what to think anymore.'

'Well I didn't, so there. I got it fair and legal. The landlord paid us to leave, if you must know!'

'He paid you! How much?'

'Enough for two passages. Where should we go? America? Everyone says it's the land of golden opportunity.'

'I don't care,' Adam replied dispiritedly, picking up his bag and moving on.

They walked mainly in silence, passing through the occasional village. The area was poor, the land hard and stony. Women stood in doorways, staring along the road with defiant eyes, children clinging to their skirts. We have nothing, their expressions seemed to say. Don't ask for charity. Of the men, there was no sign.

Adam's shoes rubbed at his heels, forming red ugly blisters. His suitcase, which had initially seemed so light, became a leaden weight. Rain threatened, sending fat teasing drops to wet his hair. Food became an obsession. Adam thought about it constantly, counting the hours between one miserable bite and the next. He saw children following the ploughs in the fields, rooting in the ground for chickweed or sorrel, or the occasional turnip cuttings left behind after the harvest.

They crossed streams that ran through green meadows, stopping occasionally to drink the cold water. Ahead, a cart lumbered into the hazy dusk and beyond, towards the cold dark outline of the mountains. Adam paused and turned, seeing his own shadow and Conor's, elongated and ridiculously out of proportion on the uneven ground.

He felt odd, out of kilter, as though he was caught in some nightmare from which he would soon wake. But this was no dream, he knew. This was his life now. The cottage was gone. His parents were gone. Conor was the only family he had left, and he had no choice but to move on.

That first night, he and Conor roasted some of those same turnip cuttings over a fire, slice by slice, burning fingers and tongues in their haste to eat. Then they rolled under thick bushes to sleep. In the morning, clothes damp with dew, they found watercress and mushrooms in the woods, and picked berries off a tree. The berries were green and left Adam doubled over with pain and sprinting for the nearest thicket of trees after a few hours.

It was this way that Adam and Conor came into Londonderry, tired and hungry. Alongside the ancient city walls they trudged, past the cannons pointing over ramparts unused for a lone time now. They were caught up in the human tide, pulled along the narrow roads. Down steep Shipquay Street they went. Whole families strode by, young children perched on their fathers' shoulders. Carts rattled alongside, piled high with belongings. Tall buildings lined the streets, hemming them in. To Adam, everything seemed too hurried, too frantic. He looked down at his own small suitcase, the only remnant of the life he was planning to renounce, and wondered how he had ever imagined the contents would be enough to take him into a new existence. Bewildered, he allowed himself to be jostled along the road, towards the docks which lay behind the Guildhall.

In the streets near the wharves, placards were posted extolling the virtues of the ships that lay at anchor in the harbour. 'Superior accommodation' or 'first class' read the signs, giving the sailing dates and destinations. There were several heading for America, though not one was sailing within the week.

Morosely, Adam stared at the surrounding warehouses, offices and taverns. His ears rang to a discord of man-made noises. Ahead, one of the shipping agents accosted a group of would-be emigrants, and pedlars were trying to sell cheese, tea and sugar to boarding passengers. He could hear sudden snatches of conversation above the din.

'Best be bringing some of your own food —'

'The offering on board's not much —'

One vendor held a chamber pot aloft for all to see. 'Ladies, decent ladies!' he cried as several women bowed their heads, blushing. 'You'll be thanking me every day of the voyage if you buy one of these.'

'Damn!' said Conor with a grin. 'I don't think our finances will stretch that far.'

They found lodgings and paid what Adam thought an exorbitant rate for the privilege. The room was dingy and smelled of tar and salt. Cockroaches ran up the walls. After a few minutes Conor let himself out the door, saying he was going to investigate the surroundings.

Adam lay back on the bed, hands behind his head, wondering if the blanket was lice-ridden. He fought back the impulse to scratch, staring instead at the ceiling. What exact moment of madness had brought him here? he wondered. Why had he left all that was familiar?

Now, in this strange place, the looming thought of departure shocked him. He let his thoughts idle over the events of the past few days. How quickly our fortunes change, he considered. He closed his eyes, trying to conjure a picture of Mam. Already she was fading from his mind, her features hazy in his memory.

He took her wedding ring from his pocket and held it towards the light, studying the dull glow of the gold. He supposed he could sell it, take it to some local pawnbroker and exchange it for a few miserable shillings. But he was loath to sever that last tangible link with his mother, and Conor had assured him they had enough funds for the trip. Better to keep it, he reasoned. There might be need of money later in this new land to which they were headed.

Conor returned, half an hour later, with a bottle of rum under his arm. 'This'll stop any seasickness,' he told Adam with a wink.

Adam frowned. 'Precious money spent on grog!' he admonished. 'For God's sake, Conor! We'll need every penny wherever we're going!'

'Relax, brother dear.' Conor threw the bottle nonchalantly onto the bed. 'I didn't pay for it.'

'You stole it?'

Conor grinned. 'That's a bit harsh. Although it's a word some of the other card players might be using.' He ambled back to the door and produced a bag, laying all manner of foodstuffs on the bed next to Adam. 'Anyway, I managed to pick up a few things while I was out. Dried codfish. Eggs packed in salt. Carrots and turnips, onions and vinegar. They should keep us going for a while.'

'Conor, about the ships —'

But Conor waved Adam's words away. 'That's the other thing I've been meaning to talk to you about. The American ones aren't leaving for at least a week, so there'll be lodgings and food to pay for until then. Why waste our money when we can be off? One of the ships is bound for Australia. It's leaving tomorrow morning.'

'Australia?' repeated Adam faintly.

'So, what's it to be?' demanded Conor, impatiently. 'I don't really want to hang around here for days.'

'I don't care,' shrugged Adam, suddenly indifferent to the destination. America or Australia: it was all the same to him.

'I know. We'll throw for it.'

Conor took a coin from the dresser and juggled it between his hands. 'Choose a side,' he ordered. 'If it comes up, we'll wait for America. Otherwise we'll sail tomorrow.'

'Heads.'

Adam watched as Conor spun the coin. It sailed high into the air, almost touching the ceiling, and then fell back against the floor. It seemed incongruous that this coin would decide their fate. One dull sixpence sending him one way or the other around the globe, careless of the outcome.

The coin clattered to a halt. Conor bent forward and grinned.

'Tails! Looks like it's Sydney Town we're headed to, brother dear. Australia! England's dumping ground for thieves and felons.'

There. It was decided. Just like that. The fall of a coin sending them in a direction Adam had not chosen.

Suppressing a feeling of apprehension, he turned to his brother. 'Thieves and felons! Perhaps Australia's a perfect choice after all, Conor. You'll feel right at home there.'

CHAPTER 5

CENTRAL QUEENSLAND
July 1867

'Jenna! Are you there, Jenna?'

The words were barely audible over the sound of the rain on the tin roof. Jenna McCabe placed an empty bucket on the shop counter, under the worst of the drips. She stared blankly in the direction of the voice, back towards the curtain that partitioned the shop from the living quarters beyond.

'Yes, Mary,' she muttered resignedly.

Her mother was always like that, screaming at the top of her voice when a simple call would suffice. Jenna this. Jenna that. There's a customer in the shop, Jenna! Or: Get yourself down to the pub and get me a pint, Jenna!

But Mary (Her mother insisted Jenna call her that: 'Don't call me mother. The men all say I'm much too young to have a daughter your age,' she'd said so many times.) lumbered to the door, arms wrapped around her belly. Her mouth was pulled into a tight uncompromising line and a frown creased her brow.

Jenna stared, a sense of unease washing over her. 'What's wrong?'

The first of the drips hit the bottom of the bucket. *Plop*. The sound seemed loud, even over the din of the rain. Mary McCabe shifted on her feet, leaning heavily against the doorway. Her mother's face, Jenna noted, was unusually pale as she swayed against the curtain.

'What's *wrong*?' Mary mimicked after a long pause. She pointed towards the floor where Jenna saw another spreading puddle and made a mental note to look for an extra bucket. 'This building's worse than a leaky old boat, this town's no better than the last, and the baby's coming: that's what's wrong! You'd better shut the shop and get Mrs Porter. *And* you'd better be quick about it, before I have the wretched thing here on the floor!'

There was a sense of urgency to her mother's voice, one Jenna had never heard before. Carefully she locked the front door of the shop and, pocketing the key, picked her way through the puddles that lay randomly along the footpath. The rain came in cold sheeting waves, carried almost sideways by furious gusts of wind. Leaves, sodden and brown, were scattered in great drifts in the gutters. Jenna shivered in the sudden chill and pulled up her collar against the rain. Already, before she had gone a quarter of a mile, her hair was a dark wet mass against her scalp.

Mrs Porter came grudgingly to the door in answer to Jenna's frantic knocking. 'Summat wrong, girlie?' she asked, wiping floury hands on her apron.

'It's my mother!' gasped Jenna. 'Mary McCabe, down at the store. The baby's coming and she asked me to fetch you.'

Mrs Porter gave a loud disapproving harrumph. 'So, she'll be needing my help, will she? Pity she didn't think about that when she refused me credit last week.'

'You will come?' pleaded Jenna desperately, sensing her eyes fill with tears. 'She said I was to bring you back and if I don't ...'

Her words died away unspoken and she closed her eyes briefly against the thought. If she didn't return with Mrs Porter, as was her mother's instruction, there'd be hell to pay. She brought her hand instinctively to her cheek, covering the bruise there.

'And if you don't,' finished Mrs Porter, leaning forward and wiping a stray strand of wet hair from Jenna's face, 'she'll be laying into you with a strap, no doubt.'

Was it that obvious? Quelling a rising sense of embarrassment, Jenna nodded and blinked back the tears. She raised her head defiantly, staring directly at the woman. Mrs Porter had kind eyes and a comforting manner. What would it be like, she wondered, to be caught up in the woman's embrace, to be smothered against the ample bosom and clasped by those floury hands? It was a long time since her own mother had held her close.

'Come on, girlie, don't be crying! Get along home and tell your mother I'll be there shortly,' the older woman said, breaking Jenna's train of thought.

Suddenly she remembered the reason for her hurried dash to Mrs Porter's house. Remembered the way Mary had leaned, ashen-faced, against the doorway, remembered her mother's words: *You'd better be quick about it, before I have the wretched thing here on the floor.* Guiltily she sprinted back towards the store, careless of the mud that splattered her boots and the rain that soaked her clothes.

Mrs Porter arrived at the store several minutes after Jenna, puffing from her brisk walk. Jenna, who had hung back near the curtain to her mother's room, reluctant to intrude, watched round-eyed as the midwife slammed a large black bag on the end of the bed and proceeded to remove several evil-looking instruments. 'Don't just stand there, girlie!' she snapped at Jenna. 'There's work to be done.'

'Y-yes,' stammered Jenna, unnerved by the sight of the instruments.

'How old are you?'

'Th-thirteen.'

'Old enough to be of some use, thank God!' the midwife muttered. 'Well, Jenna, no use hanging around like a useless ninny! You can start by filling your biggest pot with water and bringing it to the boil. Then I'll be needing all your spare sheets and towels.'

She was expected to help!

The thought jarred, causing a bubble of unease under her breastbone. She took a deep breath, wishing away the rising sense of alarm. She knew nothing about babies being born, or even how this one had come to be inside her mother's stomach. And just how was Mrs Porter planning to get it out? Judging from the intermittent moans that already came from her mother's room — signalling some kind of pain — and the row of instruments waiting at the foot of the bed like silent sentinels, Jenna didn't want to know.

'Go, then,' Mrs Porter went on with a frown. 'Hop to it, or we'll be in a right old mess if this baby decides to come quickly.'

Jenna let the curtain fall back into place and ran towards the kitchen, glad for the excuse to be gone. Quickly she took the largest pot from the cupboard and filled it with water, placing it over the hottest section of the stove. Then she rummaged through the linen press for the requested sheets and towels. There weren't many, the shelves being scantily filled, but Jenna took the worn contents to her mother's room as requested.

Mrs Porter ripped the fabric into smaller pieces. To Jenna, it seemed a senseless waste (where would they find the money to replace the items?) and she flinched against the harsh tearing sound of it. She glanced uneasily at her mother, seeking a reaction. But Mary was lying pale on the bed, her eyes closed.

The hours slowly passed as Jenna attended to her allotted chores — keeping the pot of water on the boil and generally tidying after the midwife. Occasionally the bell on the front door summoned her to the shop, where she served the assortment of customers who straggled in.

'Mary having her baby?' asked one of the women, glancing uneasily towards the occasional sharp cry that came from within. News obviously didn't take long to spread in this town. And the earlier arrival of the midwife at the shop would have been cause, Jenna suspected, of hasty gossip over back fences.

The nosey customer was the policeman's wife: that much Jenna knew. 'Mrs Hoity-toity', Mary called her behind her back. A prim and proper woman. Nose tilted imperiously. A knowing, smug expression on her face. Treating Jenna, with her words and accentuation, as someone to be tolerated.

'Poor little mite,' the woman went on, obviously referring to the baby, tut-tutting and shaking her head as she paid Jenna for the few groceries that now lay in her bag. 'Having a whore for a mother and never knowing its father. Though perhaps *that's* for the best,' she added darkly, emphasising the word.

Jenna wanted to ask her what she meant. She, herself, had never known her own father. And although she hadn't a clue what the word 'whore' meant, it was said with such venom that she instinctively drew back, distancing herself from the woman who let the door close with a bang as she marched back onto the footpath.

Finally, at six o'clock, Jenna locked the door and turned out the lamp, returning to the living quarters at the rear of the shop. Mary — Jenna could see through the partly opened curtain — lay on her side, arms bound tight around her stomach. She was keening softly. Her eyes were closed. Her cheeks were wet. From tears? wondered Jenna. She had never before seen her mother cry.

She made a pot of tea and a plate of sandwiches, though they were mainly for Mrs Porter's benefit;

Jenna found she had appetite for none of it. She nibbled at the corner of a piece of bread and sipped half-heartedly at a cup of tea. Then, not knowing what to do, she drew a chair to her mother's bedside and waited.

Seconds slid into minutes, into hours. Mary McCabe tossed and turned, intermittently moaning or crying out aloud and cursing the fate of women. From time to time the midwife poked and prodded at her mother under the sheet, the fabric rising and falling with the movement of the woman's hands. Jenna glanced away, staring at the grimy wall, feeling a mixture of fright and embarrassment. Though she couldn't see the target of those hands, she could guess at their destination. To have someone touch you — like that — seemed to invade the most private part of you.

'Nowt to be scared of, luvvie,' said the midwife, sensing Jenna's discomfort as she washed her hands in the bucket of water Jenna had provided.

Defiantly Jenna raised her head. 'Who says I'm scared?'

The woman laughed. 'It's written all over your face. Better get used to it, I say. This'll be your lot one day. Marriage and babies, and a whole lot of pain in between.'

Suddenly unable to bear her mother's distress, Jenna swallowed hard and forced back the urge to leave. Instead she considered what she could do to ease her mother's discomfort? Some part of her wanted to press her fingers against Mary's mouth, soothing away the sounds. She wanted to stroke her cheek and tell her ... What? Jenna wondered. What would she tell her mother? That she loved her, in an odd, twisted way? That somehow, despite all the things that had gone wrong in their lives — despite the drunken beatings and the cruel words Mary sometimes thrust at her — her mother had taken care of her the best she could, and somehow she was grateful for that.

Tentatively she reached out and took her mother's hand. It was worn and rough, the fingers calloused from years of hard work. 'It's alright, Mary,' she whispered.

'*Don't!*'

Her mother pulled her hand away, wrenching it from Jenna's as though she couldn't bear her daughter's touch. Jenna pushed the chair back and stumbled to her feet. In the kitchen she stood by the wall, arms folded across her chest. She stared through the window into the night, and the winking lights of the other houses. Snug cosy lights that suggested families and warm fires. Toast being cooked over the coals. Jam and cream for supper. Milky tea. Mothers wrapping their arms about children, tucking them into bed. Goodnight kisses. A solitary tear slid down her cheek. Hell! Her own mother couldn't even hold her hand.

She tried to detach herself from the scene, her mother's moans and the withdrawing of the hand, the brisk way the midwife moved about the room, familiar with the womanly ritual of childbirth that so horrified Jenna. Instead she thrust her mind back to her own childhood, seeking familiar details.

Jenna's grandmother, she knew, had been a convict, sent from Scotland to Australia at the age of eighteen for a paltry crime. And although it was thirty years since she had earned her freedom, Mary had never gotten over the bitterness that had brought her mother to this new land.

Nor had Mary accepted the role of her own father: a sailor aboard the leaky lice-infested barque. Mary's mother had traded her favours for a warm bed and a full belly, in more ways than one. He had promptly deserted her when the boat arrived in Sydney Town. It was there, in one of the slum houses near the Rocks, that Mary had been born seven months later.

Likewise, Jenna had never known her own father, though Mary sometimes spoke of him when she was in her cups. He'd been a garrison soldier — Jenna knew that much — and married. 'He took off when he found out I was having you,' Mary had often told her, maudlin and nostalgic with grog. 'Moved his wife and family right away, and didn't even say goodbye. I loved him and I miss the bastard,' she'd add, 'even now.'

However, missing Jenna's father hadn't stopped Mary being with other fellows, Jenna noted wryly. There'd been dozens over the years, hard cold men who'd come knocking on their door after dark. Her mother would take the visitor into her bedroom, shooing Jenna towards her own room with strict instructions not to come out until morning.

Lying in bed, waiting for sleep to come, Jenna would hear them through the thin walls. Murmuring of voices. Sounds of slapping. An occasional laugh or coarse grunting noise that reminded her of the pigs in the pen at the bottom of the neighbouring paddock, and the cry they made as they rummaged through the swill.

The creak of bed springs rasping through the night. *Squeak. Squeak.*

Jenna had held her hands over her ears, trying to block the hated sound.

She never saw the men leave; Mary had made sure of that. They were gone by first light, leaving a few coins on the kitchen table.

'I don't like what I do,' Mary had said one morning, coming into the kitchen and finding Jenna standing with the coins in her hand. 'But it pays the bills and you never go hungry. I don't know any other way.'

Just what exactly did her mother do? Jenna had wondered, but didn't ask. Instead she'd glanced away, staring instead at a fly that buzzed uselessly against a window pane, and tried not to notice the bruises on her mother's arms.

Mary had pulled the loose wrapper tighter across her chest and brought her arms up in a defensive hopeless gesture. 'I look after you properly, don't I?'

They'd moved a lot in those early years, from one miserable place to the next, eventually ending up here, in central Queensland. Mary had saved enough to purchase the general store. Somehow they were making a moderate success of it, though the running of the place was mostly left to Jenna these days while Mary kept long hours at the pub. 'Drumming up business,' she'd said to Jenna, though Jenna wasn't certain what kind of 'business' Mary meant. The store or ...

But Jenna didn't mind. Mostly her mother left her alone and by the time Mary came home drunk and senseless each evening, Jenna had usually long since gone to sleep.

'Men can be loving one minute and bastards the next,' she had told Jenna one night, perched on the end of her daughter's bed. 'Unreliable, that's what they are, and more than likely to leave you up the duff.'

Mary had brought the lamp into the room and it sent out long swaying shadows that licked at the dark corners. Jenna had blinked against the light. Her mother's face seemed sallow and old, tear-streaked. Her mouth was lopsided, twisting away at the corners.

'Up the duff,' she'd repeated, slurring the words so they were almost indistinct. 'Do you know what that means?'

Jenna had shaken her head, wishing her mother would take the lamp away and go to her own bed. 'No, Mary.'

'Good. You're a good girl, Jenna. You'll never embarrass me, make me sad.' She'd ruffled her daughter's hair and pulled the blanket over Jenna's shoulders. 'Go back to sleep. Don't mind my mad ramblings.'

As the months passed, Jenna had watched as her mother's belly grew fatter, unable to be hidden by her loose shift. There was talk about town, whispered conversations on street corners that ceased abruptly as she drew near. Fingers pointed. Her classmates snickered. 'Your mother's a whore,' sneered one of the older boys as she passed him in the playground.

'Who says?'

'My father.'

'Your father wouldn't know anything.'

'He says your mother's got a belly full of arms and legs.'

What had he meant, that snotty-nosed brat? Only the previous week Jenna had caught him helping himself to a handful of biscuits from the barrel under the store counter while she had been serving his mother. As though sensing her puzzlement he went on, 'She's having a kid. You know, a baby. A *bastard* baby.'

A baby? So who was the father? Certainly not Jenna's. According to Mary he was long gone. Jenna hadn't a clue, and Mary McCabe wasn't forthcoming with any information, not that Jenna asked.

Her mother took to sleeping in the afternoons, not bothering to open the shop. She became slovenly, scarcely bothering with her clothes or appearance. 'What does it matter?' she asked, staring listlessly at her daughter. 'Who'd want me, anyway?'

Who indeed? Lumbering around the shop with her bloated face, lank hair and grimy dress, her mother seemed like a parody of her former self. She swayed as she walked, a lopsided gait, hands supporting the small of her back. She swiped out at Jenna if she made a mistake totalling the accounts, nasty, hateful words spilling from her mouth.

One morning Jenna didn't go to school. 'I've left,' she told her mother.

'What'd you do that for?'

'So I can help here.'

Mary had patted her head, a rare gesture of affection. 'You're a good girl, Jenna.'

So here she was. Thirteen years old and running the store, working from dawn until dusk behind the counter. Then there was the cooking and cleaning to attend to. And soon there'd be a baby: another responsibility. Mary, from all indications, would probably pay scant attention to it.

Jenna sighed. She turned from the window, and the lights and signs of other, normal family lives going on, back towards the room where her mother lay curled on the bed. There was a dark stain of blood on the sheet and her face was contorted with pain. Sweat ran down her cheeks, making a small pool at the base of her throat.

Wordlessly Jenna took a damp cloth and began bathing her mother's face. Mary bit her lip and arched her back, seemingly unaware of her daughter's presence. After a while she began to scream — a half-animal, half-human sound.

Mechanically Jenna wiped the flannel to and fro, trying to block her mind to the noise. Her life was here, in this place; her duty was clear-cut. The room blurred away and the future stretched before her, predictable, formless and grey. And the burden of it weighed heavily upon her.

It wasn't until the sun was almost risen the next morning that Mary McCabe gave one final exhausted push. Jenna watched, speechless, as the baby slithered between her mother's legs and into Mrs Porter's waiting hands. The midwife swung the infant up by his ankles and gave him a sound smack on the behind, resulting in an indignant cry. 'It's a boy,' she said matter-of-factly.

Mary sank back against the sheets, her face almost translucent with fatigue. 'Thank God that's done,' she said, ignoring the child.

While Jenna removed the bloodied sheets and towels, Mrs Porter bathed the baby in a metal tub filled with warm water. Then, when he was dried and wrapped in one of Mary's shawls, she handed him to Jenna.

Carefully she took him in her arms, staring down in wonder at his red wrinkled face. He was so tiny, and so wonderfully perfect. His eyes were closed, his hands balled into tight fists. A thatch of dark hair curled around his temple. She took a deep breath, inhaling the clean fresh smell of him. 'Can we call the baby Michael?' she asked.

'Name him what you will,' replied Mary in a tired voice, turning her face to the wall. 'I can't be bothered.'

'Then Michael it is,' whispered Jenna, stroking the baby's soft cheek. 'Michael McCabe.'

The child stirred and stretched, suddenly opening his eyes and staring up at her. As Jenna bent her head, touching her mouth to his forehead, an odd surge of emotion rose up inside her, an ache of love that almost made her heart skip a beat. *Poor little mite*, the policeman's wife had said. But *she* hadn't counted on Jenna to care for him, feed and clothe him, teach him things.

She took a deep breath, holding him close.

He was, she thought with a surge of excitement, someone to love.

Later that night, when her mother and the child lay sleeping, Jenna took her diary from beside her bed. *12th July 1867*, she wrote. *It rained today and the roof leaked again. The baby came and I had to run for the midwife. She made me help. Mary screamed a lot and there was blood. I was scared. When I grow up, I'm never having a baby. Never, ever!*

PART TWO

New Beginnings

CHAPTER 6

Brad parks the Landcruiser ute outside the roadhouse, under the shade of a huge pepper tree, and awards me a grin. 'Don't know about you, Jess, but I'm starved. Everything okay?'

'I think so.'

'Only three hundred and fifty kilometres to go,' he adds, stepping from the car and leaning back through the window.

'Only?'

I say the word lightly, as though in jest, and force a smile to my mouth as I unbuckle my seat belt. What am I doing here? I wonder, for the umpteenth time today. What moment of madness has allowed me to follow Brad into the outback, a place I've never been before? What lapse of sanity has caused me to pack a suitcase full of sensible clothes and walking shoes, mosquito repellent and 30+ sunscreen? How could I possibly have left our home — those familiar well-known rooms where time never seems to move forward and I can sometimes imagine myself in the past — for an unknown place, hundreds of miles from civilisation? Why have I let myself be plucked from my comfort zone, from an existence that has become routine and familiar?

But Brad, my husband, is unaware of my dilemma — I've learned to hide my emotions well. Instead, I nod and smile, and stretch my legs. I'm experimenting, waiting for the pain that comes with long-distance travel. Beside me, Brad's kelpie pants from the heat.

'Come on, Harry,' calls Brad as he takes a bowl from the back of the ute and fills it with water from the tap beside the dirt-caked fuel bowser. The dog, in one fluid brown motion, pads past the steering wheel, leaps from the car and laps appreciatively at the water.

Although it's only late September, hot air blasts my face as I lever myself from the front seat onto the red hard-baked dirt. Giving Brad a cursory glance, Harry crawls under the vehicle into the shade. He lies there, panting, watching us with yellow eyes.

Several trucks, the interiors of which exude the stink of cow dung, are parked haphazardly outside the roadhouse. I walk past them, trying not to inhale, and trying not to think of the bovine occupants, feet shifting on the timber plank flooring, bound for some city abattoir. I also try not to think too closely of the T-bones Brad and I devoured for dinner the previous night at a motel restaurant en route.

Inside, at the counter, we order lunch. 'I'm going to find the loo,' says Brad. After he leaves, I sit at one of the three tables. Already I'm feeling lonely, missing Carys and my parents.

Carys is my sister. She's twenty-five — four years my junior — smart and savvy. With the same dark hair cut into a short bob, and green eyes, she's a smaller, more petite version of me. Sometimes people mistake us for twins. During the day she works as a conveyancer in a solicitor's office. In her spare time she's doing a law degree at uni.

Our grandmother bequeathed us the house that Brad and I now own: we bought Carys out because she hadn't wanted to live there. With the money she purchased a high-rise unit in the centre of the city, on the river. It's funky and modern, and at the time we'd all thought her crazy. But now, the way real-estate prices have risen over the past couple of years, it's probably worth three times what she paid for it.

Sometimes I have sleepovers at her place with a few other friends — a girls' night where we pig out on chocolate and pizza and red wine, and spend the next day regretting it. When I stay at Carys's, I like to rise early and sit on the balcony. I look down at the first dribble of traffic along the freeways, at the boats on the river: the city catamarans and sleek-hulled yachts, the rowers straining muscles against the tide as they pull in unison.

I wonder what my sister is doing now. It's Sunday lunch time so she's probably dining in one of those trendy little alfresco cafes along the waterfront with a few friends. The wine and laughter will be flowing, and afterwards they'll all drift off to a cinema and watch some arty movie or go to a play.

And my parents? Well, being Sunday, they'll be sitting down to a traditional roast dinner. I can imagine the bowl of freshly cut flowers on the table, and a jug of gravy. The roast will be beef or lamb, with crisp potatoes and beans and carrots from Dad's vegetable garden. And for afters there'll be apple crumble or steamed pudding and custard. Later, while Mum washes up, Dad will sit in his favourite chair, reading the Sunday paper. Invariably he'll fall asleep there, with the sun and the smell of freshly mown lawns coming in the window.

A loud crash comes from the direction of the roadhouse kitchen — the sound of breaking plates — and my attention slides back to the now. I gaze around the room. The walls are fly-speckled. Red and white chequered plastic cloths cover the tables. There's a puddle of tomato sauce (can't anyone be bothered to wipe the table after the previous occupants?) congealing in the centre of ours. Several milk crates containing empty soft-drink bottles stand by the door which carries the obligatory plastic strips designed to keep out flies, but seems more efficient at keeping them in.

Two men sit at the other two tables respectively, their heads bent over newspapers as they wait for their order. One is wearing a blue singlet, the other a flannelette shirt. The place radiates a feeling of faded nonchalance. I pick up a magazine from the chair next to me. The corners are tatty and someone has drawn a moustache on the face of a female politician on the cover. October 2000, reads the date. Years earlier. Old news. Idly I flick through the pages.

Without warning, my attention is caught by a picture of a woman, her face horribly scarred. In a small inset there's a photo of what she had looked like before. She'd been dark-haired and pretty. Her smile had been infectious. Now her features were misshapen and she wore a permanent scowl.

What momentous occurrence in her life caused this? I wonder, fascinated in a macabre sort of way. At what precise point in time had her face ceased to be attractive? When had beauty become ugliness? And, more importantly, what would this woman give to be able to take that moment back, to change the course of what went horribly wrong?

I stare at the words on the page, wanting to read the details, but they blur together in an incomprehensible smear. Angrily I wipe away the tears, hoping no one else has seen me at my most vulnerable. I'm embarrassed, in an odd way, by the tears. I'm also puzzled that they should surface here, in this dingy place. What does it matter, anyway? I tell myself. I don't know this woman. She's merely a face on a page, with another desperate hard-luck story to match my own.

My mind slides sideways, in a familiar pattern, and screams sickeningly to a halt. I'd give anything, I think now, to take back that split second that changed our own lives — mine and Brad's — but I can't. Time doesn't move in reverse. It simply marches ahead, taking nothing but the memories with it. That's why I've come here with my husband, to try to place some distance between the person I was and the person I am now, to try to regain some kind of perspective in my life.

Brad comes back and we face each other across the table. Suddenly I'm unsure of what to say to him.

The words won't come and I glance away, staring instead at the milk crates beside the door.

'Talk to me, Jess.'

It's not fair that he has to bear my silences, but there are times when I don't trust myself to speak. 'I can't.'

'Look, about —'

Don't, I think. Don't say her name.

'About everything that's happened,' he goes on. 'I'm sorry, but I can't change it. I'd give anything if I could.'

'Not here. Not now,' I whisper.

'When, then? When's a good time, Jess?'

There is a sense of urgency to his voice and I know I should say something — anything — to reassure him. But my words, when they come, are pathetic.

'I don't know.'

'We have to move on, let things take their course. We can't live in the past. And we can have such a good future, you and I.'

'Can we?'

There are days — black sullen days when everything seems futile and senseless and dismal — when I can't imagine Brad and me sharing any future. Too many obstacles, too many reminders of the past, separate us now. We've changed, he and I, from the people we once were. Brad's become hardened, more practical, while I . . .

I search my mind for some way to describe the woman I am now. More emotional, I suppose. More introspective and nostalgic. More distrusting.

There is spilt salt on the table and I'm aware of it,

gritty, under my fingers. Determinedly I arrange it into a pile, pushing and prodding the greyish mound. I can't look at him, can't bear to see the tortured expression on his face. Suddenly he leans forward and folds his hand over my own. 'Don't,' he says, his voice terse. 'Don't do that.'

I stare up at him. His fingers are warm. Mine are cold, despite the heat. Words fail me. What can I say to this man — my husband — who sometimes seems like a stranger? He's the one I've trusted over the years with all my secret thoughts. He knows me, I think, too well. Yet there are days when I scarcely know him — or myself, for that matter.

'I'm glad you decided to come.'

His voice softens, becomes mellow. I know what I'm supposed to answer: me, too. Agree and smile. Keep the peace. But the words jam in my throat and go unvoiced. Am I glad? I don't know. It's not an emotion that springs readily to mind.

I think about the six weeks ahead — Brad and me, alone — and feel apprehensive. How will we fill those minutes, hours and days? What words will we say to each other? How will we say them? With rancour and acrimony, or with understanding and insight?

In my mind I picture us rehashing the past as we sit around some campfire discussing the whys and wherefores. How things might have been. What we would have done differently if we'd been blessed with the divine ability to see into the future.

'Here we go. Two hamburgers with the lot, and coffee.'

Gratefully I'm distracted by the food slammed before us on the table. I focus my attention back on my surroundings and my mind begins its usual series of thoughts. If this were my place, I think, I'd have crisp cloths on the tables and vases of flowers. I'd wear a clean apron and clear out the milk crates and old magazines, straighten the place up and make it a bit more welcoming. But, I wonder, staring at the other two male occupants of the room, would anyone care out here?

I eat mechanically. The food is tasteless though Brad seems to be enjoying his. He wipes a smear of sauce from his mouth and offers me a tentative smile. 'Good, hey?' he says before taking another mouthful.

'Great,' I agree, trying to sound enthused.

We finish the meal in silence. There's really nothing we can say to each other that hasn't been said before. The words are meaningless anyway. They don't alter facts, change the way things are between us.

As we walk out the door, back to our car and the seemingly endless highway, I notice the crudely written sign in the window. BUSINESS FOR SALE. APPLY WITHIN.

The road from here is dirt. We jolt along in the Landcruiser, weaving around potholes and corrugations at an alarming speed. Behind us, when I turn my head to see, trails a plume of red dust. Hours go by. Occasionally we pass another vehicle — a livestock truck or another dirt-caked 4WD — but mostly the road ahead remains empty. Harry puts his head on the seat between us and sleeps.

I stare listlessly at the dashboard. Specks of dust hover above its surface and I focus on them, wishing for the thousandth time that I'd never heard the name Diamantina. I glance across at Brad. He focuses straight ahead, a look of concentration on his face as he steers the 4WD. The road, if it can be called that, looks as though it belongs back in the horse and buggy days.

The countryside changes constantly. The expected dry bushland never eventuates. Instead, one minute we're travelling across undulating country dotted with Mitchell grass and trees. Here and there, clumps of wildflowers carpet the ground in unexpected swathes of colour — pink and yellow, blue and cream — making a contrast with the drab green and brown. Then suddenly the landscape drops away, vast and lunar-like, almost level, broken only by ancient flat-topped hills jutting from the ground. 'They're called jump-ups,' says Brad, pointing to the distant weathered outcrops.

I glance across at him, covertly, trying to remember all his good points. His enquiring mind. An unfailing sense of good humour. The way he always managed to see both sides of any story. Qualities I find now, with the passage of time, that tend to annoy rather than attract.

'Hey, Jess!' Brad awards me a quick grin, takes one hand from the wheel and rests it on my knee. 'Everything okay?'

I used to like that, the touch of his hand on my leg, in what now seems another lifetime. It indicated an intimacy that once bound us, a sense that we belonged together, and that if we were the only two people left in the world somehow it wouldn't matter because we still had each other. But now the pressure of his fingers and the heat that radiates from his skin irritates me, and I fight the urge to push his hand away. All I want is a bath, or a long hot shower.

'Sure,' I say instead, suppressing the thoughts as I plaster a smile across my face, pretending again.

CHAPTER 7

CENTRAL QUEENSLAND
December 1867

The months passed, days rolling into each other in an untidy blur of school, work and precious little sleep. No longer was Michael a tiny helpless baby, all thin arms and legs, crying with that little bleating sound like the goats in the farmer's paddock on the edge of town. Now he laughed and held out his arms towards Jenna when she came home from school, or crawled around the floor while Mary served the endless line of customers who streamed through the shop door.

Jenna had returned to school after Michael's birth, prompted by a visit from the local teacher who informed her mother, in no uncertain terms, that Jenna's continued absence from school was a breach of the law. Ungraciously Mary gave in. She never failed to remind Jenna daily that her help was needed constantly at the counter, more so since the only other grocery shop in town had closed its doors. The owner had headed for more lucrative pickings — or so he had informed his customers — on the northern goldfields.

Jenna had turned fourteen that spring. Mary either managed to forget the occasion of her daughter's birthday or, if she had remembered, she neglected to say anything let alone tender a gift. Jenna had been reluctant to remind her, preferring to stay on the periphery of her mother's attention: Mary was even more short-tempered these days.

So her birthday passed like any other day, and instead of some celebratory meal and a specially iced cake, like Annie Rawlins had boasted of at school the previous week, Jenna spent the evening alone with Michael while her mother went to the pub, as usual.

'You know, don't you?' she whispered to her brother as they snuggled together in bed after supper. 'You know it's my special day?'

He chuckled and pulled at her hair, grasping the strands with his chubby fingers. She pretended to bite his arm, laughing and wrapping him in her embrace. He felt solid and warm, someone who returned her affection. In a few short months he had somehow become her life — the *whole* reason for her existence was to be Michael's substitute mother — and as the days and months passed she struggled to remember a time when he had not been there.

Jenna heard all the local gossip, and more, at the counter where she took over from her mother after school had finished for the day. Juicy titbits. Snatches of public scandal. Rumour and hearsay blended together in an alarming array of ire and sanctimonious outrage. The policeman's wife was the worst, making snide remarks about whoever took her fancy. Last week it had been the blacksmith's daughter running off with the baker. This week it was dancing and debauchery (she'd heard that from Hetty O'Brien, who'd heard it from the blacksmith) at the old Melville place, and the new female teacher at the school.

'She's too young and pretty, in my opinion. Still, that didn't stop her from being jilted last year. She was waiting in the church, if you please, and the bloke was riding out of town as fast as his horse would carry him . . .'

The woman's voice faded from Jenna's awareness. She tried not to listen, wanting no part of it. The thought left a sick empty feeling in her belly. She was increasingly aware that her own family provided much fodder for gossip: Michael's birth, Mary's drunken sprees, the absence of Jenna's own father and the speculation about Michael's.

There were afternoons when she arrived at the shop after school, breathless from running, to find the premises locked and an angry queue of customers waiting outside.

'Disgraceful!' the customers muttered. They pushed past her as she unfastened the door, snatching items from the shelves and thumping them down on the counter. Jenna would be torn between serving them and rescuing Michael from his cot in the bedroom, from where she could hear his dejected sobs. Mary, she knew from experience, would be sprawled drunk and senseless in the ladies' lounge at the pub.

Other afternoons she came home to find her mother holding forth in the shop, and Michael filthy from crawling around the floor all day. Once the queue of customers had cleared, Mary invariably removed her apron, even though it was several hours until closing time.

'You'll be able to manage now, luvvie?' she'd ask, peering in the mirror on the wall behind the counter, pinching colour into her cheeks. She pulled the neckline of her dress lower so the swell of her breasts was visible, then pinned up the stray strands of hair that had somehow managed to escape. Not once did she glance in Jenna's direction. She was more intent on her own reflection.

Jenna would nod and look away, her mouth unable to form words.

'Got to get myself a bit of company, relax a bit. I've been so busy this afternoon.'

None of the day's chores had ever been completed so Jenna wasn't sure what had kept her mother occupied all day. Today, there were several unfilled grocery orders lying on the bench, and stock waiting to be packed on the shelves. From all appearances, the floor hadn't even been swept. With a sigh she picked up the broom.

'You don't mind, do you?'

The question was solicitous but the tone of her mother's voice was hard, as though daring Jenna to refuse.

Jenna shook her head. 'No, go on. I'll manage here.'

What could she otherwise say? *Yes, I do mind! Michael's your child, not mine, and he needs you. I'm a miserable substitute.*

But the words remained unsaid.

'You're a treasure,' her mother said, ruffling Jenna's hair as she pulled on her hat and walked towards the door. 'I don't know what I'd do without you. Just make Michael a bit of supper, there's a love, and give him a bath.'

The door slammed behind Mary. Jenna scooped up the baby and held him to her chest. He was grubby from crawling on the floor and, judging by the smell, his nappy had probably needed changing hours ago. 'Mum, mum, mum,' he said, touching his chubby hand to her face. Playfully she bit at his fingers and he pulled them away with a chuckle.

At six o'clock she locked the front door and extinguished the lamp at the counter. She bathed Michael in a tub on the kitchen bench, fed him, then held him close, rocking him back and forth until his eyelids fluttered and became still, and his chest rose and fell with the steady rhythm of sleep.

She sat there for what seemed like ages, unwilling to place him in his cot, savouring his warmth and the clean soapy smell of him. Her mother did her a favour, she told herself, leaving them alone. For these few hours each day, Michael was hers. She wondered, watching his dark eyelashes as they rested against his cheeks, what it would be like to have a baby grow inside you. She imagined her belly pushed out hard with it, as Mary's had been. She imagined lying on that same bed as her mother, her face screwed up with pain as she pushed the child from her body. What would it feel like, she wondered, to nurse a baby at her breast?

But Michael wasn't really hers, she reminded herself hastily as she laid him gently in his cot. She had no claim on him, and the thought was one of unbearable sadness. She stood looking down on him as he sighed and curled into the sheet. And where the child's body had rested against hers, at the place where their skin had met, Jenna felt leaden and suddenly cold.

She shivered, despite the December heat. In the kitchen she made a hasty sandwich and nibbled at it half-heartedly before going back into the shop. Despondently she stood, hands on hips, surveying the mess. Several unpacked orders — biscuits and flour, sugar, tea, cans of sardines and jam — were scattered on the counter.

Jenna studied the handwritten notes and collected packing boxes, putting the items inside. She'd get up early and distribute them before school. Then she wiped the never-ending layers of dust from the shelves. Restocked those same shelves. Weighed and packed bags of flour and sugar in preparation for the following day. She was making life easier for her mother, though for what reason she had no idea. Keep Mary happy: that seemed to be her main aim in life these days.

It was after midnight before she tumbled, exhausted, into bed.

Minutes later, her mother came home. Jenna held her breath as she heard Mary rattling at the door, trying to insert the key in the lock. She heard her stumble through the darkened rooms, cursing loudly as her shin collided with a chair leg. Then she felt the mattress sag as Mary crawled into bed next to her. 'Hold me,' she said, smelling of beer as she wrapped her bony arms around Jenna's chest. Jenna longed to wriggle away from the stink of sweat and grog. But her mother held her close.

'Jenna?'

'Yes,' she mumbled sleepily, trying not to inhale the bitter stench.

'I'm sorry.'

'What for?'

'I'm a lousy mother.'

'No, you're not.'

Who was she trying to convince? Jenna wondered: herself or Mary?

'I am!' Mary cried, mock hysterical, her voice breaking. Jenna sensed the hot tears slide down her mother's face. 'I'm a whore and a hussy, that's what they say.'

'That's what who says?'

What person said those things about Mary? Jenna had to know. She needed to be prepared for the vicious onslaughts from the policeman's wife or the cruel taunts of the children in the schoolyard. She wanted to be able to defend herself, and Michael, if the need arose.

'But they don't understand, those self-righteous bastards,' Mary went on as though Jenna hadn't spoken. 'They haven't had the life I've had. No husband. Two kids to support. *Whore!* That's a bit rich! A woman needs a little loving sometimes, that's all. She needs to feel like she's wanted.'

The reply choked in Jenna's throat. Michael and I need you, she longed to cry out. We're family. You gave birth to us. You don't need the pub or ale to make you feel wanted.

But they weren't the words, she knew, that her mother needed to hear.

Instead she lay there, rigid in her mother's clumsy embrace, wishing for sleep. And when she finally woke, it was morning and her bed was empty.

* * *

Caught in that grey interval between wakefulness and sleep, Adam pushed the sheet towards the foot of the bed. Already the air was stifling, the day promising suffocating heat.

From outside he could hear the chatter of birds mixed with an odd deep-throated chuckle. The sound was foreign to him and it pulled him closer to consciousness. Something's wrong, he thought suddenly, unable to feel the pitch and roll of the boat beneath him.

He opened his eyes, blinking in the early morning light. A breeze was coming through the open window, billowing the fabric of the curtains inwards and bringing with it the tang of salt. From beyond the periphery of his vision came the whinny of a horse. He sat up, confused. Where was he? And where was Conor?

Then he remembered.

Yesterday they'd arrived in Sydney. In the middle of a sudden December squall he and Conor had stumbled from the boat, their sea legs threatening to topple them to the ground. They'd found this lodging room, planning to look for work that very morning. And the chuckle, he thought, recalling the earlier sound intermingled with that of the birdsong. Someone on the boat had told him about the laughing jackass, or kookaburra, only seen in the antipodes.

Australia: his new home.

So much to see and learn.

Adam's thoughts trailed back to the previous day. He remembered the first sight of land, a distant smear on the horizon. Everyone had crowded up on the deck, anxious to watch, and the men had set up a loud cheer. The days of tossing and turning on those briny waves were finally at an end. Then, as they came closer, the details of the land ran into each other as Adam strained his eyes to see. Tree-clad hills and ragged cliffs. Looming headlands, one on either side, through which they must pass. Then the harbour lying before them, houses dotting the shoreline and a colourful array of boats skimming across the water.

There had been several tall-masted ships docked at the wharves. Wool clippers mostly, Adam had surmised, watching the flurry of activity as the dockhands loaded the hessian-covered bales.

'Wool for the English mills!' Conor had snorted derisively then turned his attention to the mish-mash of warehouses and stores and pubs that towered along the waterfront. 'Come on. Let's have an ale to celebrate our arrival.'

Now, lying in bed, Adam heard the rattle of carts on the street below. He slid from the mattress and walked to the window, throwing back the curtain. From there he could see a pocket-sized glimpse of that same harbour from yesterday, sunlight already reflecting from its surface. It had rained during the night and everything looked fresh and clean, newly washed. Below, a milk cart and horse waited as shopkeepers swept leaves from the gutters, and a few early shoppers hurried along the wet pavement.

On the bed against the far wall, Conor was curled into a tight ball, sleeping soundly. Adam paused for a moment, studying his younger brother. Fair, where he, Adam, was dark. Lean and sinewy, where Adam was shorter, stockier. He supposed that strangers might not take them for brothers, so unlike were they. Then he leaned across and shook Conor awake.

'What is it?' Conor opened one eye and glared at his brother. 'Come on, Adam. Be reasonable. It's not yet six o'clock, surely?'

'It's way past seven and we had an agreement. Breakfast, then off to look for work.'

Grumbling, Conor pulled on the trousers and shirt he'd worn the day before, then clomped down the stairs in front of Adam. The smell of cooked meat wafted up towards them as a maid, dressed in black and wearing a white apron, held open the dining room door. 'Morning, gentlemen.'

Conor gave her a broad wink. 'Morning, ma'am.'

The girl smiled and turned a darker shade of pink. Conor, mused Adam, seemed to have a certain way with women, despite his youth. Girls gravitated towards him while Adam usually stuttered and stammered and was always lost for words. A bit like their mam he thought, remembering. Some had thought her aloof, brusque even. But Adam knew she'd been a shy woman, not given to unnecessary words. Conor, now, was like Da. He'd loved to chat and be friendly.

Breakfast was a hearty plateful of chops and eggs and several thick slabs of bread. Conor and Adam were almost finished when voice made them look up. An older gentleman stood by their table, cigar held between his thumb and forefinger. He was well-dressed, though a trifle overweight, and wore a waistcoat and cravat.

'Mind if I sit down, boys?'

'Feel free,' replied Adam, getting to his feet as the man sat, as a mark of respect.

The man took a long draw on the cigar, paused, then blew a cloud of smoke from his mouth, most of which drifted across Conor's face. Conor wrinkled his nose and awarded the man a sour look, which the man failed to notice. 'Let me introduce myself,' he said. 'George Eldred Owen McKenzie. You can call me George.'

The chap seemed friendly enough, thought Adam, introducing himself and Conor.

'So you chaps are new in town?' asked George, looking them up and down.

'We might be,' replied Conor, shovelling the last spoonful of egg into his mouth.

'Did you arrive on the ship yesterday?'

Conor put down his fork with a thump. 'Why? What's it to you?'

George raised his eyebrows at Conor's tone and, by the sudden tilt of his chin, Adam knew the lad's manner had annoyed the man. 'Just thought you might be looking for work and I need a couple of strong boys.' He made to rise from his chair. 'However I can see you're not interested. Shame really, because there are plenty of others looking for work.'

'There are?' asked Adam. Perhaps he'd been naive in thinking any number of jobs might be available to them in this new country. 'What sort of work?'

George eased his frame back against the chair and regarded them for one long moment, deliberately, Adam knew, delaying his answer. He was drawing them out, sensing there was now a flicker of interest in his proposal. 'So, you *are* interested?'

'Perhaps,' answered Adam guardedly.

George took another long draw on his cigar. 'Farm labouring, mainly. You blokes ever done that sort of work?'

Conor gave a deprecatory laugh. 'Born and raised to it.'

'That so? And where would that be?'

'Ireland, as surely you can tell by our accents. County Derry.'

'Well, the job's available, if you want to work. It's a day's ride from here.'

'What's the pay?' asked Adam.

'Fifteen shillings a week, paid monthly, plus food and board.'

To Adam, used to working for scant more than a bellyful of potatoes and a warm bed, the offer sounded more than generous. *Fifteen shillings!* Double that, for Conor would get his share too. If they worked hard for a couple of years, saved like mad, perhaps they would have enough for their own place. He glanced enquiringly at Conor, and his brother shrugged in reply.

'It's a deal,' said Adam. He offered his hand and the two men solemnly shook.

'Be outside by nine tomorrow morning. The wagon will be leaving then.'

And George Eldred Owen McKenzie touched the brim of his hat and walked away.

Later, in the hallway outside their room, Adam said to Conor, 'You didn't have to be so rude.'

'I wasn't rude. I just don't trust that man.'

'Why not?'

'I don't know. Gut instinct perhaps.'

'*Gut instinct*! For God's sake, Conor!'

'Excuse me.'

The two brothers looked up to see a man standing in an open doorway. 'I'm not meaning to stick my nose in where it's not wanted,' he said, 'but I couldn't help seeing you in the dining room, talking to George McKenzie.'

'What of it?' snapped Conor, clearly irritated.

'He didn't happen to offer you blokes work, did he?' the man asked affably, ignoring Conor's hostility.

'He might have,' replied Conor defensively.

'What wage did he offer you?'

'Look, I don't really see what business —'

'Fifteen shillings a week,' broke in Adam, silencing his brother. 'Plus board and keep.'

The man nodded. 'The going rate's eighteen, especially where you'd be headed.'

'Eighteen? That's three shillings more.'

The man turned, as though to enter his room. 'Don't be fooled. George McKenzie's a scoundrel, if ever I knew one. He takes advantage of new chums like you, so be warned.'

Back in their own room, Conor was all for forgetting the job offer. 'There'll be others,' he said dismissively. 'We're young and fit. We won't have any problem finding positions.'

But George McKenzie's words niggled at Adam. 'What if there is little work on offer?' he asked. 'We could be passing up an easy chance.'

After some discussion, they agreed to spend the remainder of the day scouring the city in search of employment. If they were unsuccessful then they'd take up George McKenzie's proposal.

'I suppose that's fair,' Conor conceded. 'That way we'll know what's available.'

They tried the warehouses and pubs, and the bond stores along the waterfront. They slogged around dockyards and factories. They even caught the train to Parramatta, a stop-start journey of twelve miles. Everywhere they went, doors were closed in their faces. 'Sorry, mate. Nothing going. You'll be lucky to pick up anything around here,' was the standard reply.

'Well, that's it, then,' Adam said as the train disgorged them, hot, tired and hungry, back at the Redfern railway terminal. 'Looks like it's George McKenzie's.' He frowned anxiously at Conor. 'You don't mind, do you?'

Conor shrugged. 'We agreed. There's no work here, so might as well head north. At least we'll have a roof over our heads and a full belly.'

* * *

At nine o'clock the next morning they waited outside the hotel for the wagon, as instructed. It was almost Christmas and there was a festive air to the city. Shop windows displayed bright decorations. Shoppers, despite the heat, seemed to have a jaunty spring in their step. Watching from the footpath, Conor felt a pang of sadness. This time last year it had been the four of them: Mam and Da, himself and Adam. They'd been a family, celebrating the holiday season and a new year. Now, twelve months later, he wondered if he would ever feel so light-hearted, so idealistic again. So much had happened in the last year, such misery and sadness and dampening of spirits. There was little to celebrate now. So far, even this new country seemed to yield little encouragement.

The wagon arrived an hour late. The man behind the reins offered no apology, and gave them mere seconds to hoist their bags onto the back and jump up. The wagon was old, Conor could see that, and the condition of the horses poor. The driver had several days' growth on his chin and smelled strongly of ale.

For one brief moment as the horses stepped forward, he hesitated, sensing that something was not quite right. Perhaps he and Adam should take their bags and get off now, before they had gone more than a few blocks, take their chances with work in the city? But how long could they last? Only a few shillings remained in his pocket, and lodgings and food were proving expensive.

He glanced across at his brother and Adam gave him an encouraging smile as the wagon rolled and swayed. Conor closed his eyes, projecting his mind forward. Maybe Adam was right in wanting to leave the city. They were country folk after all, not used to the rumble and roar of traffic, the press of people. Farm labouring: that was what they wanted. Good honest work among wide open spaces where you could see the horizon.

His attention slid back to the previous day. Rude: that was what Adam had called him after their conversation with George McKenzie. He hadn't meant to be. Hadn't thought he *had* been really. Just suspicious and wary and distrusting. The last few months had taught him that.

To get on in this world you had to keep your wits about you. Everyone, it seemed, was out to get you, one way or another, whether it was the landlord back home, or a hotel keeper or a prospective employer. *Don't trust*, said an inner voice. *Take nothing for granted.* Like he had in his former life. Mam. Da. He'd thought they would always be there, looking out for him. But they were gone — seemingly in the blink of an eye — and it was just the two of them now. He and Adam — brothers fighting their way through the muck and mire and intricacies of life.

It was late when they arrived, almost midnight. No supper was offered and he and Adam were ushered to a lean-to at the back of the stable. Conor sank gratefully onto a straw mattress, every bone and muscle in his body screaming for relief.

Tomorrow, he thought with optimism, was another day.

George McKenzie owned a pub — the Rose and Thistle — with a small farm attached. It was beside a wide river, the Hawkesbury, north of Sydney. The surrounding green hills and lush valleys reminded Adam of Ireland, although the climate soon had him wishing for cooler weather.

There were six workers in total, both for the farm and the pub, and they all bunked together in a tin shed next to the stables. The accommodation was wretched. Beds were pallets flung haphazardly on the ground, and the iron roof and walls of the shed retained the heat of the day long after night had fallen. The food was slop — 'we wouldn't have fed this to the pigs back home,' Conor grumbled — and the working hours horrendous. The men were summoned from their beds at sun-up, and did not retire until dusk, six days a week.

On the morning of his day off, Adam needed to distance himself from the place. The other men had all wandered into the pub and Conor was still sleeping. The lad was exhausted, he knew that. So he climbed a nearby hill and sat with his back against the rough papery bark of a gum tree, looking down on the farm.

From that distance, away from the grinding work and squalid conditions, it looked pretty, picturesque. Eye-squinting greenness of grass. Sunlight mirrored off the surface of the river. Crops growing in neat structured rows. Overhead a flock of birds flew high on the wind, dark specks against the infinite blueness of the sky. He heard them, shrill shrieks that came in fractured bursts, and wondered, not for the first time, what it would be like to fly free.

Ireland, he thought, suddenly homesick. In this new country, thousands of miles away from his homeland, nothing had changed. If life was a ladder then he was on the lowest rung. Conor was right: they were still living like pigs. Maybe this was his lot, he mused, destined to be poor. Perhaps no matter how hard he worked, how desperate he was to better himself, life would never improve. If so, he wondered, what was he doing here, in this place, miles from anywhere? Perhaps, in hindsight, he should have listened to the advice of the stranger in the hotel.

A shadow fell across the grass and Conor flung himself down beside Adam. 'I overheard some of the other chaps talking,' he said. 'They've been here a month longer than us and they've never been paid. Maybe we should cut our losses and walk away now.'

Adam stared down at the farm. 'Let's give it a few more weeks. Maybe things will get better. If we work hard and save, we'll have a place of our own some day. And not some runty little farm with poor soil. We'll have acres and acres, stretching as far as the eye can see, with black loamy soil and cows and sheep and horses.'

'Don't forget the pigs,' broke in Conor with a grin. 'And a few acres of potatoes. It'll be just like home.'

Adam swung slowly towards his brother. 'Home,' he said slowly, drawing the word out. 'Ireland's not home anymore. This is.'

* * *

By the end of the month, when no pay had been offered, Adam and Conor approached George McKenzie. 'Let's see,' their employer said, 'how long have you been here now?'

'Just over four weeks.'

'At twelve shillings a week.'

'You promised us fifteen!' blurted Conor.

'I did?' George sounded surprised.

'We shook hands on it,' added Adam quietly.

'All right.' The man had a smirk on his face. 'Fifteen shillings, as agreed, multiplied by four weeks. That's how much credit you get at the bar.'

'At the bar?'

'Things aren't going too well at the moment, and I don't have the ready cash to pay you. Not till the crops are sold. But you boys can have a good time drinking your wages.'

CHAPTER 8

CENTRAL QUEENSLAND
July 1871

The winter of '71, Jenna thought, was the coldest she remembered. Sleety winds blew from the west bringing icy temperatures. The shop was freezing and she dressed four-year-old Michael in layers of thick clothing, hoping he'd stay warm. At night the two of them lay under the blankets, his sturdy body snuggled up to hers.

She took comfort from the heat of him, his sweet breath, and the way he lay entangled in the sheets. He was careless of his surroundings, the way customers looked at him in the shop. *Bastard*, she heard some of them mutter under their breath, pressing past him, not bothering if they trod on his toes or pushed him against the wall. He never cried. Not once. Instead he looked at them in puzzlement, as though wondering why they rushed and shoved and gave each other scant attention.

Jenna had turned seventeen earlier in the year. She had begun wearing her hair up, the dark mass of it pinned at the back of her head. The local dressmaker had sewn her several new dresses — with low-cut, fitted bodices that her mother had chosen — that somehow made her appear, or so she thought, older than her years. Sometimes she caught sight of herself in the mirror behind Mary's bedroom door and it seemed, for one suspended moment, that a stranger stared back. She'd grown taller and her body had taken on curves where once there had been flat planes of skin. Now she had breasts and hips, and there was a new fullness to her mouth. Where had that gangly awkward schoolgirl gone?

She could have been a teacher, or so the headmistress at the local school had said. Her grades were good, her spelling and arithmetic excellent. But her mother had been adamant: Jenna was to help in the shop and there was Michael to consider. So she had left school and now worked full-time.

Without the distraction of geography and arithmetic, the job was mundane. Days dissolved into each other, none standing out as separate or distinct from the rest. From sun-up to sundown she served, stacked, cleaned and measured, doling out meagre yet cherished minutes to Michael. Most days she barely saw her mother. Mary was keeping company with a chap who lived near the pub, and only put in the occasional appearance to 'borrow' money from the till.

'Just until the end of the week,' she'd say, taking a handful of notes. 'I'll repay it then.'

Jenna knew she'd never see the money again.

Some of the local men waited until there were no other customers before coming into the store. They'd smile conspiratorially at Jenna. Then they'd lean towards her across the counter, uncomfortably close, letting their gaze rove conspicuously over her body, mentally undressing her until she blushed with embarrassment. 'I don't mind paying for extra services rendered,' was the standard offer.

'I don't know what you mean.'

She learned to toss her head and stare them down, learned to feign ignorance while fighting back the urge to slap their faces. How dare they! Men who went home to their wives and children each night, coming here, treating her like —

She'd stop then, remembering. They were treating her like her mother.

One man came into the store and locked the door behind him, pocketing the key. He pushed Jenna up against the counter, grinding his hips against hers, trying to plant his wet mouth on her lips. His hands seemed to be everywhere, pawing at her. 'Come on, darlin', just a little poke. It won't hurt and I'll spend another few quid in the store.'

She wanted to scream, but Michael was napping in the bedroom at the rear of the shop. 'Don't be silly,' she hissed instead. 'Besides, your wife usually comes in most afternoons. She'd be surprised to find you here, no doubt.'

'She won't know if you don't tell her.'

Jenna was disgusted. She averted her head and his mouth landed near her ear. 'Get away! Leave me alone!'

She pushed him, hard, and he stumbled back against the shelves, sending tins of jam and sardines rolling across the floor. He stood, face purple with fury, waving his finger at her. 'Your mother's no better than a whore, so don't you go pretending to be so high and mighty.'

After he left she got down on her hands and knees and picked up the tins. Several had been dented — who would want them now? — and she placed them angrily on the counter, tears massing at the back of her eyes. Her hands were shaking and her heart was beating so fast she feared it might burst through her chest. When the last tin was retrieved, she let her legs fold under her, sliding down the front of the counter until she sat on the floor, wrapping her arms around her calves and resting her chin on her knees. 'Oh, damn! Damn! Damn! Damn!'

There was a movement behind her: Michael. He was sleepy-eyed, his cheeks pink. Obviously the noise of the falling tins, or the raised voices, had woken him.

'What's wrong?' he asked, putting his arms around her and laying his face against hers.

'Nothing.'

Despite her intentions, the tears started in earnest. And, once begun, they could not be stopped. 'I love you, Michael,' she hiccupped. 'Always remember that.'

Gently she drew him onto her lap. He stared up at her, puzzled. 'Don't cry, Jenna,' he whispered. 'I don't like it when you cry.'

Michael: her brother. The only meaningful person in her life, and he loved her unreservedly. She should leave, she thought, take him away. This was no life for a child. But the doubts niggled. Where would she go? How could she support them? She had no talent for anything other than shop work. Perhaps she'd end up like Mary, taking men into her bed just to pay the bills. She shuddered, thinking of the man who had just left, the way he had grasped roughly at her skin and tried to put his hand down the bodice of her gown.

Oh, God! That option was worse than staying here, fending off the unwelcome propositions. Michael wriggled on her lap, demanding her attention. She hugged him back hard, feeling the weight of his body and the warmth of his embrace until she thought her heart might break.

It was late afternoon and the usual stream of customers straggled into the shop. Michael sat in the doorway, playing with a ball. It was shiny and red, and made a funny thumping noise when bounced. Jenna had been playing with it earlier, rolling it along the floor towards him. Now she could see him pushing it along the ridge of the step that led down onto the footpath.

'Michael,' she called, glancing past the line of people waiting at the counter, thinking he really should come inside. Soon it would be dark, and already a chill was creeping into the air.

'You all out of marmalade?' old Mrs Jessop asked, claiming her attention.

'No, there should be a few tins left. There, on the right.'

Jenna glanced back towards the step, but from where she was standing the sun, low in the sky, now obscured her vision. 'Hey,' said another customer, angrily thumping his purchases on the bench. 'Are you going to serve us or not?'

She was stacking the man's goods in a box when she heard the whinny of a horse and a shout, followed by a woman's scream. Almost animal-like, the sound echoed on and on, resounding through the shop like cannon fire. The customers turned towards it, murmuring. Jenna stopped, hand poised above the box she was packing. 'What's that?'

The man shrugged. 'How would I know? Come on. I don't have all day.'

A noise was buzzing in her head, like flies at a closed window. Instinctively she cried: 'No! Something's wrong!'

Then it came to her. *Michael!* It was Michael, she knew with sudden dread.

Inside the shop, a dying shaft of sunlight played upon the counter, dust motes dancing in its beam. The queue of customers shifted and realigned, a moving background. Slowly she skirted the counter. Her feet felt heavy, like lead, but she forced them to take her forward, towards the doorway.

The sun was a fleeing crimson streak over the rooftops and the air was icy against her face. A knot of people had gathered on the roadway, blocking her view. Townsfolk. Shoppers. Other shop owners. Michael's red ball lay in the gutter. Jenna stumbled down the steps, thinking *this can't be*. The ball, caught perhaps by the wind, rolled a few feet then was still.

'It's Jenna,' someone said.

The crowd parted and she moved through, nausea churning in the pit of her stomach.

Michael lay in the dirt. He looked odd, arms and legs protruding at unnatural angles. Jenna sank down beside him, gently gathering him onto her lap. His body was limp. His breath came in shallow gasps and he was bleeding from a huge gash in his temple.

'What happened?'

Her voice sounded wooden and came from far away. There was a dream-like quality to the scene. Everything seemed to be happening in slow motion. Her whole life was reduced to this one moment, telescoping into that one fraction of time and space. She took in the images, surprised she could examine them singly: the press of onlookers, Michael's white face, a pool of dark blood congealing in the dust.

'The ball,' someone said. 'He was chasing the ball and ran out in front of the wagon. There was nothing the driver could do. He came so fast, right under the wheel.'

'The driver's gone for the doctor,' added another.

She sat staring at the blood, unable to move, her mind refusing to form thoughts. Someone — the doctor perhaps? she wondered later — eventually lifted Michael from her and bore him away. Mutely she followed, someone guiding her through the crowd. 'The hospital will fix him up, luvvie. He'll be like new in a few days.'

'There, there.' A kindly pat on the arm. 'Nothing to worry about. He's in good hands now.'

How could they? she thought angrily, bracing herself against their concern. Hypocrites! Offering solicitous words when she knew what they really thought! *Whore. Bastard.* She'd heard the words so many times. Did they really think that Michael's accident could negate all that?

At the hospital she sat on a chair in the corridor, waiting for what seemed like hours but was mere minutes according to the clock on the wall. Nurses hurried past. Visitors came and went. Finally, down the length of the hallway, the doctor walked towards her. The features on his face were set, offering no hope. She rose, mutely holding out her hands, unable to talk.

'I'm sorry,' he said, taking her arm. 'There was nothing we could do.'

Strong arms guided her to a chair. She could feel them, holding her upright as her legs buckled beneath her, refusing to hold her weight. The doctor's words tangled and tripped over in her mind in their effort to be understood. There were internal injuries and bleeding to the brain. It was best he'd not survived. Intellectual damage, you know. A liability ...

'I want to see him,' she said.

She wanted to take in his features one last time, to have some final memory of him to sustain her through the days and months ahead. Wanted to see that he was really dead, wanted proof that the doctor — though she had no reason to doubt him — spoke the truth.

'It won't serve any purpose.'

The doctor led her away, down the corridor and out into the night. She walked mechanically, placing one foot before the other, careless of the cold. Each step took her further from Michael, towards an uncertain future. Past lighted windows and the random sounds of laughter she went, past neat gardens. A black wall of pain massed somewhere in her chest. Never, ever, had she felt so alone.

The shop was in darkness when she returned. Someone, one of the customers perhaps, had thoughtfully turned down the lamps and shut the door. She walked inside, seeing the surroundings in the reflection from the outside street light. Eerie, she thought, imagining she could hear a child's voice.

Jenna. Jenna.

The sound — high-pitched and child-like — slid towards her through the doors and windows, the timber floorboards. It came from outside, and from within. She spun towards it, confused, blinking in the half-light.

Jenna, look at me! See my ball!

'Michael, you're not real!'

She buried her face in her hands, trying to ignore the voice.

Come play with me!

Slowly she lowered her hands and stared around the room. She imagined the dart of shadow, fancied she could see him playing in the dust.

A wind blew through the unclosed window, sending the curtains billowing and forming the suggestion of a shape. Michael was everywhere, yet he was nowhere.

A phantom ghost. Unreal.

Now it was as though he had never existed.

*   *   *

Apart from the minister, Jenna was the only person present at the funeral. And although she had sent word, there was no sign of her mother. It had rained during the night and the trees were still dripping with moisture. An icy wind blew from the nearby mountains. But, she told herself, rubbing hard on her hands to warm them, it was colder for Michael.

Jenna watched as the small casket was lowered into the ground. Two labourers, hired especially for the occasion, stepped forward and began shovelling clods of earth onto the box. It was moist and dark, the earth, almost peaty, and fell with a thump. Jenna glanced away, unable to bear the sight. Poor little Michael: he'd never really had a chance.

She thought back to the night of his birth, remembered how Mary had shunned her tiny son, resenting her unwanted pregnancy. It had been Jenna who had held him for the first time, bathed him, who had eventually taken over his care.

'Jenna!'

The cry made her look up. Through her tears, she could see her mother approaching, staggering and sliding towards her through the mud. Her clothes were dirty and creased. In her hand she held a bottle. 'My baby,' she cried, holding out one hand as though to stop the men in their task.

Mary stumbled on the uneven ground and Jenna's arm went out, automatically, righting her. 'So, you came,' she said, the tone of her voice harder than she'd intended.

Mary stared at the dirt-covered casket. Her hair was lank and there were dark bruises along her cheek. 'Don't be so hard, Jenna. I loved that little bloke, I really did,' she whispered, her voice faltering.

'Of course you did,' Jenna soothed, knowing those were the words her mother wanted to hear.

Mary began to sob — a loud wailing that embarrassed and angered Jenna by its pretence. The minister looked uncomfortable. 'Perhaps we'd better ...' he began, obviously not knowing where to look. *Such a public display!* said the expression on his face. *How unseemly!*

How unseemly, indeed, thought Jenna, cringing with shame. Who had stayed up at night with Michael when he'd been teething or had a fever? Who had he run to for comfort? Not Mary! She hadn't cared a fig for her son. All the townsfolk knew Jenna had been more of a mother to him than Mary ever had.

Jenna tried to extricate the arm that Mary now clung to so tenaciously, but her mother simply held her tighter. 'No, Jenna, don't let go. I'll fall,' she said.

It came to her then, a sudden realisation that this was the way it would always be. She, Jenna, propping up her mother. Physically, financially and emotionally. Coping when her mother couldn't. Feigning understanding when inside she felt only disgust.

'No,' she said angrily, jerking away, leaving Mary standing forlornly in the mud. 'I must get back to the shop. There's too much to organise back there. Though you could come and give me a hand.'

She walked away, knowing Mary would never follow. Back to the shop she went, back to her lonely, lonely life and the void that now existed there. She took her diary from the drawer, opened it. *One moment he was there, and the next he'd gone,* she wrote. *Or that was how it seemed. How can I ever forgive myself? I'm sure everyone blames me, even Mary, though she was probably drunk at the time ...*

At that moment she knew she had arrived at a place, mentally, where she had never been before. She was alone now, truly alone. She could never rely on Mary, couldn't expect support or understanding from that quarter. Her mother was too absorbed in her own problems. For Jenna, her own resources were all that remained.

And also at that moment, at that precise instant in time, she knew she came close to hating Mary McCabe.

CHAPTER 9

Brad looks tired, I think, as we drive along. The preparation for this trip has been enormous, with the responsibilities falling mostly on his shoulders. 'You can't go into the outback without the proper equipment,' he'd said, weeks earlier. 'Where we're going is fairly remote. If you break down or have an accident, you could wait days for another vehicle to come along.'

So now we have a global positioning satellite (GPS) system and satellite phone — the latter mounted in the car with an external aerial — dual batteries and a sturdy car fridge. We look, I think, like seasoned outback travellers.

Brad's tentatively called his thesis 'The Ecology of Arid Zone Rivers — The Middle Diamantina', and the basis for his work is what he calls a 'boom or bust ecology'. The place where we're going, where we'll spend the next six weeks, is either dry or wet, and the climate affects the whole life around, and in, the river.

It's late afternoon before we see the sign on the gate: Diamantina Downs.

'That's it! We're here!' Brad announces, clattering the 4WD over a cattle grid. Despite my tiredness I smile at his enthusiasm. Harry gives an enthusiastic yap.

There's a sprawl of outbuildings and a huge six-bay machinery shed, where I can see a tractor and other farm machinery, and several fuel tanks up on high stands. The station homestead is in shade, banked on the western side by a row of pepper trees. In the front yard grow an assorted profusion of aerials and solar panels. It's dry and dusty. Even the straggly plants growing in the yard look tired.

We present ourselves at the homestead door, as arranged. A grey-haired woman — Betty, she introduces herself — points across the paddock to another distant building.

'That's where you'll be staying, down there. Come on. Let's get you settled in.' She glances in my direction with a frown, dusting her floury hands on her apron. 'You look exhausted.'

'You could say that.' I summon another smile.

Betty's a large woman, the wife of the station manager, she informs us. 'The property's owned by a big corporation back in the city. Probably used as a tax dodge, but we keep it running like clockwork. My Jack's good at his job. We used to have our own farm once, thirty years ago, but drought wiped us out. So now we look after other people's places. At least the pay's regular.'

She's brisk and business-like, no-nonsense. What does she make of us? I wonder as we follow her outside onto the hard-baked driveway. I feel dirty, gritty, as though the varying layers of dust that trailed from our car have somehow found their way onto my skin. Even at this late hour, heat rises in suffocating waves around us and I think longingly of a bath.

Betty rejects the offer of a ride in our car and hoists herself onto the seat of an old bicycle leaning against the front gate. 'Need the exercise,' she puffs. 'Besides, this way you don't need to bring me back.'

She pedals down the road in front of us at an alarming rate, two farm dogs in pursuit, yapping at her wheels. Harry gives an excited whine and clambers across my lap, sticking his head out the open window to see what all the fuss is about. As we follow, Brad suppresses a conspiratorial grin and reaches out to take my hand. The grin makes us allies, I think. And the linking of our fingers promises something, though I'm uncertain exactly what.

The road stretches ahead, taking me towards someone else's house, not my own. Cautiously I restrain a rising sense of panic. *Stop the car! Take me home!* I want to scream. *I'm not ready for this. I need familiarity, not change.* Yet another part of me senses a surge of anticipation, a feeling of heading in new directions and a fresh start in unfamiliar territory. I squeeze Brad's hand.

The house is low-set and squat, with a rusty iron roof. It's fibro-clad, about fifty or sixty years old, with paint-peeling walls. A tank stand is almost hidden by a clump of pepper trees, identical to the ones up at the main house. Even from this distance I can hear the hum of bees as they swarm around the flowers.

Betty leans her bike against the gate and marches up the overgrown path. Brad and I follow hesitantly. With a flourish she throws open the front door and ushers us into our new home.

'It's not much,' she says, 'but it's comfortable enough. The workers all stay here, come shearing season.' She glances around, as though taking in the surroundings for the first time. 'I keep thinking it needs a lick of paint, but there's never enough hours in the day.'

'No,' I assure her, studying the fine layer of red dust that seems to cover every surface. 'It's fine, really it is.'

Who am I trying to convince: her or myself?

I prowl through the rooms while Brad unloads the car. Betty tags along behind, pointing out things here and there. There seem to be no bedrooms, simply a hotch-potch array of bunks on the screened verandahs that encircle three sides of the house. 'There's a double up there,' she says, pointing to the far end of the verandah, which has been curtained off by what appears to be an old sheet.

There's a lounge room with a couple of old recliner chairs and a worn brocade sofa, years old. The house contains no television, but there's a radio on the bench in the large eat-in kitchen. A bucket of water, covered with a tea towel, stands next to the sink. 'Rainwater,' says Betty matter-of-factly. 'Just fill the bucket from the tank out the back. We don't drink the stuff from the tap. It's bore water.'

After Betty leaves, Brad and I unpack our belongings. I hang the clothing in the wardrobe next to the double bed, while the food and grog and contents of the car fridge are stored away in the kitchen. Brad arranges his scientific equipment on a table on one of the verandahs, and lines up the specimen jars on a nearby windowsill. 'There,' he says. 'Almost like home.'

I survey the room and shake my head. 'Hardly.'

'Oh, I don't know. A bed and a kitchen: what more could you want?'

He kisses my mouth and pushes me back onto a nearby bed. I lie there, gazing into his well-known face.

'Carys. Mum and Dad. A stereo and my favourite CDs, for a start. Cinema down the road. Takeaways.' I bite my lip, thinking about all the conveniences of modern life we've left behind, and the possibly too-few bottles of cabernet shiraz I've brought. 'What if we run out of grog?'

Too late, I realise my mistake. Brad rolls away, frowning at the ceiling, hands behind his head. I've upset him, I know. Self-accusations bombard me. Why did I say that? It was my decision to come here. No one forced me and it's not as though it's forever. It's only six weeks out of the rest of my life!

'I'm sorry. This place is going to take a bit of getting used to, that's all. But I will, and it'll be like a holiday of sorts. Besides, we'll get to spend time together. That'll be good, won't it?'

I'm babbling, plucking random words to fill the hurt between us. Tentatively I trail one finger along the side of his neck and into the hollow at the base of his throat. I can feel the faint throb of his pulse there, mirroring the steady beat of his heart. Then he turns, staring unblinkingly at me for one long moment. His voice, when it comes, is low, almost inaudible.

'This can't go on.'

There's a crow caw-cawing in the background, the sound mixed with the shrill scream of cicadas from the pepper trees outside. In the distance, a dog barks. I swallow hard, heart suddenly pounding.

'What can't go on?'

He swings his legs from the bed, stands and thrusts his hands deep into the pockets of his jeans. Suddenly he looks vulnerable, like a child. He's been hurt too, I remind myself. I don't have a monopoly on pain.

'You and me. This circling around each other and the past. We have to talk about it some time, Jess. I can't bear the not talking. I love you, for God's sake!'

He walks away. The screen door slams and I stand at the kitchen window, watching as he makes his way across the paddock. His shoulders are hunched and he's kicking at something on the ground — a stone perhaps — as he goes. Harry trots along behind at a respectable distance, as though he too senses his master's anger. The sun is low on the horizon, and Brad and the dog soon become a dark smudge against its brilliance.

Mechanically I take out the ingredients for dinner, the first in our new home. I'd planned a special menu. Fillet steak and new potatoes. Beans and baby carrots. Dessert. Bottle of wine. But now it all seems wrong. I fight back sudden tears, for the second time that day.

Brad comes back as I'm uncorking the wine. He seems more relaxed than before and he's carrying a bunch of wildflowers. They're small and pinkish-purple and have an aromatic smell.

'What are they?' I ask, searching through the cupboard for a vase or jar.

'Crush a leaf.'

I take one leaf between my thumb and forefinger, rubbing briskly. 'It smells,' I say, 'like thyme.'

'Native thyme,' Brad agrees. 'Or *Ocimum tenuiflorum* to be exact. It's trendy to use it in Aussie bush tucker food. There's a whole swag of it growing down near the dam.'

Dinner is a somewhat silent affair. Afterwards we sit on the verandah. From inside comes the muted sound of the radio. It's an old eighties song, something about love gone wrong. Away on the next rise, the lights of Betty and Jack's house wink at us out of the inky blackness. The stars seem bright in the moonless sky. There's a warm breeze blowing, bringing with it a pungent smell.

'Gidgee,' says Brad. 'Rain's coming.'

We sit in silence, not knowing what to say to each other. The past is there between us, a barrier. After a while we make small talk, inconsequential details of the day's events. Finally Brad stands, yawns and stretches. 'I don't know about you but I'm bushed. I'm going to bed. Coming?'

The implication is there, the slight inflection in his voice. Sex, intimacy, togetherness: somehow, in these unfamiliar surroundings, I can't even begin to think about it.

'No,' I say, casually. 'I think I might sit out here a while.'

I'm avoiding him, I know. Avoiding conversation and commitment. Avoiding reality, really. And when I finally do crawl into bed, an hour later, Brad stretches and rolls beside me, but does not wake.

Sometime through the night, I dream.

It begins similarly to the others. Dark streets. Me running from those same faceless pursuers. But then something changes. The men chasing me suddenly lag behind and I sense freedom. Until I come to the river.

As I stare down into the dank swirling water, I can see the back of a sedan. It's partly submerged yet, in the spangled moonlight, I can see a movement at the rear window. Tiny hands bang futilely at the glass. A white ghostly face presses hard against its surface, distorting mouth and nose. That same mouth opens in a soundless scream.

The car is sinking — silver water laced with black streaming away — disappearing slowly into the shadowy depths below. The image distorts and wavers. Darkness merges with darkness, becomes one. I want to dive in, wrench open the door, free the hands and face. But my limbs move so slowly, like I'm wading through treacle.

Then, soundlessly, without warning, the car slides under the water and disappears.

I wake, screaming. Brad is holding me, brushing strands of hair from my damp face. I can feel the strength of his arms. My heart is thumping erratically, threatening to burst from my chest. I take a gulp of air, trying to ease my laboured breathing. My head — containing the ragged remnants of the dream perhaps — seems ready to explode.

'It's alright,' Brad says, soothing me with practised words. 'Whatever it was, it wasn't real. Just a dream.'

A dream? The car, the water: I could have reached out, I'm certain, and touched them. 'No!' I cry, trying to slide across the bed away from him. 'It can't be.'

But Brad is holding me tight, allowing no escape. 'It was a dream, Jess,' he repeats in his firmest voice. 'Nothing more.'

The images shred away. My heartbeat blends with a far-off roll of thunder and, in the glare of a sudden flash of lightning, I can make out the contours of the room. It's hot and a breeze stirs the curtains, sending them inwards.

'Hold me,' I whisper.

During the night, a shower of rain falls. I hear it drumming against the iron roof and rushing noisily along the gutters. I smell the aroma of damp earth. Beside me, Brad sleeps, one arm draped across my belly. It feels comforting in an odd inexplicable way. And my sleep, when it comes again, is not filled with terrifying images, but with a low-set house shaded by pepper trees, and the distant hum of bees.

CHAPTER 10

NORTHERN NEW SOUTH WALES
January 1868

It wasn't so much that Conor had hit George McKenzie, Adam realised later, but the fact that he had done so in front of the other workers. Not only was McKenzie's nose broken and bloodied, but his pride was dented as well. The police were called from the nearest town and Conor taken to the lock-up there. Adam cooled his heels in town while he waited for his brother's release, a week later. He slept in someone's cowshed and cadged food from a sympathetic farmer. In the fracas, McKenzie had conveniently neglected to pay them for their month's work.

Adam was waiting when Conor was finally pushed, blinking in the strong sunlight, onto the footpath outside the local gaol.

'And don't cause any more trouble or you'll end up back here,' the policeman called after him as the brothers walked away.

They headed north, doing a day's work here and there, sleeping in barns at night. Finally, a month later, they managed to find permanent farm jobs. Their new employer was a fair man, but hard.

The country was different there, scrubby and dry. On the surrounding hills, the trees grew tall and straight, reaching long branches towards the sky. Their leaves were dark green on top, with pale undersides, and there were hollows where small animals lived — gliders and possums, and the occasional bees' nest. The bark of these trees was greyish brown near the base, shedding in long strips through the year to reveal a smooth blue-grey surface underneath.

'Blue gums,' someone told Adam.

After almost two years of hard work he and Conor had saved enough to buy a farm. They began casting their eyes around, looking for a small going concern. Some of the larger holdings were being subdivided, a few acres being sold off here and there.

They managed to purchase one hundred acres, a small property by local standards, and soon had a pig and several goats, and a cow for milking. Chickens pecked in the dirt. Neat rows of crops waved in the breeze.

The two men built a home. It was rough but serviceable, with a kitchen and dining room, two bedrooms and an earthen floor. Adam thought the hut reminded him of his former home, back in his previous life. But Newtownlimavady was now four years and half a world away.

He could see himself staying in this place, making a

reasonable living, eventually taking one of the local girls as his wife, raising a family, the O'Loughlin line continuing on through the years. He thought of them, his ghost children. Sons to help him in the fields (funny, he thought, that he still called these small fenced plots fields, not paddocks) and daughters to welcome him home at night.

But it was his brother, he suspected, who would find a wife first. Adam knew that Conor had been going with women for several years. Conor had made no secret of it, seemed to boast of it, in fact. He was always talking about this one and that, hinting to Adam several times that he'd been to the brothel in Main Street.

Conor the outgoing one. Conor the charmer, when it came to the opposite sex.

Why was his brother like that when he, Adam, felt so awkward, so God-damned tongue-tied around women? At the local dances he hung back near the doorway, never approaching the girls who sat against the opposite wall waiting to be asked to dance. He never knew what to say to them — couldn't manage to find those clever words like Conor — and he did not know how to charm and seduce. Meanwhile his brother never seemed to lack a dance partner, and was always surrounded by a group of women.

Conor turned twenty-one the following summer, the same month their next-door neighbour approached them about buying their farm. The neighbour was short and stocky, and had an air of arrogance about him that Adam had disliked on sight. 'You've only a hundred acres,' the man said, sweeping his hand wide as though dismissing their land. 'Not enough to live off, really. But if I amalgamate it with the four hundred acres I've already got, I'll be able to make a decent living.'

'It's not for sale,' replied Conor, clearly irritated.

'I'll offer you a fair price.' The man named a sum.

'We paid more than that for the land,' snorted Conor. 'Not to mention the crops we have in.'

The neighbour shrugged. 'Suit yourselves. But one day you'll be begging me to take it.'

'What do you mean by that?' Adam asked quietly.

But the man was already walking away.

Odd inexplicable events soon began to happen around the farm. A broken wagon wheel. A fire in the bush behind the cowshed. Two of the goats were found dead in the back paddock and one by one the chickens disappeared.

In July, as the chill winds raced through the valley, a policeman came to the door. 'Your neighbour's had several sheep dead these past few weeks. You wouldn't happen to know anything about that, would you?'

'Just as he doesn't know anything about our dead stock?' replied Conor sarcastically.

'So you *do* know something, then?'

'Hardly. It's just that strange things have been going on around here too.'

'What happened to the sheep?' asked Adam.

'Throats cut.'

'And you're accusing us?'

'You could say that.'

'Any number of people could have killed them. Our neighbour isn't well liked around here.'

'Can we see the sheep?' asked Conor.

'I believe he's gotten rid of the carcasses.'

'How convenient.'

'What's *that* supposed to mean?'

Adam could see the policeman was getting angry. 'Did you see them then?' he asked calmly, trying to defuse the situation.

'No.'

'So you've no proof that a crime was even committed. What if the man's lying?'

'Why would he do that?'

'Well, why would *we* lie?' Adam scratched his head. 'So how *do* you know he's telling the truth?'

The policeman shrugged. 'I'm just following up a complaint, that's all.'

'What makes you think it was my brother?'

'Your neighbour suggested it was. Talk around here is that he's been in gaol before.'

'So he's been assumed guilty until he can prove his innocence? He went to gaol for hitting a man, not for killing stock!'

After the policeman had gone, Adam walked up the hill and stood in the shade of the gums. It was cold there, suddenly bleak, as though all the warmth had gone from the sun. As he looked down on their small farm — the neat buildings, fences, straight rows of corn — he felt a shiver of apprehension. Something over which he had no control was happening here. Something malevolent. Unless ...

He remembered Newtownlimavady and the visit from the bailiff. *Conor's been seen snooping around*

*the landlord's fields. If something goes missing he'll
be the first to be blamed.*

He remembered the salmon lying on the kitchen
bench. He remembered Mam being ill after the baby,
and Conor saying, *I'll get meat for Mam, even if it
kills me!* And he remembered Conor coming home
with the lamb, the way he'd thumped the carcass on
the kitchen bench. If his brother had done it before,
then perhaps ...

'I didn't do it,' said a voice behind him. Adam
turned and came face to face with Conor. His face
was pale and his arms were folded across his chest.
'On the grave of our mother, I swear it wasn't me.'

There was such an earnestness about him, such an
obvious need to be believed, that Adam felt
immediate shame at his suspicions. Of course Conor
hadn't killed the man's sheep, if they had been killed
at all. It was probably some trumped-up claim to
push them into surrendering their farm and moving
on. Perhaps their neighbour, desperate for the land
and smarting under Adam's refusal to sell, would
stop at nothing to force them out.

He closed his eyes momentarily, shutting out the
view of Conor and the trees, listening instead to the
chatter-chatter of birds overhead. Beyond the
blackness of his closed eyes, the years dissolved away.
He imagined he could see the bailiff and his men
armed with rope and axes and crowbars, striding up
the hill to what had been the O'Loughlin cottage.
Men intent on destroying what was his and Conor's,
driving them away.

Was that the unavoidable shape of his life? At some

predetermined moment in his past, had some greater being determined that this was to be his lot? Always running, seeking something — land, stability, a sense of future — that could never be his? What if he was now living a dream, and he wasn't meant to be part of it? He opened his eyes and saw his brother. It was just the two of them now, no Mam or Da. His future was also Conor's and if he couldn't trust him, then ...

'I believe you,' he said, grasping his brother's hand. 'No matter what they say or do, this land is ours. We paid for it with our own sweat, and no one can take it from us.'

As the days passed, Adam's sense of foreboding grew. Why, he wasn't sure. There was simply a feeling that all was not done, that some further drama was lurking. *'Tis the bad luck upon you*, Mam would have said. Then she would have hung a horseshoe above the front door or searched the fields for a four-leafed shamrock to counter the effect. But Mam was long gone and he and Conor were Irishmen no longer. There were no shamrocks in the paddocks here.

Though he wanted to believe otherwise, he sensed his days on the farm were numbered, was not surprised when the policeman knocked again at their door.

'Where's your brother?'

'Gone into town. He won't be home for an hour at least.'

'He's been at it again.'

Patiently: 'At what?'

'Fences knocked down.'

'Show me.'

'I can't. They've been repaired.'

'How convenient.'

Adam turned to go inside but the man stopped him. 'There's more.'

He was tired of all this, made weary by the nonsense. 'What more could there be?'

'There was money stolen. Jewellery, too.'

'Well, if there was, you're wasting your time here when you could be out catching the thief.'

'Mind if I take a look inside?'

Adam had nothing to hide. Perhaps the policeman, in seeing that, would then leave them alone. 'Please yourself.'

He didn't actually see the policeman find the brooch on the shelf above the fireplace. He saw instead the man's hand open and the jewellery lying there, tiny diamonds winking in the light from the flames. 'You might like to explain this then.'

'I've never seen it before.'

'That's a likely story.'

'It's true.'

'I found it here on the shelf. Your brother will have some explaining to do.'

'My brother didn't take it.'

'If it wasn't your brother, then it must have been you.'

'That's nonsense and you know it.'

'If I thought that, then I wouldn't be here, would I? Anyway, you were seen.'

'By whom?'

'Your neighbour. The man who owns this brooch.'

'I haven't been anywhere near his place.'

'Please yourself. You can confess, or you can tell me your brother did it. Either way, I'll get one of you.'

Adam found himself in the local lock-up — oh, the ignominy of it all! The shame and embarrassment and the utter injustice of being behind a locked door, unable to walk free. He despised his inability to fight back, to prove his innocence. He had done nothing, yet here he was being punished like a common thief.

It reminded him of those dark days before Mam's death. Submitting to the authorities. Bowing and scraping and stooping to keep the land. Feeling inferior and worthless. And for what? A few miserable acres. Was the land so important to him that he was willing to subordinate himself yet again?

He shared his room in the lock-up with an old man named Dougal who'd been taken in for drunkenness, or so he said.

'Dougal of Donegal,' he introduced himself with a toothless grin, a faint lilting trace of Irish in his accent. 'You can't beat them, you know,' he said later, after Adam had told him about the processes that had brought him to the gaol.

'Beat who?'

'*Them*. The establishment. Those who hold the power.'

'I'm not trying to beat anyone. I simply want to live in peace. And I don't want to be accused of things I didn't do.'

'Maybe you'd be better off leaving here.'

'Why should I? This is as much my place as theirs.'

The man gave a bitter laugh. 'Don't you realise? You're in their way. The policeman: did you know he's a cousin of your neighbour, the man who wants your land?'

Was he? Adam hadn't known. 'No.'

'So you can't win. They'll take you and grind you into the ground until there's nothing left. If he's offering you a reasonable price for your place, my advice is to take it and move on.'

'Where? Where would we go?'

Their stop-at-nothing neighbour, the policeman, even this man, Dougal from Donegal — it seemed everyone was conspiring to push him further from his dream. He and Conor had come to this country thinking that anything would be better than their previous life. But in reality it seemed nothing had changed.

'You know, you could do worse than head up north. Apparently they're opening up whole new areas up there, more land than anyone has ever seen. It stretches from horizon to horizon, as far as the eye can see, and further.'

Though he'd heard stories about the inland, vast tracts of countryside so flat and broad and devoid of trees that you could see the line where the earth met the sky, Adam couldn't imagine it. 'Where is this place exactly?'

'In central Queensland. It's poor country, though, compared to around here. You'd need a lot of it to support livestock.'

Hours passed, though no one came with food or water. Sunlight faded. Day became dusk. The old man curled on his bunk and slept. Several times through the night he cried out and Adam, startled awake by the noise, lay there in the dark, wondering for a moment where he was.

In the morning, there was no movement from the old man. Adam, standing over him, tried to shake him awake. But it was no use. He was a limp mass of cold bones. Sometime through the night he'd ceased to be.

The policeman let him go. There was no apology, no trying to justify his actions, simply a rough push onto the street with a terse warning.

Conor was waiting in the shade of a nearby tree. His face was pale, deep furrows creasing his forehead. He looked as though he hadn't slept for days. 'It's all gone,' he said, his voice leaden.

'What are you talking about? What's gone?' Adam cried, taking hold of his brother's shoulders. 'Tell me.'

'The cottage.'

Adam came to an abrupt halt and stared at his brother for what seemed like an eternity. Suddenly he knew, the memory coming to him as clear as if it had happened yesterday. Striding towards the small woods, away from the O'Loughlin home, standing in the shade of the trees for one last look. He could almost see the bailiff and the men marching up the hill towards the hut, the thin spiral of smoke coming from the thatched roof. One bright flare — *whoosh* — then the roof alive with leaping, darting flames. But Conor, he knew, hadn't lit *this* fire.

At sunset he and Conor sat on the hill and surveyed the ruin that had been their home. Conor had told him outside the gaol, in halting disjointed words, how he had come in from the lower paddock to find the kitchen well alight. He'd tried bucketing water onto the blaze, but the fire had a good hold and the water had sizzled and evaporated even before it had neared the flames. Nothing had been saved — apart from the clothes they stood in. Even Mam's wedding ring was gone. There was no way Adam would ever find it in the black stinking mess that had once been their home.

Overhead the wind sighed through the gums. It was a mournful sound, melancholy, the music of unspeakable sadness. Even from this distance Adam could smell the acrid burnt odour. For a long while he couldn't speak, couldn't voice the words that must be said.

'We're leaving,' he said at last.

Conor rubbed one hand wearily across his eyes, as though trying to erase the scene below. His voice held no enthusiasm. 'Where will we go?'

'North-west,' Adam replied slowly. 'We'll go north-west of here.'

He saw the bark of the trees, golden brown in that late-afternoon light — great long shards of it, stripping away, revealing the mottled blue underbelly. Idly he plucked at the end of one, feeling the fragile weightlessness of it come away in his hands. It was passing, ephemeral, like himself and Conor. When they were gone from this place, when they had moved on, what would be left to tell they had ever been here?

It all seemed so pointless, so bloody irrelevant.

* * *

Adam paid their neighbour a visit. The man stood in his doorway, neither inviting Adam inside nor joining him on the path below. He was managing, thought Adam, suppressing the uncharitable thought, to keep himself higher than Adam, projecting some sense of superiority.

'You win,' Adam said, trying to keep the emotion from his voice. 'The land's yours. We can't fight you and your kind.'

'What do you mean by that?' The man had a belligerent tone to his voice and there was a bulldoggedness about his stance, the way he lounged against the doorway with his arms folded.

Adam shrugged. 'You know.'

'How much do you want for the land?'

'What's it worth to you?'

'It's obviously not worth much to you, if you're leaving.'

He named a sum, a miserable amount really, but Adam knew he would accept it and move on. There was nothing left for them here. All those years of hard work had gone up, literally, in smoke. They'd agreed, he and Conor, to head north, as the old man had suggested. The money would buy them more land. They were young and they'd start again. Surely all parts of this country couldn't be bad? Surely there were decent men somewhere?

He bade farewell to the gums, stood in their shade one last time as he looked long and hard at the land that had been theirs but belonged to them no more.

Perhaps, he thought, he'd been too hasty. Maybe he should have dug his heels in and refused to sell. He and Conor could have started over, built a new home. But he knew he hadn't the heart for it now. Best to start somewhere new where there were no bad memories, and no sense of failure. No, he thought determinedly. They were doing the right thing. He'd been too naive, too trusting. Next time, he thought. Next time he'd be more wary. No one would ever take advantage of him again.

CHAPTER 11

CENTRAL QUEENSLAND
April 1873

It was a late afternoon when Adam and Conor came to the outskirts of the village which emerged, literally, out of the scrub. One minute there was nothing but gums and the track winding through their midst. The next, Adam saw sunlight reflecting off tin roofs and heard the frenzied barking of dogs. He dismounted, stiff from hours of sitting in the saddle, and stopped to pat a yellow-eyed mongrel outside a ramshackle humpy. 'Where can we get supplies around here?' he asked the owner who had emerged from the interior.

The man pointed further along the road, where Adam could see other humpies jutting out onto the footpath, and a few horses tied to a rail. 'There's a general store up there a bit. Just ask for Jenner.'

There were no customers in the store. A young woman was sweeping the floor near a curtained opening that obviously partitioned the shop from a rear living area. Her back was to them and she was obviously engrossed in her task. She attacked the floor with gusto, dust flying from her broom. Adam rapped his knuckles against the wooden bench and she turned towards them, startled. 'O-oh, hello. I didn't hear you come in.'

'We're looking for Jenner,' said Adam.

'Then you've come to the right place,' she replied matter-of-factly, leaning against the broom.

She was wearing a white apron over her dress and her hair was pulled back into a dark curling mass, the escaping tendrils of which fanned about her face. A hint of a smile played cautiously about her mouth and danced in her eyes. She was young, Adam thought, perhaps about twenty, though she had a brisk, no-nonsense manner about her, as though she was used to dealing with people.

She was staring at them, unnerving him with those unblinking blue-grey eyes. Adam felt himself redden slightly under her gaze, felt the soft flush of her scrutiny rise up his throat.

'Well,' he said abruptly, distracted. 'Where is he?'

'Who?'

'Jenner. The owner of this place.'

'Where is *she*,' Jenna corrected. Then, as though sensing Adam's confusion, she added, '*I'm* Jenna.'

Adam took a step back. 'M-miss Jenner,' he stammered.

'No, I'm Jenna. J-E-N-N-A,' she said, spelling the name. 'Jenna McCabe. From the Coldstream Berwickshire McCabes, though they've long since had any dealings with us.'

Adam was lost for words. He searched his mind for some small talk to fill the empty space between them. Then, as Jenna stood the broom against the wall and moved behind the counter, Conor stepped forward and tipped his hat. 'Pleased to meet you, Miss McCabe.'

'Jenna,' she replied brightly. 'Everyone calls me Jenna. No one's too formal around here. Now, anything I can help you with?'

Conor stood there, a silly smile on his face. Adam glared at him, thinking, *Here we go again, Conor getting all soft over a woman.* Sometimes he really was so obvious!

Adam gave Jenna a list of the necessary supplies then the two brothers wandered about the store, checking the goods on the shelves. 'She's very pretty, don't you think?' Conor whispered as they stood behind a display cabinet. He had taken a tin from the shelf and was pretending to study the label, although Adam could see he secretly watched the young woman over the top of the shelf.

'Pretty enough,' Adam replied gruffly.

'No,' Conor persisted. 'Look at her eyes. They're not blue, yet not grey. Actually they're a sort of steely colour. And her mouth: it's just made for kissing.'

'And you'll be the one to do that?'

'Aye. If she'll let me.'

Adam turned his back on his brother and made a pretence of inspecting the goods on the shelves. He selected a few more provisions — tins of sardines and jam — and set them down on the counter. Jenna gave the two men a long appraising look. 'I haven't seen either of you before. You must be new about these parts.'

'We're just passing through, on our way north.'

'Where exactly north?'

Conor leaned forward, his elbows on the counter, smiling disarmingly. 'Wherever we can get land. Someone said there's plenty of it going cheap, further west. Big blocks. A place we can make a fist of it.'

'Farmers, are you?'

'You could say that.'

'Well, you'll need to see the land agent, next to the pub. He handles everything west of here. And speaking of the pub, you'll get a bed there at a fair price, and good yards and stables for your horses.'

Adam organised to collect the supplies the following morning and Conor gave Jenna a passing wink. 'Perhaps I'll see you later,' he said.

'Perhaps.' She put her hands on her hips and tilted her head in a defiant way. 'Or perhaps not.'

Thunder rumbled in the distance and the afternoon light had almost gone. As Adam ran down the steps of the store, he could see the line of bruised angry-looking clouds banking along the horizon. An acrid odour came on the breeze. 'Gidgee,' he said, taking a lungful as they made their way towards the hotel. 'Rain's coming. I hope we don't get much, or we'll be stuck in this place.'

Conor glanced back towards the store, seeing Miss McCabe standing at the doorway. He made a mock bow in her direction then turned back to his brother. 'I could think of worse places,' he grinned.

*　*　*

Jenna watched the two men as they made their way towards the pub. The younger one — what was his name? She hadn't even thought to ask, so topsy-turvy were her emotions — turned back towards her and dipped his hat, and an involuntary laugh bubbled under her breastbone. She tossed her head and folded her arms, suppressing a smile. Shameless and cheeky, she thought. Yet, in an odd way he was also respectful and courteous, not like the men who usually came into the store.

Something stirred inside her, a sense of wings, light and gossamer, beating uselessly against her heart. Why, when she was usually so restrained when it came to her male customers, had she made conversation with the two men? Asking questions when normally she would choose silence. Delving into their lives. That wasn't her way. But these men seemed different.

A drumroll of thunder came from the west and the air smelled sweet and pungent with the scent of approaching rain. Jenna gave a small sigh and turned back into the shop. Almost six o'clock: closing time. Determinedly she locked the front door and made her way to the kitchen beyond. Obviously Mary wasn't about to make an appearance today. Too busy with her male 'friend' — 'He's just a friend, Jenna, nothing more!' — she supposed. She raked through the coals in the stove and threw on another log, watching as the flames flickered along its length before closing the door.

As she prepared her lonely supper for one, the first heavy drops of rain began to fall and she heard them splattering against the iron roof above.

It was still raining the next morning. A grey misty veil hung over the village and puddles of water lay in the gutters along the main road as Adam and Conor let themselves in the land agent's door. Any available land was still several days' travel away. The journey wasn't to be attempted in the rain, the agent told them, shuffling through some papers on his desk. 'Creeks can come up overnight, cut roads. You don't want to be stranded out there.'

'How long is the rain likely to last?' asked Adam.

The man shrugged. 'How long's a piece of string? A few days maybe. Who knows. It's a bit early for the wet season.'

Conor asked what land was available.

'There's been a rush out there, this past couple of months, and there's not much left. Nothing decent, anyway.' He rubbed his chin thoughtfully, as though searching his mind for possibilities. 'But there's one chap about to relinquish his place. His wife's sick and he's got three young children, with another on the way.'

'How much land?'

'It's a parcel of six blocks, each a hundred square miles, with a seven-mile frontage to the river.'

Adam's attention was caught. A river meant water, and water meant feed for stock. 'River? What river?'

'The Diamantina.'

Diamantina. Diamantina. Diamantina.

The name ran through his head like a cold Irish

stream, cleansing, washing away memories of the past. An odd name, unknown yet hauntingly familiar. Perhaps this was his destiny, he thought. A place named Diamantina.

The agent was still talking and gradually his thoughts returned to the present. 'There's a cottage of sorts, though I can't guarantee its quality. And there's stock for sale. About ten thousand sheep and five hundred head of cattle.'

'How much is he asking?'

The agent named a sum, far beyond Adam and Conor's means.

'And *without* the stock?'

The agent shook his head. 'Well, there's the rub. One condition of the lease is that the land must be stocked. If you didn't buy the animals already there, you'd have to overland them from somewhere else. And that costs time and money.'

Blast! He hadn't counted on that. Hadn't counted on anything really, but had simply come, lured by the prospect of the land. And what the agent said was right. What good was the land without stock?

The agent gave them a form to fill in and bade them good day.

'What are we going to do?' asked Adam as they descended the steps. 'We've enough money for the land but none spare for stock. And if we don't have stock then we can't have the land.'

'Maybe we could stay here a while, get jobs.'

'Then we'd miss out on the land. By the time we saved enough, someone else would have taken up the offer if the place is half decent.'

They spent the remainder of the day wandering around the town. Conor had volunteered to collect the supplies from the shop and it had taken him, Adam noted, an extraordinarily long time to complete the task. The rain had grown heavier, a steady downpour, and great puddles gathered on the road and footpaths, trapping unwary pedestrians.

After supper they sat at the bar, studying the form the land agent had given Adam. It all seemed so hopeless and Adam resisted the urge to crumple the paper into a tight ball and throw it into the fire. Even after all these years in Australia, all their hard toil, they still lacked the funds to realise their dream.

It was quiet in the pub — even most of the locals seemed to have deserted the place — so Conor pulled on his coat and boots.

'Where are you going?' asked Adam, surprised.

'Out.'

He knew instantly his brother's destination: that place behind the store, the home of the woman with dark hair and eyes that crinkled at the corners when she smiled. A pang of annoyance roiled in his gut. Had he possessed more confidence, it might have been him going to visit her, but it wasn't. Trust Conor to edge in before him. 'To see that McCabe woman?' he asked gruffly.

Conor's reply was curt. 'Jenna. Her name is Jenna.'

'Conor!'

'Well, what's wrong with that? Should I be a lonely bachelor all my life?'

Adam felt a surge of anger — or was it envy? 'There's no time for courting. It's land we're after, not women.'

'There's more to life than land and work.'

'And there'll be plenty of time for women later.'

'I doubt there'll be many where we're going.'

Annoyed, Adam pushed the form the land agent had given them across the bench. Conor stood for a moment, studying it, then quickly picked it up and put it in his pocket.

'What do you want with that?' Adam asked

'Nothing. I just want to read it.'

Adam snorted. Conor had spent more of his childhood avoiding school than attending it, and his reading skills were negligible. 'That'll take a while.'

Conor grinned. 'Perhaps I'll have Jenna McCabe read it to me, then.'

'I don't want anyone in this place knowing our business.'

'Relax, brother dear. I'll be very discreet.'

Adam stood at the door and watched Conor leave, shrugging his shoulders against the misty rain as he walked away into the dark. Incensed, he sat back at the bar and ordered another drink. He wished long and hard it was him heading for Jenna McCabe's welcoming kitchen. She seemed nice, not shy and reticent like some women. She was forthright and confident, traits that came, he supposed, with the responsibility of running a store in a rough bush town.

The thought rose again in his mind. Why couldn't he be more outgoing like his brother? Why couldn't he say clever words, seducing with his mouth and tongue? Was he destined always to be second-best when it came to women? Opportunities might come and go and he'd still be dithering about, working up the courage to say even one word.

Angrily he drained his glass and went to bed.

Conor knocked on the front door of the shop. It was dark inside, the shelving and counters a shadowy blur beyond the glass door. But from the light spilling from a side window and under the curtain separating the shop from the rear quarters, he supposed Jenna was home. He hunched his shoulders against the rain and waited.

After what seemed like ages, the door opened. She stared at him and he returned her gaze. 'Oh, it's you,' she said. 'I thought it might have been one of the locals wanting something after hours. I almost didn't answer.'

'Can I come in?'

She hesitated. 'I suppose so.'

She stood aside to let him pass then closed the door behind them, ushering him through the darkened shop, past the shelves filled with groceries, to the brightly lit room at the rear.

It was a kitchen. A fire burned merrily in the stove. The remains of a meal sat on the bench. Jenna had obviously been reading as a book lay, opened, on the table. Now she stood with her back to the fire, arms crossed as she regarded Conor. 'So,' she said, 'to what do I owe the pleasure?'

Pleasure? She didn't sound pleased. Wary and defensive like a trapped animal, more likely. Sizing him up as though she had, Conor thought, long since forgotten how to trust. A sudden idea occurred to him: maybe he had made a mistake in coming here. He'd gone along blindly, supposing she had wanted to see him — had he really had the audacity to believe he was so irresistible? — yet in hindsight he realised she'd not given him any encouragement, or any indication that she was interested in him. Maybe she already had a boyfriend.

'Well?' she added, breaking his chain of thoughts as she uncrossed her arms and slid into a chair.

Conor slipped his hand into his pocket and withdrew the land agent's form. 'I was hoping you'd help me fill this in.'

'Why can't you fill it in yourself?'

He shrugged. 'Because I can't read and write, that's why.'

'Didn't you go to school?'

He laughed. 'Oh, school. Yes, I suppose so. Some days I went, but there were usually more important things to do. I suppose I'm regretting that now.'

'What about your brother? Can't he read and write either?'

'He can do it right enough.'

'So why don't you ask him to help you fill it in?'

Conor gave her a wide smile. 'Because then I'd have to find some other excuse to come here and see you, that's why.'

'Oh!' Jenna averted her head and he saw the slow flush spread across her cheeks.

'I'm sorry. I've embarrassed you.'

'No!' She turned back towards him, frowning. 'It's just that you don't seem like other men.'

Other men: he was at a loss to know what she meant. But the tone of her voice did not invite further questions on the subject. 'How old are you?' he asked instead.

'Nineteen.'

'And you run this place by yourself?'

'Actually it's my mother's but she's hardly ever here.'

'I know. I've seen her —'

'At the pub,' Jenna broke in, staring at him hard, as though daring further comment. Testing him somehow, studying his reaction. 'She's *always* at the pub.'

'Do you have brothers or sisters?'

Jenna closed her eyes for a moment and, when she opened them again, he could see they were bright with unshed tears. 'Why all the questions?'

'I want to know everything about you.'

She swallowed, offering him a tentative smile. 'There was a brother once, but that's a long time ago.' Suddenly her smile seemed artificial, as though she was trying to mask some inner hurt. 'So it's just me now. I run a good business here. This is the only store for miles around and I do a regular trade.'

She made a pot of tea and placed a cup before him. Black: just how he preferred it. How had she known? He sipped the hot liquid, watching her over the rim of his cup as she busied herself at the bench. When he'd finished, she took the cup and rinsed it, then ushered him to the front door. 'When are you leaving town?'

'I don't know. The rain ...'

His voice dwindled and he could think of nothing to say. Instead he pondered the unbearable possibility of never seeing her again, and a pain rose up in his chest.

She opened the door and he could see the rain misting in the light from the street lamp. Some part of him wanted to stay within the warmth of the shop, not caring to walk away at all.

'May I come and see you again before we go?' he asked.

CHAPTER 12

The rain continued, reducing the landscape to a grey blur. Trees and buildings merged with the watery sky. Even the birds that sat on the pub verandah railings were wet and bedraggled. There was no talk of moving on. Creeks were up, according to the local mailman, impassable in most places. Adam and Conor managed to find a few hours' employment each day at the pub, rolling barrels in the cellar and cleaning behind the bar. There were no wages but the publican had offered to forego the cost of their food and board.

Conor discovered that Mary McCabe, Jenna's mother, was the pub's most regular patron. She was always propping up the bar, one man or another at her elbow. Mary and Jenna: Conor wondered how two women could be so unlike, so totally opposite. Mary was nothing but a harlot — though he'd never say that to Jenna — while her daughter was dependable and conscientious, almost staid by comparison.

He went to Jenna's most evenings, under the pretext of study. She had offered — out of pity, he thought — to teach him to read and write. However the lessons were progressing slowly, the time taken up mostly with Conor relating their colonial experiences and Jenna making copious cups of tea. She still seemed wary of him, cautious, guarded in her comments. Even after two weeks he sometimes thought he knew scarcely more about her than on the day they had first met.

During the intervening daytime hours, he couldn't stop thinking about her. At odd times he walked past the shop, careless of the mud on his boots and the steady downpouring of rain. He stopped in front of the window, hoping to catch a glimpse of her, his heart dancing with sudden joy when she looked up from serving a customer and smiled at him.

And, oh, what a smile! The warmth of it filled his heart and made him happy. But the rain had brought many of the outback men into town. Conor saw them in the store, leaning nonchalantly on the counter, imagined them flirting with Jenna and felt a jealousy he had never known before.

Mary McCabe called in late one afternoon, just as Jenna was closing the shop. 'Someone said there's been a man hanging around here at night,' she said to her daughter, without preliminaries.

'How are you, Mary?' Jenna asked affably, trying to deflect her mother. But Mary was not easily placated. She stood, hands on hips, demanding an answer.

'Well, is it true?'

Patiently: 'Is what true?'

'That the young man — Conor someone — who's been staying at the pub has been calling at the shop after hours.'

'His name's Conor O'Loughlin.'

'So you *do* know him then?'

'We're friends.'

'*Friends!*' snorted Mary. 'Men are never *friends*! They're bastards, first and foremost. Take, take, take: that's all they ever do. Then they leave you.'

'Conor's not like that.'

Wasn't he? Jenna wasn't certain, but felt bound to defend him anyway.

'Really?' Mary sneered. 'We'll see about that!' She went to the till, took a handful of notes and stuffed them in her pocket. In her haste, several fell to the floor and went unnoticed. 'The shop's going well, I see.'

'Passable, despite the rain.'

'Well, then,' Mary sniffed. 'At least something's right in my life.'

'Your life? What does the shop have to do with you? You're never here, except to take money.'

The words were out before Jenna had time to think, and instantly she regretted them. She saw her mother's hand tracking through the air towards her, palm outstretched, and felt the stinging slap against her cheek as her head snapped back with the force of the blow.

Mary's eyes were dark glittering orbs in her face. Her lips compressed with anger. Without speaking, she walked away, down the steps and out into the darkening evening. Jenna could see the street lamps were now lit and the last of the birds were winging their way home across a damp indigo sky.

'You disappoint me, Jenna. I thought I'd raised you better than that,' Mary shouted when she reached the place where the footpath met the road. 'You need to know the meaning of respect. And if you take my advice, you'll not get mixed up with that Irish scum. Believe me, he'll only break your heart.'

Jenna held her hand against her stinging cheek, blinking back tears. She would not cry, wouldn't waste her emotions. This was the way of her life, so she'd better get used to it. Mary would be back, days or weeks later when her money ran out, desperately needing cash for grog and acting as though the scene had never happened. No use fretting about it. Grin and bear it, she thought.

'My mother means nothing to me,' she whispered as Mary tottered in the direction of the hotel, weaving her way into the gathering dark. 'Nothing! Nothing! Nothing!'

Conor called later that evening. He arrived with his notebook under his arm and sharpened pencil in his pocket. Somehow they legitimised his visit and made Jenna feel more comfortable. This time he knocked on the rear door.

'Who's there?' she called.

'It's me, Conor.'

Tentatively Jenna opened the door. 'Aren't you going to ask me in?' he said.

'I-I wasn't really expecting ...' The words died in her throat.

'I'll go then,' he offered, not wanting to leave at all.

Her hair was loose, the dark mass of it cascading across her shoulders and down her back. She was wearing a white nightgown, with ruffles up to the top of her throat, and it was all he could do to restrain himself from grazing his mouth across that creamy skin. Momentarily he swallowed hard and closed his eyes against the sight of her, unable to bear her close proximity. Then she was pulling him into the room, abruptly, glancing up and down the laneway as she did so.

'What's wrong?'

'Nothing.'

Her voice was flat, lacking its usual warmth. Her cheeks were unnaturally flushed, her eyes bright. Too bright, he thought, wondering if he could see the glimmer of tears. And he could tell by the way she moved her hands, jerkily, that something had upset her.

'I *can* go,' he repeated, not knowing what else to say.

'*NO!*'

The force of the word took him by surprise. 'Jenna,' he began.

But she was pacing the room, one hand held to her cheek. 'I'll not let them dictate the way I live my life.'

'You'll not let who?'

She flung her arms wide. 'Gossips. Snoops. My mother. Everyone who comes into this shop, probably. That's the trouble with small country towns. Everyone knows the others' business.'

'What's happened? You're not making sense.'

'It makes me sick,' she went on, as though she hadn't heard him, striding backwards and forwards across the room. 'Sometimes I'd like to pack up and leave. Walk away. Go to the city. No one knows me there.'

'Stop!' He took her roughly in his arms, forcing her to a standstill. 'Tell me what's wrong.'

Suddenly she was telling him a story about a little boy named Michael. She was crying now, tears rolling unchecked down her cheeks. Her words came fast and furious, tripping over each other in their effort to be said. It was a miserable story, wretched in its outcome. Mary McCabe's virtual desertion of her unwanted baby. Jenna's attempts to be a substitute mother. How she had tried to organise her life around her schooling, her brother and work at the shop.

'I'm not complaining,' she hiccuped, burying her head in his shoulder. 'I just wanted you to know how it was, and how I felt when he was gone. After what happened with the buggy, I blamed myself. If only I'd been more vigilant.'

At her words, he thought his heart might break. 'It was an accident, nothing more,' he soothed, brushing her hair back from her damp face. 'You could go through life apportioning blame, but it won't change what happened.'

'Sometimes I think he's still here. I hear sounds. A laugh maybe, or the bounce-bounce-bounce of a ball. But when I look, there's nothing.' She gave a mirthless laugh and pulled away, jerking from his embrace. 'Oh, I don't know why I'm telling you this. I've never told anyone before.'

'You haven't?' Somehow that knowledge meant something, raised his hopes.

'It's all in the past now. And I don't know what has gotten into me, thinking you'd be interested in all this.'

She was standing at the kitchen bench, looking out the window at the darkness beyond. Conor could see her reflection in the glass, could see the rise and fall of her shoulders and chest. Warily he approached, placing one hand on her arm. 'But I am,' he tried to reassure her. 'I want to know everything about you.'

At his touch she flinched away, stumbling wild-eyed across the room. 'Please,' she said, biting her lip. 'Don't feel sorry for me: I couldn't bear that. I have a reasonable life, really, and there are lots worse off than me. One day I'll be married with babies of my own, and all this pain will be just a memory. They say time heals all wounds.'

'Don't,' he begged, unable to bear the thought. Jenna married, other children replacing Michael. He'd never forget his own dead brothers and sisters, or Mam and Da. 'Don't ever say that.'

She stood watching him, hands fluttering by her side like moths around a lamp. 'You should go,' she muttered, her voice unsteady.

'Why? Don't you want to be with me?'

One hand came up towards him, reaching out, trying to make contact, and all at once she seemed so vulnerable, so alone. He took a step forward, two.

Wrapped his fingers around hers, drawing her towards him. 'Why are you avoiding me?'

'I-I'm not.'

'Kiss me then.'

He half expected her to pull away again, but shyly she raised her face to his. He felt the pressure of her mouth. He inhaled the sweet smell of her hair and skin. Her hand came up, fingers parting the hair at the nape of his neck, pulling him closer. Her mouth was demanding, taking him to places he hadn't been in a long time.

'I've wanted to do that from the very first moment I met you,' he said at last.

'You have? Why?'

'How can you ask?' He nuzzled along the side of her neck and she shivered, kissing him soundly once more.

Somehow — he was later unable to remember the exact process that had taken them there — they were both in the bedroom, beside a big brass bed. Jenna had unbuttoned her nightgown and was standing in her underclothes. Scarcely daring to breathe, he took in the milky skin, the soft swell of her breasts. Cupped his hands around those same breasts, and the nipples were hard, like tiny stones. 'Oh, God!' he groaned, burying his face in her hair, an unbearable ache in his groin.

He drew her onto the bed, easing off the last of her clothing. Then he lowered himself over her, parting her legs with his knee. There was an initial resistance and she pulled back with a soft moan, pain mirrored in her eyes. 'I've hurt you,' he cried, mortified.

'No. Don't stop,' she pleaded, silencing his words with her mouth.

He was slow and gentle, in deference to her obvious inexperience, guiding her hands and mouth. Pulling back, teasing. Playing out the emotion and longing until she cried out, 'Sweet Jesus,' then he allowed himself to find blessed release. He shuddered into her, spilling his love and desire and desperate need. And somewhere, deep within his heart, there was a sense of unavoidable grief that he was both loath and unable to explain.

'I love you, Jenna,' he said later, tracing one finger lightly across her belly. 'You have to believe that.'

'Have you ever been in love before?'

'No. Not like this. Have you?'

'What! With one of the lecherous old men around here?'

'So, do you think you could love me?'

She studied his face for what seemed like a long time. A smile curved the corners of her mouth. 'I might,' she replied mischievously. Then, 'What if we've started a baby?'

'I'd marry you.'

'Really? Just like that?'

'Why not?'

'And if we had started a baby, would you love him too?'

'Who says it'd be a boy? Maybe it'd be a little girl with dark hair and smiling eyes like her mother.'

'Oh, silly.'

She gave him a gentle push and he caught her to

him, sliding his hand along the small of her back. 'I love you,' he said again, simply. 'Marry me.'

'I scarcely know you.'

'I feel like I've known you all my life.'

'What if we didn't like each other after a while?'

Defensively: 'I'd *never* not love you. You have to believe that.'

She was thoughtful for a moment. 'I can't marry you. You're going away and I can't leave here.'

'Why not?'

'The shop, that's why. I make a good living here. I can't sell, because it's not mine. And Mary's incapable of looking after it. I can't simply walk away.'

'Well, there's a possibility we may not be leaving after all,' Conor offered tentatively.

She glanced at him, puzzlement creasing her brow, and Conor longed to kiss away the fine lines there. 'Why not?'

'Because Adam and I don't have enough money to buy the land. Or rather,' he went on with a grimace, trailing a finger along the contours of her throat, 'we can afford the land, but there's not enough left to buy stock, which is a condition of the lease. So maybe you won't be rid of me that easily.'

It became a regular conspiracy: Conor knocking on the back door each evening and Jenna spiriting him inside, pulling him impatiently into the bedroom and onto the brass bed. The curtains were closed against the night and prying eyes — 'so they can't see. I don't want to be the brunt of their gossip,' Jenna said, anxious and distrustful of the local townsfolk.

Tender loving moments played out against the rumpled sheets, tracing fingers over flesh. Intimate seconds faded into minutes and hours. Great stretches of time when their world included only him and Jenna, cocooned against the night. Their lovemaking was the most joyous experience, carrying Conor through the ensuing days. No matter how long they spent together, no matter how many times she acquiesced to his desire, and her own, he could not get enough of her. And though he knew she was willing, often instigating the intimacy, sometimes he sensed it was in a hesitant, defiant kind of way, as though her morals were colliding with her needs.

He loved her dark curly hair that fell to her waist. She pinned it up during the day, keeping it from her face as she worked in the shop. At night he liked to remove the pins and clips and watch as it tumbled down across her neck and shoulders like a cape. He took handfuls of it and held the strands to his face, breathing in the scent of her. Sometimes, unable to sleep himself, he watched as she dozed, her face relaxed in the light of the lamp left burning. Overhead the rain still fell, sleeting down, and he could hear the comforting sound of it on the tin roof.

One morning, over breakfast, she offered to lend Conor and Adam the necessary money so they could buy their land and stock. 'I've been putting my wages aside for years. There's little to spend it on out here and I've saved a sizeable amount.'

Conor's first reaction was refusal. 'No, I couldn't possibly ... Adam and I couldn't —'

'Why not?' she broke in. 'One day you'll be able to pay me back.'

'Because Adam wouldn't agree. He wants us to do it by ourselves.'

'It's a loan, not charity. A business agreement. You'd borrow from a bank, wouldn't you?'

'A bank would hardly lend *us* money.'

'Well, then, it seems you have no other option.'

Practical, business-like Jenna. He stared at her amazed. That she would offer to finance their land, when he knew she was reluctant to let him leave, seemed like a supreme sacrifice. He grinned at her, reached out across the table and took her hand. 'So you want me gone, then?'

She looked wistful. 'Hardly. I can't imagine this place without you. But the land is why you came here. And maybe sometimes you'd come back, visit me.'

'Of course I'd come back. Just let anyone try and stop me.'

After six weeks of constant rain, the sun had been out for several days. The air was steamy and clouds of bush flies crawled into unprotected eyes and nostrils. The local mailman announced that the surrounding seasonal creeks, swollen with rainwater these past few weeks, were now reducing to their usual trickle. It was time, Adam knew, for he and Conor to make some decisions about their future. Stay here or move on? That was the question. The land they'd come for seemed unattainable now. If only they had more cash. For the first time since coming to this country, he felt in limbo, without goals.

He'd hardly seen his brother lately, scarcely spoken to him. For weeks now, Conor had spent every evening at Jenna McCabe's store, arriving home only in the mornings, whistling, smiling to himself in a secretive, pleased manner. Adam could only imagine what was happening there.

Jenna McCabe. From the day he'd met her, she was a mystery to him. She was pleasant, cordial. Yet privately she reduced him to a tongue-tied jealous misery. Why? It was true that he felt an attraction towards her. An attraction he could never act upon, had he the courage, for she was obviously Conor's woman.

He was surprised to find them both, Conor and Jenna, waiting when he came up from the cellar at lunchtime. They ushered him outside, to a table and chairs set out in the shade of a pepper tree. 'What's the matter?' he asked, surprised.

'It's about the land.'

'We can't afford it, Conor, you already know that,' replied Adam flatly.

'Jenna has come up with a solution.'

He let his gaze move between them, curious. 'She has?'

Jenna took a deep breath. 'I'll lend you the money.'

'No!'

The word came automatically to his lips. A woman funding their venture? The idea was unthinkable. But Conor was holding his hand up, silencing him. 'Don't be so quick to object. Just listen to what she has to say before you make a decision.'

Jenna glanced at Conor as though for reassurance, and his brother reached out and took her hand. Adam found himself staring at the entwined fingers, a surge of envy fighting its way through his gut. 'It would be a partnership,' Jenna was saying as he forced his mind back to the topic at hand. 'I'll contribute one-third. Added to your money, that should be enough to buy stock and carry you over for at least twelve months. Later, when the land becomes financially viable, you can repay me and I'll have no further involvement.'

'What do you know about farming?'

Jenna smiled. 'Absolutely nothing. I'd be relying on the pair of you to look after my share of the investment.'

Adam stared hard at her, studying the slow curve of her mouth and the way her dark eyelashes rested against her cheek. Her skin was so smooth, creamy, and he fought back a sudden laughable impulse to place his mouth there, at the hollow at the base of her throat. 'You scarcely know us. Why would you lend us money? And, more importantly, how do you know we'd repay you?'

Jenna and Conor exchanged a conspiratorial smile. 'I trust you,' she said simply, looking deeply into Conor's eyes.

Conor ran one hand through his hair. 'I can see, brother dear, that you don't agree with our proposal.'

'Why?' asked Jenna. 'It makes perfect sense to me. I have money to spare and you have need of it. It's merely an investment, a business arrangement.'

Conor laughed. 'Adam hates to be beholden to a woman, that's why.'

Adam shifted uncomfortably in his chair. 'That's not quite true,' he stammered. 'It's just that Conor and I planned to do this by ourselves.'

'So you'd rather lose the land than accept outside help?'

'No-o.'

His answer was long, drawn out, thoughtful. Here he was, being offered an easy solution to their dilemma. Jenna didn't want to be an active partner, involved in the running of the land. She was content to stand back and let them do things their way. She had already admitted to knowing nothing about farming. The money was a loan, straight and simple. No strings attached.

He drew himself up, straight and tall in the chair. 'Very well, Miss McCabe. Your offer's a generous one and Conor and I would be foolish to refuse. You'll be repaid in full, plus interest. No —' he shook his head, silencing her imminent protest. 'I insist that be a condition of the loan.'

'I didn't want to involve a third party,' he said to Conor later, back in their room.

'Jenna's hardly a *third party*. I love her. One day, God willing, she'll be my wife.'

So it had come to this! 'Conor! What about the plans we had? The land —'

With an exasperated sigh, Conor threw himself into an armchair. 'They were always your plans, Adam. But I promised I'd go with you, and I'll not go back on my word. I'll stay six months in this place called the Diamantina, see you started. Then I'm coming back for Jenna.'

'You're bringing her back to the land? It'll be no place for a woman out there.'

'Relax, brother dear. That'll never happen.'

'What do you mean?'

'Because she's got the store. What would she do with that? It belongs to her mother. She can't sell it. We'll live here, in town, make our own way. Besides, you heard what she said. She's not interested in the land.'

'How can you be certain?'

Conor laughed. 'Certain? That's another thing altogether. With a woman you can *never* be certain.'

She'd known his departure was imminent, yet some small measure of hope inside Jenna had flickered and died when Conor told her the news earlier that evening. 'Hey,' he said, cupping her chin in his hands. 'Why so sad, pretty lady? I'll soon be back.'

A glimmer of expectation surfaced. 'You will? When?'

'As soon as possible. I've told Adam I'm not staying out west. But I promised him I'd help him get the stock set up, check out the fences, that sort of thing. I'll be back in six months, maybe sooner. We'll be married then.'

'What did he say?'

It was important to her: Adam's consent. Except for Mary, who hardly counted these days, she had no family of her own, and Conor had only his brother, though how two men could be so unalike was a mystery to her. One fair, the other dark. They were like the sun and the moon, water and fire. Black and white.

There were days when she didn't know what to make of Adam O'Loughlin. Where Conor was easygoing, Adam seemed surly, aloof and distant in a preoccupied kind of way. She suspected he disapproved of her relationship with Conor. He was impatient with her in the shop, brusque sometimes almost to the point of rudeness. He knows, she thought then, feeling a slow flush creep along her cheeks. He knows about Conor and me, and what we do when we're alone in the big brass bed.

'Adam was disappointed, naturally.' Conor had begun undoing the buttons on her blouse. They were small and fiddly, requiring his concentration.

'Perhaps he'll try and change your mind.'

He hugged her to his chest, fiercely. 'Just let him try.'

'What about the land? It was what you wanted too.'

'It means nothing without you. When I come back we'll run this store together.'

Jenna couldn't bear the thought of a single day without Conor, let alone months. She thought about the empty hours ahead, the loneliness. 'Six months,' she whispered despondently. 'It'll seem like years.'

'Promise me you'll wait, that you won't go running off with the blacksmith.'

Despite herself, Jenna laughed. 'I promise.'

They lay in the bed for the last time, Conor's arms wrapped around her, holding her close. They had just made love, a frenzied final coupling that Jenna knew would have to sustain her for the weeks and months ahead. Now, listening to the rhythm of his breathing, she knew Conor slept. But that same sleep eluded her. Instead she lay beside him, her thoughts in turmoil, watching through the window as the sky turned from black to indigo to the palest of blue.

The shrill call of birds in the trees outside finally woke him at dawn. He stirred, rolled towards her, ran one finger lightly across her breasts. 'I have to go.'

'I know.'

She watched as he dressed, and heard the rustle of fabric and the snap of belt buckle. The minutes seemed to be running into each other too fast. Slow down, she wanted to scream.

By the time Conor had finished breakfast, Adam was waiting outside with the horses. Jenna walked down the steps of the shop into sunshine, suddenly shy. Conor bent down from his perch high on the horse, kissing her one last time. 'Goodbye, Adam,' she said to Conor's brother, feeling some sort of acknowledgement was in order.

She stood on the front steps and watched them go down the street, horses and supplies at a steady plod. At the last moment, before they turned the corner, Conor swivelled in his saddle and tipped his hat. She fought back an overwhelming urge to run to him, to let him swing her up on the horse behind him. Then they'd ride off into the bush together, leaving this place forever. She blinked back sudden tears, cursing herself for her lack of control. Be strong, she told herself. The time will go quickly and, before you know it, he'll be back and it'll be like he's never been away.

By the time her vision had cleared, the road ahead was empty.

She walked back inside the shop, locking the door behind her. It was still an hour until opening time. In the bedroom she stared down at the bed she and Conor had shared the previous night, the rumpled sheets thrown back in a tangled mess, evidence of their lovemaking. Something lay on the floor, blue fabric. It was the shirt Conor had worn the previous day, forgotten in the morning's rush. Jenna picked it up and pressed it to her face, breathing in his musky smell.

The loss of him felt aching and raw. Although she hadn't known him for an inordinately large amount of time, she felt as though she'd understood him in other ways. Understood his needs, the desperate sense of loneliness he'd hidden under that cloak of blatancy. Understood his capacity for emotion.

Already, though mere minutes had passed, she missed his presence, the way he'd come up behind her and cup his hands around her breasts, that gentle lulling teasing that took them somehow from the kitchen to the bedroom and that wide soft canopied bed that had cradled both their bodies. She would, she knew, miss the way he enticed her into compliance, aroused in her those passions she'd never known before.

Somewhere, from the past, her mother's words came to her then.

A woman needs a little loving sometimes.

Finally she, Jenna McCabe, had found someone who loved her. Now, how could she bear the weeks till she saw him again?

She was roused, minutes later, from her reverie by a loud banging on the shop door. 'Alright, I'm coming,' she called crossly, throwing the shirt on the bed.

The local policeman stood on the front step, his face strained. Her first thought was of Conor. Had something happened?

But it was not her lover that the man had come to see her about.

'Miss McCabe,' he said, pale eyes blinking. 'I'm sorry to inform you that your mother has been found dead, down the embankment behind the pub. I'll need you to come down to the morgue to formally identify the body.'

PART THREE

The Diamantina

PART THREE

CHAPTER 13

Brad says I'm the sort of person who, when walking along a beach, prefers not to look ahead but rather looks back. He says it in an uncomplimentary way, as though it's a failing on my part. 'What's the point, Jess?' he insists, emphasising the word 'point'. 'Anything behind us is all in the past. You can't change it.'

He's a forward thinker, my husband, a go-getter. Onwards and upwards: all that sort of reasoning. What he doesn't realise is that I enjoy looking back. I like seeing my footprints in the wet sand; I take pleasure in pondering over the zigzag course I've taken — stopping to look at a shell perhaps, or a beached jellyfish — when in fact I thought I'd been walking in a straight line.

And although commonsense tells me it's pessimistic and self-defeatist to look backwards and not ahead, during the past year I've come to accept that my life's like a time warp where nothing changes or progresses. It's become a habit to wallow in my emotions, in the whys and wherefores and might-have-beens. Some people believe the premise that tragedy is supposed to teach you something — life skills perhaps — or make you reprioritise your existence. But in my case it's simply brought me to an emotional standstill.

I fight it, rail against the unfairness if it all. But to no avail. There are days when I wish I could miraculously rerun my life like a movie, in reverse, frame by frame. Then, when I reached that particular point in that particular scene, the one that keeps jamming in my mind, maybe I could change the plot or move the action sideways. Select a better ending.

In this place called the Diamantina, I've started to wake early in the mornings, around the time when night fades gradually into dawn and the sky is shell pink. There are purple clouds on the horizon — I can see them just above the distant tree line — but I know they'll disperse later in the heat of day.

I'm not certain what brings me to wakefulness. The screeching of birds or the deceptively cool breeze that finds its way past the glass louvres, perhaps. Or maybe the far-off barking of one of the station dogs, or the ragged remnant of some dream. Whatever reason, my body clock's changing and sleeping in has become a habit of the past. So I slide from the bed, careful not to wake Brad, slip on a pair of shorts and a shirt, and walk away from the cottage, Harry the kelpie in tow.

There's a peacefulness, a sense of solitude out in the paddock, a heat haze gathering already on the horizon as I walk in the direction of the dam. Why is it, I wonder, that, given a choice, we always head towards water? Beaches. Creeks. Rivers or dams. Me with my dream. Brad with his work. What draws us?

The ground is dotted with Mitchell grass and I step carefully around the clumps, alert for snakes. Harry noses his way forward, stopping to sniff at a pebbly pile of animal dung. Suddenly he throws his head up, ears alert, as the air is filled with a shrieking sound. It's a flock of corellas. I can see them ahead, a white fluttering mass, as they lift above the trees and settle again.

By the time I return, half an hour later, Brad is sitting on the front step and nursing a cup of tea. There's an affable smile on his face. Casually he throws a few biscuit crumbs towards the dog. Why is he always so God-damned cheerful early in the mornings?

'You're up early. Couldn't sleep?'

I nod and kiss his cheek in passing, and head towards the kitchen and my first cup of coffee for the day.

Already, after only a few days, he's well immersed into his research and field-study trips, and within an hour I know I'll be alone in the house. So far the time has passed quickly. I've been reading, working my way through the pile of books I've brought, wallowing in self-indulgent indolence. But today, I think, I'll find something new to occupy my time.

After Brad leaves I tidy the house. It takes so little time: there's scarcely any mess with only the two of us here. If I was home, back in the city, I'd spend a few hours in the yard, pruning and clipping and yanking out the annuals that have ceased to flower. But here there's no garden to speak of, just a leggy jade plant and a few straggly geraniums growing next to the front steps.

Instead I do the washing, scrubbing the clothes in the old cement wash tub in the lean-to at the rear of the house. By the time I hang them on the line, the hair at the back of my neck is damp with perspiration. Then, at a loose end, I make another cup of coffee.

What would I do now, if I were home? Go to the movies or meet Carys for lunch? Phone my mother, perhaps, or take a leisurely stroll through the local park? No, not there, I think, remembering the playground, the swings and slippery dip. Maybe instead I'd dash down to the supermarket or butcher. Plan a nice evening meal for myself and Brad.

'Cooking,' I say aloud, a sudden idea forming.

I open the one and only recipe book I've brought and gather the ingredients: flour, water, yeast, a pinch of salt. I measure the required amounts into a basin and stir, then set the bowl aside on the windowsill, out of the sun. It is warm there and, according to the recipe, the dough will soon expand, doubling in size. But when I look, half an hour later, the lump seems as flat and lifeless as before. Dispirited already, I shape it into something that resembles a cob loaf of bread. But when I take it from the oven after the allotted amount of time, it's a hard little ball, not edible at all.

'You haven't kneaded it enough,' says Brad, throwing it in the bin when he comes home.

Patiently he reselects the ingredients and mixes

them in the bowl, then slaps the dough on a floured board. I stand, mesmerised, watching the mixture beneath his hands, the way it squishes through his fingers. Kneading and folding. Rhythmic. Push. Roll. Push. Roll. His hands are working at the dough, making the process look easy, though I know from my previous attempt that it isn't. His fingers dance, proficient and nimble. Why do I feel ridiculously like crying?

'I didn't know you could make bread,' I say, hurriedly blinking back tears. Then the thought occurs to me that maybe, after all these years, there are other things I don't know about my husband.

'I can't. Leastways, I never have before. But I used to watch my grandmother when I was a kid. She rolled it like this, to let the air into it.'

He flips the dough over, kneading it with the base of his hand, stretching it, and then he pushes it together into a tight ball before repeating the process.

'Want to try?'

I nod. Cautiously I dab my hands in the flour then take the lump of dough. It feels firm between my fingers.

'Like this,' says Brad. He is standing behind me, his arms over mine as he guides my hands. Then he stops and runs the tip of his tongue down the side of my neck, which gives me instant goose bumps.

'Don't,' I laugh, pulling slightly away. 'You're supposed to be teaching me how to make bread, remember?'

I find pleasure in the repetitive pummelling movement, the flick of wrist. There's a sense of accomplishment as the dough, covered with a tea towel on the bench, slowly begins to rise.

After a while the aroma of baking bread fills the kitchen. I stand at the sink, looking out. The landscape seems alien in that late-afternoon light and I feel out of place, removed somehow from the scene, as though I'm merely an onlooker, and a reluctant one at that. The paddock stretches away, dusty brown, and I can see the dull grey-green line of coolibahs circling the distant dam. Brad comes up from behind and wraps his arms around me. I let myself fall back against him, resting my head on his chest.

It is a moment shared, when all the past hurts fade into inconspicuousness. It feels right, my body encircled within his strong arms: as it should for husband and wife. Besides, I'm feeling lonely, neglected. I've had enough of days by myself in a house that is not my home.

'Tomorrow,' I say later as we're turning down the cover on the bed, 'I'm coming with you.'

Brad raises his eyebrows. 'It's a 7 am start.'

'No problem. I think I can manage that. Anyway, who's been getting up early around here?'

'Okay. Point taken.' He grins and raises his hands in defeat. 'I'll be expecting you to wake me then.'

He walks around the bed, to the place where I'm standing. Gently he cups my chin in one palm and raises my face to his. He stares into my eyes for what seems like an inexorably long time. I feel bare, exposed. As though he's looking through me, into my soul. Can he tell what I'm thinking?

'I love you, Jess,' he says at last. 'And I've missed you, missed us.'

I blink and glance away, unable to meet his gaze. Instead I take his hands and press them against my mouth.

'Prove it, cowboy,' I challenge, diverting his attention.

I am wearing a silk kimono, a souvenir of our long-ago trip to Bali. It is black and splattered with crimson hibiscus, and makes a swishing sound when I walk. The sash is loose and dramatically I tug it away. The front of the gown falls open. Brad's hand encloses one breast, my nipple hardening at his touch.

I sigh and lean against the weight of him. His mouth is raining light kisses along the length of my neck. My hands come up, fingers tangling in his hair, pulling his face towards mine. I taste him, long movements of mouth and tongue that leave me aching for something more. Whatever we have become as a couple, despite the times when I despair that the memories will never leave and our marriage return to that previous easy normalcy, the sex is always good.

Brad's hand moves lower, trailing across my belly then between my thighs. A need begins there — a raw throbbing emptiness — in the hot swollen core of me, as his fingers tease. My own hand follows and I cup his hardness. 'Oh, God, Jess,' he groans, pulling me onto the bed.

We join, become one: the most intimate of acts. Rocking back and forth, to and fro. It is like a dance, a swaying rhythm of motion. Sensual erotic movements that carry me perilously close to the edge. Then I stop, waiting until the moment subsides, and begin the ritual again.

Brad's mouth is demanding. His tongue slides, hungrily searching the interior of my mouth. I can't get enough of him: lips, teeth and breath. His hands are stroking my breasts, kneading, and there's an image of the bread dough and the floury board and Brad's hands working, working. My hair hangs over us like a veil. Our skin, where it touches, is damp.

Suddenly the rhythm changes. Brad is moving faster now, a motion he seems unable to stop. So I move with him, releasing all control. For one brief moment I am a bird soaring beyond the memories and heartache. I am eternal, flying free.

'Now!' Brad says urgently, his voice hoarse.

I poise, then fall. Brad spills himself into me with a shuddering gasp.

'Oh, my God! Oh, my God! Oh, my God!'

Have I voiced the words or are they silent within my mind? Heat explodes. It rises up, engulfing me. Juddering circles of pleasure mixed with exquisite pain radiate outwards, leaving me breathless. I collapse, satiated, letting myself fall against my husband.

'I love you, too,' I placate in those first flushed moments.

I feel magnanimous, complete. Intensely feminine. Lying naked in the bed, sheets pushed back, as Brad's finger slowly circles my breast. Thinking: this feels so right, so right ...

Then Brad starts talking and ruins it all.

'Jess,' he begins tentatively and I stiffen at the tone of his voice.

'Mmnnn ...' Feigning sleep.

'Don't you think it's time we tried for another baby?'

I am beyond words. Or rather, I am beyond saying them. For a few moments I lie there gathering my thoughts, forming a suitable reply. My voice, when it comes, is tremulous, wavering.

'No.'

'Jess, please. We can't simply stop our lives.'

The air catches in my lungs and I find it difficult to draw breath. My heart's thudding erratically in my chest. Does he know how much I've dreaded this eventual conversation, how many times I've mentally tried to circumvent it? Dozens and dozens, over the past months.

'I don't want to talk about it,' I say now, sliding off him. The bed creaks and sags alarmingly, protesting at the shift in weight.

'Well, I want to talk about it.'

There's a tone to Brad's voice that demands attention: a steely quality, a slightly pissed-off timbre. Why can't he leave it? Why drag it all up now, spoiling the mood, the evening? I'm tired, wishing for sleep, not some argument that can never have a satisfactory conclusion. I take a deep breath.

'You can't replace a child.'

'I'm not trying to replace Kadie —'

'Don't!' I cry, closing my mind to the word. 'Don't say her name!'

The pleasure from the last few minutes is now completely gone and I'm left with an awful sick churning in my stomach. Somehow the evening is going horribly wrong, not how I'd imagined it at all.

'It was an accident, Jess. Just a bloody accident. We have to move on eventually. We can't stay bogged down in the past.'

'Accident?' I give a shaky laugh that sounds more like a sob. 'How could you call it an accident? A drunk driver and a rainy afternoon sounds more like a recipe for disaster to me. My daughter's death was no *accident*!'

'Kadie was my daughter too. You don't have the monopoly on grief, Jess.'

Unable to stop the tears, I roll to the far side of the bed, presenting Brad with a view of my back. It's purposeful rejection, showing my contempt for his words. How can he simply just dismiss everything that's happened? It's not as though he doesn't care — I know he does — but his ability to let go of the heartache both puzzles and infuriates me. I want — no, *need* — someone to blame for my own unhappiness. I want to dwell on it, let the details churn around in my mind.

I don't *want* to forget.

That night I dream again.

As usual there are dark streets and the pursuers, stark fear and laboured gasping breathing. But when I reach the river there's no car, no tiny white face pressed against the back window. Instead I dive into the swirling inky water and strike out for the other side.

Wet and exhausted, I clamber up the opposite bank and throw myself on the ground under the shade of a coolibah tree. Amazingly, here the sun is shining. The wind is blowing and clouds, tinged pink, skim overhead. Paddocks stretch away to the horizon, dotted with clumps of Mitchell grass. It's Diamantina country and no one is chasing me. As I sit and catch my breath, there is a movement to my right.

A little girl is running towards me.

Kadie, I think. *It's Kadie!*

But something is wrong.

This child's hair is dark, where Kadie's was blonde. It's longer, falling in tight ringlets where Kadie wore hers in a short bob. And there's something odd about the way she's dressed — kind of formal and old-fashioned. She's running towards the bush, the stout boots on her feet flying over the cracked earth and the hem of her skirt tangling around her ankles, catching burrs and twigs in the thin fabric as she moves. As she draws level with me she turns, looks directly into my face. I reach out, trying to stop her, but she brushes past, running, running. And there's no sign of recognition, for either of us.

I blink, stare harder.

I realise, in that fleeting glance, that the little girl isn't Kadie at all.

CHAPTER 14

The next morning we drive for about twenty minutes along a dirt road, beside the meandering coolibah-lined channels of the Diamantina River. The 4WD kicks up dust behind us. Harry is in the back of the utility, barking uselessly at every tree we pass. The sunlight is dazzling, reflecting off the dashboard. Birds flit across the track. For several minutes an emu runs alongside the car on long spindly legs, then veers off suddenly into a sea of spinifex. Already a heat haze shimmers on the horizon.

Away from the station homestead, the landscape slowly changes from medium-dense bush to gibber-stone flats. Above a distant line of trees there's a cone-shaped mountain rising out of the layers of branches and leaves. The car seems to be alternately rising and falling, navigating the maze of lignum and dry river channels. The sky above is blue and cloudless.

Eventually Brad drives under a coolibah tree, on the bank of a large water hole. He unloads several storage boxes from the back of the ute and arranges the contents on the ground. I set a folding chair out in the shade. Then I flick my novel open at the appropriate page. Harry sits beside me, panting lightly.

Instantly I'm immersed in the book. I've always had a fascination with words and stories, plots and characters, and my job as a researcher has given me a good background in general knowledge. I love the rhythm of sentences. I enjoy the way they flow over and around you, creating images, blocking out other, darker thoughts.

After what seems like only a few minutes I glance up. Brad is standing in knee-deep water, brandishing a long-handled net. He walks backwards, sweeping the net to and fro across the water as he goes. His arms are brown and his muscles ripple in the sunlight. A shock of blond hair flops untidily across his forehead. There's a frown of concentration on his face. I stare at him for a moment, seeing a stranger.

'What are you doing?' I call, curious. A trickle of perspiration runs down the length of my spine and I shift in the chair, angling myself towards a slight breeze that comes across the water.

He pauses in his work. A smile creeps across his face and even from this distance I can see his teeth, white against his tanned face. He dips his head towards me.

'I'm taking samples.'

'Of what?'

He splashes out of the water and climbs up the bank, empties the contents of the finely-meshed net into the lid from his esky. I imagine something gasping, squirming against the sudden exposure to sunlight and air. Brad selects a glass pipette from a tray on the ground and puts it to his mouth. Water rises along the length of it as he sucks inwards, his cheeks concaving. Removing the pipette from his mouth, he holds it towards me, as though inviting inspection.

'Want to see?'

'Creepy-crawlies.' I smile and shake my head.

Brad empties the pipette into a specimen jar containing the usual alcohol and water mix, then he writes on the waterproof label with a graphite pencil. He throws me the jar and I catch it, glancing at the murky water inside. The contents — several tiny snails barely discernible to the naked eye — lie suspended, already dead.

For the next few hours my attention wavers between Brad and my book. Covertly I watch him splashing about in the water, holding the net, knowledge jolting at me. Why, after all these years, am I just discovering Brad's work routines, the finer aspects of what his job entails? Have I been so caught up with myself, with my own life, that I've neglected to ask? Brad has always been interested in my career, but until now I've only ever seen the results of his work — jars of specimens on my kitchen windowsill and Brad slumped at the kitchen table writing his reports, rows of neat letters and figures detailing his findings. I never thought to ask exactly how the specimens were caught, how he put them into the jars.

I stare at the jar, at the place where Brad's hands have so recently rested. For one moment I resist the urge to place it against my cheek, as though to capture some warmth from his touch, some sense of familiarity. But the glass is cold against my hand and any remnant of heat is long gone.

I place the jar on the ground. Something's biting at my leg, distracting me. I feel a sensation somewhere between a pain and an itch, and my attention wavers. I slap at my skin, resisting the urge to scratch.

'Sand flies,' says Brad, glancing up at the noise. 'They're worse after rain. Apparently they had a few millimetres the week before we arrived. There's some insect repellent in the glove box in the car. You don't want to end up with Ross River fever.'

I rummage in the car, find the tube and slap cream along my arms and legs. There's a local map in the glove box. I take it out and lay it on the seat, studying the squiggles and scrawls that are the roads and creeks. I can see the name of the property where we're staying, and the fanned-out blue lines that mark the course of the Diamantina River. And there are circles indicating the ancient-looking jump-ups that rise so suddenly, so unexpectedly, from the flat ground.

'See that hill over there,' I call to Brad, pointing to a craggy rise that juts above the distant tree line on the other side of the water hole. 'According to the map, it's called Mount Misery. And the waterway that runs alongside is called Murdering Creek. Odd sorts of names, don't you think?'

Brad sets the net on the river bank and puts one hand on his hip. He shields his eyes with the other hand, squinting against the glare. His hair, in that light, seems almost silver.

'According to old Jack, Betty's husband, there was supposed to be a massacre of Aborigines there over a hundred years ago.'

He says it offhandedly — a titbit of information casually flung across the void between us. A shiver runs across my shoulders and I resist the urge to turn and stare again at the hill. I know I'll see nothing there except trees and red eroded rock. There'll be nothing out of the ordinary, nothing unusual.

I haven't yet met Betty's husband, Jack, but Brad's been up at the homestead, fuelling up the car and catching up on some of the local knowledge. Massacre? I think again, puzzled. There was no mention of it in the potted local history I'd read.

'What about lunch? I'm starving,' Brad calls, breaking my chain of thought.

I've made sandwiches with the bread Brad baked yesterday, and there's a flask of coffee which is a welcome change from the water we've been drinking all morning. When we're finished, Brad fiddles with the two-way radio in the car. He's supposed to call the Environmental Protection Agency base at Longreach every day, to report in to his superiors and let them know we're okay.

'VKC289.'

He's speaking into the microphone, holding it close to his mouth. I see his lips moving, forming words. A crow, perched in a nearby tree is cawing, loud raucous sounds that distract me. Then I hear a crackle of voice on the other end of the radio.

'Receiving you. What's your position? Back.'

Brad relays our location, according to the global positioning system in the car. 'Any messages?' he asks.

The reply is lost in a stammer of static and I can only hear Brad's side of the remainder of the conversation.

'I'll be topping up with fuel. Back.'

'Hot and dry. Dust storms? Back.'

'Water level's down. Bit murky. Back.'

'Excellent. I've already got a few good samples. Back.'

'Yeah. We'll take it easy. Back.'

'Standing by.'

Brad clicks the two-way off and replaces the microphone on the holder. Little awarenesses are bumping against my consciousness. For the second time today I'm seeing a side of my husband that has somehow, over the past eleven years, managed to elude me. Proficiency on the two-way? Talking the right lingo? Baking bread? Where was I while he was learning those skills?

I study him from under the brim of my hat, trying to see him as others might. Good-looking, I concede, with blond hair that flops over his tanned forehead. His hands are expressive, his manner is confident and capable.

Brad has always been affable, in a relaxed easy-going way, not threatened by other people's opinions. We'd met back in our university days, on a winter's afternoon. I'd been working part-time in the uni library and Brad had come in looking for research books. I remember him as he was then, leaning casually against the front desk, alternately blowing on his fingers and frowning over a list of reading matter.

There had been one book in particular, necessary reading for his course, but there were already a dozen holds on it.

'No matter,' he'd said nonchalantly, digging his hands deep in the pockets of his jeans as he rocked on the heels of his boots. 'I'll just have to wait.'

He'd stood there, staring at me as though he was aware of something that I wasn't. 'What's the matter?' I'd asked, disconcerted. 'Spinach in my teeth?'

He'd smiled then, suddenly and without warning — a disarming grin that ridged his face and crinkled up his eyes. 'What time do you finish work?'

Something inside me lurched, then righted itself. I'd felt a sense of balancing on the rim of something momentous, deciding whether I'd purposely let myself topple, just to experience the impression of falling. Even now I have a clear recollection of that moment — a slow heat burning up my neck, trying desperately not to blush under his scrutiny; the sensation that although we were strangers, we had somehow already met. Did he feel the same?

'Another half hour,' I'd shrugged, trying not to seem too eager. Suddenly all I wanted was to spend time with this man, get to know him. All the old clichés came rushing at me, mocking: soul mates, love at first sight. Was there such a thing as love across a crowded room? — although the library was far from congested on that chill blustery afternoon.

'Let's go for coffee then?'

'Okay.'

The start of our relationship: as simple as that.

We'd sat in a booth in some dingy inner-city café, talking until midnight. The conversation flowed, random and haphazard, interspersed with several cups of surprisingly good coffee. We talked about my studies and his, my passion for research, his for the environment. Reading. Bicycling. Italian food.

'Pollo alla griglia? You love pollo alla griglia?'

'Especially when it's washed down with a decent shiraz.'

We lurched easily from one subject to another, minutes flowing into hours, topics and scenes intertwining in my mind until they became a kaleidoscope of ideas and impressions: Brad's fingers wrapped around the coffee mug; the dim overhead light creating shadows under his jaw line; our reflections in the mirror tiles on the opposite wall. We had so many interests in common, plus several, as we soon discovered, shared friends.

'If you know all these people, how is it we've never met before?'

'Fate. Destiny. It wasn't meant to be, until now.'

I'd glanced at him, puzzled. There was an earnestness about him, a lack of pretentiousness that I found addictive. I wanted the night to go on and on, never ending. I didn't want to walk away from this man, ever.

'Do you really believe that?'

'That all things happen for a purpose at a given time? Sure.'

I'd toyed with some grains of spilt sugar, pushing them into a neat pile. Brad brought his hand forward, enclosing it over mine. His skin felt warm and tingles ran along my arm as I fought back a sudden urge to reach forward and run one finger along the line where fair hairs sprouted at his temple.

'As Aeschylus said,' he'd gone on, obviously oblivious to my chaotic thoughts, 'things are where things are, and, as fate has willed, so they shall be fulfilled.'

'And as Elizabeth Bowen said,' I replied, staring boldly into his eyes, watching for some reaction to my words, 'fate is not an eagle, it creeps like a rat.'

Immediately I'd cringed inwardly. Why had I said that? No guys, it seemed, were interested in women with intelligence, and I'd been told more than once by men that they found me intimidating.

He'd laughed then, a deep, full-bodied sound that made other heads in the room turn. 'I've never thought of myself as a rat.'

The waitress brought another round of coffee to the table. 'Ten minutes till closing time,' she warned.

The thought of my empty flat was suddenly unappealing. 'So much caffeine,' Brad observed, looking deep into my eyes. 'I'll never sleep.'

Then I'd said: 'Come back to my place.'

Just like that. An invitation, casually extended. Me, Jess, usually so conservative, scarcely daring to breathe, waiting for his reply. Please say yes!

'Okay,' he'd shrugged. 'Why not?'

We'd left then, grabbing our coats and hurrying out the door, Brad's arm slung proprietorially over my shoulder. Outside the wind was icy, racing along the footpath. I shivered and Brad, as though sensing the shudder that coursed through me, stopped and spun me towards him, cupping his palms against my cheeks.

'Oh, Jess,' he'd said, and his voice was like a long, drawn-out sigh. 'I've been searching for you for years.'

He'd kissed me then, and somehow it felt right. Mouths and hands fusing, becoming one. Something inside me had melted and I felt a sudden heat rising up, engulfing me.

Things are where things are, he'd said. Fate. Destiny. Call it what you will, but it seemed, on that long-ago night, that all the powers in the world couldn't have kept us apart. We might have been a regular couple who had been hanging out for years, that was how I felt with him. Right from the start, from that night on, our relationship had been comfortable, like an old shoe.

Until now.

'Jess?'

Brad's calling me and my mind seesaws unwillingly between the past and the present. These days the past seems so much more desirable.

'Were you asleep?'

'No.' I roll onto my back and look upwards towards the Diamantina sky. 'Just thinking.'

There's not a cloud to spoil the interminable blue. Instead the colour is broken, fragmented into sections by the dark shapes of several hovering birds.

'Time to pack up. I want to check out another site.'

We drive further along the river, away from the long water hole. On the way, Brad tells me about the food chains in water. Macro-invertebrates — animals with no backbone, ranging from yabbies down to microscopic beings — form a food source for birds and fish. Phytoplankton and zooplankton are the microscopic plants and animals right at the base of the food chain, the first vital bits of a healthy ecosystem.

I listen, the words washing around me, scarcely heard. I'm more aware of the dog beside me, panting slightly, and the rolling lurch of the car. There's something niggling at me, some awareness demanding to be heard. There's also a tenseness lying between us — can Brad feel it too? — a murky undercurrent which, as the day progresses, is becoming stronger.

We stop at a smaller water hole. The water here is still and there's a smell of something rotten. Brad leans out the car window, one hand shielding his eyes.

'Look at that,' he says, pointing towards the scummy pond. Several large fish lie unmoving on the surface, scales silver in the sunlight. 'There's been a fish kill.'

Great! I think, searching for a handkerchief to cover my nose.

'A fish kill,' Brad informs me as though it's a topic I need to know about, 'is usually associated with low dissolved levels of oxygen in the water.'

I try to sound interested but the smell makes me feel nauseous. 'And that's caused by ...?'

Brad shrugs. Perspiration beads his temples and he raises his upper arm, wiping it away. 'A flood that brings lots of decaying matter into the water, or simply by the water hole drying up, becoming stagnant.'

He carries out GPS tracking for our location then methodically does a water-quality test. Taking the camera from his bag, he photographs the site upstream and downstream, making notes as he goes. Using a thermometer, he records the water temperature then tests the acidity level with a special meter. Lastly he takes one of the largest fish and lays it on a board, next to a long-bladed knife.

A slight wall of panic rises up in my chest and I will it away. 'You're not seriously going to chop that thing up?'

'Yep.' He slices at the side of the fish's head and removes a chunk of flesh. 'This is the ear,' he says matter-of-factly. He holds it out and I glance away, fighting back another surge of nausea. I'll never understand how he can do that, slice into flesh, even though it's only a dead fish.

'I've never really considered fish as having ears.'

'They're small hard stones made of calcium carbonate, called otoliths, and they function as a fish's gravity and sound receptor. But in a way they're similar to tree trunks. They develop a growth ring every year, so you can tell the age of the fish by the number of rings. This one's a yellowbelly, and it's about four years old.'

He's still slicing into the fish, laying strips of it on the board. Momentarily I close my eyes against the sight, blocking out also the dappled shade that falls across the ground. All I can hear is the excited chatter of birds in the nearby trees and the sound of the knife.

Chop. Chop. Chop.

But Brad is still talking, unaware that I'm scarcely listening. '. . . just like tree rings we can judge the seasons. Widely spaced rings means a good season. Narrow rings means a bad year of growth.'

I feel I have to say something, add to the conversation. 'Because of drought?'

'Probably. Or bad water quality, for whatever reason.'

I still can't bring myself to look back at the fish lying there, its head sliced open. 'What's this!' I say flippantly, trying to divert the subject. 'A natural science lesson?'

Brad shoots me a wounded glance and I see his mouth forming a wedge of disappointment. He shrugs, moving slightly over the cutting board until I am presented with a partial view of his back. 'I thought you'd be interested, that's all. It was your idea to come today.'

He takes the fish and wraps it in a plastic bag, puts it in the esky. 'No problem,' he continues, still avoiding my gaze. 'I'll take it home and store it in the freezer, examine it later. I can see you've had enough for today.'

'Brad, I —'

'Forget it, Jess,' he cuts off my words with a terse reply.

We repack the car in silence. Even Harry, as Brad leashes him in the back next to the esky, seems to sense the mood. I'm angry, with myself mainly, for demeaning Brad's work. It's the reason we're here after all, and the completion of his thesis is something he's been striving towards for ages now. I search my brain for something to say, some words of apology, but nothing comes. I've upset him with my jokey remark, and there's a strained silence filling the space between us as the car lurches forward along the river bank.

Brad seems to be aiming the car towards every pothole and washaway. We pass trees that seem mere inches away. Is he trying to frighten me? The seat belt jerks at my chest, making it suddenly difficult to breathe. My eyes slide down. Brad's field notes are attached to the clipboard that lies on the seat between us. Shockingly, the date on the top catches my attention.

I shut my eyes, trying to blot out the sight. But it's too late. The numbers, in black and white, dance tauntingly behind my closed lids. This is what I've been trying not to think about: tomorrow — the anniversary.

The dread has built up inside me like a living thing. I don't want to remember, want instead to block those last images from my mind. But my thoughts slip sideways, uncontrollable, no longer on the fish or the argument, or the air that squeezes from my lungs. The passing trees seem to surround me like bars on a cage, and I fight back the urge to open the door and throw myself from the car. There's a stinging sensation behind my eyes. For a second the trees blur into the sky, merging with the blue. How odd, I think, that my body can still produce tears, when the core of me seems so hard and dry.

Has he realised, I wonder, what tomorrow is?

Then suddenly that thought seems so ridiculous. How could he forget?

The scene stabs back at me. Brad is fastening Kadie into her safety seat in the back of the car. Those first drops of rain are beginning to fall on the driveway. Kadie is smiling and I'm waving goodbye.

'Blow Mummy a kiss.'

Brad is staring at me over the roof of the car, saying, 'Are you sure you won't come with us?'

'You know I've got to get the proposal finished by tomorrow.'

He frowns. 'Work! Work! Work! It's Sunday, for Christ's sake! We never spend time together anymore. Kadie never sees you. She'll forget who her mother is.'

Kadie, our daughter, is almost three. She's bright as a button, with blonde hair cut into a short bob and a ready smile. She loves wearing zany clothes — encouraged by my sister Carys — purple and pink and lime green mostly, and her favourite food is sushi. My mother, who believes in such things, calls her an 'old soul'.

I bend down and smile at her through the closed window. I mouth the words again — 'blow Mummy a kiss' — and she obliges, awarding me with a grin as she does.

'Hey, babe.' I straighten and stare past Brad, upwards towards the sky where dark clouds have gathered. A splotch of rain lands on my face. 'Next weekend, I promise. Anyway, looks like today's going to be a wash-out.'

Brad shrugs and I know from the tight line of his mouth that he's annoyed. He slides into his seat and slams the door with a resounding bang, not bothering to reply. I stand on the driveway, forcing my mouth into a smile that's more for Kadie's benefit than Brad's, watching as the car pulls out onto the road. I can see Kadie's hand still raised in a silent wave.

'Next weekend, babe,' I say aloud. 'I'll make it up to you next weekend.'

Except I'm not to know there will be no next weekend for the three of us.

It's raining harder now — fat drops that plop against concrete and tar. I walk back inside the house, my mind on Brad's accusation rather than the task ahead. It's true: we hardly spend time together as a family. Brad's work, mine, Kadie's weekdays spent in childcare: all conspiring to keep us apart. We'd been planning today's picnic for several weeks and now I'd gone and spoilt it all.

'You have to learn to say no,' Brad had said the previous night. 'Switch off. Prioritise. Kadie will be starting preschool soon. Perhaps it's time we thought about another baby.'

'Hey, cowboy, I'm just getting back on track with my career. I don't want to stop now.'

'What about us, our family? That has to mean something too?'

Little niggly arguments, words like arrows, silences that seemed to go on for days: what was happening to us? I could manage, couldn't I, juggling the demands of a career and home and family? Other women seemed to cope. But underneath I was struggling, borrowing precious moments from Brad and Kadie's lives to placate work superiors. A promotion was looming and I was certain I'd make the grade. I couldn't bear to fail.

I'd have done things differently, of course, if I'd known. In hindsight I would have said to hell with the proposal. I would have also suggested a different route that Sunday, not along the dirt back road over the wooden one-lane bridges. Perhaps I would have seen the driver ahead, obviously drunk, weaving through the pouring rain across the centre of the road, heading for the side of our car. Maybe, unlike Brad, after that first awful explosion of metal, I would have been conscious when the car catapulted through the bridge railing, able to scrabble about in the back until I'd found my daughter and unstrapped her from the child restraint, before the car slowly sank into the water.

Maybe, maybe, maybe.

I remember certain images, flickering snapshots of the hours and days that followed. The policeman at the door, his hat held in his hands, funereal expression on his face. A low animal-like moan comes from the depths of me. A blank space, blessed darkness, then family and friends moving around the house, heard through a fog of sleeping tablets. Carys crying. My mother making endless cups of tea. Dad talking on the telephone in muted tones, making arrangements. 'Sshh,' I'd hear someone say. 'Jess's sleeping.' Brad's arm in plaster. Ribs strapped.

I remember sitting dry-eyed at the funeral, eyes sliding towards that tiny, tiny casket. An uncontrollable fury beats in my chest. How dare someone — anyone — destroy my daughter's life!

Now I glance sideways at Brad. His mouth is drawn tight into a line of concentration and he's staring straight ahead, eyes glued to the road. I reach out and run one finger along his tanned forearm. Still he stares ahead, ignoring me. What's to become of us? I wonder.

There are days when I think Brad and I would be better off apart, starting afresh with new partners, not trying to climb over the mountains of baggage we seem to have accumulated in the past year. And there are days, like today, when it seems too difficult, too damned mentally exhausting, to go on. Sometimes the memories of Kadie are so tied to him that simply looking at my husband hurts. Same smile, same shade of hair colour. Same blue eyes and jutting obstinate chin. Every time I look at Brad I see my daughter, and my heart breaks into tiny pieces yet again.

I lean my head back against the car seat and watch the trees scudding past, closing my mind against the images, not wanting to remember those awful, awful days, yet unable to forget.

There's a note tucked under the front door when we arrive back at the house. *Come for dinner*, it reads. *Eight o'clock. Bring mozzie repellent. Betty.*

There has been a light shower of rain while we were unpacking the car and bathing, and the breeze has a certain coolness to it, which seems odd after the heat of the day. However the clouds have gone and the stars are bright in the sky overhead as we walk across the paddock towards the lights of Betty and Jack's house. Brad has a torch, the wavering beam of which snakes before us, highlighting the unevenness of the ground. Dutifully we follow its path.

Brad and I are not the only guests. A battered Toyota 4WD is parked at the front of the house under a pepper tree and as we walk along the verandah I can hear voices and laughter. There's music playing softly in the background and a few moths flutter around the lamp next to the front door. A smell of something delicious comes from the interior of the house. We knock and Betty calls, 'Come in. We're all out on the back verandah.'

There are handshakes all round as Brad introduces me to Jack, Betty's husband. Then Jack introduces his other guests, Stan and Ella. They're an Aboriginal couple, about the same age as Jack and Betty: mid-sixties.

'Stan does some stock work for me, and a bit of fencing,' says Jack. 'They've got a place about two miles down the river.'

We talk: the usual get-to-know-you stuff. Weather. Brad's research progress.

'There's been a lot of your mob coming up here lately,' says Stan, 'doing tests and other scientific research.'

Ella turns to me. 'Your mob!' she repeats, laughing. 'Don't mind Stan. He thinks anyone who doesn't live out here deserves the same label.'

I smile back, taken by her warmth. 'That's okay.'

'Let's see,' says Stan, ticking off on his fingers. 'In the past six months we've had an archaeologist, a couple of hydrologists, even a bloke studying dust and wind. What was he called again, Ella?'

'Dunno, love.' She gives me a wink. 'Some fancy "ologist" name. We called him the dustbuster, though. He had these little windmill things all over the bottom paddock.'

'What did you say you were again, Brad?' asks Stan.

'What sort of "ologist", you mean?' Betty adds.

'I'm an aquatic biologist.'

'You don't say.' Stan rubs the tip of his nose. 'So you study water, right?'

'That's right. Aquatic animal life and vegetation, and water quality.'

'Fancy that.' Stan seems quite impressed. 'Water quality? Never thought much about studying that before.'

'Well, the quality of the water pretty much determines the plant and animal life. Factors such as turbidity, salt and pH levels are all important. And once the dissolved oxygen levels fall below a certain range, water can't support fish. Speaking of which, we found a fish kill today in that small water hole about five kilometres upriver.'

Jack and Stan are talking with Brad about nutrients. My attention's wandering and I hear only random words such as 'phosphorous' and 'nitrogen'. My thoughts slip back to the morning and in my mind's eye I can see Brad as he was, standing knee-deep in the water hole, sweeping the net across the water.

I swallow hard and see him again, the memory surfacing oddly. Brad holding the pipette to his mouth, deft fingers stoppering the end. Water splashing into the jar. His fingers, strong and capable, holding the pencil.

'So, Jess, what do you do?'

The mention of my name brings me back to the present. I turn to find Ella staring at me, intent on making some sort of conversation. She really is very kind, I know, wanting to include me. She's also well meaning and probably curious and, although tonight I'd rather be left alone, I can't ignore the question.

I shrug helplessly. 'I used to be a researcher for one of the television stations.'

There I go, defining myself as usual by my former occupation, as though the job validates me as a person. Why don't I also add, I wonder fleetingly, that I used to be a mother and a proper wife, not full of pretence as I am now. Then I feel panicky. Maybe this woman will see through the wall I've thrown up around myself and catch sight of the real me, not the fake one I parade for everyone to see.

But Ella smiles and takes my elbow, steering me towards the kitchen where I can hear the clank of crockery. Her mind seems to be following another path altogether. 'Let's go and help Betty set the table,' she says. 'Television, now! Imagine that! Stan and I were on the telly once. A camera crew was out here doing some sort of documentary . . .'

After dinner we go outside, onto the back lawn. Jack's built a fire there in an old forty-four-gallon drum, and there's a line of empty chairs semi-circled around the flames.

'It's not as though it's really that cold, but there's something about a fire, don't you think?' says Betty.

The conversation drifts along, words washing over me. I'm feeling drowsy after the meal and lay my head against the back of the chair, listening.

'The min-min lights,' Stan is saying. 'They're a bit of a tourist thing now, especially out Boulia way. But we've had them around here.'

'They used to call them the devil lights, back in the old days,' adds Ella.

'Devil lights,' I murmur, fascinated, opening my eyes. 'Have any of you ever seen them?'

Jack shakes his head. 'Not me, and I've lived here for thirty years. Reckon it's a bit of bullshit myself, if you'll excuse the language.'

'Ah, such a disbeliever, Jack,' Ella chides.

'Have a few too many rums, Ella, and you'll see strange lights too.'

Betty takes another sip of her drink and looks thoughtful. 'According to the legend, anyone who chases the light and catches it will never return to tell the tale.' She gives a mock shudder. 'Spooky, isn't it?'

I feel a sudden chill across my shoulders, and the hairs on my arms tingle.

'Brad and Jess are interested in the history of the place,' says Jack, breaking the mood. 'They've got a copy of that local history booklet the historical society in town put out a while back. You could fill them in on a bit more local knowledge, Stan. Some of the stuff that isn't in the book.'

There's a silence among the group, a space between words that looms ominously. For some unknown reason, the morning's names have fought their way up, through my consciousness: Mount Misery, Murdering Creek. 'So, Stan, your family's from around here, then?' I ask, filling the gap.

'Not originally. My great-grandmother, Ngayla, came from another tribe further up the river.'

Everyone is still, listening to Stan's words. Jack and Betty. Ella and Brad. Me. I see the fire reflected in the old man's face. As the flames rise and fall, the shadows dance, flit away, then skulk back. The darkness beyond the fire seems as though it might go on and on forever, like outer space, although I've never quite been able to comprehend the concept of infinity. Everything must end some time, surely. This evening. Our stay on the Diamantina. My self-imposed retirement. The raw aching pain of losing Kadie that slams back at me, even now.

Yet tonight my world is somehow encompassed within this circle of firelight, in the company of these people. I feel calm, though detached, as though I'm poised on the brink of something. Like that rainy afternoon years earlier when Brad had said *things are where things are* and I'd let myself fall, willingly, into an unknown future.

Stan lifts his hands expressively, laying his palms flat towards the stars, and begins to tell the story. 'It was back in the 1870s,' he says, 'as it's written in the book Jess read.'

I have the oddest sensation then, a feeling of déjà vu, that I've been here before in this same place, doing this same thing, and somehow I already know the words Stan speaks, even before he voices them.

CHAPTER 15

DIAMANTINA COUNTRY
September 1873

It seemed to Adam, even after only a few months, that he had lived in this land called Diamantina country forever. He sensed he had somehow come home, to a place where he felt at ease, where all troubles that had gone before seemed to fade away and finally become the past. Maybe here, among the dry river channels and spinifex, his luck might prosper and good fortune eventually come his way. He was certainly willing it and, God knows, he had waited long enough. He was twenty-five years old. It was six years since he had left the Old Country.

In his mind he'd laid his parents to rest, and all those tiny siblings. He'd forgiven his former neighbour, the man who had managed to force them from their land — had the man not ultimately done him a favour? That place of the blue gums seemed far away now, belonging to another life.

He'd also pardoned Conor for his last-minute betrayal. The land had been a long-time dream for both of them, or so Adam had always thought. But the woman named Jenna had changed all that. Conor was twenty-three now, Adam was forced to remind himself, and could make his own choices. Mam and Da had already been married at the same age. At least Conor had promised him six months to help him on his way, for which Adam was grateful.

He and Conor had arrived at the property bearing a letter from the land agent, noting that the lease had been transferred. The former owner had gladly accepted the proffered cash for the hut and the sheep and cattle. The man and his family had thrown their few meagre belongings in the back of their wagon and left that very afternoon, after a few hurried instructions on care for the livestock. The man's parting words were: 'Don't trust the blacks.'

Adam had been amazed when he'd seen the interior of the hut. How a family of six had managed to squeeze in there, let alone eat and sleep, was a mystery to him.

'Nothing like togetherness,' Conor grinned as he surveyed the stark interior.

Walls were rough-hewn timber and the floor was dirt. The chimney was badly constructed and smoke billowed into the room when the fire was lit. The roof was built from thatched boughs and, as they eventually discovered, leaked when it rained. Somehow that hut reminded Adam of Ireland but he didn't care. This was his place — well, his and temporarily Conor's and, because of the money she had lent them, Jenna's too. Given time, he'd make it better.

Adam named the place Diamantina Downs, in deference to the nearby river, although *river* seemed too grand a name for the chain of muddy water holes strung out across the countryside. He fixed the hut's fireplace and roof. Then he and Conor began exploring, noting the boundaries, hills and streams. They left each day at sun-up, not returning until dark. Already, though it was only early spring, the sun poured unaccustomed heat onto the dry baked earth. The rainy season was a few months away and it would be prudent, Adam told Conor, to check the lie of the land now.

Several miles north, the surrounding countryside rose up in a long curving line on either side of the river, forcing the course into one narrow passage. Adam and Conor left their horses below and puffed their way to the top, amazed by the view.

Beyond, the land dropped away and levelled out into a wide well-grassed plateau with few trees. The ridges further out were a smudged misty blue and seemed to sway in the mirage heat. Below, snaking lines of coolibah marked the maze of braided channels that made up the river. From that height the channels seemed more like deep dry furrows in the ground, but the previous owner had assured them that once the annual rains came they would fill and overspill, and water would fan out over the land.

Ground, water and air: it seemed that everywhere Adam looked there were birds. The water holes were alive with black swans and ducks, geese and pelicans. Native quail and plovers — with their harsh shrill cry — darted among the sand hills through the straggling clumps of spinifex and Mitchell grass. During the late afternoons, flocks of pink and grey galahs hopped along the ground pecking at grass seeds, looking awkward with their stiff-legged gait. Brightly-coloured finches and budgerigars flitted through the leaves of the trees that lined the water holes. Cockatoos and corellas sat sentinel on the branches, shrieking protest and rising into the air in one mass if anyone came near. And above, soaring on unseen currents of air, hawks were dark specks against the blueness of the sky.

Choosing to ignore the former owner's warning, Adam tentatively approached the local Aborigines. A small group was camped beside one of the nearby water holes and Adam took a bag of flour and several wads of tobacco down there late one afternoon. There were half a dozen men and two women and they could, he discovered, speak halting English. So he offered them all work.

Two of the men — Yapunya and Pigeon — would do odd jobs about the place, such as fencing and cutting wood. Wongaree, in deference to his age and seniority, was to be head stockman. Wandi, the youngest of the tribe, was put in charge of the horses.

Adam asked Aleyne, the older of the two women, to help out in the hut with the cooking and cleaning. Lalla, Aleyne's fifteen-year-old daughter and Wongaree's girl-wife, came every second day to attend to the washing.

Aleyne's name, he discovered, meant 'tongue', and he sincerely hoped he would not be the recipient of hers. She was about forty, he supposed, formidable looking, with a face covered in scars and several of her front teeth missing. 'Ah, you men,' she said with a toothless smile, the first day she came to the hut to work, 'you can't get along without woman. You need woman, yes?'

As the weeks passed, routines were established. Aleyne was busy in the makeshift kitchen. Lalla kept the two men in a supply of clean clothes. A new pile of firewood grew alongside the hut and already there were the makings of a vegetable garden. As the weather became hotter, feed was becoming scarce near the hut so Adam suggested moving the sheep further away, up to the grassy plateau they had discovered.

It was decided that Conor would go. 'No point in both of us traipsing up there,' he said. 'Someone needs to stay here and keep an eye on the place.'

'Take Pigeon,' Adam offered. 'I don't like the idea of you going by yourself.'

'And what's going to happen to me, I might ask?'

Adam shrugged. 'It just seems safer, that's all.'

'Ah, sometimes I like just being by myself. No one to argue with.'

And so it was settled. He waved his brother goodbye as Conor rode off at dawn one morning, the kelpie shooing the sheep before him. He was taking two weeks' supply of food.

'I'll stay up there a while and start laying out for fence lines. We're going to have to think about fences, you know,' he said sternly to Adam, watching as the sheep skittered and jumped, 'else this mob will just wander off.'

Adam was so used to his brother's company that it felt strange with Conor gone. He wandered around for a while, not knowing what task to begin. Eventually he set to, fixing a broken gate on the home paddock.

He was so engrossed in the task that he missed lunch altogether, and it wasn't until mid-afternoon when one of the dogs began barking furiously that he looked up. He could tell, by the approaching man's uniform, that he was the commander of the local native police. The man was accompanied by eight mounted black trackers and four packhorses.

The commander brought his horse to a halt next to Adam and sat there, high in the saddle, staring down.

'Who's the owner here?'

The man had a belligerent air about him and Adam disliked him on sight. 'I am,' he replied, frowning under the brim of his hat.

The commander looked him up and down, a smirk on his face. 'You don't say.'

'I just did, actually.'

The smirk vanished. Aleyne and Lalla had come to the front door of the hut and were giggling and pointing towards the group of men. 'You the only white bloke here?' asked the man, eyeing them.

'Just me and my brother. He's out there.' Adam pointed towards the blur of a distant hill. 'He's taken the stock further out where there's better feed. Is there a problem?'

'I'd be bringing him back, if I were you. It's not safe out there.'

'Why not?'

'There's a group of blacks coming along the river. We've had reports of stock being killed, and we've seen tracks around the water holes and the remains of fires. The locals say they're not from around here. We think they're part of the mob that killed the wife of a station owner further north.'

'Killed?' Adam glanced towards the black trackers. They sat sullenly on their horses, not meeting Adam's gaze, staring forlornly down at their saddles instead. There was an air of compliance about them, a beaten look.

The commander awarded his men a contemptuous sneer. 'Retaliation, apparently,' he went on. 'It seems one of the white stockmen on the property was seeking ... aahhh ... favours with one of the native women. He promised her money but when it came time to pay he shot her instead. She had a small baby. The child was killed as well.'

Adam thought of Conor, heading off alone that very morning. A flicker of fear rose in his chest. 'And they're coming this way?'

'Don't worry. We'll clear them out for you. That's why we're here.'

The man, Adam saw, was pompous and arrogant. He wore a smart coat and a silk shirt, clothing quite unsuitable for the bush. Who was he trying to impress?

'What do you mean by "clear them out"?'

'Get rid of them.'

'*Kill* them?'

'Whatever.' The man shrugged, a careless uplifting of his shoulders, then turned to go. 'You can be assured that when we're finished, they won't be coming back to bother you.'

Adam leaned forward and grabbed the horse's bridle. 'Let's make one thing clear,' he said in the most authoritative voice he could muster. 'There'll be no killing on Diamantina Downs. Just make your presence known to these people and they'll probably be gone in a day or two. Meanwhile, you can set up camp by the river and you're welcome back up here for a meal tonight.'

The commander arrived at the hut at dusk, leaving his 'boys' to fend for themselves back at their camp. Under one arm he carried a bottle of rum. In the other hand he carried a gun.

'Never go anywhere without it,' he said nonchalantly. 'You don't know when you'll need it.'

'I doubt you'll be needing it tonight,' Adam replied dryly.

Aleyne had cooked a stew earlier in the day and the two men sat down at the kitchen table to a plateful. Talk was general and Adam's thoughts kept drifting to Conor, out there in the dark alone except for the dog. Was there a real threat? The man sitting opposite him seemed to think so, but that could simply be scaremongering, the commander trying to provide justification for his job.

Though Adam's personal knowledge of the native police force was non-existent, he'd heard plenty over the previous few months in town, in the bar and on the verandah of the pub. The local landowners had been very vocal, and disparaging. Gradually, over dinner, the conversation drifted towards the subject.

'Generally,' said Adam, 'you're seen by most settlers as doing more harm than good. We're getting along alright by ourselves, but lots of areas seem to have no end of problems once you chaps go through, when there were none before. You come here, stirring the blacks up. Then you go and leave us with the mess.'

The commander pushed his empty plate away and laughed. 'This is the bush and you have to be tough with vermin like these. Treat them rough and they'll respect you for that. If you're soft they'll walk all over you.'

Adam pushed his plate away too. Though his meal was only half-eaten, his appetite was suddenly gone. 'It's all very well you coming out here and throwing your weight around, and your guns. The black trackers you bring with you are bloody petrified of what you'll do to them if they don't obey you. I wouldn't fancy being tied to a tree trunk and whipped. So out of fear they'd happily mow down their own kind, for no other reason than they stole a sheep and cooked it on their campfire. You have to understand the ways of the natives.'

The man's mouth tightened, fine lines of annoyance radiating from his lips. 'I don't have to understand anything! They're thieving mongrels, nothing more! And when you've lived here for a while, maybe you'll realise that.'

'What rubbish!' Adam was becoming incensed now. 'We come here and take *their* land, so doesn't that make us the thieving mongrels?'

'People like you need us — we keep this place safe for you. Take your stock, for instance. The blacks consider whatever moves is fair game. Maybe you'll feel differently when you start to notice lambs missing.'

Adam took a deep breath. 'Kangaroos, emus, sheep: it's all food to them. We're wiping out *their* food so they're taking ours. Seems like a fair exchange to me. And *you* blokes! You think you're a law unto yourselves! You don't care what you do to the local tribes, and you don't care who knows it. I give you permission to camp on my land, then what if you start wiping out the blacks on my run? You go back to wherever you came from but I have to live here and bear the consequences of your actions. The blacks will think I'm behind it somehow, or at least that I agree with what you do. I've worked bloody hard to get to a state of friendly relations with the local tribe around here. I don't want to find myself with a spear in my back after you've gone.'

The commander looked thoughtfully at Adam for a moment. 'Have you ever had a black woman?' he asked at last.

Adam was shocked. 'No!'

The man laughed and brought out the bottle of rum, waved it towards Adam. 'Then you don't know what you're missing. Best damn fuck you'll ever have.'

He offered a tot of rum, which Adam accepted.

'Ah, let's not argue,' the commander went on.

'You and I are the only two white blokes for miles. It'd be a shame to completely ruin what might be a pleasant evening.'

Adam sipped the liquid and felt a hazy warmth settle in his chest. Eventually the anger slid away. No use fighting it, said an inner voice. There's nothing you can do.

Instead the two men chatted on, moving to neutral topics. Adam was eager for news from the towns further north. The commander asked about Adam's plans for the land, to which he happily replied. From time to time he thought about Conor, wished he was there. Conor, with his smooth tongue and quick way with words, would have been able to put this man more firmly in his place, would have been able to present a better argument.

As midnight approached the commander stifled a yawn and both men agree to retire to bed. 'We'll be off early in the morning,' the other man said. 'We've got a few miles to cover.'

Adam walked the man to the door. He stood in its opening and stared, for one brief moment, towards the sky. The moon was a crescent slit, poised just above the horizon. The stars were bright pinpoints juxtaposed against a darkness that seemed to go on forever. He stared back at the man, seeing him in the pool of light spilling from his own doorway. 'What I said earlier,' he cautioned, folding his arms across his chest, 'I mean it. There'll be no blood shed on Diamantina Downs.'

He cleared the plates from the table. Then he lay on the bed and closed his eyes, waiting for sleep. But it seemed to have deserted him, despite the late hour. From outside he heard the squeak of bats and the far-off howl of a dingo. There was a sound of something thrashing through the nearby grass — a large lizard perhaps, or a night bird foraging for food.

Some time during the night a cool breeze came up. It blew steadily, jostling through the trees and bringing with it the sweet scent of rain. Adam stirred and reached for a blanket, aware of the splatter of the drops against the roof. Then he slid back into the dream.

In his dream Da and Mam, Conor, and all those tiny babies he'd seen buried, were gathered about his bed. He stared at them in turn, resting his eyes on their faces. Da and Mam were blurred at the edges, their features barely seen. The children were blank-faced with black holes where their eyes and mouths might have been. Only Conor seemed real.

They were all carrying gardening implements: rakes and hoes, axes and shovels. 'Come on!' shouted Da, pointing to the doorway that led outside. His voice was hoarse and raspy, as though from years of disuse. 'Get out of bed. There's work to be done and we're here to help. No time to waste.'

'You're dead,' replied Adam. 'You can't help me.'

Da stopped and stared at him for what seemed like a long time. 'Well,' he declared hesitantly, taking Mam's hand. 'If that's the case, we'd best be off then.'

He beckoned the children and they shuffled towards the door, Conor in their midst. With each successive step they became smaller, even less distinct, until they merged with the darkness in the room.

'No!' cried Adam, 'don't go!'

He was calling to Conor mainly. The others might be long dead, but his brother was alive, real flesh and blood, his companion in this rugged land. But it was too late. Conor had gone and he was alone in his dream.

Too soon the rain passed, leaving only the sour odour of gidgee and damp earth. Eventually Adam woke to a grey dawn filled with the chorus of birds. He stumbled to the kitchen bench, the after-effects of the rum leaving his thoughts fuzzy around the margins. Had he imagined the visit from the commander? But no, there were the two used plates on the bench, and through the window opening he could see a column of smoke winding its way through the trees down by the water hole where the man and his trackers had made their camp.

They were leaving this morning, Adam remembered, and he thought he might go down and say goodbye, reiterate the instructions he'd given the previous evening. However he could see Wongaree hurrying towards him from the direction of the stockyard, a frown of concentration on his face.

'Horses gone, boss,' he said as he came alongside.

'Both of them?'

Wongaree nodded and Adam had a fleeting thought that maybe someone had taken them. The commander, perhaps, or one of his men? He himself had checked that the animals had been properly secured the previous afternoon.

'How did they get out?'

'Gate broken. See.'

He held forward the metal latch, which was now in two jagged pieces.

The two men walked across to the stockyard where Wongaree made a great production of studying the ground. He alternately bent and straightened, peering at the marks. He brushed his hands across the dirt and stood back, hands on hips.

'Well,' asked Adam. 'Which way did they go?'

Wongaree pointed towards the upper reaches of the river. 'Along there. Towards water.'

Adam weighed the broken latch thoughtfully in his hand, not liking the idea that came to him. He glanced back towards the place where the commander and his men were camped. The men were saddling their horses — he could see the dark shapes of them moving around — obviously ready to move on. He counted the horses. There were thirteen in total. An unlucky number for some.

'Wongaree, do you think someone's been down here, playing about with the gate?'

The stockman shrugged and inspected the ground again. 'Dunno, boss. Mebbe. Can't say for sure.'

'There's no footprints?'

'Those horses mucked up plenty good. Nothing here now.'

The commander and his men were walking their horses in single file now, heading in the direction of Adam's own errant beasts. They were too far away for Adam to call, asking for a ride on a spare animal.

Adam took two bridles from the hook in the feed shed, and reluctantly he and Wongaree followed on foot. God only knew how far the horses had gone. His boot rubbed against his heel. No doubt there'd be a blister there shortly.

Already, the day had a bad feel to it.

CHAPTER 16

Time seemed to move slowly as Adam and Wongaree thrashed through the underbrush. They were heading towards the main river channel, following the horses' hoofprints. The weight of the bridles was heavy on Adam's shoulder.

Already the clouds had lifted, leaving blue sky, and the sun heaved its heat upon them. The previous night's rain was but a memory and the ground hard-baked already. The commander and his men had long since disappeared from view. From time to time Adam had heard a shout or the whinny of horses, but now there was nothing but silence ahead.

Adam's thoughts kept turning to Conor, alone in the bush and unaware of the possibility of marauding blacks. That would be his first priority, once the horses were found, *if* they were found. He would ride out and check on his brother, alert him to the danger, persuade him to come back to the hut until things settled down.

The landscape seemed different at ground level, used as he was to being astride his horse. Several times he and Wongaree disturbed large lizards that stood up on two feet and loped through the grass. The black man watched them go with a regretful frown. The lizards, Adam knew, would have made a fine feast down at the camp, baked over hot stones. However the recovery of the two horses was uppermost in both men's minds. Adam made a mental note to send an extra bag of flour down to the camp with Aleyne to compensate Wongaree and the others for the missed opportunity for food.

Wongaree ran ahead, scouring the dirt for signs of the horses. His back was bent, his head low. The ground seemed a mass of colour — purple candytuft, the yellow buds of wild boronias, dainty white native heliotrope, red saltbush berries. A snake slowly unwound itself from a rock under a clump of Mitchell grass and sat looking at them with contempt. Straggling clumps of spinifex and lignum grew in zigzag lines along the sand hills that reared, red and crumbling, from the otherwise flat ground, interspersed with spreading mats of nardoo grass.

Standing on top of one of the sand hills, scouring the countryside for some sign of the horses, Adam's attention was drawn to the horizon where the rugged sandstone ranges rose out of nowhere. They had been an indigo hue when the men had left the shack. Now, several hours on, they were burnt orange.

The two men stopped occasionally, taking a swig of water from their bottles. Sweat ran along Adam's brow and stung his eyes. Just when he thought there was no chance of finding the horses, Wongaree swung left through the bush and clapped his hands, pointing to two dark shapes standing in the shade of a creek wilga, munching happily on grass. 'We find 'em, boss,' he whooped loudly. 'Wongaree track 'em plenty good.'

They were in a narrow gorge and the horses stood waiting expectantly as the two men approached. As Adam swung the bridle onto his horse, a green and yellow parrot swooped out from the underbrush. It passed mere inches from his face — he could feel the disturbed current of air from its wings — alighting on a nearby branch where it sat, glaring balefully at the two men.

Wongaree froze, a look of terror on his face, and pointed wordlessly towards the bird.

'What's wrong?' asked Adam.

The stockman bent down until he was almost level with the bird. 'He says danger. He guardian of the sacred ground,' he whispered on a deep breath.

'What sacred ground?'

'*This* sacred ground. Spirit-bird say we shouldn't be here.'

'Well, it's a little late for that,' Adam replied with a laugh that sounded more nervous than confident.

The laugh seemed to startle the bird. It fluffed its feathers and gave several loud shrieks before flying back into the underbrush. Wongaree's eyes grew large in his face. He threw the bridle across his horse's head, quickly pulling the animal towards him. 'Quick! Quick! We gotta leave here, boss. Plenty danger, orright? We all tumble down and die!'

'Hey! Slow down.' Adam put his hand on the man's arm, stilling him.

Slowly Wongaree turned to face him and Adam could see clearly that the black man was terrified. Beads of sweat dotted his brow. His chest rose and fell. There was no use pushing him, in case he turned tail and fled, leaving Adam to manage two horses back to the hut. Well, they had found what they had come for. Time enough left in the day to return home and saddle the horses properly before setting out to check on Conor.

It was then, in that moment's silence between words, that the first volley of shots rang out further along the river. The noise echoed, seeming to come from all directions, exploding off the rock walls.

'Bloody hell!' Adam whispered as the sound died away.

For a moment there seemed an unnatural quiet. Not a bird sang. The cicadas in the trees were silent. Even the breeze had stilled. He and Wongaree stared at each other. 'We must go,' said Adam, nodding his head in the direction of the shots, 'and see what those bastards are up to.'

Wongaree hung back, a look of fear on his face. 'No, boss. Bad — *jung-ga* — spirits along there.'

'We *have* to.'

'No like, boss. Wongaree stay here.'

'You can't. Come on. Those men won't hurt you. Not while I'm here.'

Slowly, reluctantly, Wongaree climbed up onto the horse's back. He sat there, looking uncustomarily awkward, waiting for Adam to move.

'Yes, boss,' he said, his voice little more than a whisper.

Ngayla leaned her back against the trunk of the lignum bush, letting her gaze roam around the camp site. They had arrived here the previous night. This morning they would move on, yet again. They couldn't stay, the elders of the tribe had said. A mob of men were following — one whitefella boss and a traitorous few of their own: native police trackers on whitefella horses.

Why they were being chased, no one knew. There were tales of whites being killed back north, up the river. It had nothing to do with them, yet still the trackers followed. Ngayla and her tribe had seen the smoke from their fires and heard the far-off whinny of horses, though for several days now there had been no sign of them.

Maybe now they were safe? Perhaps those who followed had realised their mistake and moved on?

The previous evening, one of the old men had taken a stick and drawn a line around the perimeter of their camp, to keep out the evil 'debil-debil' spirits. The circle had kept them safe during the hours of darkness. Now, with first light, some of the group were crossing its boundaries and making their way to the creek and fresh water.

Ngayla closed her eyes. Behind her she could hear the babble of voices and smell the smoke from the fire. The wind stirred in the leaves above and they rubbed against each other, making a pleasurable rustling sound. Then, over it all, she heard her mother's voice, chastising one of the younger children.

Her thoughts slid past the present, remembering all the changes that had happened in the last few weeks since the tribe had decided to go walkabout. First, there'd been a new baby. Her older married sister, Mingul — with her brown bulging belly — and Ngayla's mother had gone off into the bush and, when they returned, Mingul had been carrying a boy-child, smeared with a mixture of animal fat and ash. He was long and lean and cried a lot, and sucked hungrily at Mingul's breasts.

Meanwhile, Ngayla's own body seemed to be changing daily. At thirteen, she was the youngest of her family. She was small for her age, but already small buds of breasts had formed on her chest and her hips had become shapely. A few weeks ago the blood had come between her legs. She'd been frightened at first, thinking she'd caught some terrible whitefella sickness. But her mother had calmed her then shown Ngayla how to put wads of grass there, to soak it up. For the few days it lasted, she'd had to sleep separately from the others, and had been forbidden to walk along the same tracks as the men.

'Why?' she'd asked her mother.

'Because it is our way,' was the stern reply.

Ngayla was promised already to Yanda, a shy boy two years older. She wondered what it would be like to be a married woman, to sleep away from her mother and have a baby grow inside her. She had put her hand on Mingul's belly, before Mingul had gone off into the bush, and felt the rippling movements.

'Plenty of time yet,' her mother said, when Ngayla asked when Yanda would become her husband. 'You still *mi-ri* — too young. Gotta grow some more.' She moved her hands about her own body, outlining the shape of her breasts, hips. 'Must be older — *ka-na-ri* — before marriage and babies.'

'How do you get a baby?'

Her mother had given her a quizzical look. 'Ah, child. So many questions.'

'But how?' Ngayla persisted.

'Well,' began her mother. 'When a man takes a woman to his *gundi* and they set up camp together, the spirits come down and by 'n' by there's a baby.'

'Spirits? In your belly?' Ngayla had asked, round-eyed.

'But like I said, plenty of time yet.'

Now, remembering, Ngayla opened her eyes. A few of the tribe were straggling from the direction of the creek up towards the camp. The sheep — someone had found it wandering, bleating piteously in the bush — was obviously well-roasted, and one of the women had taken it from the coals and was handing out chunks of meat. Her mother brought her some laid out on a piece of bark. Ngayla took a bite but the food was hot and she felt it sting her lips. She pulled a face.

'Blow on it,' said her mother. 'Like this.'

Her mother screwed up her mouth and puffed towards the meat. It looked funny. Ngayla laughed. Her mother smiled.

On the edge of the camp, someone was singing. Several children squabbled over the sheep's carcass.

A baby cried. Mingul's? Ngayla was barely aware of it all, the noise a background hubbub as her attention focused on the meat.

Suddenly she jolted upwards, senses jarring. Something was wrong. There were men riding into the camp on horses, yelling and scattering children as they came. Ngayla's mother looked towards them, the meat part-way to her mouth and a look of puzzlement on her face. One of the elders ran towards the spears lying in an untidy heap near the fire. There was a loud exploding noise and the old man pitched forward onto the dirt, a dark red stain spreading across his back.

Ngayla put her hands over her ears and shut her eyes. Someone — was it her mother? — picked her up and began to run. She could tell they were moving by the way she was bumped along, and by the tree boughs that whipped against her face. There was another loud bang, and another, on and on the noise went until her ears, even though they were still covered, seemed to explode. Then there was a sensation of falling.

Whoever was carrying Ngayla had landed awkwardly on top of her. She had an immediate sensation of being unable to breathe, as though all the air had been forcibly ripped from her chest, so she struggled to push her way clear of the unmoving weight. Finally she was free and she lay next to the body, panting. It was her mother, she realised, fighting back a scream. Her neck was twisted at an odd angle. A thin stream of blood ran from her mouth. Her eyes were open, staring unblinkingly, yet

Ngayla knew with awful certainty that her mother could no longer see.

Her immediate instinct was to hide: she needed to distance herself from the yelling and loud banging sounds. Wildly she glanced around. They had come a short way from the camp site and the river-bank location was now unfamiliar to her. Spying a thick clump of bushes, she scrabbled across the dirt towards it, careless of the sharp stones that tore at the flesh of her knees.

Her heart was beating so fast she thought it might burst from her chest. The leaves of the bushes were sharp and spiky. She thrust herself past them, burrowing deep into their mass. Then, when she thought she was hidden from view, she hunkered down in the dirt and bound her knees with her arms, rocking backwards and forwards.

She waited, holding her breath and biting back a scream, for someone to force her from her hiding place. But seconds, then minutes, passed. No one, it seemed, had seen her go.

The loud banging sounds suddenly stopped and Ngayla peered through the mass of leaves. Bodies lay everywhere, arms and legs at grotesque angles as they had fallen. They were women and children mostly. The whitefella boss who had ridden into the camp was striding about, kicking out his boots at anything that still moved.

One of the black trackers picked up a baby by the legs and hurled it towards a nearby tree trunk. It was Mingul's boy-child, Ngayla knew with certainty. His body was limp, arms and legs flopping uselessly. No screams came from his mouth. She watched, bile rising into her mouth, as he landed with a thud against the bark. Then his tiny body slid down the long length of the trunk until it lay in a twisted mound in the dust.

Ngayla spat the contents of her mouth onto the ground and wiped her lips against her forearm. Her legs, stuck in a squatting position, had begun to ache. Her forehead seemed unusually hot and beads of perspiration had gathered there. Momentarily she closed her eyes, thinking that if she could simply go to sleep she would wake later and find this was nothing but a bad dream.

A long low scream hung on the air. As Ngayla brought her head up, she saw a flash of movement. It was Mingul, still alive, trying to claw her way past several black trackers towards her child. The men were darting and weaving before her, blocking her progress. Suddenly one of them laughed, a loud throaty sound, and pushed her to the ground.

Mingul lay staring up at the men, a confused and panicked look on her face. One lashed out with his boot. She shied from the blow, rolling onto her side, curving her body to protect her belly. The man unbuckled his belt and pulled down his trousers, egged on by the others. 'Hurry up,' she heard one of them call. 'Don't take all day. We all want a turn.'

Though Mingul tried to crawl away, screaming and kicking and bucking like a big goanna, Ngayla knew her sister was no match for the man. He lowered his arm and slammed his fist against her jaw. As her body sagged backwards, the man climbed on top of her.

Mingul stopped thrashing about and lay still. Her face was turned away from the man, towards the underbrush where Ngayla lay. Tears ran down her cheeks, leaving muddy tracks. Ngayla could see the man's bare buttocks rising and falling. Mingul's body rocked with the movement. Finally he struggled to his feet and buttoned up his pants. One by one, the other men all lay on top of Mingul.

It seemed an eternity until the last man stood and refastened his trousers. Mingul lay motionless in the dirt, her eyes now closed.

'Look at me, bitch!' the man yelled, nudging Mingul's thigh with his boot.

Mingul didn't move.

The man nudged harder, his voice louder. 'I said, look at me!'

Mingul's mouth tightened and formed a silent 'no' of denial.

The man raised his foot and aimed it at Mingul's head. Ngayla heard the dull thud as the boot connected with her sister's temple. Mingul's head slewed sideways, then stilled. Her arms, which had been tensed at her sides, folded away and slid into the dirt.

'Stop!' Ngayla wanted to scream. 'You can't do this to my people!'

But the words were only in her head, not her mouth. These men were big and strong, and outnumbered her. To alert them to her hiding place would mean the same treatment.

One of the men walked towards her. He bent down, mere feet away, and picked up something from the ground. It was a piece of meat. One of the women must have carried it with her from the camp as she ran. He held it towards his nose and took a deep breath. 'Lamb,' he said loudly, calling across the clearing to the whitefella boss. 'Serves them bloody well right. They've been killing sheep.'

All this for one animal?

A whimper escaped Ngalya's lips and she quickly put her hand there, pressing it hard against her mouth. She was shaking, unbearably so. Tears filled her eyes and she squeezed them shut, trying to block out the images.

Time dragged on, measured not by the passing of the sun's rays through the dappled shade, but by the sounds that burned themselves into her memory. Laughter. A whip cracking. Several more loud bangs. Whitefella words ran together excitedly, scrambling in her brain until they made no sense at all. How long had she been there? she wondered. Squatting in the dust. Legs screaming with pain. She desperately needed to pee and, as the minutes passed, the urge became a dull ache in her belly.

After what seemed like an eternity, the men left. Ngayla heard the laughter and receding sound of the horses' hooves as they moved off along the river bank. In desperation she scratched away a few handfuls of earth beneath her and gratefully released a stream of urine. She felt it splashing wetly against her leg, fizzing into the dry ground. Habit made her scrape the dry earth back over the wet patch. Then, cautiously, she parted the thick branches of the underbrush and peered out.

Nothing moved on the river bank. No lizards darted into the sun to bask on a rock. No birds flitted among the trees. No women scooped water to take back to the camp and no children splashed at the water's edge.

There were just bodies lying haphazardly on the ground, dark pools of blood congealing in the dust, and lignum, tea-tree and coolibah overhanging the pink-stained water.

CHAPTER 17

Adam and Wongaree raced along the river bank in the direction of the gunshots, jumping logs and small gullies. The undergrowth was thick there, slowing them, and the two men slipped and slid on the backs of the saddleless horses. Several times Adam had almost fallen to the ground, his firm hold on the bridle the only thing saving him. At times they were forced to dismount, Adam leading the horses through a rough patch while Wongaree searched for tracks. As the minutes ticked by he cursed under his breath.

The gunshots had sounded deceptively close. Miles flew under them yet there was still no sign of the commander and his men. Had they missed them? Adam wondered. In this dense patch of bushland you could easily pass by someone twenty yards away and not see them.

'How much further do you think?' he asked Wongaree.

The black man shrugged. 'Next hill, boss, or mebbe longer. Hard to tell. Bad spirits muck up everything, tell lies. P'raps they send us wrong way altogether.'

Unbearable thought. All this energy wasted when they might have been able to get there sooner, stop what Adam suspected was senseless slaughter. But so much time had gone by. 'We *can't* be going in the wrong direction,' he argued. 'You followed the tracks further back, remember? We were going the right way then.'

'Yair, boss, but them tracks come and go.'

Was Wongaree — terrified by what he might find, as well as those bad *jung-ga* spirits — purposely leading him astray? Adam pondered on the possibility for a few moments as they splashed the horses through the remnants of an almost dry water hole, then he dismissed the thought.

At last, riding up from one gully over an hour later, they came to a clearing near the river. In the centre stood a large wilga tree, a lifeless shape hanging from one of the branches. Several others lay in a bloodied mass at the base. The ground all about had been trampled. Blood was splattered through the matted grass, dark pools of it congealing under the hot sun. Thick crusts of flies gathered on the surface. A hot metallic smell filled the air.

The two men dismounted. Wongaree hung back, his eyes large and white in his face as Adam approached the hanging shape. He was dark-skinned, a young male about twenty years of age, naked except for a grass necklace and a belt, which appeared to be made of human hair, which encircled his waist. A length of rope was fastened securely around his neck.

What to do? He couldn't leave the body there. Wongaree had slid down onto his haunches and bound his arms around his knees, setting up a steady wailing sound as he rocked to and fro.

Adam walked over to the stockman and shook his shoulder. 'Stop that!' he commanded in the sternest voice he could muster, hoping Wongaree couldn't hear the waver in it.

'Bad spirits here,' whispered the black man as he scrambled to his feet, glancing warily about the clearing. 'Tell us go back.'

Adam took a knife from his belt and moved towards the tree. 'We can't go back. Not yet. You've got to help me first.'

Wongaree took one hesitant step backwards. 'No, boss.'

'*Yes*, boss,' Adam corrected firmly.

Still Wongaree did not come forward. Adam gave an inward groan. He couldn't manage by himself. He needed the black man's help.

'The men who did this,' he cautioned, hating himself for the words to come. 'They'll say Wongaree lazy man. Perhaps do the same to Wongaree.'

Wongaree's eyes grew even wider. 'You'd tell them?'

'I might if you don't help.'

'These fellas not from 'round here,' said Wongaree, pointing his finger northwards towards a distant range of hills as he reluctantly helped Adam cut the man down. 'They belong longa there.'

One by one they uncovered other victims lying nearby in long grass. All had been shot in the back —

obviously they had been trying to run away — and at close range. None had been carrying weapons. Their spears lay untouched in a pile by the smouldering fire.

Adam had seen death before, but not this way. Not this senseless culling of ordinary decent people. Chances were these men had never harmed anyone in their lives, despite what the commander had said.

'Looks like they'd been eating when they were disturbed. They were totally unprepared and never stood a chance.'

Adam stopped for a moment and faced the stockman. 'Wongaree,' he said earnestly, grabbing the man's forearm. 'You know I had nothing to do with this. I'd never hurt —'

His voice choked to a halt in his throat and, for a moment, he was unable to go on. Wongaree looked away, back towards the distant range that had once been home to these people. 'Not you, boss. You good fellas, you and Mista Conor. Those other blokes — they did this.'

Conor. During the past few minutes he'd forgotten about his brother. It wouldn't take long for the word to spread, blackfella-way, about the killings. What if there was some retaliation? Conor was alone with the sheep miles from here, a sitting target. Nausea had begun in his belly and the contents of his breakfast threatened to disgorge themselves. He walked a few yards away from the black man, bent over and retched, a stream of disgust and contempt spewing onto the dust.

One by one Adam and Wongaree carried the dead men to a central area near the fire, laying them out in a row. 'Cold-blooded bastards!' exploded Adam as he counted the bodies. There were twelve in total.

'What about women?' queried Wongaree. 'Must be women.'

'Maybe there were none,' offered Adam hopefully.

Wongaree shook his head. 'All go walkabout. Children too.'

Children. He hadn't considered that.

Wongaree pointed towards a trail of trampled grass that led towards the river. 'Mebbe they longa there, boss.'

Adam moved forward, a ball of dread forming in his belly.

After a few hundred yards he found them, their bodies lying haphazardly along the track. Old gins. Several children. A young woman who had obviously been raped. The body of a tiny baby boy lay curved around the base of a sapling. He was naked, his head bloodied. Gently Adam picked him up, feeling the insubstantial flaccid weight of him in his arms, and stumbled back along the track towards the clearing.

'What you gonna do?' Wongaree yelled after him. 'What you gonna do about all these dead people?'

Tears blurred Adam's vision. Words failed him. What *was* he going to do? He glanced back towards the black man. 'I'm going to put this baby with the others,' he yelled in return, his voice sounding strangely unfamiliar. 'Then you and I are going back to the hut to get shovels. The others can come back with us, help bury them.'

'Yapunya and Pigeon orright, but not Wangi. Wangi not see this, he just a boy.'

'All right, not Wangi.'

Wongaree pointed towards the sky. The sun was past its zenith and already shadows were beginning to spear out from the surrounding trees. 'No time today, boss. Next morning p'raps.'

Adam laid the child's body with those of the men and walked back towards the creek. He was thinking, eyes fixed on a clump of bushes. Odd, he thought, wondering if he had really seen a movement among the leaves. He peered harder, trying to make out the blurred shape. 'Who's there?' he called.

The sun beat down through the overhanging trees, sending dappled shadows skittering across the dirt. From somewhere to his left came the harsh shriek of a bird. Hesitantly he took one step forward. 'Is anyone there?'

There was a rustling in the leaves and the sound of footsteps. A small dark figure burst from the hiding place and ran towards the river. 'Wait!' Adam cried, springing forward and giving chase.

He was pounding through the scrubby trees, past gidgee and lignum and prickly acacia that slashed at his skin. Boughs stung, whipping at his face. Quickly he pushed them aside, stumbling over the rough ground. 'Stop!' he yelled. 'I won't hurt you. I'm a friend.'

A young girl sprinted away from him on brown spindly legs. She was wearing nothing, the soles of her feet flying upwards in a fast rhythmic beat as she darted and wove around the trees, agile as a goat. On the periphery of his vision Adam could see Wongaree moving nimbly on his left, trying to stop her escape. So intent on running was she that she failed to see the stockman until he stepped in front of her, blocking her path. Blindly she spun around and ran back towards Adam, who grabbed her as she passed, swinging her to a standstill against his chest.

'It's alright,' he soothed in his calmest voice possible.

She was about twelve years old, he supposed. Her face was bloodied and her chest heaved from a combination of fear and the effort of running. Adam could feel the pounding of her heart through the fabric of his own shirt as she squirmed and wriggled in his grasp, kicking out with her feet at his shins. But he held her firm.

Wongaree approached, said something to her in his own language that Adam didn't understand. The young girl slowed then stopped her frenzied struggle. Her large brown eyes filled with tears and they ran, unchecked, down her cheeks. She made no move to wipe them away as Wongaree reached out and lifted her from Adam's grasp, carrying her like a baby, pressing her face against his broad chest to shield her eyes from the carnage that lay around them. Silently they walked back to the horses.

'We'll take her back to the hut,' said Adam. 'The rest' — he indicated the bodies laid out side by side in a straight row with a wide sweep of his arm — 'will have to wait until tomorrow.'

It was a slow trip home.

Aleyne met them at the fence, her mouth a round 'O' of surprise at the sight of the young girl. Wongaree handed her to the older woman.

'Look after her,' Adam instructed. 'The rest of her tribe have been killed. She's lucky to be alive.'

He spent the rest of the afternoon loading shovels and supplies onto the cart. The following morning he and the other men would go back and bury the dead. Then he'd continue on to Conor, persuade his brother to come back home until things quietened down.

It wasn't until dusk that the commander and his men returned. Adam stormed down to their camp. 'I know what you've done,' he challenged the group, awarding their leader a look of disgust.

The man smiled — a contemptuous sneer — and shrugged. 'I don't know what you're talking about.'

'What sort of a mongrel act was that?' Adam went on. 'And don't bother denying it. I've seen the bodies! What did those people ever do to harm you?'

'Personally? Nothing. But let me put it to you this way. The killing of the white woman I was telling you about has been avenged.'

'What proof do you have that that particular tribe was even involved?'

'Proof?' the man laughed, goading Adam. 'I don't need proof.'

'And why *was* the white woman killed? In retaliation for stockmen raping the native women, or because the flour, given to the blacks by some 'generous' landowner, was poisoned with arsenic?'

The commander shrugged, dismissing the question. 'One colour. One kind. They're all the same mob, when it comes down to it. It doesn't matter who pays, as long as someone does.'

Adam was speechless. He stared at the man, despising him, hating his ideals. He wanted to slam his fist into the man's face, wipe away that supercilious air. Momentarily he closed his eyes against the sight of him, forcing his anger down, and swallowed hard. 'I told you there was to be no killing on Diamantina Downs,' he said at last.

'You can't stop me. I'm the law.'

'There's a name for what you're doing.'

'And what might that be?'

The man was baiting him, egging him on. Adam knew he should have turned and walked away — the man had already won.

'Cold-blooded calculated murder! I'll report you.'

'You'd be wasting your time. Nothing would ever happen. We're here to protect you and those people were a threat.'

'A threat? Women and babies? You think your uniform provides an undisputed licence to kill?'

'Those babies grow up to be hunters. And if we kill the women, there'll be no more babies. It's that simple. You have to understand the rules, mister new chum.'

Adam raised his hands in defeat. 'You know, this has all got to stop somewhere.'

'It'll stop when the last one is dead.'

'You low-down bastard. I want you and your men off my land! Now! I'll not be giving hospitality to murderers.'

And he turned away, disgusted, making his way back to the hut.

* * *

After supper, Adam took a pen and sat at the table, the lamplight casting a dull glow across the paper as he wrote a letter to the governor. Laboriously he recounted the events of the day, every last grisly detail, reliving the ordeal himself as he did so.

Earlier Aleyne had taken the young girl to the nearby camp, promising to keep watch over her. Now the only sound in the room was the scratching of the pen and the crackle of the fire. With Conor gone, the place seemed unnaturally quiet.

When he'd finished, Adam reread the words. They jumbled around in his head, like something out of a book or a bad dream. The account seemed inconceivable — far-fetched, impossible — even though he had witnessed the aftermath. How could the governor, sitting in his Brisbane office, believe what he, Adam, had written?

You have to understand the rules.

He remembered the commander's words, feeling a wash of frustration. What good would it do, sending the letter? Nothing would ever come of it. Recounting the facts could never undo the wrong or bring justice to the culprits.

It doesn't matter who pays, as long as someone does.

That was the sad truth: those who made the laws condoned this behaviour and he'd be a lone voice crying in the wilderness. With an angry sigh Adam screwed the paper into a tight ball and lobbed it into the fire. Then he took the station journal from his desk and re-recorded the events there. Someone, some time in the future, would know the truth.

* * *

Munwaal and Wadjeri limped onto the rocky outcrop above the white man's river-side camp almost on dusk. Overhead, flocks of birds screeched their way to the nearby water holes. The sun was a red ball of fire sinking over the western horizon. Below, the two men could see a mob of whitefella animals and the dog that guarded them.

The white man was tending the fire, his back to them. On a nearby rock lay a killing machine. It was like the ones owned by the whitefella mob, that had made loud noises and knocked their own tribesmen to the ground as they stood.

Exhausted, the two men slid down onto the grass, their backs against the trunk of a tree, and waited. The sky grew dark. The air was shrill with the shriek of cicadas and the mournful honk of frogs. Flames from the fire below sent shadows flickering through the trees and along the rock walls. The smell of roasting meat teased its way towards them on the breeze. It had been several days since they had eaten. Only the women and children had received their food before the whitefellas had ridden into their camp that morning.

The two men had escaped by pretending to be dead. Lying next to their slain tribesmen, trying not to breathe in the stench of blood and urine and faeces, retribution seemed the only recourse. But how to fight back against an enemy who so easily overpowered them? Surprise, they agreed later as they fled the scene. Like the whitefellas had surprised them by riding into their camp without warning, catching them unawares. Ambush and attack seemed the only way, giving no time for retaliation or the whitefellas to use their killing machines.

Wadjeri's leg was shattered below the knee bone and a steady trail of blood had coursed down his calf all day. He'd tried to staunch the flow by packing the wound with a mixture of mud and grass, but there had been no improvement. Each step had been agony yet he knew he had to distance himself from the morning's camp, put as many miles as possible between himself and his attackers. How he had managed to walk this far was a matter of sheer willpower. Now, hours later, he was almost delirious with the pain.

Munwaal had been hit in the shoulder. There was a wound there, raw and gaping, and it was all he could do to lift his arm, so intense was the agony. Revenge twisted, a dark mass in his heart. And despite his injuries, hunger knotted his belly. He glanced across at Wadjeri and nodded. It was time to make a move.

Wadjeri shook his head. His blood was running out of his body and he felt odd, like everything around him was tumbling, slow motion, into a whirling spiral. He wondered if he could even stand, let alone make his way to the whitefella's camp below.

Munwaal made a tsk-tsk sound of disapproval and Wadjeri levered himself to his feet, steadied himself against the trunk of the tree. Silently they padded between overhanging branches, trying not to dislodge any stones as they made their way down the rocky slope towards the camp site. They moved inches at a time, downwind, pausing between steps to ensure they had not been seen or heard. With every step, Wadjeri thought he might pass out from the pain.

The flames of the fire darted and scurried according to the wind, sending shadows leaping about the man's camp. Beyond, where Munwaal and Wadjeri waited, it was dark, a velvety blackness that hid them like a cloak. As they neared, the dog growled and stared in their direction, hackles raised. Wadjeri could see the flames reflected in the white man's face as he laid a hand on the dog's neck, calming him.

'It's okay, mate,' he soothed.

For a moment he stared in their direction then, obviously seeing nothing, turned back to the fire.

The man was singing, a soft floating sound. Not the songs that Munwaal and Wadjeri knew, but whitefella music. They heard snatches of words. The rest were caught by the wind and taken some place else. Something about 'true love' and 'promises', whatever that meant.

Wadjeri moved forward, motioning Munwaal to do the same. As he did, a spiral of pain ran the length of his leg and he drew a quick breath. A low groan escaped his mouth. If only he didn't have to walk, to move.

They were close now, almost at the edge of the camp. Munwaal took another step forward and a twig cracked beneath his weight. The sound seemed inordinately loud in the still night air — almost thunderous. He jerked his head up, annoyed. The pain in his shoulder was making him careless. Wadjeri glanced anxiously at him and he paused, foot poised in mid-air.

Without warning, the dog ran towards them, snapping and growling. Wadjeri saw the white man hesitate, then run towards the killing machine that lay on the rock. Despite the pain and a faintness that was threatening to lay him on the ground, he stepped from the shadows into the firelight, his spear in his hand.

But Munwaal was running towards the rock too, screaming, the dog snapping at his heels. The white man hesitated, obviously confused, and Munwaal was there first, snatching the killing machine out of the man's reach. He was careful to use his good arm, flinging the gun in a wide arc where it landed yards away, in a clump of bushes. The whitefella jolted to a standstill and stared back at him, a look of fear on his face.

Wadjeri remembered the way the attackers had ridden into the camp that morning. He remembered the way his tribesmen had fallen, the screams of terror from the women. The pain in his leg told him that maybe he too would soon die. He had nothing to lose, and someone had to pay for the day's events. Summoning his remaining strength, he thrust his spear towards the white man's chest.

The spear flew through the air, making a soft whistling sound. It hit bone, jarred. The man clutched his hands to the spot. He had a surprised, shocked look on his face. Quickly Wadjeri limped forward and pulled it free. He raised it again, aiming carefully.

'Stop!' the white man screamed, holding his hands out in front of him in a gesture of surrender before turning and stumbling away.

The dog was worrying at Wadjeri's leg, barking and nipping and making a racket. Wadjeri rammed the spear again, this time into the man's back. The man staggered then fell forward, lying face down in the dirt. His body twitched several times then was still.

He and Munwaal glanced at each other, nodded. 'It's done,' Munwaal whispered, his face shiny with perspiration in the firelight.

They went to the fire and took handfuls of food before limping back into the darkness, kicking out at the dog as they went.

It took almost until noon to bury the bodies. Adam felt nauseous with worry and fatigue. He'd slept scarcely a wink the previous night. And when he had, images of what he had seen that day had paraded themselves in all their sickening glory. Now, beckoning Wongaree to accompany him, he sent the other black men back to the hut. His immediate concern was to check on Conor, warn him home until all the antagonism had died down.

As the two men rode along, Adam scanned the bush around him for signs of anything unusual. But there was nothing. Birds sang. Cicadas shrilled. A faint breeze stirred the leaves in the trees. In comparison to the previous day, this journey seemed uneventful by its ordinariness.

'Conor?' he called, letting go of the reins and cupping his hands about his mouth as they neared his brother's camp site. A few sheep had wandered and were nibbling grass along the river bank as they approached. The animals looked up then lowered their heads once more.

There was no reply, no answering whistle or coo-ee. Nothing except the regular sounds of the bush.

Something caught in Adam's chest — a frisson of concern — but he pushed it away. There was a logical explanation, he told himself. Maybe Conor had gone ahead with his horse, marking out lines for the new fences? Perhaps he hadn't heard Adam's shout.

'Conor?'

A dog barked, away to his right. The sound bounced back from several directions and he glanced upwards, towards the rocky crag that overlooked the camp site. Had something moved? He couldn't be certain. The sun was shining there, sending fractured rays spinning through the branches of the trees, distorting his vision. He blinked hard then looked again. Nothing: he was certain of that. Wongaree was impatient, already riding ahead, and he turned to follow.

They found Conor on the river bank. He was sprawled in the dirt, a spear embedded deep in his back. The kelpie barked at them several times, as if to acknowledge their arrival, then went back to herding the sheep.

It seemed to Adam that he couldn't move, couldn't breathe. The air caught in his lungs and he stood, rooted to the spot, unable to go on. He felt disoriented, as though caught in some weird space of time where nothing mattered. But this couldn't, *shouldn't*, be happening. Conor didn't deserve this.

Wongaree knelt down beside the body, feeling for a heartbeat. He shook his head. There was obviously none. Bewildered, he turned and looked back at Adam. 'Them bad spirits been here, boss,' he whispered and the words seemed like drum rolls.

'No bad spirits. Bad men.'

Wongaree nodded. 'Two of them. See the footprints. Mebbe wounded, boss. There's blood.'

They searched the immediate area, Wongaree following the bloodied trail along the river bank for a while until it petered out where the attackers had waded through water. The ground on the other side was too rocky to hold any clues. 'Them all gone,' Wongaree shrugged. 'Gone long way. Mebbe die.'

Back at the camp site, the spear protruded from Conor's bloodstained shirt like a gross obscenity and Adam was unable to tear his eyes from it. It hung there, a finely whittled piece of wood, proof that something out of his control had determined his fate, and Conor's, yet again.

Why? Bloody hell, *why*?

Adam felt his mouth, lopsided and suddenly uncontrollable, and the scene blurred before him. He closed his eyes against it and when he opened them again he could see the black man, as though sensing his distress, trying to dislodge the pole.

Somehow Adam moved forward as the spear came away with a soft plop. Wongaree stood there, holding it awkwardly, as though unsure of what to do with it. 'Throw it over there,' Adam ordered, nodding towards a clump of bushes. 'Get it out of my sight.'

He sank down beside his brother, cradling him in his arms. Conor's body hung limply, the skin bloating already. 'Get the shovel,' he said tersely to Wongaree. 'It's tied to my saddle.'

When Wongaree returned, Adam took the shovel and began to dig a hole in a high patch of ground, in the shade of a broad-branched tree. He worked single-handedly, refusing Wongaree's offer of help. Sweat ran into his eyes and down his temples, and soon his hair was plastered wetly to his scalp. He was reminded of that day, back in the Old Country, when he had taken the tiny rag-wrapped bundle from the end of his mother's bed, consigning it to a similar fate. How long ago had that been? Six years? He shook his head, pushing the images away, the similarities.

At last the task was done. Aided by the black man, he lowered Conor's body into the hole. Numbly he began to re-shovel the dirt. It fell across his brother, obscuring his face and then his chest, his legs. Wongaree approached, offering to take over, but Adam waved him away. When at last he had finished, he broke off an overhanging tree branch and drove it into the ground to mark the spot.

Numbed by grief and exhaustion, Adam hunkered down on the dry earth and said his farewell. He heard the words fall from his mouth, dry as the dust beneath his feet as he buried his face in his shaking hands. He was losing control. He felt it slipping away, taking him to the boundary of his sanity. All that was precious had been snatched from him. Mam and Da. All those tiny babies. And now Conor. There was no one in this world he could claim as his kin. Desolate, he pressed his knuckles against his brow.

There was a movement at his elbow. It was Wongaree, his dark face creased with concern. 'You orright, boss?'

He struggled to his feet and grabbed the shovel, not knowing how to reply. No, he wasn't *orright*. He was lonely already, without his brother, and frightened for the future. When would the killing stop? Who would fire the last shot and call it quits?

It was a lonely God-forsaken place, he thought as he rode away. Miles from the hut. Bleak and windswept. Sometime soon he'd come back, erect a fence around the grave. Make it into a proper cemetery, though, Lord knows, he hoped Conor would be the last to be buried there.

There was someone waiting at the hut when he and Wongaree returned. A woman, Adam realised with surprise, wearing a bonnet and a full-skirted dress. As he came closer, he saw it was Jenna.

Why was she here?

How did she get here?

Oh, Lord! He'd be forced to tell her about Conor …

He was in no mood to talk to her or recount the events of the day. All he'd thought about during the ride home was climbing onto his bunk, waiting for the blessed release of sleep.

She waited expectantly as Adam dismounted and walked towards her. 'How did you get here?' he asked, his voice sounding more brusque than he had intended.

'The local mailman obligingly gave me a lift.'

'Why are you here?'

'Well, that's not exactly the kind of welcome I was expecting.'

She smiled and he was instantly aware of how beautiful she looked standing there, late-afternoon sunlight making her hair and skin glow. She brought her hand forward in a gesture of greeting but he ignored it.

'What *were* you expecting?'

She stared at him, obviously confused, a small frown creasing her forehead. 'I was expecting Conor,' she said in a low voice. 'Where is he?'

He walked up the steps and took her arm, propelled her inside and motioned towards a chair. 'You might like to sit.'

'I'd prefer to stand, if it's all the same to you.'

His tongue seemed glued to the roof of his mouth. His thoughts were going in a dozen different directions at once. There was no pleasant way he could relay the news. 'Conor,' he said, spacing out the words, hating having to say them. 'Conor is ...'

'Yes,' she prompted.

'Conor is dead.'

She stared at him, her eyes suddenly huge and dark in her pale face, and swallowed hard. 'He-he can't be,' she stammered. 'We were to be married.'

Tears filled her eyes and she let them run down her

cheeks and along the tip of her nose, not bothering to wipe them away.

Adam took her hand, forcing her to sit in the chair as he recounted the events of the past two days. In all practicality she couldn't remain out here and he told her so.

'It's too dangerous, no place for a woman. This hut could be attacked! Obviously you'll have to stay until I can organise some transport —'

'I *can't* go back.'

'Why not?'

'My mother's dead and I've sold the shop. There's nothing — no one — to go back to.'

Somehow he put together the makings of a meal and they ate in silence. Jenna washed up the dishes and he dragged a bunk bed to one of the lean-to sheds. 'You can stay in the hut,' he told her, 'and I'll sleep out there. We'll talk some more in the morning.'

She walked with him to the door, waiting as he walked across the clearing to the shed. He knew she waited, by the way her shadow loomed out across the dirt beside him, an odd elongated caricature. At the entrance to the shed he stopped and glanced backwards, seeing her outlined against the lamplight.

'There's another reason I can't go back,' she called uncertainly, her voice small and lost in the space that surrounded them.

Adam waited. She hung in the doorway, swaying slightly.

'Why,' he prompted at last. 'Why can't you go back?'

'Because I'm pregnant. I'm carrying Conor's child.'

PART FOUR

Lovers and Liars

CHAPTER 18

The past completes me.

It's strange how words and phrases stay in your mind, long after the memory of the exact time and place of their origin has gone. And that's the one phrase I know that defines me: Jess.

I can't remember where it came from: a book, perhaps, or a movie? Maybe it stemmed from one of those girly films that makes you grapple for your handkerchief two minutes from the end, and you just dread walking out into the foyer afterwards, with predictable red-rimmed eyes like every other woman. Or maybe I read it in one of those insightful novels that draw you in, spellbinding you with words and images until you feel part of the characters and plot.

But wherever it came from — book or movie — at the time the words felt right. They leapt towards me, burrowing into my subconscious. Occasionally I take them out, examine them. And it's true. Only in the past do I feel complete, a whole person.

In the present I feel disjointed and fractured, as though a whole chunk of me has fallen away. I'm no longer a mother. I'm barely a wife. My career has dissolved. Grief overwhelms me. I stumble from one day to the next, disoriented, as though I'm living in body but not in spirit. Nothing interests or excites me. I'm existing in a vacuum, performing like a puppet. Some days I feel I can't go on.

'The past completes me,' I tell Brad when I'm at my lowest, my most vulnerable. I thrust the words at him, waiting to see how they fall.

'You can't live in the past.'

'It's where I want to be. There's no pain there.'

He takes my hands, presses them against his cheeks. His expression is one of sadness and regret. Regret at all we have lost, and sadness that the pain is still inside me. 'Don't talk like that. I love you. We still have each other. Doesn't that count for something?'

My eyes fill with tears. 'I miss my daughter,' I say. 'I miss Kadie so much that it hurts.'

'I hurt, too.'

I shake my head, not to negate his feelings but to emphasise my own. To me, my grief seems so much greater than his — a mother's anguish — and he couldn't possibly understand. It was my body that carried her for nine months, felt those first tremulous butterfly movements. It was me who felt those initial pangs of labour. It was my breasts she nuzzled instinctively after her birth. How could Brad know the emptiness I feel?

He puts his arms around me and buries his face

against my neck. He is breathing hard, like a man who has been running. I wait, not knowing what to do, until finally he pulls away and holds me at arm's length.

'I want us to be a family again.'

For one long moment I cannot speak, cannot bear to hear that word: family. It has connotations of Christmas and opening presents around the tree. Kadie's first birthday party. Winter mornings when she ran into our room, wriggling under the blankets between us. Summer afternoons at the beach.

I can see her now, laughing as she runs towards the waves, Brad following close behind. I'm holding the camera. Click. The photo is in my wallet where I can see it every time I open the clasp. Kadie frozen in time, the colour already bleaching from her face, her clothes. Kadie fading inexorably into the past.

One of my aunts suggests — shortly after Kadie's death — that perhaps it is meant to be. 'Nothing is ever permanent in this world,' she tells me. 'Our children are simply on loan to us, and we must be grateful for the time we have with them.'

The words, heard through a haze of grief and anti-depressant pills, make me cry. They sound like a cop-out. 'There, there,' she adds. 'It'll feel better in time.'

But I sense I'll never feel better about this. It's something monstrous and incomprehensible. Maybe 'in time' I'll be able to live with it better, but now, a year later, it's still raw and shocking.

Why is it no one wants to see me grieve? Is my pain something I should hide away, bring out only when I'm alone? Does it make other people uncomfortable? Does my anguish remind my family and friends that this too could happen to them? Is it the there-but-for-the-grace-of-God-go-I syndrome? Perhaps, for the well-being of others, I should retain a bright chirpy face and push my sadness into an unreachable place.

In the days and months after the accident, my grief over Kadie grows bigger than me. It creeps over me like a dark mantle. It swamps me. It swallows me up. Suddenly I am no longer the Jess I used to be. Her death makes me smaller, more self-deprecating. More critical. Where have I failed my daughter? Where have I gone wrong? As her mother, I should have been able to protect her. Self-doubt slinks in. Perhaps if I'd been a better mother, she'd still be alive.

It is Carys who understands me best during that time, which seems strange now because my sister has never been a mother herself. She appears at the house at random times, checking up on me, quietly jollying me out of whatever mood I've found myself in.

One particular day I'm sitting around in my pyjamas. It's midday. The bed hasn't been made nor have the breakfast dishes been washed. The containers from last night's Chinese takeaway are still sitting on the bench, surrounded by a congealing puddle of satay sauce. Wearily I answer the knock on the door.

Carys stands there. She's wearing a yellow suit and high heels. Her hair is pulled back into an elegant chignon. She looks smart and attractive.

'Hi,' she says.

I run my fingers through my own lank hair. I can't even remember brushing it this morning, or the last time I washed it. I must look terrible, I think, but Carys says nothing.

'Hi yourself,' I reply, though my voice lacks any enthusiasm.

I stand aside as she walks through the door, then I close it after her.

She hugs me, her arm resting across my back a fraction longer than normal, the pressure of the embrace a little firmer. She's reassuring me through the sense of touch that she cares. Then she hands me a small paper package. 'It's my lunch hour and I'm between clients. So I've brought a couple of sandwiches.'

Chicken and salad: my favourite. Tears well in my eyes and I give her a return hug. She sits with me on the sofa. We open our packages and pick at the contents. I can see she doesn't have much of an appetite either, but we're both trying, making small talk.

There's a framed photograph on the coffee table: Carys and Kadie. It was taken six months earlier, on an outing to the zoo. I see Carys look at it, then glance away. Her mouth tightens and she takes another determined bite of her sandwich.

'Where does love go when someone dies?' I ask as she's preparing to leave. 'That love: it can't suddenly disappear, and you can't transfer it to someone else.'

'No,' she agrees. 'It just sits there, consuming you.'

Why am I thinking of that now? Why do snatches of scenes and disconnected jumblings of words surface suddenly, overtaking the present?

'Hey,' Brad tips my face back, offering me a tentative smile. He doesn't know what's happening inside my head. 'Life doesn't come with any guarantees, Jess. Love and pain are often part of the same experience. Sometimes you can't have one without the other.'

'Then maybe I don't want either.'

It seems so simple, so true. Life's master plan. A recipe for survival. Throw in a pinch of happiness then dampen it down with a dash of unexpected heartache. Stir thoroughly.

Odd little comparisons filter through my subconscious. Now and then. Past and present. What was, and what is.

'Why won't the dough rise?'

'You're not kneading it properly, Jess.'

'Like this. You have to try harder.'

'I'm trying. I'm trying.'

'Harder.'

Brad's words draw us together, yet somehow hold us apart.

Mid-morning, two days after our impromptu dinner up at the homestead, a utility shudders to a halt outside our cottage. Betty clambers out. She's brought Ella's husband, Stan. I can see him, arms dark under his rolled-up sleeves, as he leans into the back of the ute and lifts a large wooden box.

'Yoo-hoo,' Betty calls, advancing up the path that leads to the front door. Stan trails in her wake. 'You there, Jess?'

'Hi, Betty, Stan.'

Politely I hold the screen door open as they tramp inside. Stan dips his head towards me in acknowledgement, in lieu of his otherwise occupied arms. I notice Betty glancing around, taking in the house. Am I being assessed? I wonder, thankful that the bed is made and the place tidied for the day.

Stan deposits the box on the kitchen table with a resounding thud.

'There you go,' states Betty, tapping the lid. 'We thought you might like to go through this.'

'We?'

I stare stupidly at the box. The badly-fitting lid is covered in a thick layer of dust. A couple of daddy longleg spiders, obviously disconcerted by their journey across the paddock, venture out from one corner and scuttle across the laminex table.

'What's in it?' I ask.

Am I the only one who doesn't know what's going on?

Betty shrugs. 'Dunno, really. Old stuff. It was Jack's idea, you seeing this. Ella said you used to be a researcher and the other night you said you were interested in the local history.'

So, they'd been discussing me.

I lift the lid and peer inside. There's a mass of loose paper on the top. It looks chewed around the edges. 'Mice,' I say, watching as several pebbly droppings slide onto the table.

'Or cockroaches,' adds Stan matter-of-factly. 'Those big ones.'

Betty fingers the top pages. 'Jack found all this stuff a couple of years ago, out in one of the old sheds. He told me to throw it out but I couldn't bring myself to do it. It might be important, you know, historically. I thought I might take it into town the next time I go, give it to the museum. They'd be grateful.'

Do I really want to wade through the half-chewed contents of the box? Just the thought of the mouse droppings makes my skin crawl. 'I'm sure they would,' I agree, secretly hoping Betty will change her mind and march right back out the door with the container.

But Betty shows no such inclination. 'Meanwhile, if you want to have a look through, go right ahead. Just bring it all back over to the house when you're finished. Look at this one —'

As though on cue, Stan lifts the sheaf of loose papers out of the way and brings forward a leather-bound book. He hands it reverently to Betty who wipes her hand across the cover, leaving a scar in the film of dust. The numbers '1873' are inscribed in the leather. 'Jack says this is a station journal. See the date? It's very old.'

'One hundred and thirty years.'

My curiosity stirs and I press the feeling away. Brad and I are only here for a few more weeks and it'd be silly to start something I'd not be able to finish.

'It's the same year,' breaks in Stan, 'that my great-grandmother Ngayla came to Diamantina Downs. Remember I was telling you the other night?'

Betty is removing the contents of the box, one by one, and placing them on the table. It is, I realise, a foregone conclusion that I'm interested.

'Jack and I thought it might give you something to do,' she continues, obviously not sensing my hesitation. 'Help pass the time.'

I could tell her, I suppose, that I need nothing to help me 'pass the time'. My time is mostly occupied by my thoughts, and my thoughts are mainly of Kadie. I spend most of my waking hours thinking of her, of what might have been, and isn't.

Reluctantly I force my attention back to the present and the assortment of paperwork that now litters my kitchen table.

There are more station journals — five in total. A paper bag filled with loose receipts. Several chequebook butts, very old. Another two leather-bound books, smaller than the first. I pick one up, weighing it in my hand. A diary, I know instinctively as I open the cover. 'Jenna McCabe', the words inform me on the first page, and I close the cover with a snap.

'What is it?' asks Betty.

'A diary.'

'Don't you want to read it?'

I suppress a smile. Does she want me to go through it now, with her peering over my shoulder? 'Later, maybe.'

'Maybe?'

There's a slight querulous tone to her voice and I wonder if I've upset her in some way. Should I have appeared more pleased, shown more excitement?

'Well, thanks for thinking of me. You're very kind. But the writing's very faded and I'd need good light. It'd be best to have a pen and paper handy, too. To write notes.'

I'm finding it difficult to explain the true reason why I'm loath to open the pages and read the words. It feels like prying, of sorts, as though I'd be snooping through someone's private thoughts.

Meanwhile, Betty and Stan are standing in my kitchen, waiting. The silence between us is a growing void. 'Now, tea, anyone,' I say brightly, knowing Betty's love of a cuppa and a bit of a chat.

Betty beams. 'That'd be lovely, dear. Right, Stan?'

One of the things I hate most are the well-meaning getting-to-know-you questions. You know the scenario. Dinner party. New acquaintances. A lull in the general conversation. That's when the woman sitting next to me invariably turns and tries to strike up some sort of discussion.

'So, Jess.' She falters, just for a second, a frown wrinkling her forehead. 'It is Jess, isn't it?'

Am I that forgettable? I nod, waiting.

'Cynthia,' she introduces herself. Or Pauline or Margaret or Jo.

'I know,' I remind her. 'We were introduced earlier.'

She gives a short, silly laugh. 'Oh. So we were. I really am so absent-minded.'

Then she spends the next ten minutes complaining about her son's eczema problems, the exorbitant fees orthodontists charge and the fact that her local supermarket no longer stocks her favourite brand of smoked salmon.

I nod my head and sympathise, aware that I'm only encouraging her yet unable to extricate myself cleanly from the conversation. I should excuse myself and go to the loo, but no, I sit there like a masochist, waiting inevitably for her attention to focus on me.

It's almost a relief when we begin the gamut of questions. I have to wait no longer. We're closer to the truth, the inevitable outpouring of information. What do I do for a job? Where do Brad and I live? How did I meet the hosts?

Then the inescapable: 'Do you have children?'

What can I say? Yes, I had a daughter but she died? Or take the easier way out and say no? But that denial negates Kadie, makes her non-existent and she wasn't. She was real, bright and funny, and part of me.

The truth, I know, will cause embarrassment on behalf of the woman. I already know her reaction, in advance. She'll become flustered and go red in the face, not knowing where to look. Then she'll say something clichéd and meaningless like, 'Oh, I didn't know. I'm so sorry.'

Why should she be sorry? She doesn't know us, didn't know Kadie. She'd never seen my daughter's smile or the studious frown on her face as she tried to tie her shoelaces. She'd never heard my daughter's voice or laugh, or howl of indignation at bedtime. No, I think, she didn't know Kadie at all.

Then I'd feel uncomfortable about the woman's embarrassment and go to great lengths to assure her, no matter how untrue my words were, that it was okay. Why did I do that? Denying my own emotions. Pushing my own pain aside so as not to hurt someone else's feelings. Somehow, later, it never made sense.

But no matter how much I prepare myself, the question always shocks me. My considerate friends try to warn other diners in advance. 'Don't ask Jess about children,' I overheard the hostess, a close friend, confiding to a dinner guest one night.

But now, Betty asks none of these questions. Has she been warned by Brad, I wonder?

Instead she is chatting away, talking about an outback festival that's being organised in town, guaranteed to pull a few tourists. She goes on and on about the attractions planned. 'Of course our Beverley probably won't be able to make it,' she says.

'Beverley?' Have I missed something?

'Our daughter. She and her husband live on a property the other side of town. Her first baby's due soon.'

'Your first grandchild?'

Betty beams. 'That's right. Isn't it, Stan?'

She glances at Stan, as though for confirmation. Stan nods.

'You must be so excited.'

'Well, yes. Jack and I have been hoping for a baby, ever since her wedding. That's what life's about, isn't it? Having children, then your children having babies. That way there's a part of you going on, long after you're dead and buried.'

Then the memory stabs back, catching me unawares.

I am six months' pregnant, standing naked, frowning, in front of the mirror in the bathroom. Brad comes up behind me and cups his hands around my belly, cradling the shape of our daughter. I say 'daughter' in hindsight, although at the time I suspect it's a girl. During my last scan, a few weeks earlier, the technician kept referring to the baby as 'she'.

'What's wrong?' Brad asks.

'Nothing.'

'Something's wrong,' he persists. 'I can tell.'

'Am I so transparent?' I laugh away the question, not wanting to answer. Although it's important to me, it's a woman thing. To Brad, it'll probably sound silly and inconsequential.

'Yes.'

'Well,' I begin tentatively, 'I've spent most of the day looking for a wedding dress.'

'And ...' he prompts

'And, nothing.'

His confidence is amazing. 'You'll find something.'

'I've only got a week.'

He lowers his head and nuzzles the side of my neck. 'My about-to-be wife: the shopaholic. I have faith in you!'

'Brad! This is no joking matter!'

Tears spring into my eyes. I pull away from his mouth and his words fall flatly in the air. I hadn't pictured my wedding like this.

'It's not the dress,' I say, angrily wiping the tears away. 'It's me, the way I am. Look at my belly! Every dress I've tried on makes me look like a beached whale!'

'A beached whale? When did you last see a beached whale?'

'Well ...'

'When?' he insists. There's a hint of a smile turning the corners of his mouth upwards.

'Actually, never. It's a metaphor.'

We stand, watching each other in the mirror for what seems a very long time. Then Brad runs the tip of one finger down the side of my cheek. 'Look at you!'

'There's a lot of me to look at.'

'So? That means there's twice as much to love.'

I feel my anger slipping away. He always has that effect on me, makes me see sense. 'Don't tease.'

'I'm not. I'm serious.'

He turns me, slowly, until we are facing each other. My belly presses against his and the baby, as though sensing my upset, thumps madly. He moves his hand to the spot, hesitating. Then he cups my face in his palms. 'I don't care if you look like a so-called beached whale. It's the wedding that's important. You and me making a commitment to each other and our child. Not the dress, for Christ's sake! Who'll remember the dress ten years from now?'

A chair scrapes and suddenly I'm back in the now, in a kitchen somewhere on the Diamantina, and the dress, duly purchased and worn, has been sitting in the back of my cupboard for almost four years. Betty gathers up the cups and saucers and takes them to the sink. 'Well, we'd better be off,' she says. 'There's things to do.'

'By the way,' says Stan as they are leaving, 'Ella said to ask you to come up and see her some time. No matter what day, but make it for morning tea.'

'There's an old bicycle out in the back shed.' Betty nods approvingly and points towards the river, in the opposite direction to which Brad has been going each day. 'Just follow the track that runs back along there. It won't take you long. About two miles. You can't miss the house.'

After Betty and Stan leave, I sit looking morosely at the contents of the box. The five station journals, I think, will probably reveal nothing more important than records of rainfall and station expenses. I sort them — one for each year, beginning in 1873 — into chronological order and stack them in a neat pile on the end of the table. Then I place the cheque-book butts into the bag containing the loose receipts.

There's something I haven't noticed before. It's a large piece of paper, almost cardboard-like in thickness, that's been folded several times. On the top fold is the notation 'Bignall & Sons, Architects, Brisbane'. Below, in faded ink, is the date: 1874. Carefully I open it out and spread it on the table.

It's a plan of a house, although the word 'house' seems rather a plain and insignificant description. At the front there's a large entry with a set of stairs leading upwards. To what? I wonder. There's no sketch of any second floor. Several formal rooms lead off a hallway to the left. They are all named in neat lettering: drawing room, library, study, music room and dining room. The kitchen and pantry, the latter appearing to be almost as large as the former, lie along the rear of the house. On the right there's another long hall. This side of the house appears to be devoted to sleeping and bathing. I count the bedrooms. There are eight in total.

Odd, I think, that this plan should be here. This house isn't suited to the outback. It's a gentleman's residence, a city home. Curious, I refold the paper and put it in the bag with the receipts.

Then I finger the tattered leather-bound diaries for the second time that day. Jenna McCabe, the inscription had said inside, yet I had never heard the surname McCabe mentioned before. Who was she? Servant? Governess to the O'Loughlin children? Come to think of it, I had never heard anyone even mention a wife for Adam O'Loughlin, the first man who had settled this area.

Stan had told the story of Adam and Conor, and the massacre. How his great-grandmother Ngayla had come to Diamantina Downs and Conor's subsequent murder. Maybe that had been enough to send Adam O'Loughlin running back to the city? The small local history book I'd brought with me from the city hadn't contained any additional information about the man. Just that he'd been one of the early landowners.

It occurs to me that these diaries might provide answers to some of my questions, yet for some awful unknown reason I cannot bring myself to read them. Perhaps later, I tell myself. In a day or two, when I get used to the idea of reading someone else's private words.

'What's wrong with reading them?' Brad asks later. 'Have you thought that this woman —'

'Jenna!' I interrupt. For some reason I can't bear that he doesn't say her name. 'She's called Jenna!'

Brad awards me a quizzical look. 'Okay,' he placates, continuing. 'Has it occurred to you that this Jenna might have wanted someone to read them and know her story? Maybe that's why the diaries were left here, as some sort of a record.'

I shake my head. 'But what if she didn't have a choice?' I counter. 'Maybe someone simply took them and put them in this box. Maybe Jenna would have wanted them destroyed. Would you want someone reading through your personal notes?'

Brad shrugs. 'Over a hundred years after I'd written them? I don't think I'd be too worried.'

CHAPTER 19

DIAMANTINA DOWNS
September 1873

Adam lay awake long into the night, staring through the open doorway of the lean-to at the pale rectangle that was the sky outside. From time to time he heard the mournful cry of a nightbird, the howl of a dingo. He thought of the sheep, miles from the hut, unattended now. Sometime in the next few days he'd have to decide what to do with them. Leave them out there, or bring them back in to poorer pasture?

No wonder he couldn't sleep — the ordeal of the last few days had left him wide-eyed and distracted. The massacre and subsequent burial of the murdered blacks. Conor's death. Jenna McCabe's unexpected arrival. His head throbbed. His eyes hurt, stinging in the darkness. A build-up of grief had massed there, unable to be released. He hadn't cried for Conor. Couldn't. The core of him was brittle and dry, without tears. There was, he thought, nothing left that could shock him. He'd seen more hideous sights in the past two days than any man should bear witness to in an entire lifetime.

It seemed a thousand random thoughts jumbled in his tired mind, like some ghastly nightmare, sliding into each other until they blurred and became one.

And, over all, Jenna's words surged through his mind, niggling insistently, waiting to be acknowledged and dealt with. *I'm pregnant. I'm carrying Conor's child.*

Could she be mistaken? he wondered. Maybe, with Conor dead, it was wishful thinking on Jenna's part. And how did she know, if it *was* the truth? Adam didn't understand how Jenna could tell these things, but he supposed it was possible. It was her body, after all.

The logistics of the situation overwhelmed him, and a mixture of commonsense and convention told him she couldn't stay. A lone white woman, unmarried and pregnant, living with her dead lover's brother? That fact alone would give the gossipmongers — and he was sure there were some, even out here — plenty to talk about.

Then there was the safety aspect. What if the hut was attacked? It was a scant three months since he had come to the Diamantina and there was so much to do. Clearing. Fencing. Sometimes he could be gone into the paddocks for days. He couldn't babysit her. Also, what if there were complications with the pregnancy? There was no doctor within a hundred miles.

For the second time that day he thought of his mother and the babies she had lost.

Jenna was used to living in a bush town, but not the bush. Did she have any idea of the loneliness, the isolation? It was all very well her coming here to see Conor, but Conor was dead and he, Adam, needed the responsibility of another person like he needed — what?

He searched in his mind for a comparison and found none. Instead he remembered the way she had looked earlier in the lamplight as she ate her meal. Her eyes had been dark hollows in her face, her skin almost opaque with fatigue. Yet there was something about her, an unconscious dignity, that had made him loath to take his eyes from her.

Her voice, when she had spoken, was low and tremulous. Her hand, as she brought the fork to her mouth, had shaken, ever so slightly. He remembered wanting to reach out, place his own fingers against hers, calming her. 'It's alright,' he'd wanted to say. 'Somehow we'll get through this.'

But he'd said nothing. Instead, aware that he'd been staring at her, he'd risen sharply from the table, almost knocking the lamp in his haste, making some excuse about needing to sleep as he had to be up early the next day.

'I *can't* go back,' she'd said again as he'd lugged the bed towards the door, telling her he'd sleep in one of the sheds. 'I mean it, Adam.'

He'd known then that behind that fragile beauty lay steely determination. So, what if all reasoning failed and she simply refused to leave? How could he force her? Would he pick her up bodily and carry her away? Hardly! He imagined Jenna kicking and screaming like the young Aboriginal girl, Ngayla, when he'd cornered her near the river bank the previous day. They were feisty, both of them. Purposeful and bloody-minded. But there the comparison ended.

Then, lying there, staring at the night sky, the reality slammed at him. There was no way he could make her leave. Legally she had as much right to live on Diamantina Downs as he did. They had all held equal shares, he, Conor and Jenna.

Why had he given in to Conor's argument all those months ago? He hadn't wanted to, and his first instinct had been to refuse her offer. But it was Conor who had swayed him, Conor who had dangled the possibility of borrowing Jenna's hard-earned money.

So you'd rather lose the land than accept outside help?

In reality he'd had no choice.

What were the legal ramifications now Conor was dead? There had been no will, of that Adam was certain. Did it mean that he and Jenna were now joint owners? Or could the child — Conor's son or daughter, Adam's own kin — have some sort of automatic claim over Conor's share after it was born?

Bloody hell! What a tangled mess, legally and emotionally.

His mind was exhausted. In his head he'd gone through what seemed like hundreds of options, and discarded them all. Now, almost senseless with fatigue, he'd lost the ability to reason. All sense of rationality was long gone.

It wasn't until the sky began to lighten with the first hint of dawn that Adam felt sleep descending — dark, soft and comforting — and he was powerless to stop it.

'In the morning,' he mumbled to himself. 'In the morning we'll talk about all this, logically and without emotion.'

Jenna woke to the shriek of birds. She struggled back to consciousness, feeling a sense of inexplicable panic, not knowing for a moment where she was. The bedroom walls were rough-hewn timber. The floor was hard-baked dirt. There was neither glass nor curtains on the window openings. Outside, grey dawn was breaking and she could see the trees moving in the breeze.

Then, on a deep breath, she remembered. Conor was dead.

The words hung like poison in her head and there was a huge void where she imagined her heart to be. For the last three months she'd missed him unbearably. Since she had bid him farewell, she'd counted every hour, knowing that with each passing day she was closer to seeing him again. And by the time she had arrived at Diamantina Downs on the mail cart the previous afternoon, her excitement had reached fever pitch.

She'd imagined him standing by the gate as the mail cart drew up, imagined flying into his open arms. Imagined, later when they were in bed, telling him about the baby. He'd be delighted, of course, insisting on an immediate wedding. She had dreamed, all those hours sitting in the cart, about the dress she would wear and the words they would say, the promises ...

But Conor had not been there.

There'd been no one waiting by the gate or the hut. Instead, the front door had been opened by a black woman. Aleyne, she'd introduced herself in halting English, explaining that Mista Conor had gone 'longa way', and that Adam wasn't expected home until nightfall. So she had sat on a chair on the verandah, scanning the surrounding bush, willing someone to appear.

It wasn't until late afternoon that she'd seen the dark speck coming along the track. Conor, she'd thought, her heart beating fast in her chest. But it had been Adam, she'd realised with dismay as he drew close. Dark-haired, staid Adam: not her golden fair-haired Conor at all.

Then Adam had said the dreadful words.

It seemed the sun had dimmed and the birds quietened. The only thing she'd heard was his voice resounding from the walls of her own despair. It couldn't be true, she'd told herself. It *couldn't*. What was to become of them now, she and the baby? Later she'd been forced to tell Adam about the child, though God only knew what his reaction had been. Luckily it had been too dark to tell.

Now, in the raw light of a new morning, Jenna knew with awful certainty that nothing had gone as planned. Heartbroken, she slid from the bed and pulled on a robe. Silently she stepped through the front door into the dawn light and started walking.

Past the lean-to where Adam slept, she went. Past the stockyards and through the gate, towards the river.

She came to a wide water hole. Further along, through the trees, she could see the outline of the blacks' camp and a curl of smoke that rose dark against the pale sky. A flock of corellas flew screaming overhead. Out on the water, a lone pelican slid effortlessly across the water.

She sank down on a low rock, binding her arms about her as she rocked backwards and forwards. In front of her, the gossamer threads of a cobweb dangled between two trees. Several beads of dew were caught in its mass and she stared hard at them. Her eyes were raw and aching. The dew wobbled in and out of focus.

Determinedly she looked further afield. In the distance, winding away, she could see the wavering lines of green that denoted the river channels, and the red sand hills that loomed abruptly up from the landscape, catching the first rays of sun. Here and there, breaking the harsh colours, were carpets of spring flowers, patches of pink, yellow and mauve.

Where was Conor? Jenna wondered. In what God-forsaken spot had he died and been buried? She would have liked to have seen him one last time, to pay her final respects. She wasn't afraid of death. God knows she'd seen much of it during her life. Perhaps she'd ask Adam to accompany her to the place. Surely it wasn't too far distant. She could take a bunch of the wildflowers.

Tears flooded her eyes, reducing the scene to a smudge. She buried her face in her hands, unable to stop the dry racking sobs that came from deep within. She was crying for herself and her own lost hope. She was crying for Conor, who would never know his child. And somehow her tears were for this unfamiliar country she now found herself in, this land of ridges and spinifex and dry river channels.

The tears went on and on, until she thought she might never stop. When at last they subsided, a muffled cough made her look up. A young black woman stood under a nearby tree. She was wearing little and carrying an armful of dry brush. For her fire, perhaps? wondered Jenna.

'What you cry for, Missy?' she asked in a low sing-song voice.

Jenna rubbed her eyes, embarrassed at being caught. No doubt she looked a sight, eyes red and streaming. 'Oh dear, I didn't realise I was being watched.'

The young woman grinned. 'No mind. Lalla not tell.'

'Lalla. Is that your name?'

Lalla nodded shyly. 'My mother Aleyne.'

'Ah, yes. From up at the house yesterday. We met.'

'She say you come for Mista Conor. But Mista Conor ...'

Her words died unspoken and she waved her hand vaguely in the direction of the distant sand hills. Then she stared at the ground.

'Lalla?'

'Yes, Missy.'

'My name's Jenna.'

'Missy Jenna.'

'Do you know where Mista Conor's buried?'

Lalla shook her head. 'Wongaree, he know.'

'Wongaree?'

'My man, Wongaree. He go with Mista Adam, dig hole.'

'So Wongaree could take me there?'

Lalla shrugged. 'P'raps. Have to ask first.'

Jenna closed her eyes and felt the first rays of the sun warm her face. Suddenly she felt very tired. 'How old are you, Lalla?'

'My mother says fifteen.'

'So young. And Wongaree's your man?'

'That our way, Missy.'

'How long have you lived here?'

'Always, Missy. Born here.'

'You're very lucky, do you know that. To have a home and family.'

Lalla made an odd tsk-tsk sound and Jenna opened her eyes. 'You people lucky ones. You got our land. We got nothing now.'

'This is not my land. Not really.'

'You come here. No one make you. I think land belong you now.'

'Maybe.'

The girl was right, she had to concede. Jenna had chosen this journey. No one had forced her to sell the shop and head further west. It was Conor, and the thought of their life together, that had drawn her. But no one had *made* her come. However, Conor was dead and that part of her dream had died along with him, pulsed to a halt with his last heartbeat.

Lalla was staring at her, frowning. 'Perhaps you learn to like?'

Jenna let her gaze travel the landscape. The sun was well up now and the colours, so harsh and rich, made her eyes hurt anew. Brilliant cobalt blue of sky. Cinnabar red of hill. The dark verdant celadon of the trees. She would have loved it all, if Conor were here. But the land seemed bleak and empty with him gone.

But there was still the child.

Unconsciously she brought her hand down until it lay flat across her belly. Conor's baby. A living being inside her. Part of him, part of them both. She had to go on, make a new life. If not for herself, then for the child.

Lalla pointed to a haphazard pile of white rocks near the water line. 'See the stones,' she said. 'They spirit stones. Maybe you talk longa them. P'raps they tell you 'bout this place. Then you learn to like.'

'Spirit stones?'

'Yair. We got spirits look after the land. Long time past, man and woman came here from a tribe far away. Set up camp in sand hills, down by 'nother water hole. By 'n' by spirits come down and make babies for the woman, give the couple a song to sing and a story to tell. We got our own songs, our own stories, you know.'

'And the spirits?'

Lalla grinned. 'Them spirits bring us sun and rain and food. But we don't need so much food now. We got white man tucker.'

'Adam gives you food?'

'Yair. Me and Aleyne work in the house. And the fellas help with the sheep and fences, chop wood. Mista Adam gives us stuff.'

Jenna thought about what it would be like, losing everything, having to rely on someone else for her most basic needs. And when she put it into perspective like that, her own life didn't seem quite so dismal. Certainly she had lost Conor, but in some small way she was recompensed by the child.

She was four months gone already, by her own reckoning. Maybe it'd be a boy, with his father's fair hair and cheeky smile. Someone to remind her of those few precious months they'd shared. She also owned a stake in the land, and money from the sale of the shop. She wasn't destitute. She could pay her way on Diamantina Downs. There was no way she'd be forced to rely on Adam O'Loughlin for anything.

Jenna brought her head up with a defiant toss. She was here, and somehow she'd make the best of it. Presently she'd walk back to the hut. Surely Adam would have risen by now. They'd sit down in the kitchen and talk rationally over a cup of tea, make plans.

Mind made up, she rose briskly to her feet and waved goodbye to Lalla.

Aleyne was waiting on the front steps of the hut when she returned, a sullen expression on her face. 'Where's Adam?' Jenna asked.

Aleyne shook her head and pointed to the lean-to where Adam had dragged his bed the previous night. 'Him still in there,' she said flatly.

Jenna marched past her, into the kitchen. What to

do? Adam obviously hadn't risen and she wasn't used to sitting around all day. Her eyes took in the hut. Now, in the harsh light of day, she could see the interior was in a terrible mess, with dust and cobwebs everywhere.

What this place needs, she thought, is a thorough clean. She opened the stove door, finding nothing but cold ashes. 'Come on,' she said briskly to the older woman. 'You can help me light the fire. We need boiling water and there's work to be done.'

'But Mista Adam —'

'Mista Adam's still in bed, sleeping the day away.'

Aleyne eyed Jenna warily. 'How long you stay, Missy?'

'Long time.'

'How long 'xactly?'

'Missy not going anywhere, so you'd better get used to it.'

It was late, the sun well up in the sky, by the time Adam woke. Carefully he moved his tongue across his teeth. Christ! His mouth tasted like the interior of an old boot. He moved his head and the room spun. An ache had started there, in his temple, as though he'd consumed the contents of a bottle of whisky the previous night, though, in truth, he'd had none.

Tentatively he levered himself into an upright position and waited for the room to stop revolving. Then he pulled on his shirt and trousers and made his way to the hut. He was met at the front steps by the aroma of baking. Bread and what? he wondered, suddenly ravenous.

Jenna was busy at the stove. She turned at the sound of his footfall. 'Ah, there you are,' she said. 'I was wondering when you'd be up.'

Was it an observation or criticism? Adam didn't know. He stood awkwardly before her, like an errant schoolboy, his mind forming an explanation. 'I don't usually rise so late,' he began defensively. 'But I didn't get much sleep last night.'

'That makes two of us.'

She took a tray from the oven and upended it onto the bench. Small cakes tumbled onto the surface. She was moving in a jerky, animated way. Her mouth was set into an unusually firm line. What had he done to upset her? Adam wondered. Sleeping in hardly constituted a crime.

'I'm sorry about what's happened,' he began, not really knowing where to start. Well, actually, in all practicality he'd like to start with a cup of tea and some solid food to calm his grumbling stomach. One of those little cakes, perhaps. Or two.

As though reading his mind, she took the teapot from the shelf and ladled several spoonfuls of tea into it. Then she took a kettle from the stove top and poured water on top. He could hear it, fizzing and spitting.

'You don't have to say sorry to me. What happened to Conor wasn't your fault.'

Wasn't it? Despite his own reservations, he'd let his brother go by himself with the sheep, when he should have insisted on one of the men accompanying him. Two of them might have stood a chance. Then again, if the commander hadn't shot most of the walkabout tribe ...

'No,' he replied despondently. 'I suppose it wasn't.'

'He was your brother. I know this has been upsetting for you, too.'

'He was the only family I had left.'

An empty wretched feeling settled in the pit of his stomach. His mind tunnelled back, remembering. Conor with the dead sheep for Mam. Conor watching, smiling, as fire destroyed the Newtownlimavady cottage. Conor in the boarding house in Londonderry, urging Adam to throw a coin to decide their destination.

One of the ships is bound for Australia. It's leaving tomorrow morning.

Conor taking a coin from the dresser and juggling it between his hands.

Choose a side. If it comes up, we'll wait for America. Otherwise we'll sail tomorrow.

Adam remembered the scene as though it had happened yesterday, so clear was it in his mind. Heads, he'd said, remembering now how Conor had spun the coin high into the air.

Tails. Looks like it's Sydney Town we're headed to, brother dear.

The fall of a sixpence sending them halfway around the globe, sealing Conor's destiny, deciding his own. How random was that? What if the coin had fallen head-side up? What fate would have been waiting for them in America? Would Conor still be alive, or was it his fate to die, wherever they'd gone?

He had a sudden thought: perhaps your life was already mapped out for you from the moment of your birth. If so, Mam and Da and Conor and all those tiny O'Loughlin babies were destined never to lead full lives. And what about himself — what was his own future? Could the remainder of his own life be measured in days, weeks or months?

'Neither of us has anyone now,' said Jenna, bringing him back to the present. She turned abruptly to Aleyne who, Adam knew from experience, had been listening to the conversation. 'Aleyne,' she said, taking the dark woman by the arm and steering her towards the door, 'I'm going to need help here today. I'd like you to go down to the camp and bring Lalla and Ngayla back.'

'But this not Lalla's day for workin' up here,' Aleyne protested, hands on hips. She glanced towards Adam, as though for support, but he shook his head at her. Goodness knows why Jenna wanted the other two at the hut, but at least Aleyne's departure would give him and Jenna a chance to speak in private.

'Do as Miss McCabe says,' he confirmed.

Aleyne flounced off through the door and down the steps into the sunshine. Adam watched her go across the paddock towards the camp. 'Aleyne's the oldest female in the tribe. She's not used to having another woman giving orders.'

'I didn't order her. I asked.' Jenna put two cakes on a plate and pushed it towards him, across the table 'Why don't you sit down?'

It seemed more a command than an invitation. Adam pulled out a chair and lowered himself onto it, sensing a frisson of discomfort. Since Mam had died, he'd never been waited on by any woman, especially one as young and pretty as Jenna McCabe. He barely knew her, yet here they were, isolated, miles from anywhere.

They were bound together inexorably by their grief that, in itself, seemed an odd thing. Conor had been a brother to Adam, a mate. Yet Jenna had known Conor, if the story about the child was to be believed, in the most intimate way possible. He tried to picture them together as lovers, and failed. He knew little about such things. But if events had been different, if Conor had lived, Jenna would have eventually been part of the O'Loughlin family too, and the baby, Conor's child, a niece or nephew.

Jenna took two mugs and placed them on the bench, filled them with steaming tea and handed him one. His eyes slid to her trim waist and the apron she had tied there. 'You don't look pregnant,' he observed, the words coming from his mouth before he could stop them.

She stood next to the table, watching him over the rim of her mug. Her skin was still as pale as it had been the previous night, and there were purple smudges under her eyes, evidence of her disturbed sleep. For a while she said nothing, simply stood watching him, as though thinking of a suitable reply.

'So, you're an expert on having babies, are you?' she said at last.

'Not exactly.'

'Just how am I supposed to look?'

He shrugged. 'How do you know you're pregnant?'

'Do you think I'm lying?'

Why did she keep answering his questions with another question? 'No. Mistaken, maybe.'

'I am not mistaken.'

'Have you seen a doctor?'

She gave a short mirthless laugh. 'Hardly. The news would have been all over town in a day.'

'So how do you know?' he insisted.

'A woman can tell these things.' She frowned, regarding him thoughtfully. 'It is Conor's, if that's what you're wondering.'

He jerked to a halt, a piece of cake midway to his mouth. 'I never suggested it wasn't.'

'I'm not a slut.'

Adam sat back, shocked. 'Jenna —'

She drew herself up to her full height and he felt somehow diminutive, sitting before her. Part of him wanted to stand, to be on more equal footing, yet another part of him wanted to sink into some imaginary hole in the ground.

Then, abruptly, she sat at the table, in the chair that had been Conor's. The tea slopped over the rim of the cup but she made no attempt to wipe it away. Her eyes swam with unshed tears. Her body sagged in a defeated way. Somehow she reminded him of Mam and the way she had set her mouth, refusing to hear anything bad about Conor.

'I didn't choose Conor's death, Adam.'

'Of course not,' he denied hotly.

'And I didn't choose to bring a fatherless child into this world. But I loved your brother and part of me is glad and honoured to be carrying his baby.'

'Jenna,' Adam began, not knowing how to say the words. 'This is no place for a woman, or a child. I watched my mother die from the complications of childbirth. There's no doctor here for — oh, probably a hundred miles. What if something went wrong?'

'I'm young and strong and healthy. Nothing will go wrong.'

'You don't know that! It's too risky. Why not make a fresh start in a place where no one knows you?'

'No one knows me here, except you.'

'You make it sound so, so ...' He searched his mind for the right word, badly needing her to see reason. 'So uncomplicated. You want to stay here on Diamantina Downs and have your baby? What about proprieties? What will people say?'

'About my child?'

'Yes. No. About us. You and me living together, not married.'

'But we're not living together. Not in that way.'

She made it sound distasteful, as though no woman could ever want him. 'They don't know that,' he replied, trying to keep his voice even.

'Ah, the mysterious "they". People who decide how we must live, if we let them.'

There must be, he thought, some strange feminine logic in what she was saying, though for the life of him he couldn't figure it out. 'That's a bit rich. It was you who wouldn't even go to the doctor in town because of the gossip.'

'That's different. Those people knew me, knew my family. Do you know what they used to call my mother?'

'No. And I don't —'

She put out a hand, silencing him. 'This is not going to be easy — I know that — but I've made up my mind. I won't leave, and you can't make me. This place is as much mine as yours. Don't worry. I'll never be a burden to you and I won't interfere in the running of Diamantina Downs. Maybe, one day, you might even find it useful having a woman about the place.'

'I have Lalla and Aleyne,' he replied stubbornly.

'And they can't even keep this place clean!'

'This is the bush, Jenna, not some fancy city house. It gets damn hot out here in summer, and when it rains we're liable not to leave the place for months. If the flies don't get you during the day, the mosquitoes will be waiting at night. Then there are the dust storms when the sky turns red and you can't see more than a few feet in front of you. Housekeeping is the least of my worries.'

He hadn't meant to be harsh, but he heard it creep into his voice. Abruptly she scraped her chair back and struggled to her feet. As she averted her face from his, Adam could see tears coursing down her face. 'I'm sorry,' she hiccupped. 'I told myself I wouldn't ...'

'Wouldn't what?'

'Cry. It's so pointless and unproductive. It won't change anything, and it won't bring Conor back.'

He felt ridiculously like crying himself, though he'd never admit it to Jenna McCabe. Instead he stood and rummaged in his shirt pocket, distracting himself from her grief by bringing forward a clean handkerchief. He held it towards her and she stared at it for one long moment. 'Go on,' he urged. 'Take it.'

It seemed she couldn't move. Adam stepped closer, dabbed at the tears on her cheek. At any moment he thought she might flinch away, but she stood there like a docile child, staring at him. Then somehow she leaned into him, against one outstretched arm, and suddenly he was holding her in a clumsy embrace.

Through the thin fabric of his shirt he could feel the shuddering that came from her chest and the dampness of her tears. Her head had come to rest in the hollow at the base of his throat. Her hands were clasped hard around his shoulders, pulling him close. A tenderness rose up inside him, a need to protect her — to protect them both, Jenna and the child — from further heartache.

It seemed they stood there a long while, though it was, in reality, less than a minute. Eventually a discreet cough made Jenna pull away. Aleyne, Lalla and Ngayla were waiting in the doorway, arms folded.

'Ah, there you are,' exclaimed Jenna briskly, stepping away from him. His skin, where her hands had rested, suddenly felt cold, and he watched her go with a stab of regret. It had felt comforting somehow, the way she had clung to him, needing support.

'You want to see us, Missy?' asked Lalla.

'Well,' Jenna replied, giving Adam a sideways glance. Her chin had come up at a defiant tilt and her voice was firm. Gone were the tears. There was a purposefulness about her, a sudden briskness that seemed at odds with her recent behaviour. 'Seeing I'm to stay on, we'll need some changes around here.'

'What sort of changes?'

'If the women are going to work up here in the hut, they'll have to dress decently. I can't have them walking around half-naked.'

Aleyne raised her hands in protest. 'But, Missy —'

Jenna pointed to the corner of the room, to one of the large trunks that had arrived with her on the mail cart the previous day. 'No buts, Aleyne. You'll find some clothes in there, old dresses and petticoats that will scarcely fit me for much longer.'

She threw open the lid of the trunk, dragging several garments from its confines and thrusting them at the black women. 'You can try them on in there,' she added, pointing to the bedroom.

The women stood holding the dresses, looking at Adam for endorsement. 'Better do as Missy says,' he said, suppressing a smile.

Much grumbling, mixed with the occasional laugh, came from the bedroom. After a few minutes, Lalla came out wearing a gingham dress, several sizes too large. The buttons at the front had been done up unevenly and Jenna helped her get them right. Aleyne and Ngayla followed, looking awkward.

'Good,' Jenna nodded. 'That's one thing out of the way.'

'There's more?' Adam asked innocently.

'If I'm to stay then I have to earn my keep,' she said to his enquiring glance. 'This place is a terrible mess. By nightfall you won't recognise it.'

And she shooed him from the room, brandishing the broom.

CHAPTER 20

The day's activities became rituals. Washing, cooking, cleaning: it seemed to Jenna that her hours were mapped out, unending, before her.

The hut had been in a terrible mess and patiently she had shown the women how to do the most basic tasks. She taught them to cook — properly — and, despite the vagaries of the oven, they were soon preparing tasty casseroles and scones. Aleyne had been stand-offish at first, reluctant to follow Jenna's orders. But Jenna persevered. Finally she had come around, began bringing her small gifts — a striped creek pebble or a bird's feather — and offering to do chores.

Monday was washing day. The sheets were stripped from the beds and Aleyne and her daughter Lalla pummelled the fabric in the rough washing trough Adam had set up. Then they wrung the sheets by hand in the yard, giggling as they worked. Jenna invariably found Ngayla standing in the doorway of the hut, pausing in her work to look wistfully in their direction. There was a sadness about her, a lethargy that was hard to define.

Adam had told Jenna the story of the massacre and how he had found Ngayla, the only surviving female of the tribe. She was young, he said, and she'd soon assimilate into her new surroundings. They were, Jenna thought as she observed the girl, two lost souls, she and Ngayla. Losing all their loved ones. Starting afresh in a strange place. Eventually, after a few weeks, she set up a small bed in the corner of the kitchen and brought Ngayla to the hut to live permanently.

Jenna's birthday — her twentieth — came and went without anyone knowing. And the weather, already warm when she had arrived at Diamantina Downs, became hot. She lay in bed at night after Adam had gone to his own bunk in the lean-to shed, feeling guilty that she had evicted him from his home. Perhaps they could build an extension? She'd need more room when the baby came. Adam had told her that a family of six had lived there previously, and Jenna wondered with bemusement how they had even fitted around the dinner table.

She felt the first movements of the child, those tremulous butterfly flutters when she wondered for a moment if she had imagined them. She'd pause in whatever she was doing and stand still, waiting, hand expectantly against her belly, with wondrous excitement.

Her waistline expanded and most of her dresses no longer fitted. Instead she sewed loose shifts that she wore under her apron. As her pregnancy began to show, she often turned to find Aleyne and Lalla staring at her, whispering, glancing away when discovered. Eventually she took them aside.

'I'm having a baby,' she said simply.

Aleyne nodded. 'We guess, Missy.'

'Conor is my baby's father.'

'We know, Missy. Can see it in your face. You sad sometimes. Think about him alla time, yes?'

'Yes.'

'But a baby, now. That makes you happy?'

'Happy, yes. But sad about Conor.'

'Wongaree and me like a baby,' added Lalla wistfully.

'Must be patient,' soothed her mother. 'Spirits come soon, make plenty babies.'

Of Adam, she saw little. He came in for supper each evening and they often ate in silence. As soon as he'd finished, he'd scrape his chair back and, taking the axe from behind the kitchen door, disappear out into the yard. The wood chopping was Pigeon's job, but Adam went anyway, adding to the already large pile of cut logs. Jenna could hear him out there, the thump-whack of the axe.

It was as though he'd rather be outside than inside the hut with her. Did he resent her presence that much?

Quietly she and Ngayla attended to the washing up, stacking away the clean plates and pots. Then, the young black girl dispatched to her bed, Jenna sat by the lamp, reading, her mind only half paying attention to the open book on her lap, not knowing what else to do. Should she, out of politeness, wait up for him? Or should she simply ignore him and go to bed?

In the yard, the light from the hut spilt out across the uneven ground, highlighting the dips and bumps. Sometimes she stood at the window and watched as Adam raised the axe high above his head and brought it down with a steady thwack. Down by the water hole, frogs screeched a chorus for rain, and the cicadas in the nearby trees put out a high-pitched shriek. Sometimes she could hear bats flapping overhead, a far-off howl of a dingo and the answering call of its mate.

It seemed to Jenna that everything came in pairs, or groups. Frogs, cicadas, dingos. Yet she sat alone most nights, lonely for a male voice, desperate for conversation, however trivial. No sound came from the interior of the hut except for the regular ticking of the clock and the sound of an occasional page turning, though if asked, she would have been hard pressed to relay what she had read.

Random thoughts ran through her mind, like how different things would have been if Conor was alive. She imagined him coming home to her every night, how she could have shown him her love in the bed that she slept in alone. Imagined waking him with kisses every morning.

Her sigh filled the silence. There was a movement at the doorway. Glancing up, she saw it was Adam, his shirt damp with perspiration. 'Goodnight,' he said.

'You're going to bed?'

'Tomorrow's another day.'

How well she knew. 'Yes, well, goodnight.'

Abruptly he was gone and she was left sitting there, with no company except for the few moths that fluttered uselessly against the glass of the lamp.

In early November, purple clouds gathered overhead one afternoon and the sky darkened until it seemed like night. The wind rose, whipping the branches of the trees into a frenzy and stirring up dust. A jagged spear of lightning lit the surrounding countryside with a blinding flash, followed by a clap of thunder that set Ngayla scurrying towards the stove.

'Big wet comin',' said Aleyne as she stood at the doorway of the hut, looking out. Jenna, walking up behind her, watched as a veil of white swept across the landscape.

It poured for two solid weeks.

'River's up,' said Adam, coming in a few days later, stamping drops of water onto the verandah.

'Are we safe here? The water won't come this high?'

Adam shrugged, looking concerned. 'Honestly, I don't know. We'll just have to wait it out.'

The water rose, eddying around the fence posts of the home yard. Inside, it was a continuous task to empty the buckets placed under the worst of the roof leaks. In a brief lull in the rain, Jenna borrowed a pair of Adam's boots and waded through the mud to a high vantage point. There she saw the river courses running with water, spreading into brown swirling streams that rushed and twisted through the sand hills.

She felt a sense of peacefulness as she looked down on the network of braided channels. Thousands of birds — pelicans and geese, black swans and ducks — had gathered there, dipping and diving into the water. The heads of trees, like green ghosts, peered from the swirling current. She might have been anywhere, she thought, miles from here.

But eventually the sun shone again, and each day seemed hotter than the one before. The air became humid, and tiny bush flies crawled up noses and into mouths and across every available surface. She called the tribe up to the hut, both men and women, and gave them all a dose of castor oil.

Some of the men still seemed wary of her. There were days when she found their existence not a threat, but an overshadowing presence on a different plane. They were important to her: she sensed that, but the importance was unknown, a shadowy thing. She was aware of the vibrations of them, their constant thrumming on the periphery of her own life. She was tied to them somehow, yet separate, though she couldn't distinguish the cords that bound them, now or in the future.

Despite their differences in the past, Adam missed Conor unbearably. There were times when he thought to turn to his brother and offer some remark about his progress with the fences or the fact that a dozen or more sheep had already lambed, or to say, 'Remember when ...' But at the last minute he brought himself up short and the words died on his tongue, unsaid.

Conor wasn't there anymore. There was no one left to link him with his past.

Instead, Adam sought to distance himself from the hut. There were plains, further out, where he had never been — flat expanses of rock-littered land where nothing seemed to grow. Accompanied by Wongaree, he took supplies and a gun, staying away for days on end. As the weeks passed he came to know the paddocks intimately, like a lover, recognising every dip and hollow, every rise. The land was part of him and he never tired of riding its boundaries. It restored his spirit when he felt low.

It seemed strange, on those nights when he returned home, having Jenna there. In the beginning he couldn't bear to be near her, couldn't find the words to say. The mere presence of her reminded him of Conor and what he had lost. But she was determined to stay, and there seemed nothing he could do to persuade her otherwise.

Despite his initial misgivings, she had slotted unobtrusively into life on Diamantina Downs. She was good-tempered and, he had to admit, always had a ready smile and a kind word for everyone. He often found her humming or singing in the kitchen, pulling tasty treats from the interior of the oven. He also admired the brisk, no-nonsense way she dealt with the blacks.

'They have to earn their keep,' she said when the men came up to the hut, bartering jobs for supplies of flour and tobacco, even though Adam's own supplies were scarce. She treated them firmly, but respectfully. 'I won't let them be lazy.'

'I intend to be fair,' Adam added. 'When I can afford it, they'll get a few shillings.'

'There's nothing to spend money on out here,' she countered. 'You'd be better off giving them blankets to keep them warm, and clothes.'

To Adam, women were a mystery. One minute they were practical. The next they were totally opposite, all caught up with silly romantic notions and dissolving into tears. They thought and acted differently from men, and he'd always felt awkward around them, tongue-tied and tense — not like Conor who'd been flippant and easy-going, able to make effortless conversation.

Yet, despite his discomfort, he was intensely aware of Jenna's femininity. As the weeks and months passed he began to notice small things about her: the way she moved about the stove at day's end, stirring something in a pot or taking roasting meat from the oven; the curve of her cheek in the lamplight, the soft lilting cadence of her voice. He watched with fascination as the child grew inside her, a gentle swelling that even her apron could no longer hide.

Conor's child.

Something rose up inside him, emotions both painful and soothing, and a vague fluttering sensation inside his chest, like his heart was beating too loudly.

It was times like that when he took the axe into the yard, even though Pigeon already had a ready supply of wood cut. By the light that spilled from the windows into the yard, he brought the blade down against the timber, gaining some joy from the repetitive thudding sound and the jarring that shook his body. He worked hard, blotting out the memories, keeping the thoughts of her from his mind by sheer physical force.

She could never desire him, he knew. It was Conor she loved, Conor's child she carried. And to think otherwise meant a betrayal, of sorts.

At odd lonely times he rode through the paddocks to the place where he had buried his brother, and sat beside the mound. Animals had defecated on the grave. Weeds grew there in wild abandon and he pulled them from the dirt. Maybe, he wondered in hindsight, he should have brought Conor's body back to the homestead, buried him there. But no, he thought, staring about him at the rugged beauty of the landscape. It was right that this should be his final resting place.

One morning Jenna asked if he could take her to the grave site. He felt a momentary pang of alarm, a quickening in his chest that he sought to subdue. That clearing by the river was the one place he felt at peace with his brother, and to share it with her meant relinquishing the only tenuous hold that remained.

'It's a hard half-day's ride,' he replied curtly, 'and you're in no condition to travel.'

'*Condition*! I'm not sick. I'm just having a baby.'

'I don't care,' he replied stubbornly. 'If something happens out here, there are no doctors. I won't have the responsibility.'

'Then I'll assume responsibility.'

'So I can look forward to burying you too. No!'

'Look,' he said later, 'I'm sorry if I sounded gruff. It's just if anything happened …'

His words died away, unsaid. Terrible thought, he considered, that anything *could* happen to her. How could he live with himself, the guilt? Jenna's baby must be protected at all costs.

'All right,' she conceded. 'But can you build a fence around the grave and put up a cross? Conor's grave needs to be marked, so that in years to come people will know someone's buried there.'

'We know he's there,' Adam replied hotly.

'But we won't necessarily always be here.'

He stared at her, silent for a moment, unable to comprehend the thought. Leave the land? What was she thinking? He'd worked long and hard for this place and wasn't about to give it up.

When he spoke, his voice was rough, as though from years of disuse. 'I'm not going anywhere. And years from now everyone will know the story of Conor and what happened. Everyone will *know*.'

Still, one morning he took fence posts and wire, and the makings of a rough wooden cross with the words *Conor O'Loughlin 1851–1873* chiselled onto one side. Carefully he dug the loose sand away from the grave, erected the posts and strung the wire. Then he stood back, surveying his handiwork. Even Jenna, he thought, would have been impressed.

The rains came again: shrouds of white descending across the land. He began staying indoors after supper, using the rain as an excuse, helping her clear the plates and pots away. The first time she'd glanced at him in surprise, but said nothing. Had he caught the hint of a smile playing at the corners of her mouth?

After the cleaning was done, he sat at the table with the station journal spread before him, pages open as he glanced occasionally at Jenna. She was always sewing these days, some impossibly small garment for the baby, her head bent over her task and unaware of his scrutiny. She also kept a diary, he knew that. Some nights she spent an inordinately long time writing in it, and he came to find the sound — the scratch-scratch-scratch of the pen nib against the paper — comforting.

When the rains stopped and the skies cleared, he suggested sitting on the verandah one evening, where the errant breeze made life more bearable. They made small talk mostly, though gradually he began dropping small snippets of news about the station. Several lambs had been lost and the water had stopped overflowing from the big water hole. He didn't know if she was interested or not, but she listened politely and the conversation filled those empty night-time hours between sunset and bedtime.

He couldn't, in retrospect, pinpoint the night when he began telling her about his own life back in Ireland, or exactly when Jenna, bit by bit, reluctantly brought forward details of her own: Michael's birth and death, her own mother.

'They used to call her a whore,' she said. 'That's why I could never stay in town once I knew I was expecting Conor's child. I could just imagine the snide remarks. Just like her mother, they'd say.'

'But you're not!' Adam cried, suddenly aware that

he was defending her and indignant beyond belief at the thought of such gossip.

'No, I loved Conor. It was something that just happened, that felt right.'

Felt right: suddenly he knew what she meant. He was struck by how much he had become used to her company. How lonely it would be, he thought, if she decided to leave. Something inside him had altered, realigned itself.

She sat on the front step, rocking to and fro, hugging the shape of her child. She seemed preoccupied, looking out over the land, yet there was a sadness about her that evening, a certain neediness that Adam was at a loss to define. Something inside him pulsed with immeasurable tenderness and awe. It seemed like a miracle of sorts that, although Conor was dead, part of him still lived on in the child. He had begun thinking about the baby's arrival, making mental plans to take Jenna to town a few weeks before the birth. He must ask her, he thought, when she thought the baby was due.

'I don't know exactly,' she admitted. 'Another two months, perhaps longer.'

He knew then, with surprising clarity, what he must do.

'I'm going into town tomorrow,' he said, easing himself into the conversation. 'It's almost Christmas and we need supplies.'

'There are things I want for the baby. If I give you a list, can you bring them back?'

'Of course.' He took a deep breath, bracing himself. 'But there's something I want to ask you before I go.'

'Yes.' Slowly she spun her head towards him.

'Will you marry me?'

She stared wide-eyed, saying nothing.

Adam took her silence for hesitation and ploughed on. 'I know you loved Conor but you've the babe to think of. I'll give your child the name O'Loughlin.'

Jenna considered him gravely. 'It wouldn't be fair to you, Adam. Maybe one day you'll meet a woman —'

'What! Out here?' He gave a short mirthless laugh. 'I'm not Conor and I can't take his place. In fact, I'm a damn poor substitute. But I'll be honest and true to you, and a good father to your child. Maybe in time you could learn to love me a little.' He forced a smile to his face. 'I'm not such an ogre, really.'

'Of course you're not. You're good and kind, and I really don't deserve this —'

'You deserve better,' he broke in. 'You deserve *Conor* and I'd do anything to have him here.'

Slowly she reached forward and took his hand. In the lamplight Adam saw, to his surprise, that her eyes had filled with tears. 'Yes,' she said.

'Yes,' he repeated stupidly, confused.

'Yes, I know you would, and yes, I'll marry you.'

'Well,' he said, stunned. 'That's that, then. I suppose I'd better send for a minister.'

He was suddenly at a loss what to do. She had just agreed to be his wife and he supposed he should mark the occasion in some way. Perhaps, he thought, he should kiss her but her face was angled slightly to one side. Instead he leaned forward and clumsily brushed his mouth across her forehead before pulling away and releasing her hand.

'Time for bed,' he said, running a hand through his dark hair. 'Goodnight. See you in the morning.'

And before she could answer, he found himself heading out the door.

Reverend Carlyle arrived one week before Christmas. At Adam's request, he brought a photographer. 'You can't afford it,' admonished Jenna as she watched the two men alight from their horses.

Adam shrugged. 'So I'll be broke, but at least we'll have something to remember the day by, long after it's gone.'

Wongaree and Lalla had agreed to witness the ceremony. Lalla, wearing one of Jenna's cast-off dresses, looked shy, overawed by the occasion. Wongaree arrived wearing a battered top hat. Adam confided to Jenna with a grin that the hat had been given to the black man years earlier by a party of surveyors who had passed through.

They were married down by the water hole, under the shade of a coolibah tree. The others were there too — Aleyne and Yapunya, Pigeon, Wandi and Ngayla — waiting expectantly in a semi-circle around them, dark faces shiny with perspiration. Jenna felt disjointed, as though time was jangled, seconds and minutes running in mad disarray. She heard the words dance around her, mixing and mingling with the hot breeze. 'We are here today, to unite this man and this woman ...'

She closed her eyes, fighting back a flutter of panic. Was she doing the right thing in marrying Adam O'Loughlin?

The question had stayed with her since the moment she had accepted his marriage proposal. She had agreed on impulse, though, if pressed, she could not have given a logical reason. True, Adam was a kind and decent man, and he was Conor's brother. Her child could do worse than be raised by his uncle. On the other hand, she wasn't destitute. She had money. She could have gone anywhere, another town or the city perhaps, and spun some story about recent widowhood, the lie reinforced by the purchase of a cheap wedding ring. No one would have questioned her.

So why Diamantina Downs and Adam: a man she did not love? Did she feel some sort of automatic kinship to him, because of Conor? Was it her destiny to be here? Perhaps something out of her control, some force bigger than her, had made this her place to *be*.

So many questions required answers, and yet she had none. She took a deep breath, trying to quell the bubble of anxiety that had lodged in her chest, and glanced towards the minister. He was eyeing her warily, his eyes sliding down to her belly. I don't care, she thought, bringing her head up defiantly and awarding him a challenging stare.

'Do you, Jenna McCabe, take this man ...'

Automatically she made her reply.

Afterwards, there was tea and sandwiches back at the hut. Adam insisted on photographs of everyone, which seemed to Jenna to take a very long time. The photographer bobbed and darted under his black cloth, holding the flashbulb high. Jenna, standing behind Adam who was sitting on a chair, tried to keep the smile from sliding off her face. She was exhausted and the baby had kicked mercilessly for the past hour. The day had seemed interminable already.

Mid-afternoon, the reverend and the photographer announced their imminent departure. Jenna went to her room and hastily scribbled a note. Adam came in while she was slipping it into an envelope. 'Are you alright?' he asked.

'I'm fine. Just tired.'

'Stay in here and rest. I'll just tell them you're indisposed. I'm sure they'll understand.'

'I'm sure they will.' She gave Adam a wry smile then handed him the envelope. 'Would you mind giving this to Reverend Carlyle?'

'What is it?'

'A message for the bank manager in town. I've asked him to engage a builder on our behalf, and I've given him permission to draw money from my account.'

'A builder?'

'Adam,' she explained patiently, 'we can't keep on living in this shack. It's stinking hot in summer and when it rains the roof leaks. I can't bring up a baby like this.'

'No,' Adam replied stubbornly. 'I'll be the one to provide a house.'

'You don't have to provide for me. We're married now and what's mine is yours. I have money from the sale of the shop, enough for a fine house and furniture. It'll be my contribution.'

He stared at her, unblinking.

She leaned forward and placed a hand on his arm, a gesture of peace. 'If you won't agree for my sake, then do it for the baby's,' she said quietly. 'And just for once can you forget your damn male pride?'

He shrugged and turned towards the doorway. 'Alright, I give in. But only because you're right about one thing — this hut is no place to bring up a child.'

It was dark by the time the women had cleared away the food.

'Wongaree reckons lot of fuss,' Lalla told Jenna and Adam with a grin. 'He say just live together, blackfella way. No need for this *marriage*.'

'Ah, but this is *our* way,' countered Adam.

'Still, lotta muckin' 'round. All that cookin' and cleanin' up.'

'Never mind, Lalla. It's all over now.'

While Lalla and Adam were talking, Jenna beckoned Aleyne aside. 'Would you mind taking Ngayla back to the camp with you?'

'What she want to come down to our camp for?'

'She doesn't. *I* want her to. Just for tonight.'

'That's alright then, Missy,' Aleyne agreed, giving Jenna a knowing smile. 'She sleep down there longa us. No worries.'

Jenna and Adam sat in silence on the verandah when the women had gone. It felt awkward, Jenna thought as she stared out into the night. Adam was now her husband; only hours earlier she'd promised to honour and obey him. Yet in many ways he seemed like a stranger still. They'd never kissed, never held hands. But if it had been Conor sitting there with her now ...

Her thoughts trailed away. Stop it! she told herself angrily. Conor was gone but Adam was here. She had to make the best of it now, get on with her life. No use wishing for the moon, as her mother had been fond of saying.

'Can we talk?' she whispered.

Abruptly Adam rose from his chair. He walked to the end of the verandah where he stood, resting his hands against the rails. In the lamplight they looked like fine hands, Jenna thought. Strong and capable. She imagined them cradling her child, rocking him to and fro.

'Oh, Jenna,' he said, and his voice sounded like a sad echo. Then he turned and clattered down the steps, striding across the yard towards his own bed.

She let him go, saying nothing. She could have called him back, insisted he stay. But she sensed he felt just as awkward as she did. Instead she went to her own room, taking off her clothes and letting them fall to the floor.

Earlier she had filled the room with wildflowers. They were in old bottles and jars, on the makeshift dresser and in the corners. Now, hours later, the aroma of them was subtle. Next she lit the candles she had placed around the room, until the walls were bathed in golden wavering light. Then she took the jug and filled the basin with water, adding sweet-smelling cologne.

She took her time bathing. She was in no hurry. She had all night. What were a few more minutes compared with the rest of their lives? By the time

Jenna towelled herself dry, according to the clock half an hour had passed. Pulling on a robe, she took a deep breath and picked up the lamp. Then she made her way across the yard to Adam's lean-to.

The door was ajar and she slid inside, holding the lamp high. Adam was asleep on the bed, curled on his side, fully clothed, his dark hair tousled. She placed the lamp on the chair next to the bed and stood for a minute studying his features. The thought ran once more through her consciousness: how could two brothers be so unalike? One dark, one fair. One full of laughter, the other serious. If Conor had been the sun, then perhaps Adam was the moon?

On a deep breath she placed one hand on his arm. 'Adam,' she said softly.

He stirred, stretched. Slept still.

'Adam,' she began again, a little louder.

Instantly he was awake, struggling up in the bed towards her, a look of confusion on his face. 'What's wrong? It's not the baby?'

'No.'

A lone moth fluttered, beating its wings uselessly at the glass of the lamp.

'Well, what?'

'We're married now,' she said matter-of-factly, trying to keep the tremor from her voice. 'So we might as well start acting like it. There's no need for you to sleep out here.'

She knelt beside him, awkwardly because of the baby, and placed her mouth over his. His lips yielded to the pressure of her own. She tasted him, flicking her tongue over his. He gave a groan, barely heard.

'Come,' she said, pulling her mouth away. 'Come inside.'

She took his hand and led him back across the yard. The moon had just risen: a blood-red orb hanging above the eastern horizon. 'Look,' she said. 'It's an omen.'

'Good or bad?'

'Good, silly.'

They tiptoed through the hut, like errant children. 'It's alright,' she laughed. 'Ngayla's down at the camp tonight.'

She drew him into the bedroom. He stood, taking in the candles already half burned, and the smell of the wildflowers. Then he wrapped his arms around her. 'Witch,' he whispered into her hair. 'You planned this.'

She nodded.

'I wanted to ... you know ... out there, before. I wanted to hold you and kiss you.'

'I know,' she replied simply.

'But I didn't know how to begin. I didn't know the words. I'm not clever like —'

Jenna placed one finger across his lips, silencing him. 'Shhh. Don't talk.' Then she took a deep breath before letting the robe slide from her shoulders to the floor.

He gave an audible gasp. Slowly, unhurriedly, she began unbuttoning his shirt, his trousers. He stood, running his hands through her hair. She paused in her task from time to time, standing on tiptoe and kissing him. When she had removed his clothes, she ran her hands down the length of him, cupping one palm around his hardness. 'Oh, God! Jenna!' he groaned, pulling her onto the bed.

Their mouths fused, joined for what seemed a very long time. He ran his hand along her, urgently, touching first throat then breast. She could feel him, skin brushing skin, damp in the heat, the hard prod of him pressing insistently against her thigh. One by one the candles flickered and died.

Moonlight slid through the open window, faintly lighting the room. Carefully she guided his hand between her legs. It was damp there, like summer rain. 'Now,' she said, sitting astride him, letting him slide into her.

'Sweet blessed Jesus!'

His hands moved across her in wonderment, touching face and breast and belly — the solid jutting shape of the child — as she rose and fell against him, a steady rhythm.

'Kiss me,' she commanded, her mouth moving forward to meet his.

Moonlight washed over them, highlighting the contours of body and bed. A desultory breeze stirred the air. Jenna felt herself sliding away, Adam's thrusts taking her somewhere else as they danced like pagan fairies.

CHAPTER 21

The next morning I stand in the shed, looking up at the bike. It's slung from a hook on the wall, just out of my reach. Cobwebs link the spokes. The tyres are layered with dust. Several spiders glare balefully from under the seat, as though daring me to disturb them.

There's a movement behind me. Brad's standing in the doorway, his body outlined against the early-morning glare.

'There you are. I was looking for you. Want to tag along with me today?'

He's asked me to go with him every day since the last. But I always refuse. It's easier, somehow, to stay away. I wave his offer away with a smile.

'No, I've been summoned. Ella sent a message with Stan to come for morning tea. So I thought I'd ride over today. Do you think you could lift the bike down?'

Once it's on the ground, Brad eyes the bike doubtfully and gives the back wheel a cautious turn. 'It's pretty rusty and the tyres are flat.'

The feeling of anticipation inside me collapses. I haven't realised, until this moment, how much I've been looking forward to getting away, doing something by myself. Something, I think guiltily, that doesn't involve Brad.

'Don't worry,' I counter despondently. 'Perhaps I'll walk.'

'Hang on a sec.'

He rummages further in the depths of the shed and brings out a can of oil and a bicycle pump. He dribbles a few drops of oil on the chain, whirls the back wheel again and pumps up the tyres. We stand around, arms folded, waiting for the tyres to deflate — it seems to be that kind of bike: unreliable — but the air holds.

After a few minutes, Brad dusts off the seat and climbs on. He rides once around the yard, pedalling hard, head down, dodging the clothesline and several straggly trees. He's being silly and that makes me laugh.

'There, madam,' he says, sliding to a halt in front of me and pointing to the garden hose. 'Your little red sports car awaits. I'd give it a quick run through the car wash first, though. You don't want any creepy-crawlies tagging along.'

Brad leaves and methodically I finish my chores. Washing up, making the bed, sweeping away the endless layer of dust that gathers on the floor and the surfaces of the furniture. I pause over the contents of Betty's box, still sitting on one end of the kitchen table. The diaries look drab and forlorn. The cover of one is torn and I fight back an impulse to hunt for some glue and paste it back, restoring it to its proper condition. But I push aside the urge. The sun is shining and I need to be out in the fresh air.

I'm normally a social creature, and my self-imposed exile since Kadie's death is uncharacteristic. I've missed seeing a lot of my friends, foregone the impromptu outings and dinner parties. I could never be bothered, couldn't summon the energy or the enthusiasm. I need structure and planning in my life to counteract the chaos in my head, or so I tell myself. Or am I simply punishing myself for being alive while Kadie ...

'No,' I say now, aloud. 'Don't think of that.'

I allow my mind to slide back a few days, to the anniversary. The day after my last field trip with Brad. The day before Stan and Betty's arrival with the box. The lost day. The day I spent lying on my bed, staring up at the ceiling and wishing I could rewrite the past.

I was reliving, yet again, that whole awful interval. Brad fastening Kadie into her seat in the back of the car. Me holding my hand out, catching those first drops of rain. Waving Kadie goodbye.

Blow Mummy a kiss.

Will those words ever leave me?

Kadie bringing her hand to her mouth, pursing her lips, flinging her imaginary kiss in my direction. She's wearing varying shades of pink — girl colours — and, sitting in the back of the car with her blonde hair falling around her face, she looks like a plump little cherub. A cherub with a happy smile.

Brad frowning. Work, work, work. We never spend time together anymore. Kadie never sees you. She'll forget who her mother is.

The words run into each other, accusatory, spinning round in my memory.

Blow Mummy a kiss.

Slam of car door. Kadie waving. Rain falling harder.

It had seemed a day like any other, nothing out of the ordinary. Why didn't I have some premonition, some sense of wrong? I was her mother, dammit! I should have known!

'Talk to me, Jess. Say her name,' Brad had said later on that anniversary day, coming in from his work mid-morning. I opened my eyes to find him standing over me, a look of concern on his face. Why was he home so early? Was he checking on me?

I shook my head and turned away, presenting him with a view of my back. 'I can't.'

'For Christ's sake! You can't pretend she never existed!'

Incredulously I turned back towards him. 'You think that's what I'm doing?'

He'd run his hands distractedly through his hair, fingers moving mechanically. 'I need to talk about her, not hide her away like some shameful secret. We're not the first parents to ever lose a child. I want to say I had a daughter and her name was Kadie, and she was the prettiest, loveliest little girl —'

His voice broke and I'd felt him drawing away, sensed the distance growing further between us, yet I'd been at a loss to know how to repair whatever damage had been done.

For the remainder of the day Brad had been solicitous and caring, and so bloody nice that afterwards I'd hated myself for being so self-absorbed. Go away, I'd wanted to scream. This is my misery. Let me wallow in it. But of course I didn't say the words. They sounded so damn pathetic. It was his misery too.

Yet in some slight way the day hadn't been as bad as I'd expected. Being here on the Diamantina — away from home — is changing me in small ways. There's less to remind me, day to day, of my daughter. Kadie never had a bedroom in this house. She never ran through the rooms or played in the yard. Her toys were never scattered on the floor. Other children may have lived here, but never Kadie. There are no memories here linking me to the past, no emotional attachment.

It's been several nights since I've had the dream. Funny, I think, that I have to come to this place, so far removed from my own home, to find my life reverting to some semblance of normality. And today, tired of my own miserable company, Ella's offer of morning tea seems too good to refuse.

After giving the bike a quick wash, I sling a backpack over my shoulder and wobble my way along the track. It's been years since I've ridden but the adage is true: you never forget. I soon get the swing of it, the intricacies of the pedals and the way the handlebar seems a bit skewed.

I try out the bell, but instead of a brisk ring it makes a kind of kerthunk sound, scaring a flock of spinifex pigeons from the nearby grass. They rise in a squawking cloud, the tufts of feathers on the tops of their heads pushed back in indignation.

After a kilometre or so, I stop beside a muddy water hole. Several pelicans laze on its surface, barely glancing in my direction as I remove a bottle of water from my backpack and take a swig. It's peaceful here, unhurried. Just as I imagine it would have been over a hundred years ago. Had the mysterious Jenna McCabe ever stopped in this same place? I wonder. At some point in time, long past, had she too watched the birds?

I note the swirls in the water, radiating outwards from the birds. Strange to think that one day this land can be dry and barren and the next, teeming with fish and wildlife. Resilient, I think. Always bouncing back from the brink of something. Hot or cold. Wet or dry. Nature picking itself up and, metaphorically speaking, dusting itself off.

Stan and Ella's house is a clone of the one in which Brad and I are living: a squat fibro box surrounded by a deep welcoming verandah. A few straggly trees cast patches of shade on the ground. Washing flaps on a clothesline at the side. I knock on the front door.

There's no reply so I walk around the back, calling Ella's name.

'I'm out here,' she shouts, her muffled voice coming from the direction of one of the sheds near the rear fence.

Ella's making ginger beer. She straightens when I appear in the doorway, waves me inside. 'Come in. I won't be long. Just got to put the tops on these.'

There are dozens of brown bottles lined up in a neat row, waiting to be capped. The aroma of ginger is overpowering, but nice. Ella moves with deft fingers. Her dark face is shiny with perspiration.

'Here. You can help me,' she says, bringing down the handle of the capping machine with a quick thrust. 'Then it'll only take half as long.' She wipes the back of one hand across her forehead, pushing aside a stray strand of hair. 'Gee, I could do with a cuppa.'

We work in silence. Ella crimps on the tops while I pack the finished product into boxes which we push under the bench. 'It's cooler under there,' she says with a grin as we shove the last one into place. 'Don't want the bottles exploding. Lost six in the last batch. What a mess. Glass and ginger beer everywhere. The ants had a ball, though.'

In the kitchen, we wash our hands and Ella fills the kettle. While it comes to the boil she puts a few home-made biscuits on a plate and ladles tea leaves into the pot. I can see through the doorway into the dining and living rooms. There, standing against the walls, are a surprising number of pieces of beautiful furniture — long sofa and several armchairs, chiffonier, piano. Over the fireplace hangs an ornately framed mirror. In the dining area there's a huge wooden table which takes up most of the space, with eight balloon-backed chairs and a matching sideboard. On the sideboard stand the remains of a dinner set. It's Doulton and Co, I know that much, and very old. There's a pretty floral pattern on it and the surfaces are crazed.

I run my hand along the table. 'Solid walnut from England,' says Ella, coming up beside me. 'Isn't it lovely?'

I nod and venture into the living room, staring at the piano. The timber on the case is unmarked and polished to a high sheen. I lift the cover: the ivory keys are intact, but discoloured. Tentatively I press one and a sound, slightly discordant, fills the room.

'Do you play?' asks Ella.

I shake my head. 'No. Tone deaf.'

'It's a Broadwood from London. Circa 1870. Needs tuning but Stan and I have never bothered. We don't play either.'

'It must be worth a small fortune.'

The kettle on the stove is whistling shrilly. Ella shrugs. 'Depends on what sort of value you put on things, I suppose.'

'True. It's all relative. But some of this stuff's very old. How did it come to be out here?'

'How did it come to be in a blackfella's house, you mean?' She softens the words with a wry smile.

Instantly I'm mortified. Is that what Ella thinks I intended? 'Oh, n-no, not at all,' I stammer. 'The Diamantina just seems an out-of-the-way place for what would have been expensive furniture of its time.'

But Ella is laughing, waving away my embarrassment as she walks back into the kitchen and lifts the kettle from the stove. 'That's okay, Jess. I was only kidding. Stan always says I have a weird sense of humour. But I reckon if you can't poke fun at yourself then the world's a pretty miserable place. Right?'

Hesitantly. 'Right.'

Over tea and biscuits, Ella tells me about the furniture. 'It belonged to the O'Loughlins originally, and it was all stored up in the old house when they left this place. Stan and I went up years ago and brought everything down here — what was salvageable anyway. The rain had gotten into some rooms, and the heat out here isn't too kind to some types of wood.'

'What do you mean by the old house? Jack and Betty's place?'

Ella shakes her head and takes another bite of biscuit. A few crumbs fall on the table and absent-mindedly she prods them into a neat pile. 'No. The original O'Loughlin homestead.' Then, 'You haven't been up to see the place?'

'I don't know anything about it. Where is it?'

Ella points to a nearby ridge. 'Just along the river a bit and back in the sand hills. There's a road. It only takes about five minutes by car.'

'And by bike?'

Suddenly I have a need to see the house, the place where this furniture had its origins. But Brad's busy most days and I'd rather go by myself anyway.

'Twenty minutes, maybe.'

'So it's easy to find?'

'Here.' Ella takes a piece of paper and pen from a kitchen drawer and draws a rough mud map. 'You can't see it from the main road, but if you follow this track, just past the claypan, you can't miss it.'

I take the map and open my purse, stash it inside. There's a photo of Kadie inside the front flap of the purse. I catch a glimpse of fair hair and smiling mouth. Ella sees the photo too. 'What a pretty child!' she exclaims. 'What's her name?'

'Kadie.'

The word cracks through the air like a whip. I snap the purse shut, closing off my daughter's face. I turn away, stow the purse in my backpack and, when I turn back, Ella is staring at me, a bewildered expression clouding her face.

'Jess, I'm sorry. I didn't mean —'

'So,' I say, interrupting, changing the subject with one short word. 'You were telling me about the house. Is there much left of the place?'

'The house! Umm. Well, I'd be careful poking around. The structure could be a bit dodgy and you wouldn't want something to fall in on you. There's also the chance of spiders and snakes this time of year.'

'Oh.' Now my interest is aroused, is she trying to dissuade me from going?

'But it's worth a look if you're keen.'

'Oh, I am.'

'Well, you might like to see this then.'

Ella shows me an old sepia photograph of a man sitting on a chair, with a woman standing behind him. It's mounted on thick board. 'Remember Stan was telling you a few nights ago about how the O'Loughlin brothers first came to the Diamantina? Well, this is Adam and Jenna on their wedding day.'

'Jenna McCabe was Adam O'Loughlin's wife?'

Ella shrugs. 'I don't know what her surname was before she married. But Jenna's not a very common name, so I suppose it has to be the same. Why?'

'I have her diaries back at the house.'

'I didn't know she'd left any.'

'Betty brought me over a box of old stuff yesterday and they were among it all.'

'So what do these diaries say?'

'I don't know,' I admit sheepishly. 'I haven't looked.'

A frisson of curiosity is building inside me. Everywhere I go, someone seems keen to tell me the story of the O'Loughlins. And the box of old paperwork that Betty has brought me — well, its arrival in my kitchen now seems more like fate than coincidence. Suddenly I know that when I go home I'm going to take the diaries and transcribe them, reveal their contents.

'I'd be interested to know if there's any reference to Stan's great-grandmother,' Ella is saying.

'Ngayla?' See, I've remembered her name.

'Yes, Ngayla. We know certain things from the stories that have been passed down the generations, but a diary, written at the same time perhaps that Ngayla came to Diamantina Downs — that'd be something, wouldn't it?'

As I'm leaving, Ella gives me the photograph of Jenna and Adam, and two bottles of ginger beer. 'Put the photo with the diaries,' she says. 'It belongs there.' Then she places the bottles of ginger beer in a plastic bag, one of those supermarket types which I sling over the handlebars of my bike. 'Take care, Jess,' she says, and there's a softness to her voice, a hint of compassion.

'Thanks. You too.'

I stand there, not knowing what to say, wishing in some way that I could blurt it all out. Kadie. The accident. The fact I can't seem to accept what's happened. How it's driving Brad and me apart.

Part of me wants to open my purse again, show Ella Kadie's photo. That's my daughter I want to say. She was bright and funny and I'd give anything to have her back again. But I know that mentioning Kadie's name will cause something inside me to burst. I'm like a dam wall, I think, with water lapping the top.

'Feel free to come over again whenever you feel like it. And let me know if there's anything in the diaries.'

I turn away, wishing for a moment that I could simply hug Ella, feel her arms holding me tight too. I have a need for closeness with someone, anyone — except Brad. I don't need sympathy. I especially don't need someone telling me that I have to move on or that I have to say Kadie's name, as though the actual voicing of the word will make everything right.

But the timing seems awry. I scarcely know this woman, Ella. And what would she think of me, unburdening myself? Brad's always telling me to stop worrying what other people might think, but it's an ingrained response, mostly out of my control.

With a final wave, I wobble back down the track, heading for home. Ella's place merges with the bush and the only noise, apart from the warble of birds and scrape of tyre, is the clink of ginger-beer bottles. All the way home, with every rotation of the pedals, they bash against my knee.

There's no one home when I arrive back at our house, so I take a writing pad and pen, and open the first of the books. 'The Diary of Jenna McCabe' it says inside the cover, in large child-like lettering. The paper is age-speckled and there are a few water stains, but it's good quality and, as I turn to the first page, I see that the writing is reasonably legible. Pen poised and ready to transcribe, I begin to read.

Jenna was, I soon discover, surprisingly literate for her age and the words flow easily, taking me back over a century in time. I can almost imagine myself there, part of that country-town life. I share with her the moment of Michael's birth, her own fear. I suffer with her Mary's emotional abandonment, the snide comments by other townsfolk. I shed a quiet tear as she describes the screams and whinny of horses, and how she found Michael's crumpled body lying on the road.

We have suffered similar pain.

The thought is so sudden, so abrupt, that it almost causes a physical ache. The words, the table, even my hands, blur together into a shapeless mish-mash as I thrust the diary aside, unable for a moment to read further. I take a deep breath, hold it in my lungs for what seems like a long time, then exhale. Then I bring my hands up, resting my elbows on the table, holding my fingers against my temples as though to quell the feeling of grief welling up inside.

I feel an immediate emotional kinship with this woman. Jenna had experienced the death of a child — okay, granted she had not given birth to Michael, but during his short life he had become like a son to her — and had battled similar emotions to my own. Resolutely I bring the diary forward and take up the pen again, anxious to know more.

It's almost dark when Brad comes in. He's been out sampling and he deposits his usual collection of jars and test tubes on the other end of the table. I'm scribbling madly, barely glancing in his direction. 'Hi,' I mumble, trying to decipher a word.

'Hi yourself.' He bends down, nuzzles the side of my neck. 'What's for dinner?'

'Oh, look at the time!'

Reluctantly I drag my attention away from Jenna's words. According to the clock on the wall, it's after six and I've done nothing towards preparing a meal. And now, at this late hour, I can hardly summon the enthusiasm.

'How about toasted sandwiches? I'll cook,' responds Brad, obviously sensing my reluctance. Then, trailing the tip of one finger along the contour of my cheek: 'I missed you today.'

'Really?' I don't even look at him. My attention's more on the page than his words.

'And you: did you miss me?'

Why does he need confirmation of my feelings, this constant reassurance? 'Of course,' I answer matter-of-factly, scraping my chair back and heading towards the kitchen bench.

'Of course? What sort of answer's that?'

How can I tell Brad I've barely thought about him, about us, all day? How can I confess that my attention's been caught instead by the writing of a woman who lived over a hundred years ago, so much so that he hasn't even crossed my mind? There was a time, in the distant past, when we would banter continually in this mode. Confirm this, prove that:

words and intimate touching that proclaimed our love to each other. But these days I don't have the patience for it.

So I tell him what he wants to hear, resorting to deceit and half-truths.

In short, I have become a liar.

CHAPTER 22

Christmas came and went, without fanfare. Adam and Jenna had agreed not to exchange gifts; Adam's finances were poor and he'd known she didn't want to embarrass him. Her determination on paying for a new house was bad enough.

He'd thought long and hard about the house. Some masculine part of him felt worthless, both by her proposal and his reluctant agreement to the idea. As the husband, he should be the provider. What man let his wife finance the building of the family home? He'd had his plans. A couple of years spent getting the sheep numbers up, fencing, making do, saving his money. Then, when Diamantina Downs was thriving and he'd accumulated enough capital, he'd been prepared to build a house bigger and better than any for miles around. A fine house. A country squire's home. Something he could be proud of.

But Jenna wouldn't wait.

'It's not important who pays for things,' she said

when he'd brought up the subject again, several days after their marriage.

'It is to me.'

'Oh, Adam.'

The words had come on a drawn-out sigh and she'd moved towards him, wrapping her arms around his chest. She'd held him tight for a brief moment, before releasing him. Even now he remembered the clean fresh smell of her hair.

'It's only money,' she went on. 'It won't buy us happiness but it may provide a measure of contentment. There's nothing else out here to spend it on. Why not be comfortable?'

Why not indeed? From the little she had told him, Adam knew Jenna had led a miserable life. Meeting Conor had been a bright spot in the midst of several dark years. Now that Conor was gone too, who was he to deny her? What she'd said on the day of their marriage had made sense. The hut was unbearably hot in summer and freezing in winter. A dirt floor was no place for a child to play and the space was very cramped. Conor's son or daughter deserved more than a smaller replica of the cottage they'd grown up in in Ireland.

'Here,' she said later, sitting beside him with a large sheet of paper. 'Let's do some rough sketches then we'll have plans drawn up.'

They'd had fun for a few nights, designing the house. Adam had thought something modest with two or three bedrooms, a parlour and kitchen. But Jenna had other ideas. She wanted a study and music room, and a formal dining room with space enough to seat twenty people. The kitchen must have a pantry, she insisted, the size of a small bedroom. And speaking of bedrooms, she planned at least half a dozen. 'For guests,' she told Adam firmly. 'And there'll be more children.'

She had grand designs for a tennis court and cricket pitch, and a small race course. 'I can just see it,' she exclaimed, clapping her hands together with excitement. Adam had never seen her so enthusiastic. 'We'll be like the English landlords. Hunting and fishing. Horse races. Games on the lawn. What about croquet? As this land around here becomes more settled, people will come from miles away to visit. We'll never be lonely.'

'Are you?' he asked.

'Am I what?'

'Lonely?'

She sat still for a moment, considering the question, frowning. Then she smiled and scraped the chair back, reaching automatically towards her apron which lay discarded on the bench. 'Lonely? Goodness me, no. I haven't time to be lonely.'

He watched as she fastened the ties, the fabric stretched taut over her belly. Her face was turned away and he saw only the profile of cheek and nose, the dark mass of her hair.

Yet again, something about her reminded him of Mam, and he was struck once more by the similarity. His thoughts flew back over the years, remembering how his mother had sat in the kitchen in the cottage in Ireland, the same day the bailiff had first come. Adam had seen none of her features then either, simply the silhouette of her face outlined against field and sky. Mam and Jenna: years and worlds apart yet there was the same proud thrust of chin, and apron swelling out with the shape of the child.

'Jenna?' he ventured tentatively.

She turned, faced him. There was a set, resolute tightening of her mouth, a defiance of sorts. 'I'm fine, Adam,' she said, the tone of her voice not encouraging confidences. 'Don't fuss. Really, I'm fine.'

Who was she trying to convince? he wondered as he turned his attention back to the house plan. Herself or him?

His own contribution to the design was a small second-floor tower that would be reached by an internal staircase. He wanted, he told Jenna, to be able to sit up there, as high as the roof when the need overtook him, and look out over the land. 'It'll be like a lighthouse without the sea,' he explained. 'A vantage point.'

Finally, when neither of them could add any more suggestions, on the advice of the bank manager in town Adam forwarded the sketch to a firm of architects in Brisbane: Bignall & Sons.

Suddenly it was a new year — 1874. Jenna and Adam stayed up until midnight to mark the occasion. He had some whisky, left over from the bottle he'd purchased to commemorate their wedding, and poured her a small measure. 'To celebrate,' he said, raising his glass towards her in salute. 'You and me.

Our marriage. A new year. The safe arrival of Conor's baby.'

They were sitting on the verandah, facing each other. The night was very dark with no moon to illuminate the countryside. From the lamplight that spilled through the open window, Adam saw the sad expression on her face.

'Another year gone and so much has happened,' she said, looking pensive, her chin resting in her cupped hands.

'Perhaps this new year will bring welcome change?' he offered.

'I dare not hope, because hoping may jinx us.'

'My mother used to say "the bad luck that is not on us today may be on us tomorrow". Is that what you mean?'

'Something like that.'

'What if there is no more bad luck?' he persisted. 'What if each person is allotted only so much misfortune in their life, and you and I have already used ours up?'

Jenna took a deep breath. 'I try to be optimistic, really I do,' she assured him. 'But some days it seems so hard.' She rose, putting one hand on the verandah railing to steady herself. She was exhausted, he knew, and midnight had come and gone. 'If you don't mind, I think I'll go to bed.'

He watched her move towards the interior of the hut, her body cumbersome with the child. As she passed, she leaned down and brushed her lips across his forehead.

'Goodnight, Jenna.'

'Goodnight, Adam.'

Sometimes, he thought, relations were so bloody civilised between them. Certainly she had taken him to her bed on the night of their wedding, and for that, and the subsequent nights they had shared that same bed, he was grateful. However, as the weeks wore on, he was aware of something lacking. There was no spontaneity to their lovemaking. It seemed more like a ritual, a duty she had decided to perform. As though she owed him something, though what he wasn't sure.

She didn't love him, he knew that. Not that she'd come right out and said it, but it was something he sensed. Her cheerfulness sometimes seemed forced. On several occasions he'd come home unexpectedly during the day and found her crying. She'd turned away, dabbing furiously at her eyes. 'Look at the time!' she'd said. 'Almost noon already and the washing not yet finished!'

Hiding her emotions, not including him, surprising him with her sudden about-changes: this wasn't how Adam had imagined marriage to be. At times like these he badly wanted to take her in his arms and stroke away her tears, but she'd put up a barricade between them with those clipped words.

Once, in the advanced throes of lovemaking, Adam thought she called his brother's name. It came to him on the wind, a breathless drawn-out sigh, tossed and buffeted by a surging froth of emotion. *Conor*, he imagined she'd said, the word dying away in her throat. Later he wondered if he had dreamed it.

She was tiring more easily these days, relying more and more on Ngayla's help. Sometimes the nights were worse than the days and he knew she slept badly. In the dark, long after the lamp was extinguished, the heat simmered inside the hut, trapped by the thick log walls and brush roof. The air was alive with the buzz of mosquitoes, and their skin was damp with sweat. He often woke to find her sitting up in bed, hugging her knees. Or sometimes the bed would be empty altogether, and he'd go to the kitchen and find her sitting at the table, a wide-eyed, worn expression on her face, elbows propped on the rough timber as she sipped a cup of tea.

'Can't sleep?' he'd ask lightly, sitting beside her.

'No.'

He'd rise, not knowing what else to say to her — sorry seemed such a useless, useless word — and press his mouth against her hair.

'Come back to bed. I miss you there.'

'Soon.'

Sometimes he'd find her in the front yard, pacing up and down the dirt in the moonlight, arms wrapped around herself, or hands running distractedly through her hair. 'Come back inside,' he'd say, worry starting low in his gut.

'It's too hot,' she'd reply, so he'd walk with her a little, talking quietly about inconsequential things, calming her, eventually leading her back to bed.

In the mornings, she seldom remembered.

Thoughts of Conor were never far from Jenna's mind. She missed him unbearably, hating the days, weeks and months since she had last seen him. Yet, despite her grief, she was comforted somehow by the child, the way it kicked solidly against the wall of her belly, or seemed to roll and tumble inside her, making her catch her breath with wonder. Conor's baby. A son to carry on the O'Loughlin name. A fair-haired blue-eyed boy. She couldn't wait to hold him, touch him, and the waiting seemed intolerable.

Jenna counted the days until she thought the child was due, marking them off in her diary. Thirty. Then twenty. *There are always people coming and going from the hut*, she wrote by lamplight in the diary after the day's chores had been completed. *Stockmen, the women from the camp who come to help me, help I need now more than ever. Some days I am so tired ...*

Her disposition alternated between despondency and elation, often hovering somewhere in between. During the daylight hours she found herself consumed by a restless energy. Cooking, cleaning, sewing: filling the time with sometimes unnecessary tasks. She was afraid that if she stopped for a moment and was still, then the memories would come rushing back. Conor, Michael and her mother: previous sorrows that lingered. Their faces would merge, tangling together in her mind, coming at her when she least expected them and sapping her strength. So she tried to close her mind to all but the present, letting the minutes slide by unnoticed until suddenly it was night again and she was one day closer.

The hours of darkness passed more slowly. When sleep eluded her, she slipped from the bed she shared with Adam and made her way to the kitchen, preparing a cup of tea. Sometimes he'd stumble into the room later, screwing his eyes against the light, a look of concern on his face. 'Don't fuss,' she'd say, 'go back to bed. I'm fine, really I am.'

At times like this she didn't need his company, didn't want to talk and lay her feelings bare. That was what Adam expected, to dissect it all, dredge up past hurts. He seemed to think that by talking, the misery would somehow be made less. But all she wanted was to be by herself, to savour the solitariness. It was her pain and she wanted to contain it.

On other nights she walked down the front steps into the dark. It was cooler there, under the trees, a faint breeze rustling the leaves. She heard the shriek of crickets and cicadas, the flap-flap of a night bird's wings as it passed close overhead.

She paced restlessly up and down the outer length of the hut, trying to suppress the ravages of grief that threatened to overtake her. Small puffs of dust rose as she turned and her footprints made a wavering track in the dirt. Then she would stand still, taking deep breaths of air into her lungs, trying to quell the rising sense of panic as she hugged the shape of her child. 'You are my everything,' she said aloud, stroking the curved outline of her belly. 'You will make me whole again.'

This child, she thought. Conceived in love. A miracle, made more so by Conor's passing. Most days, its existence seemed her sole reason to go on.

Sometimes there would be a movement on the periphery of her vision and she would glance back towards the hut. She knew, even before she saw him, that Adam waited there, watching her, his body outlined against the light. Then he'd come down the steps until he was standing before her.

It was moments like these that she felt trapped, cornered. Why had she remained on Diamantina Downs? she sometimes wondered. Had she thought that she could one day replace Conor with his brother; that over time she would come to love Adam? Or had she thought that by staying in this place, where Conor had met such a violent death, that she would somehow remain connected to him?

But it was Adam who held his hand towards her, leading her back into the hut and the bed they shared. Adam brushing the hair from her face as he held her wildly beating heart close to his own. Adam's body, not Conor's, that stirred to hardness above her as emotions were played out on sheets damp with perspiration.

She tried not to make comparisons. Tried hard instead to pretend it was Conor's hands and lips upon her, not her husband's. Desperately she tried to block out the knowledge that the father of her child was dead, imagining instead that it was months earlier, back in town in the large soft bed they'd shared.

Conor, she told herself, over and over again, deceiving both herself and Adam by the thought. Summoning his face to memory, his smile, those laughing eyes.

Conor. Conor. Conor.

Adam was gentle and slow, in deference to her advanced pregnancy. He took time to please her as well as himself, arousing her with long kisses that left her breathless, and hands that cupped and teased. Eventually she felt herself arching towards him, powerless to stop herself as he joined with her in that most intimate of acts, stroking and pleasuring her until she heard her own animal cries as though from far away — not her own voice at all — from another time or place.

And in the morning it would all seem unreal, that night-time pacing and worrying, the caressing and kissing and lovemaking, and she wondered if, in fact, she might not have dreamt it, so blurred and indistinct were the details in her mind.

Excitement ran high in the hut and down at the camp. Aleyne and Lalla chatted and giggled as they went about their work, their attention not fully on their tasks, until Jenna was forced to scold them. 'Girls! Girls! Back to work!' she'd order, waggling a finger at them until they dissolved into puddles of laughter. Nothing, it seemed, could upset them.

The gaiety in the hut was infectious. 'What's going on?' Jenna asked Aleyne, finding her watching from the south-facing window.

'Lookin' for smoke signal, Missy. Or messenger man from 'nother tribe to tell us time to leave.'

'Where are you going?'

Aleyne pointed towards a distant blue-grey ridge of hills. 'Night time full moon — *jiba* — now. Gotta go while plenty light.'

'How long will you be gone?'

'Dunno, Missy,' Aleyne shrugged and shook her head.

'According to Wongaree, there's going to be a corroboree,' Adam told Jenna later. 'It's several days' walk away. They're planning to leave soon.'

'They're going walkabout?'

'That's the general idea.'

Ngayla, as the youngest female and a member of a different tribe, wasn't to go. Instead Adam insisted she would accompany him and Jenna into town, in a few days' time, where they would wait for the birth of Jenna's baby. There was a doctor there, a makeshift hospital and a spare room at the local pub.

At last the messenger came. At first he was a mere speck moving towards them across a distant plain, growing larger as he came closer. The sky was a shimmering blue. On the horizon, heat waves danced up towards the sun. It hurt Jenna's eyes to look. Meanwhile Aleyne and Lalla took it in turns to run to the window, commenting on the man's progress.

It was late afternoon before he arrived at the camp. Adam and Jenna stood at a distance and watched as the messenger hunkered down under a creek wilga, waiting until the tribe members welcomed him with a smouldering firestick. Then he was taken to the humpy that Wongaree and Lalla shared.

The camp slept little that night. Jenna lay on the sweat-soaked sheets, listening to the sounds that came on the slight breeze — clunk of ceremonial stones, chanting that rose and fell. The flames from the fires sent a glow into the surrounding sky.

She thought she'd never sleep, her mind projecting past the goings-on at the camp, to the trip to town and the prospect of the baby. She wasn't afraid. Hadn't she watched her own mother birth Michael? There had been pain, certainly, but the result had been worth it.

Conor's baby.

The words ran through her mind, over and over. Beside her, she knew Adam slept by the slow regularity of his breathing. He was a good man, and kind, and he'd promised to treat the child as his own. She put her hand on her belly, sensing the slow movement within. The mound hardened, then went slack again.

In the dark, Jenna smiled.

'Soon, soon,' she whispered.

By morning, the camp by the water hole was empty. Jenna, accompanied by Ngayla, walked past the deserted humpies and still-smouldering fires. *It seems odd*, she wrote later in her diary, *that they are gone. I have come to depend on the women and their presence is company for me. Now there is just myself, Adam and Ngayla, and it is so quiet. Tomorrow we will leave for town.*

She spent the day tidying the hut and packing clothes into a suitcase, stopping occasionally to rest. The heat was unbearable, sending a constant trickle of perspiration across her brow and down her back. Late afternoon, the three of them walked to the water hole. Adam helped her down the bank and she paddled in the shade of a sprawling gum, wriggling her toes in the water. Her feet ached and the water felt cool and soothing.

It was as she was walking back to the hut that she felt the first pain. It was sharp and sudden, bringing her to a halt.

'What's wrong?' asked Adam, concerned.

'Oh, nothing.' Quickly she dismissed it; the baby wasn't due, surely, for another fortnight. 'Just a niggle. I've been having them for days now.'

Though none so severe as this, she didn't add.

It was another hour before the next pain came, hard and strong. She was standing at the kitchen bench, peeling potatoes, and the contraction sent her feeling for a chair. Gratefully she sank onto the seat. 'You're *not* alright,' said Adam, glancing up from a month-old newspaper he was reading.

'No,' she admitted. She brought the palms of her hands up, covering her face as she took a deep breath.

Instantly he was beside her. 'The baby's coming.'

'It can't be. It's too early. A false alarm, maybe.'

The moment passed, only to repeat itself ten minutes later.

Adam led her to the bed. 'Just rest,' he ordered. 'It's been a hot day and you're exhausted. We'll leave for town in the morning.'

She took his hand, squeezed it. 'You'd best be forgetting town,' she said. 'Somehow I don't think this baby's going to wait until morning.'

The hours passed, agonisingly slowly. Dusk became night. Midnight came. One o'clock, two. Adam boiled water as Jenna instructed, and tore old sheets into manageable squares. From time to time he held a glass of water to her lips, urging her to drink. Sometimes she did. Other times she turned her head away, her eyes dark and hollow in her face. Pain was etched there, across her brow and in those same eyes.

At midnight he sent Ngayla to her bed in the kitchen. 'I'll call you,' he assured her, 'if I need you. Meanwhile, one of us should get some rest.'

Silently he berated himself. Why hadn't they gone to town earlier? One day, that was all that was needed to put Jenna into safer care. But out here ...?

He didn't know what to do next. Grimly he remembered Mam's last baby, how he'd waited outside on the step, hearing her screams, and felt a shiver of apprehension. But Jenna didn't scream. Instead he watched as she arched her back, closing her eyes against the regular relentless pain. She bit her lip — already there were small flecks of blood on her skin. He took a damp cloth and wiped it across her forehead. He stood at the window, staring out into the night, feeling inadequate. He paced the room, back and forth, waiting, waiting.

Nothing seemed to be happening.

At daylight, with Ngayla's help, Adam bathed Jenna and helped her into a fresh nightgown. The morning was hot already, oppressive, threatening rain. He wished long and hard that the heavens would open, pour torrents of cooling water onto the earth. From time to time he heard the drum roll of thunder and the clouds hung low, hugging the distant hills.

But nothing came of it.

Inside the hut was like a furnace. Adam offered to carry Jenna outside, into the cooler shade of the surrounding trees, but when he tried to lift her she cried out with such intensity that he was forced to lay her back on the sweat-sodden sheets.

A breeze finally came when the day drew long shadows outside and the air was shrill with the scream of cicadas. Inside the hut, Jenna was lethargic and pale, her breath long and shuddering.

He drew Ngayla aside. 'It's taking too long. I have to do something.'

'Maybe baby stuck. Happens sometimes.'

He went to the basin and washed his hands thoroughly with soap and water. Then he dried them and went to Jenna's side. 'I'm sorry,' he said. 'This is probably going to hurt but I have to feel for the baby's head.'

She nodded and closed her eyes. 'Do whatever you have to. I can't ...'

Her voice faded and the thought crowded in his mind: *we're going to lose her.*

Frantically he felt his way under the sheet and between her thighs. Obligingly she raised her legs. 'Can you feel anything?' she asked on a deep breath.

He probed further, felt something hard: the baby's head.

'It's just there,' he said.

His hand, when it came away, was covered in blood.

'You gotta sit up, Missy,' added Ngayla, crouching down on her haunches in the middle of the room. 'Like this. Blackfella way. Much easier.'

Amidst protestations, Adam helped Jenna into a squatting position on the bed, he and Ngayla supporting her on each side. He didn't know if this was the right or wrong way to birth a baby, but he sensed Jenna had little choice. She was weak and sagged against him. 'I haven't the strength', she whispered. 'Please let me lie down.'

'You can do it. Come on, think of the baby.'

There was blood dripping beneath her onto the bed. It spread in a slow dark stain. Would she bleed to death? Adam felt her body tense with another contraction. 'Push, Jenna!' he shouted.

Her voice came on a whisper, dry as paper. 'I can't.'

'You have to push this baby out. It can't do it by itself.'

She gave one half-hearted thrust.

'No! Harder! You have to push harder!'

His voice held a hint of desperation. She raised her face to his and stared at him with glazed eyes. 'If you don't,' he added bluntly, 'then your baby will die. Is that what you want?'

She shook her head and tears clouded her eyes.

'Then for God's sake, Jenna! Push! Do it for your child. Do it for Conor.' She clutched his arm, fingers digging into flesh. *Please, God, give her strength*, he prayed silently. *Let this child live when so many others have died.*

She bore down.

He could see by her face, the way her cheeks puffed out with the exertion and the deep furrows that criss-crossed her forehead, that she was summoning the last of her strength. If the child wasn't born soon, he sensed he'd lose both of them, and the thought was unbearable.

Jenna exhaled the last of her breath and took another, pushed again. A dark mass appeared between her legs then receded.

'That's it!' Adam yelled. 'It's coming now. Keep pushing.'

Gasping, Jenna brought one hand down and touched the top of the baby's head. 'Oh, my God,' she said, her voice filled with awe.

'See,' he encouraged, 'almost there.'

Somehow that one simple act seemed to renew her strength. Jenna sagged forward onto her knees and painfully, inch by inch, the baby's head appeared. And just when he thought she could push no more, when he believed she had used whatever reserves of energy remained, the baby slithered into his waiting hands.

Exhausted, Jenna fell back against the sheets, bringing her hands to her face as the baby gave one loud cry. Adam could see tears beneath her fingers.

'Is it alright? What is it?' she cried out. 'Tell me. There's nothing wrong?'

Gently Adam wiped the baby clean and Ngayla cut the cord. 'It's a girl,' he said, placing the baby in a clean shawl and handing her to Jenna.

'I have a daughter?'

She unwrapped the shawl, counting fingers and toes, marvelling over the tiny hands and feet. Then she shed a few more tears and Adam felt his own eyes mist over. If only Conor could be here, he thought, to see this miracle of birth.

'Thank you, Adam,' she said later. 'I couldn't have done it without you.'

'Nonsense. You would have managed.'

She gave a shaky laugh. 'I doubt it.' Then: 'What do you think of the baby?'

'Well, she's quite perfect, and the prettiest girl for miles around. Except for you,' he assured her quickly. 'She'll have her work cut out to be prettier than her mother.'

'Oh, Adam, you say the silliest things.'

'I'm serious. I think you're beautiful, Jenna, and when I saw you there with the baby for the first time ... Well, I wished that Conor could ...'

His voice caught in his throat and for a moment he was unable to continue.

She reached out and took his hand, and her fingers felt comparatively soft against his calloused palms. 'It's no use looking back, Adam. What's done is done and there's no changing that. We're a family now, and that's what we have to think about. We'll never forget Conor, and we know he lives on in our little girl.'

They were silent for a while and there was no other sound coming from inside the hut except for the ticking of the clock. 'What do you think we should call her?' Adam asked at last.

Jenna looked thoughtful. 'I've always thought Kathryn a pretty name.'

'She'd be called Katie.'

'Katie,' she repeated, sounding the word. 'I like that.'

'Me, too.'

So it was decided. Adam stood looking down on the baby after Jenna was asleep. Tiny miracle, he thought. Dark thatch of hair like her mother. Pale milky skin and rosebud mouth. Fingers that curled and uncurled, clutching at air. He put his own finger there, under hers, and for a moment he felt the pressure of her hand against his.

Kathryn O'Loughlin. Katie for short.

He felt a surge of love — so strong, so pure, that he thought he might cry out with the wonder of it — towards her, this child of his brother. Katie was his future, his and Jenna's, and their reason for going on. Somehow they'd make a fist of this marriage, despite its inauspicious beginning. And they'd make this place, Diamantina Downs, one of the finest properties in the area, a legacy for this newborn child who lay sleeping before him.

CHAPTER 23

For several days the sky is grey, and periodic showers drift like a white veil across the landscape. Pulling on his Wellington boots, Brad goes out each morning to the closest water hole, a kilometre away. He's tried taking the 4WD but the black-soil mud simply cakes on the tyres and they spin uselessly. So he's abandoned the vehicle and it's just him and Harry the kelpie walking away from me across the paddock, head bowed and shoulders hunched against the sleety rain.

There have been some heavy storms up north. Brad informs me the river level is up and that the mild flooding means the fish will start breeding. He's in the process of completing a bird survey, inspecting certain bends in the river where the waterbirds are nesting in large colonies, and he's hoping we're still here when the chicks hatch.

Only yesterday he brought home a large speckled egg which had been kicked out of one nest and gone cold. Thoughtfully I'd weighed it in my hand, feeling the leaden substance of it, wondering what mother bird could be callous enough to cast aside her unborn young, and pondering upon the vagaries of nature. Here on the Diamantina, birth and death depend on chance and luck. Survival is a lottery. I suppose that applies to birds as well.

Two letters arrive: one from my parents and one from Carys. I read their words through a haze of homesickness. How are you, Jess? they've written. How's life in the bush? I remember how they were after Kadie's death, just twelve months earlier. They'd been devastated, of course, walking around dazed, saying little but hugging each other constantly. That's one thing about my family: we're a bunch of huggers.

We've not had much to do with Brad's family. I'd never known my father-in-law; he died before Brad and I met. There's a brother, who lives overseas, and Brad's mother, naturally. 'She's not a particularly nice person,' Brad had told me early in our relationship. 'She's cold and manipulative. After my father died she moved to the opposite side of the country. Western Australia. I keep my distance.'

I'd only ever met her twice in all the years Brad and I have been together. The first time was at our wedding. She was tall and angular, thin almost to the point of gaunt, immaculately groomed, with a perpetually sour expression on her face. She gave us a hideously expensive (and hideously unattractive) vase as a wedding present. I keep it in a cupboard, locked away. The second time was when she turned up, unannounced and unexpected, at Kadie's funeral.

She moves constantly, from house to house and town to town. Although they rarely connect, Brad receives an occasional postcard, informing him of her new address. 'She's unhappy,' he tells me. 'So she thinks that by moving, by finding the perfect place to live, she'll somehow be miraculously transformed. But what she doesn't realise is that happiness doesn't come from four walls. It has to be inside you in the first place.'

Over the years he's rarely mentioned her, seems reluctant to discuss her with me. In due course, Kadie and I became his family, a substitute for the people who should have been there for him, but weren't.

Meanwhile, in this place called Diamantina, I'm content to curl up in one of the comfortable armchairs on the verandah, listening to the rain drumming on the roof as I methodically work my way through the station journals and Jenna's diaries. The weather has turned cooler and I'm glad of the jumper I decided to pack at the last minute. I stop from time to time and make a cup of hot chocolate, which I sip while staring out over the bleak sodden landscape. There's a comfort to be found sitting on the verandah, snug and dry, watching as the moisture drips from the trees and clouds scud across the grey sky.

These diaries and station journals have been the first things, apart from the occasional weekly women's magazine, that I've read for ages. Since Kadie, in fact. I'd always been a bookworm, even as a teenager — hadn't I loved the job I'd had in the library where I met Brad? — but since Kadie I've lost the heart for it.

Until now.

Over the years I'd worked my way through the classics. Tolstoy, Steinbeck, Waugh and Dickens. Then for a while I had a penchant for women writers and I'd eagerly devoured the Brontë sisters and Austen. Then there was poetry — Coleridge and Keats, Tennyson, through to Auden and Slessor.

Slessor was my favourite — 'Five Bells'.

> *Deep and dissolving verticals of light*
> *Ferry the falls of moonshine down ...*
> *Night and water*
> *Pour to one rip of darkness ...*

Had the poem been a prophecy, a porthole into the future? Now the words remind me of my recurring dream, of those faceless men chasing me through the night and the cold water of the river I must swim across.

> *So dark you bore no body, had no face,*
> *But a sheer voice that rattled out of air ...*

Then later in the poem, all I can think of is Kadie.

> *Where have you gone? The tide is over you,*
> *The turn of midnight water's over you,*
> *As Time is over you, and mystery,*
> *And memory, the flood that does not flow.*

Remembering, I blink away the threatening tears.

After Kadie's death I'd found myself wallowing in a mire of mindless television instead of reading. It's a medium that doesn't require me to think or analyse, or pay close attention, where I can let my mind wander where it chooses. So, in a way, these old books are a return to the former full-of-life Jess, to the me that was.

The pages of Jenna's diaries are old and sometimes brittle. Some have been eaten around the edges — by mice or cockroaches? — and the ink has faded with time. I've borrowed one of Brad's blank notebooks and I'm transcribing mostly as I go, copying Jenna's faint, sometimes almost indecipherable, words into my own legible ones. Sometimes my progress is slow. I pause occasionally over a sentence, trying to make out a letter here or a word there. In the margins of my pad I jot little reminder notes to myself. Check this. Find out more about that.

I try to imagine what it would have been like for Jenna, coming to the Diamantina over a century earlier. *This is a strange place*, she'd written during her first week. *Sometimes I think Aleyne resents me for being here. Maybe she's hoping I'll leave so she won't have to clean away the cobwebs and blacken the stove ...* Then: *Perhaps I'm too hard on them.*

Jenna had arrived on the Diamantina full of hope for her own future and Conor's, and that of their unborn child. Then suddenly, with Conor's death, that hope had been torn from her. How many lonely tears had she cried at night into her pillow? How many times had she picked herself up and gone on, when all around her seemed hopeless? She'd married Adam, though it was clear from her words that she didn't love him. Admired and respected him certainly, and was thankful he'd given her baby his name.

Kathryn O'Loughlin.

Katie.

Kadie …

The names blur in my mind, become one, and my thoughts slip back to the day of my own daughter's birth. That morning had started like any other, Brad and I enjoying a late breakfast in bed. Brad had cooked bacon and eggs and huge slabs of crunchy toast. I remember the crumbs falling on my belly, where my pyjama top had ridden up, and how Brad had bent forward and licked them off.

'Don't! It tickles!'

Laughingly I'd squirmed away from him, pushing him with my hands. So he'd grabbed my fingers, biting them playfully. 'Mmnnn, toast crumbs. Tastes good.'

'Silly.'

He'd kissed me then, long deep kisses that tasted of coffee. His hand had circled my breast and I felt his fingers moving against my skin. There was something about the morning — the pale early-morning sky perhaps, or the way the wind thrashed the branches of the mulberry tree against the nearby window — that made it seem right to stay there, among the rumpled sheets, tracing out fantasies and yearnings against warm skin.

Later, I stumbled out of the shower, my heart racing. Brad was leaning against the basin, shaving. Instantly he'd known by the expression on my face that something was wrong.

'What's up?'

'I'm bleeding.'

He'd stood staring at me for a few seconds, disbelief clouding his face. Our baby wasn't due for another month.

'You're sure?'

My words had a slightly hysterical edge to them. 'For God's sake, Brad! I know blood when I see it.'

'Shit!'

I remember little of Brad's frantic drive to the hospital. There are blurred memories of someone pushing me in a wheelchair, of doctors and nurses hovering, poking and prodding. Hurried whispered words. Images of pads soaked in bright blood, of someone helping me into a hospital gown. I'm lying on a trolley and there's another frantic dash through corridors smelling of antiseptic to the operating room. Huge orb light above. Muted voices washing over me like a sea. Brad's face peering across my shoulder as the world spins into darkness.

Not for me hours of agonising labour or a home birth like Jenna, but the antiseptic sterile confines of a hospital. I'd woken later to a jangle of drips and bandages and a bank of machines that monitored my every movement. 'You were lucky,' the doctor said later. 'The baby's cord was wrapped around her throat. The placenta was coming away and that's what caused the bleeding.'

Lucky! I didn't feel lucky. I felt sore and weak and, in part, a failure. I'd wanted so badly to have a natural birth, to see my daughter's entry into the world. Now all I felt was cheated, robbed of an irreplaceable moment.

The staff kept Kadie in a humidicrib for a week,

and Brad and I had to make do with letting our daughter wrap her hands around our fingers, and stroking her thin legs. The day I'd finally held her in my arms for the first time, I'd cried so hard that I thought my tears might wash us all away — me, Brad and this tiny, tiny baby who had been a part of us both and was now a human being in her own right.

Now, as I stare out over this harsh, sometimes hostile land I know that if I'd given birth out here over a hundred years ago, I would have died. Unconsciously I run my finger under the band of my jeans and across the scar. Hard ridge of flesh level with the top of my pubic hair, still unnoticeable when I wear a high-cut bikini. I sigh and return to Jenna's diary, the one where she describes holding her daughter for the first time. *I held her to my breast and somehow the memory of all the pain and anxiety and discomfort of the past day has dissolved. I'm in awe of this tiny perfect baby,* she'd written. *My daughter. Kathryn. Katie.*

I know how she felt.

Carefully I copy her words.

After several days, the rain stops and the sun comes out. It's hot and humid. Thousands of little black bush flies have appeared from nowhere and they crawl over every available surface, up noses and into eyes. Every time Brad comes in through the door he swipes his back and a cloud of them floats away.

We've been here for three weeks now — halfway through our stay — and Brad's marking time, impatiently waiting for the dirt roads to dry. One day he stays home and we play cards and make pancakes. At times I'm tense, waiting for him to mention Kadie, or the fact that he's ready to be a parent again, even though I'm not. But the words don't come. Instead he's his normal affable self and it almost seems like old times.

That night, for the first time in several weeks, the dream returns.

I'm looking into the back of a car, a sedan, which is being driven away. There's a child there, a small girl. But something's wrong. Like in the previous dream, weeks earlier, this little girl's hair is dark, almost black, whereas Kadie's was fair. And instead of Kadie's short bob, this child has old-fashioned ringlets falling around her face. A lace collar nestles at her throat, and lace cuffs on the long sleeves fall about her wrists. I can see a gold bracelet, half-hidden by the cuffs, on one wrist. I blink, look again, certain I must be mistaken. My mind is playing tricks, trying to confuse me. The child is Kadie. It *has* to be.

She's not in her kiddie seat, which is unthinkable. Instead she's kneeling on the back seat, pale-faced, her tiny snub nose and hands pressed against the rear panel of glass. Her eyes are wide and dark. Her mouth is a gaping hole which opens and shuts, like a fish underwater. Where is my daughter? I ask myself, panic rising. And who is this unknown child?

Mummy! Mummy!

Her pitiful cries are muffled. Her hands curl into fists and bang ineffectually against the glass. As the car pulls away, metre by metre, I sense something terrible is about to happen. Dread fills me and I know I should stop the car, wrench open the door and gather her safely into my arms, this child who is not mine. But my legs refuse to work and my voice is momentarily frozen. The car turns the corner, presenting me with a different profile of the little girl. Slowly it slips away, out of sight. Only then can I feel my throat working, the sound releasing upwards, exploding, like a bubble of air.

Kadie!

My own scream reverberates through my subconscious.

Someone is shaking my shoulder, insistently calling my name, jerking me back to the present. My heart is thumping and there's a wave of panic fighting its way upwards in my chest. A film of sweat coats my forehead. Disoriented, I swing my legs over the edge of the bed, feeling with my toes for the floor. Feeling for something substantial and solid. My eyes are trying to adjust to a room barely illuminated by faint pre-dawn light.

Brad stands before me and takes both my hands in his. His fingers knead mine, claiming my attention, and I raise my face to his. 'Jess, what is it?'

How to explain? I take a deep breath and let the question settle. 'Nothing,' I say at last in a flat voice.

'It was something. I heard you scream.'

'Just a bad dream. It's gone now.'

He's stroking my cheek, wiping my damp hair away from my face. Then he leans forward and pulls me to my feet. We're standing there, inches apart, though it feels that a chasm separates us. Slowly he gathers me into his arms and I rest my cheek against his chest, feeling the solidity of him.

'Jess, precious Jess,' he says, in a voice soft with emotion. 'Don't shut me out. Tell me about your dream.'

I shake my head. 'No,' I mumble, unwilling to share.

Already the images are fading in my mind, blurred by time and space.

The next morning, after Brad has driven off in the 4WD, I think about my home, that tiny inner-city workers' cottage that I've left behind. I remember how I saw it last, as we drove away all those weeks ago. The blinds and curtains had been drawn and already it had seemed abandoned in my mind.

Now, weeks later, the house seems a world away — *is* a world away — from this outback place, and I'm surprised to realise that it's been at least a week since I'd dwelt on it last. Maybe, I think, this place, the Diamantina, is growing on me, becoming more familiar.

I think about my friends, Carys, my parents, and wonder what they'd be doing now. Then I have to remind myself, with a quick calculation on my fingers, exactly what day of the week it is.

It's easy to lose track of time out here. The weekdays have no special meaning, no definition, and our time is governed only by Brad's research. Weekday or weekend: it doesn't matter. And it's odd to wake in the morning and lie there, unrushed, knowing there's nothing more pressing in my life than preparing our next meal.

It has to end, I tell myself. Some time soon this will all be over and we'll be back to timetables and schedules, and eventually I'm going to have to do something meaningful with my life, like go back to work or have another baby. One way or the other, I can't keep stalling, putting my life on hold indefinitely.

On a deep sigh I take the photo of Adam and Jenna from my bag, where it has been since the day Ella passed it into my care. Curious, I turn it over. *Adam and Jenna O'Loughlin* it says in spidery almost-faded ink, followed by an indecipherable date.

Ella had told me the photograph had been taken on the couple's wedding day. If so, the year was 1873 and the month was December. Adam would have been twenty-four years of age and Jenna twenty.

Photographs, I muse, can be deceptive. They're flat and one-dimensional, and they rely on the depiction telling the truth when, in fact, that's not always the case. Move the camera, change the angle, and the result can be quite opposite.

In this one, Adam is sitting on a wooden chair, wearing what appear to be his Sunday-best clothes. And, although you'd never guess from the image, the coat buttoned carefully up to his chest, he must have been unbearably hot on that long-ago summer's day. Jenna is dutifully standing behind him, half-hidden, one extended hand resting informally on his shoulder. She is wearing a dark dress and I study the outline, holding the photo to the light, trying to make out the telltale swell of her belly, some indication of her pregnancy. But there is none, so hidden is she by her husband, even though I now know from the diaries that she was seven months along.

What is a photograph, anyway? I think, pushing it aside. A captured moment in time preserved forever? A superficial pretence comprising outline and contour, and light and shadow? In a photo we only see what the camera wants to reveal. All or nothing. Or some grey ill-defined area in between.

Whatever, the body language between this newlywed couple seems all-telling. Husband and wife are both staring directly at the camera. Jenna is slightly turned away from her husband and Adam's shoulder, beneath his wife's hand, seems rigid, not relaxed at all. And the placing of Jenna's hand on that same shoulder seems more acquiescent than proprietorial. What would the body-language experts make of that? I wonder.

Years ago, on the morning of our wedding, I remember my mother-in-law looking at a photograph that her younger son, Brad's brother, had sent from England. He was sitting on the bonnet of a car with his arm slung around the shoulder of a young English woman. She seemed pretty, with blonde fly-away hair and a shy smile. 'It'll never last,' Brad's mother had declared. 'She's not right for him.'

'How can you tell?' I'd asked, puzzled. Was she trying to read something more into the image, characteristics that didn't exist?

'Well, there's her mouth, for one thing — it's kind of mean-looking. And she's too thin. Look at the way her bones stick out ...'

It had seemed like the pot calling the kettle black, as my own mother would have said. Brad's mother could have been describing herself. I'd turned away, both amused and annoyed. 'How can you know someone from a piece of paper?' I'd asked Brad later.

'You can't. Don't take any notice of her.'

'But photographs aren't like getting to know people,' I'd persisted. 'That's the wonderful thing about close-up personal contact, becoming familiar with someone's moods, their likes and dislikes. What they prefer to eat for breakfast, for instance, and their astrology sign. Whether they like the smell of rain. You can't tell any of that from a photograph.'

'It's her way,' Brad explained patiently. 'My mother doesn't want to lose her son to a woman in another country. She's imagining reasons why he should come home and not get involved. Marry an Aussie girl, not some foreigner.'

Well, Brad's brother had come home, married someone else, then promptly divorced. Then he'd gone overseas again. The last we'd heard from him — a hastily scribbled note telling us how sorry he was about Kadie — he'd been in Mexico.

I'd wondered later if maybe Brad's mother had been wrong. What if the girl with the shy smile and fly-away hair *had* been the right one? And if she had, how would Brad's brother, or his mother, have known? How does anyone know?

I have a friend — twice married and twice divorced — who believes it's totally unrealistic to expect to go through life with the same partner. *The man who's right for you today mightn't be so in ten or twenty years,* she argues. *People change over time, their expectations alter.*

Does that mean that the Brad I met in the uni library, on that cold blustery afternoon over a decade ago, might not be the perfect partner for me now? It's an interesting theory. I shake my head, not knowing, and place the thought firmly aside.

I turn my attention back to the wedding image of Adam and Jenna. Their faces are stern, staring directly at the camera lens. Over the years I've learned enough about photography to know that back in those days it was almost impossible to hold a smile for the length of time it took to take a picture. Yet, despite that, there seems something tense, almost formidable, about their expressions. What had happened to give them such grave faces? The late arrival of the minister or photographer, perhaps? Some farm matter that had soured their day? Or maybe Adam's knowledge that Jenna was still in love with his brother?

Whatever the reason, the photo has endured. And that single stern moment captured on bromide when the shutter clicked, doesn't necessarily indicate the eventual state of Jenna and Adam's marriage. Only the diaries, if Jenna wrote of her true feelings, can tell me that.

I glance at the wall clock, surprised to see it's only ten o'clock. Suddenly I feel the need to get out of the house into fresh air and sunshine. I want to distance myself from the diaries and journals and those long-ago words. I want to see fresh sights, hear new sounds. And the roads seem dry, the rain long gone.

Impulsively I decide to cycle over to the old homestead, to see for myself the house that Jenna and Adam had built.

PART FIVE

Old Ghosts

CHAPTER 24

Jenna laughingly thought Katie the most spoilt baby she had ever known. The black women who came up to the hut fussed over her and picked her up the moment she cried, dandling her on their laps. Adam paced the floor with her at night when some unknown pain made her scream furiously. Even Wongaree came to visit, standing staring at this 'new whitefella baby', offering a pot of native honey. But it was Jenna's breast she searched blindly for during those first days and weeks after her birth, and Jenna who watched the steady rise and fall of her chest as she stood over the rough crib Adam had made.

My daughter, she thought with a constant gasp of wonder. Tiny miracle.

It was the dark hours she enjoyed the most, when it was only herself and Katie awake, the baby's mouth tugging insistently at her nipple. The drowsy hours, when she heard the cry of a night bird and felt the solid substantial weight of her child in her arms. The hours when she inhaled that talcum-soft baby smell, and knew with happy certainty that Katie was hers, and would never be taken away.

A month after Katie's birth, several wagons arrived, carrying the building supplies for the new house. Timber and roofing iron. Glass for the windows. On the top of one wagon sat a white claw-foot bath.

The supplies were followed a few days later by the builder and his labourers. The builder was a florid rotund man who, Jenna soon discovered, was partial to rum and not averse to young girls. Warily she watched Ngayla. She was fourteen now, and impressionable.

Only a few days earlier Ngayla and Jenna had walked down to the water hole, carrying Katie. It was cooler down there, a breeze beginning to stir in the trees. They had paddled in the knee-high water and a few of the native men had come down and were swimming in the deeper section, laughing and splashing each other. Suddenly Ngayla had been quiet and Jenna had glanced up to see her staring towards a straggle of nearby bushes.

It was dusk, the light fading. Jenna saw a dark blur that dissolved with the shadowy leaves. 'Who's there?' she'd called and Ngayla had glanced at her sharply.

A young male had stepped forward and stood by a clump of spinifex, spear in hand. It was Wandi.

He'd said nothing, simply stood staring intently at the young girl. Quickly Jenna gathered up Katie, who had been asleep on a rug. 'Come on,' she'd said brusquely to Ngayla, grabbing her by the arm and dragging her away. 'There are things to do back home.'

Back at the hut, she'd quizzed Aleyne. What did Wandi want? What were his intentions?

'Wandi 'bout to become a man,' Aleyne had replied flatly. 'He needs a woman. Wandi wants Ngayla go longa his *gundi*.'

'Get married, you mean? Become husband and wife?'

'Yair. Make babies like you. Wandi ready.'

'Well, Ngayla isn't. She's too young. You tell Wandi he'll have to wait awhile.'

'How long I say to him?'

'A year at least.'

Aleyne had sniffed and walked off in the direction of the camp, presumably to relate to Wandi the sorry news. Jenna could imagine her, dark face bobbing earnestly up and down. 'Missy says no,' she'd say, awarding a scowl towards the direction of the hut.

'You stay away from Wandi,' Jenna told Ngayla later when they were alone.

Meanwhile, month by month as the house rose from the ground — foundations and floor, walls and roof — and Jenna kept a watchful eye on Ngayla, Katie grew. She smiled and gurgled. She rolled over then crawled. By her first birthday she was tottering around on unsteady legs, laughing as Jenna followed her. She was a delight really, the one common thread that drew her and Adam together.

Jenna tried not to compare, tried not to search for similarities between this precious adored baby — Conor's daughter — and Michael, the brother she had lost. She also tried — oh, how *hard* she tried — to think of Adam as Katie's father, and not the devoted adoring uncle that he was.

'What's my little angel been up to today?' he asked every afternoon. It was a ritual, him coming in before dark and whisking her away to the bathroom.

'Dadda! Dadda!' she'd cry, stumbling in her haste to run to him. Then Adam would swing her high before taking her for a bath.

Jenna would hear the crow of her daughter's laughter from the hallway, the sound of splashing water, and smile.

Meanwhile, she and Adam had waved a relieved goodbye to the builder and his staff, and had moved into the new house a week before Katie's first birthday.

Emerging from the low-lying scrub like an oasis in the desert, the sprawling homestead had been built on a rise, about two miles distant from the hut. A perfect location, Adam had assured her. High enough above the river's highest flood level, though Jenna couldn't imagine water so high, and positioned so it caught the breezes that swept up through the valley. And from the wide verandahs that circled three sides of the house, shielding it from the summer sun or driving rain, there was a view across the river towards the distant blue-grey ranges.

The pepper trees Jenna had planted along the western boundary of the house were quickly growing and now provided shade for those late summer afternoons. Wongaree and Pigeon had built a chook house and stables for the horses nearby, and there were usually half a dozen hens scrabbling in the dirt under the trees. Aleyne's job was to tend to the vegetable garden. Once the tomatoes and cabbages had been established, she planted flower seeds, to provide cut flowers for the house. Now there were stocks and sunflowers, and netting trellises covered with sweet peas, and pansies turning their comical faces towards the sun.

In the house there were several bedrooms, one of which Jenna had decorated as a nursery for Katie. It was large and airy, and spacious enough to contain a cot and robe, and a rocking chair that Jenna placed before the window so she could look at the view while she nursed her daughter. She spent hours there, rocking to and fro, sometimes long after Katie had fallen asleep in her arms. Then she'd place her sleeping daughter in her bed, looking down on her as she slept.

To Jenna, her new home represented previously unknown luxury. The furniture and fittings for the rest of the house — bedrooms, dining and sitting rooms, library, bathrooms, kitchen and study — had been ordered from the city by catalogue, and their arrival was another cause for celebration. There were sofas and chests, beds and lowboys. Mirrors and paintings for the walls. The latest Doulton & Co crockery. Sheffield cutlery. A solid walnut table with matching chairs and sideboard almost filled the dining room. A proper 'Dover' wood stove took pride of place in the kitchen and Ngayla, under Jenna's careful supervision, made endless supplies of scones and cakes and tarts.

When Katie was older, Jenna told herself, her daughter would learn to play the Broadwood piano she'd ordered for the music room. Already she could imagine sing-a-longs and parties, with Diamantina Downs the hub of entertainment for miles around. They'd come from the neighbouring properties — husbands, wives and children — and this large still-echoing house would be filled with laughter and music.

There had been initial resistance from Adam, on all counts. He had wanted, he'd told her, to be the one to provide the contents of their home. 'All in due course,' he'd said, frowning as she'd flipped through the pages of the catalogue, ordering this and that.

'I can afford it,' she'd replied stubbornly. 'Why exist like paupers when we can live like kings?'

Adam had shrugged. 'We're not kings. We're ordinary folk.'

She'd walked towards him then, laying her face against his. 'We're not ordinary!' she'd replied fiercely. 'We're special, and don't you forget it! I spent my childhood being sneered at by *ordinary folk*, and your family existed only from one day to the next. We've managed to fight our way up and out of the mire, you and I, and our children deserve the best.'

'Children?' He'd pulled back, holding her at arm's length, looking amused.

'Yes, children.'

'Well?' He'd traced one finger down the curve of her cheek, then tilted her mouth towards his, kissing her soundly. 'Then we'd better do something about these *children*, hadn't we?'

Later she lay there in the dark, under the weight of him, praying for another baby as he shuddered into her. 'Oh, Lord,' he groaned, burying his face in her hair.

She was still for a while, lying in the curve of his arm, the sheets on the bed thrown back. It was a warm night and the breeze, billowing the sheer curtains over the windows, was a welcome one. Moonlight shafted into the room, highlighting the bed and the dark bulk of the dresser, reflecting off the ceiling. The only sound was the whirr of cicadas in the trees outside.

'Thank you,' she said at last, placing her hand on his chest, near where she imagined his heart might be.

'For what?'

'For marrying me and giving Katie your name. I respect you for that.'

He was quiet for a while and all Jenna was aware of was the rise and fall of his chest. It was like that between them, this kind of formal relationship where she danced around the edges of her feelings, treating him more like a father than a lover or husband. She searched her mind for words to fill the silence between them, but none came.

'Respect?' he said at last, and there was a slightly cynical tone to his voice. 'I married you because I love you.'

Why couldn't she say those same words to him in return?

Because she *didn't* love him.

He knew, she could tell, by his wry smile and the sad way he sometimes looked at her. It was a regretful look, an expression of grief that somehow became tangled up with Conor and that great swirling mess of emotions that had been her past, and his. Would it always be like this? She hoped not. He was a kind considerate man and a wonderful father to Katie. But something was missing, Jenna knew. That spark. That heady feeling that she had known with Conor. Two men, born of the same parents yet worlds apart. Somehow Adam didn't have Conor's joy for life, or the same larrikin appeal.

Perhaps, she sometimes thought, if they had a child together, her feelings for her husband might change. But the months had come and gone, bringing with them those first telltale cramping signs that maybe she would never be a mother again.

Though almost two years had passed since his death, Jenna's thoughts regularly turned to Conor. Sometimes she'd picture him there with them now, could imagine him swinging his daughter up in the air, making her laugh. Could imagine the feel of his hands on her body, the pressure of his mouth on hers.

She dreamed of him. She was running towards him at a frantic pace, calling his name. But no matter how hard she sprinted, how desperate she was to reach him, he seemed to come no closer. Then she'd wake, almost expecting him to be beside her like old times, the dream had been so real. But it would be Adam lying there — solemn, reserved Adam who wanted her so badly to love him.

Then there were dark days when she could scarcely remember Conor's face, his features blurring into an indistinguishable mass. If only she'd had a photograph to remember him by. But there was nothing. Except Katie.

The months wore on. Katie's second birthday came and went, and Lalla and Wongaree celebrated the birth of their first baby. Under pressure from the other members of the tribe, and Wandi, Jenna finally bid Ngayla farewell. Adam insisted on performing his own improvised marriage ceremony where he bound the couple's hands together then cut them loose with a sharp-bladed knife. It was symbolic, he said, of severing his own ties with the girl, and those responsibilities he had assumed for her that day on the river bank, years earlier.

Jenna watched Ngayla head towards Wandi's *gundi* with a mixture of sadness and regret. The girl was only fifteen.

Meanwhile, good summer rains meant lush stockfeed. The last two lambing seasons had been excellent and stock numbers had almost tripled. Adam went into the paddocks most days with the Aboriginal men. Night-times he spent poring over the ledgers and writing up the day's events in the station journal. 'Finances,' he told her, 'are on the up-and-up. Maybe next season we can take a few weeks off, go south for a break in the city.' He placed one hand under her chin, tilting her head upwards. 'Katie will love it and it'll be the honeymoon we never had.'

Jenna thought of the city and the hustle and bustle, and knew she'd feel a stranger there, just as she often felt out of place here. She'd tried to fit in on Diamantina Downs, had tried to love the same things

Adam did about the land. But she felt an emptiness here that the rugged hills and wide flat sweeps of grassland could never fill. She'd built and furnished a lovely home, hoping to ease her pain by surrounding herself with beautiful possessions. But pianos and sofas, paintings and carpets were no substitute for what she'd once had, and lost.

At odd times she thought back to that first morning at Diamantina Downs, the day after she'd learned of Conor's death. She'd wandered down to the water hole and spoken to Lalla about the land, had looked at the sky and hills and trees. 'Perhaps you learn to like?' Lalla had asked hopefully.

But she hadn't.

Why had she stayed? she wondered now. Why had she married Adam and condemned herself to this lonely life? Had she thought that by being here, in this place where Conor had last lived, that she might somehow feel closer to him? But Conor, she remembered, had had no attachment to the land. He'd been planning to leave here as soon as Adam was settled.

There were days when she thought of leaving, but the idea was fleeting. Somehow she couldn't bring herself to take Katie away from Adam who loved her like his own. Besides, she had made a commitment to her husband by agreeing to marry him, and her conscience would never allow her to leave. 'Please God,' she prayed. 'Let there be another child and let me love this man.'

Some nights after Katie had gone to bed, she climbed the stairs with Adam to the small tower room at the top of the house. There they stood at the window, looking out over the unyielding landscape. If the night was moonlit, she could see the outline of trees and the glint of the nearby river. Perhaps, if she stared hard, she might see the fires from the blacks' camp further back and the resulting glow in the sky.

It was peaceful up there. Adam would throw open the window and they'd lean out, taking great lungfuls of air, listening to the night noises. A bat might flap past or a mosquito buzz noisily about her face. It was times like these that she felt closest to him. He'd put his arm around her, drawing her close. 'Look,' he'd invariably say, pointing upwards into the darkness. 'There's Sirius and Orion.'

They shone, those distant stars, pale and cold like diamonds.

One particular night she noticed a wavering light coming towards the house, through the paddocks. 'Quickly,' she called excitedly to Adam. 'It looks like a buggy lamp. We have visitors.'

Adam went downstairs to greet the arrivals while Jenna watched their progress from the tower. The light dipped and wobbled, bouncing from side to side. The buggy was obviously having trouble negotiating the gullies and washaways. After a while Adam came back upstairs. 'No one's arrived. Where are they?' he asked, peering out into the night.

Jenna shrugged. 'Still in the same place. They don't seem to have come any closer. Perhaps they're bogged,' she added although that seemed unlikely. There had been no rain for several weeks.

Adam decided to saddle up one of the horses and ride out. Jenna lit a spare lamp and gave it to him. From her vantage point she saw his progress in the direction of the buggy. He circled the area, keeping a fair distance from the light. What was wrong? she wondered. Why wasn't he moving closer?

She waited and waited, impatient with his progress, drumming her fingers against the windowsill. *Over there*, she wanted to call, directing him, but she knew her voice would never carry that far.

Eventually Adam returned to the house. 'What happened?' she asked. 'Why didn't you bring them back?'

'There was no one there,' he replied quietly.

'Of course there was. How could you miss them? You circled around the light. I *saw* you.'

'Jenna!'

He gripped her shoulders, staring hard at her. 'Believe me, from down there I could see no light. And that bit of countryside is so uneven there's no way a buggy could ever negotiate it.'

'Come back upstairs, then,' she challenged, 'and see if it's still there.'

She ran ahead of him, taking the stairs two at a time. 'Look!' she exclaimed, leaning out of the window. 'How could you miss —'

Her voice died in her throat, the words unsaid. There was nothing below but darkness. No light. No shimmer of illumination. Not even, at this late hour, the glow of the fires from the blacks' camp further back.

Jenna turned to face Adam and they stood for a

moment, watching each other. Adam looked as puzzled as she felt, and a frisson of fear was building inside her, sending a shiver across her shoulders. 'Well?' she said at last. 'If it wasn't a buggy lamp, then what was it?'

Adam shook his head.

'Adam!'

He leaned forward and closed the window with a bang, and the light from the room shone against the glass, blocking out the view. All Jenna could see was the reflection of her own concerned expression. Resolutely she turned away, facing her husband. 'It can't be *nothing*! You saw it. I saw it. We couldn't both have imagined it.' She paused for a moment, contemplating her words. 'Could we?'

Adam shrugged and picked up the lamp. 'I don't know. The only fact I'm certain of is that no one was there. *No one.*'

The image of that dancing bobbing light stayed with her for days. At random times, both day and night, she stole up the stairs and watched from the window. But the view stayed the same. Adam scoured the area for tracks and found none. There was, he told her, no evidence that anyone or anything had been in the vicinity.

Finally, several days later, Jenna told Aleyne about the unusual sighting. The black woman listened in silence, her eyes growing rounder as Jenna recounted her story. When she reached the part where Adam had saddled the horse and gone in search of the light, Aleyne took several steps backwards. 'No, Missy,' she whispered, looking fearful. 'Me no want to hear.'

'Why? You know what it is, don't you?'

Aleyne shook her head, her dark hair bobbing around her face. 'Bad spirits there. You tell Mista Adam stay away from debil-debil light.'

Slowly, piece by piece, Jenna prised the information from the black woman. The natives were clearly terrified of the mysterious lights that appeared at irregular intervals, wavering and beckoning in the darkness. Sometimes there were years between sightings. At other times they appeared frequently, though at no particular time of the month or phase of the moon.

Of one fact, though, Aleyne was adamant. Anyone who followed the light and caught it would never return to tell the tale.

Jenna decided to put the whole episode aside. There was some logical explanation for the light, but Aleyne had tied it up with Aboriginal lore and her own version of spirits and devils.

Jenna didn't have time for such nonsense.

'Forget it,' she told Adam later. 'We've more important things to deal with.'

It was late summer and Adam was away for a few days, mustering stray stock. As evening fell, Jenna fed Katie and put her to bed. It was too hot to eat, she thought, running herself a cold bath instead. As she lay there, the water warming around her, her thoughts turned to the babies she feared she'd never bear.

It was over two years since her daughter's birth. Each month she waited anxiously, only to have her hopes dashed. She and Adam had both spoken of their wish for a large family — children to fill the sprawling house she'd built in anticipation, brothers and sisters for her daughter. Katie needed playmates. And although he loved Katie, Adam, she knew, wanted a child of his own. With Conor she had fallen pregnant so easily — too easily — yet after two years with Adam she still waited.

Unconsciously she ran her hand across her still flat belly and down between her legs, feeling a tremor of desire. If only Adam was here now. She would take him to their bed and —

Her thoughts were interrupted by a loud banging on the bathroom door. No matter how many times she had instructed Ngayla to be quiet, the girl only made noises at full volume. With a sigh Jenna slid from the water and pulled on a robe. 'Shhh,' she said, opening the door. 'Katie's asleep. Don't wake her.'

But it was Lalla, not Ngayla, who waited at the door. She was breathless, as though she had been running. 'You gotta go longa camp,' she puffed.

'Who says?'

'Aleyne. She say come quick.'

'What does she want? Is something wrong?'

Lalla shrugged. 'Dunno, Missy. She just say you go now.'

'What about Katie?'

'Lalla stay.'

'You won't leave her?'

Lalla shook her head. 'I mind her. You go. Quick!'

Fearing some problem, Jenna wished for the second time that night that Adam had not chosen to be away. She pulled on her dress and smoothed her hair. She'd unbraided it earlier and now it flew about her face. Should she put it up? The thought was fleeting. 'Quick!' Lalla had said, and there was no time for such frivolities. Taking a lamp, she hurried towards the blacks' camp.

There were three of them waiting under a tree on the outskirts of the camp — Aleyne and two older women, obviously from some other nearby tribe, whom she had never seen before. 'Come,' said Aleyne, pulling her into their midst. 'We go this way.'

They were moving away from the camp. 'Where are we going?' asked Jenna. The women weren't acting as though there was an emergency of any kind. In fact they seemed quite composed.

'Missy too curious. Just wait and see.'

They continued on through the bush, walking in single file for what seemed like ages. Jenna, not wanting to return to the house alone, had no option but to follow. She thought of Katie asleep in her bed, sensing alarm for one brief moment. But Katie was safe with Lalla. The black woman, she knew, worshipped the little girl.

Across a dry channel of the river they trudged, through a bank of trees. The three women broke off several branches as they passed. 'Here,' said Aleyne, handing Jenna a branch. 'You keep. Bring good luck.'

They moved alongside a stony ridge, breathing hard, for the grade was steep. Jenna's lamp highlighted the unevenness of the ground and the sheer rock wall that rose up to her left. She held one hand against the wall for balance as she walked. On her right, barely distinguishable in the dark, the ground appeared to slope treacherously away. One missed footing and she knew she'd tumble.

At last they came to an opening in the wall. 'In here,' ordered Aleyne, leading them into an arena of sorts. Jenna felt a rush of relief.

Two small fires were burning. The flames sent out dancing shadows which bounced along the rock walls, lending an eeriness to the scene. As Jenna's eyes adjusted to the light, she realised there were several women — older married gins — already seated in a ring. They were naked, rocking backwards and forwards, either beating sticks together or slapping their hands against the insides of their thighs. Ngayla sat, still clothed and cross-legged, on the ground in their midst.

'What's going on?' asked Jenna, puzzled.

Aleyne pointed to Ngayla. 'She and Wandi together a while now, but no babies.'

'She's very young,' replied Jenna doubtfully. She'd had reservations all along about this 'marriage'.

'No,' replied Aleyne firmly. 'She ready. This is our way. We come tell spirits make plenty babies for Ngayla. And for you too, Missy.'

'Oh, no,' replied Jenna with a laugh. Obviously this was some sort of fertility ceremony, meant not only for Ngayla but for herself as well, and she was thankful for the shadows that hid her blush. How could she extricate herself without offending the other women? Quickly she searched her mind for a reason. 'This is Ngayla's night. It mightn't work if there are two of us.'

'S'orright,' replied one of the other gins, waving her closer. 'Sometimes we have five or six others.'

Ngayla was removing her clothes, slipping the fabric down her slim body until she stood naked in the firelight. Her breasts were small and pointed. The triangle of hair between her legs was dark. Embarrassed, Jenna hugged her arms to her chest, suddenly conscious of her own fully-clothed state. 'No. I don't think so. Maybe I'll just watch.'

'You don't want more babies?' asked Aleyne, crossing her arms.

'Of course I do.'

Aleyne indicated Jenna too should take off her clothes and smear her body with ash and ochre, like the other women. 'You have to please spirits first, then they plant seed inside you. Seed grows.' She used her hands, expressively curving them out in front of her to mimic the shape of a pregnant woman. 'Get big belly, yes?'

Cautiously: 'Yes.'

'Come, then. Besides, we all women here. We got nothing to hide. Alla same.'

Jenna hesitated. What harm could come of it, joining in?

Aleyne, as though sensing her indecision, took her by the arm, leading her aside. Slowly Jenna undid the buttons on her dress and stepped from it. Two of the other women approached, dipping their hands in the red and ochre paint. Jenna could see the colours reflected in the firelight, could feel the pressure of their fingers as they wiped the paint in vertical lines on her brow. Then they all sat in a semi-circle and waited.

Jenna heard the call of the curlew — a shrill scream — and the shriek of other night birds. The fires spat and crackled, burning low. A breeze blew and she shivered, not because it was cold but because she was just the slightest bit scared. To distract herself, she tried to focus on pleasing Aleyne's spirits, and the baby she might one day conceive with Adam. It would be a boy, she knew, a son to carry on the O'Loughlin name. Perhaps she'd name him Michael in honour of her own dead brother.

Stars faded and died, merging at last with the pale dawn sky. Eventually the women rose, beckoning her to join them. Though she had not slept all night, Jenna felt strangely invigorated, not tired at all. And her legs, though she had been sitting for hours on the hard ground, were not stiff.

'We wait for morning,' said Aleyne, 'for blessing of dawn wind. You are one of us now.'

She wiped the ochre from Jenna's brow with a handful of grass. It was all done quickly, with little fuss. The other women re-lit the fires, throwing small branches on the flames. Afterwards Aleyne passed around a bowl of honey and one by one they all dipped their fingers into the amber liquid. 'You go now,' she told Jenna. 'Go back to Katie.'

Katie! In all the strangeness she'd forgotten her daughter and how Lalla was minding her. Quickly she pulled on her clothes and hurried along the track towards the house.

Katie was still sleeping. Gently Jenna roused the black woman and sent her on her way. In the bathroom, she stared at herself in the mirror. There were faint traces of the paint on her forehead and she touched her fingers to them.

She lowered herself into a warm bath and scrubbed away the reminders of the previous night. The water cooled as she sat there, an ochre scum swirling on the surface. Images of fires and darkness, the sound of beating sticks, blurred and became one in her mind. Had it really happened or was it merely a dream? Suddenly she felt very tired.

Exhausted, she slipped a nightgown over her head and crawled beneath her sheets. The images slipped away, like water flowing along a swift and silent stream, and she was aware of nothing until Katie climbed into her bed an hour later.

CHAPTER 25

After the accident, everyone said I had to go to grief counselling. Family. Friends. Even those who scarcely knew me. It seems they all decided, from my pale sleep-deprived appearance, that I was coping badly.

And I was.

I couldn't eat. Instead of sleeping, my mind kept replaying the whole scenario, from me waving Brad and Kadie goodbye, to my imagining how the accident happened, and what I might have done differently had I been there. There were days when I thought I might have been able to save her. There were days when I blamed Brad. Then followed the weeks when I blamed myself.

Basically, I was sceptical that counselling would help, but I had little to lose. I was exhausted, sluggish. My mind refused to form coherent thoughts. So I went.

Once.

I insisted Brad accompany me. He was hesitant at first.

'Do you think that's a good idea?' he asked. 'Not that I mind going, but perhaps we should do this separately.'

But I was adamant. I'd go only if he went too. There was no way I was going to endure this torture alone.

It was as bad as I'd expected. The counsellor was young and pretty, and comforting in an earnest kind of way — a way that made me want to weep. I sat in a chair in her cluttered office, trying to digest her words. I let them wash over me. I tried to make them mine. But they were only useless platitudes that changed nothing.

It was not that I was indifferent or opposed to help. I wasn't. It was the level of understanding that I questioned.

'Have you ever had a child?' I interrupted after a few minutes.

The counsellor shook her head. 'No.'

'All the training and textbooks in the world can't prepare you for what it's like.'

'But —'

'So you couldn't possibly understand how I feel!' I added firmly.

'How *do* you feel, Jess?' she asked gently. 'Tell me.'

It was a ploy, and a not particularly subtle one at that, to make me talk. She wanted me to open up, reveal my innermost emotions. Treat her like a confidante, a special friend. She leaned across the table and took my hand. Her grip was vice-like.

I stood, clumsily, wrenching my hand from hers.

'What is it like?' I repeated dully, shaking my head, unable for a moment to find the words. 'Take the worst kind of pain imaginable, then triple it.'

'Jess!' Brad rose from his chair and moved towards me. 'Please, you're not giving this a chance. Be fair, Jess.'

'Fair!' I flared, placing my hand over the door handle. Suddenly the room seemed claustrophobic. 'There's nothing fair about losing your child! What about the life she's never going to have, the life we're never going to share with her?'

He looked so vulnerable then, his emotions so God-damned exposed. 'Perhaps, Jess,' he said slowly, softly, 'things are where things are.'

I stared at him and felt a disconnection, a drawing away so sudden, so abrupt, that I swayed against the force of it. And in that moment, caught up in the rush of words and emotions, I realised he'd become a stranger to me.

I flung open the door and stepped outside. 'Jess!' I heard them call in unison — my husband and this childless, well-meaning woman.

But I couldn't go back.

Down the hallway I ran, heading for the pale rectangle of light that was the reception foyer, the front door. I heard the sound of my own footfalls, the click-clack of my shoes against the polished tiles, and the rasp of my laboured breath.

How could I ever accept that kind of reasoning, when it came to my child? I hated the way things were and I would have given anything to have my life restored to the way it had been, the way it should be.

*　*　*

Clutching Ella's mud map, I set out for the old Diamantina homestead, an easy twenty minutes away by bike. The air is clean and fresh after the recent rain, and the colours of the landscape seem sharper, more in focus, as though the layers of dust have been washed away. The tree leaves are greener, the distant hills redder. Even the cloudless sky is so blue, so bright, that I blink against the glare.

I turn off the main road at the claypan, as per Ella's instructions, and follow the rutted track. The corrugations set my teeth rattling and I dismount, finding it easier to walk. After a few minutes several roof lines loom towards me out of the bush.

First, there's a collection of outbuildings. Cautiously I step inside what appears to be the remains of the stables and coach shed. It's snake season and Brad has warned me about the explosion of the local long-haired rat population after the recent rain, and how they attract the western taipan, one of the deadliest Australian snakes. But nothing seems to move inside this derelict building. There's no hiss, no uncoiling of scales. Just a swirl of air where I walk and dust motes outlined in the shafts of sunlight that spear through a hole in the roof, spiralling in my wake.

There's a long central corridor, with stalls leading off at regular intervals. I stand on tiptoe and peer over a gate leading to one of the stalls. There's nothing remaining but the vague smell of chaff and molasses. How long, I wonder, since someone has passed through here? Briefly I look inside the nearby blacksmith's forge, and the station store with a counter and shelves lining the rear wall. Then I turn my attention to the main house.

Several small lizards bask in the sun on the front verandah steps, and immediately they scurry off at my approach. Tentatively I make my way along the verandah. Several of the boards look dodgy and I test my weight on each one before moving forward. The front door is ajar, hanging lopsided from rusty hinges. It creaks as I push it open, a sound that seems to shiver through the house.

I'm standing in a high domed entry, and I know instantly that this is the house designed by Bignall & Sons, whose plan I've seen in the box with the diaries and journals. There are hallways leading off to the left and right. I take the right and find myself peeking into a succession of bedrooms. There are the skeletons of beds, but no mattresses. A few articles of clothing, shredded by mice, still hang in an occasional wardrobe. Here a bathroom, mould flowering along the walls. There a dressing room, hanging rails bare. In the corner of one bedroom there's a nest of shredded paper and the stink of mouse pee.

Back along the hallway, in the opposite direction, I prowl around the kitchen, peering in the rusty oven. It's box-like and rather elaborate, and stands on four moulded legs. The word 'Dover' is faintly visible on the door. In the cupboards there are a few chipped plates. There are pieces of cutlery in a drawer, spotted with either mice or cockroach droppings.

In the study, bare shelves line two of the four walls. In the living room, dark damp stains spread randomly on the carpet.

Despite the once ornate fixtures and extravagant size of the house, there's a sense of wretched abandonment in these rooms. The air seems heavy with despair and I'm weighed down by something larger than me, some sense of brooding. If walls could cry, I imagine these weeping silent tears. I feel ... well, unsettled and apprehensive are two words that come readily to mind.

What has happened here?

Despite the heat outside, it's cold in these rooms and I wrap my arms around myself. Then, closing my eyes, I take a deep breath, inhaling the ambience of the building.

There are odours of staleness, of mould, the smell of disuse. I let them waft through my consciousness, no one taking precedence over the other. Here, in this place where she wrote the latter part of her diaries more than a century earlier, I feel an empathy with Jenna. I think of the expectations she had of this house after her miserable and abusive childhood. I imagine her presiding over the 'Dover' stove, perhaps tipping a tray of steaming scones onto the workbench that still stands in the centre of the kitchen, or sitting in the damp-carpeted parlour, or in the music room idling at the keys of the piano that now graces Ella's lounge room.

I consider the similarities, the parallels, that link us. We'd both been heavily pregnant when we'd married. We'd both come close to death while giving birth.

We'd both suffered through the death of a child — me with Kadie, and Jenna with her brother Michael.

But there the similarities ended. Unlike me, that experience hadn't stopped Jenna moving forward, having a child of her own.

I weigh that thought carefully in my mind. Why is it that two people, faced with similar circumstances, react differently? What special qualities did Jenna have to enable her to carry on with her life? Perhaps they were made of sterner stuff, these colonial women. They expected to lose a percentage of their immediate family to disease or accident. Untimely death was such an ongoing and constant part of their lives that maybe they shrugged it aside and moved on. Yet, in Jenna's diaries, I sense her ongoing sadness, that lurking feeling of grief, which sometimes seems to compound my own.

I've seen enough of the house, so I turn and make my way back to the front door, planning to leave. But there, to one side of the entry foyer, I see a set of stairs I had somehow missed before. Curiosity prevails. What is up there?

Ella's cautionary words come back to me. *I'd be careful poking around*, she'd said when she'd told me about the house, *could be a bit dodgy and you wouldn't want something to fall in on you*. With thoughts of dry rot, I test one foot against the first tread. It creaks, but holds. Carefully I make my way up.

I'm in some sort of a tower. There are large windows and I can see out over the countryside in every direction. There — a tiny dark spot among the trees — lies our own cottage, and in the clearing to the left, Betty and Jack's homestead. I can see the huge machinery shed that houses the tractors and farm implements, and the tall stands holding the drums containing the station's diesel supply.

The realisation comes to me, unexpected and insistent. This is the room Jenna had spoken about in her diary, the one where she and Adam had seen what Aleyne called the debil-debil light. I let my gaze wander lower until I'm staring into the rear yard of the house. Underneath the pepper trees and date palms, the garden is a snarl of weeds and overgrown shrubs. Further back, a few hundred yards away, I can see the remains of an old fence poking from a tangle of scrub.

'Mummy!'

The cry is sudden and sharp and I throw my head up. Kadie! I think instinctively, my pulse beating frantically at the base of my throat. I take one step forward then swing around. I search with my eyes, trying to see something extraordinary. The cry was so real, so near.

'Who's there?' I scream.

The words come back to me, heavy and lifeless. All is quiet. There are no child's footsteps here, no peals of laughter. Have I imagined it? I look down at the floor, at that stained and muddied carpet. It wobbles, colours and textures merging for the briefest time, then readjusts itself. A gust of wind, coming in through the open front door and up the stairs, catches at a pile of leaves, sending them scurrying past. I watch the dancing shapes. For the briefest moment they are dark, like the petals of blood-red roses.

I shiver, despite the heat of the day, and acknowledge my rising sense of panic. I need to distance myself from this house and the immediacy of Jenna. Part of me wants to run, but I press back the urge, forcing myself to walk cautiously back down the stairway until I stand, blinking in the sunlight, at the front door.

Outside, the October air is heat-heavy and stifling. Perspiration dots my forehead and face. Small rivulets of sweat run down my back, dampening my shirt. Nothing moves, not even the leaves on the trees. Strange, I think. No wind out here. Even the birds are quiet. I take several deep breaths, calming myself, and walk to the rear of the house.

There, past the jumble of weeds and shrubs, is a fenced plot. Two wooden crosses lean drunkenly, the surfaces so weathered that the inscriptions are indecipherable. Sand has built up over the graves and weeds sprout randomly. I bend forward and pull at one — some sort of native pigweed — and it comes away easily. I scrape the sand from one grave with my hand. Underneath there's a low wrought-iron railing. Small. Contained.

Immediately I know.

This is a child's grave.

I kneel, staring at the railing, unable for a moment to draw breath. My mind turns to Kadie's death, tossing up random memories of those awful first days and weeks afterwards. I close my eyes and blink back the eternal ever-present tears. It has been a mistake, I know, coming here.

As I scramble to my feet, planning to return to the bike, a shadow falls on the ground beside me. Startled, I glance up.

It's a man. Stan — Ella's husband — I realise with surprise. He's wearing a checked shirt and an Akubra pulled down low over his eyes.

'Good morning,' he says, and his mouth crinkles at the corners as he smiles.

Bloody hell! Here I am, stuck in the bush, kilometres from the nearest substantial town, and still there's no privacy. I brush the tears from my face, angry and embarrassed that he should find me like this. 'Hello, Stan,' I mutter uncharitably in reply.

'I was just on my way to check on the paddock further down when I saw your bike. I figured you must be here somewhere.'

'How do you find your way around?' I ask, changing the subject. 'Ella drew me a mud map so I could find this place. Without it I'd still be looking. The countryside all seems the same around here.'

Stan laughs and it's a warm comforting sound. 'Ah, the countryside changes,' he explains, sweeping his hand wide. 'Every coupla miles it'll look different to the experienced eye.'

'With my sense of direction, I'd be forever getting lost.'

'Na. You'd get used to it eventually.' He pulls a cigarette from his pocket and nods towards the graves. 'Bit of a mess here. Keep thinking I'll come down and give it a clean up, but I never seem to get the time.'

'It does seem like a sacrilege,' I admit.

'Tell you what,' he suggests. 'I've a spare half hour and there's a couple of shovels in the back of the ute. What if we make a start?'

'Now?'

'No time like the present. And it'll be twice as quick with two of us.'

He disappears in the direction of the utility and returns with two shovels, hands me one. Bracing myself, I dig it deep into the sand. 'Just like a pro,' Stan compliments.

The sun beats down. Perspiration rolls down my back as I work but I don't care. For the moment I'm this man's companion, his equal, and the hard physical work is diverting me, taking my mind away from other things. We work quietly together, no sound breaking the silence between us except for the occasional out-puff of air.

After half an hour, Stan calls a halt. 'Well,' he says, 'at least we've made a dent in it. Cuppa?'

'Why not?' I shrug.

He produces a flask from the ute and a couple of cups. The tea is hot and black. Stan obviously doesn't use sugar. I sip tentatively. 'Best thing on a hot day to quench thirst,' he says.

'Black tea?'

'Yep. Most people think water's the go, but it's tea that really hits the spot. You don't want to get dehydrated out here.'

'I suppose not.'

Stan changes the subject. 'So how's that husband of yours going with his research? Found out enough yet?'

'I don't think scientists ever finish researching. It's an ongoing thing.'

'Yair? No kidding!'

'Well, it's like a compulsion, this eternal quest for knowledge. They get a kick out of it.'

Stan is quiet for a moment, digesting my words. He pushes his Akubra back and scratches his forehead. 'So, when are you heading back?'

'Actually I was just about to leave when you arrived.'

'No, I meant back to the city.'

Mentally I tally the days. 'Two weeks.'

'Good. We'll be able to get this place cleaned up by then, you and me.'

This is the longest conversation I've ever had with Stan; he's usually a gruff old bloke, a man of few words. Now, for what seems like an awfully long time, he watches me over the rim of his mug. 'I heard about your little girl,' he says at last, his voice low. 'Rough thing, that.'

I stare down at my hand, still holding my mug, and find it trembling. I don't know what words to form in reply. An anger bubbles inside me. How could he possibly know about Kadie, unless Brad had told him?

I wait for the usual platitudes, the 'I can imagine what it must be like' or 'time heals all wounds, Jess' statements that invariably follow. I have no patience for people who feel the need to reassure me that they, too, can feel my pain. How can anyone who hasn't lost a child even try to imagine what it's like? I bite back a reply to the old man, and bring the mug savagely to my mouth.

But Stan isn't like most people. 'I couldn't begin to understand how you feel,' he says, sweeping aside all my assumptions. 'It'd be a right bugger. Must be a hard thing to get out of your head.'

I feel myself slipping, sliding back to that dark hole in my past. I can almost hear Kadie's laughter and feel the warmth of her arms around my neck. I can smell her, that fresh-from-the-bath talcum-powder aroma that washes over me, catching my breath. Memories track, stark and real. And each one is almost like a physical blow. *Blow Mummy a kiss*. Rain falling. Falling. Or is it tears?

'Jess!' Stan's voice is sharp and insistent, jerking me back to the present. I lift my head and stare at his crinkly weather-beaten face. It has softened somehow around the edges, and his eyes are bright, enquiring. I don't see pity etched in his features, more an expression of compassion. Suddenly I feel the need to elaborate.

'It's odd,' I begin slowly, searching for words. I've never told anyone this before, not even Brad, so it's difficult to explain. 'My head tells me she's gone, but in my heart I feel as though she's still here. Sometimes I sense a presence, a faint touch on my neck, my arm, and I'll turn, expecting to see her but —'

I stop, unable to go on.

'But she's not there?' Stan supplies the words.

Numbly I shake my head. 'No.'

'And that still hurts.' It's a statement, not a question.

'Yes.' I swallow hard and blink, trying to stop the tears that gather. 'You probably think I'm crazy,' I mutter instead.

'No.' He gives a wry smile and nods his head in the direction of the old homestead. 'I get the same feeling when I go in there. It's as though the O'Loughlins are still around, or some essence of them.' He leans forward and whispers conspiratorially, 'I thought I saw something in there once, years ago.'

I remember the cry I'd heard earlier, the sense that someone was there. 'What did you see?'

'Dunno. Must've been a shadow or something. But at the time I thought it was a child. A young girl. Course it couldn't have been real. No one has lived here for years.'

A memory stirs inside my head. 'Did she have dark hair?'

Stan tilts his head, thinking. 'Maybe.'

'And was she wearing an old-fashioned dress, one with a high lace collar? Boots?'

'Why? Did you see her too?'

'I might have. In a dream.'

'Crikey!' He throws his hands up in a gesture of defeat. 'You'd better not tell Ella. You know what she thinks?'

'What?'

'She says I've gone soft in the head.'

The old man is quiet for a while, digesting the threads of our conversation as he downs the last of his tea. When at last he speaks again, his voice comes to me, soft like snow. 'What was her name?'

I take a deep breath, drawing air into my lungs. My tongue seems glued to the roof of my mouth and I know that if I try to say the word it'll come out all wrong. My heart is beating an erratic tattoo in my chest.

'Jess?' Stan prompts.

I close my eyes, willing myself.

'Kadie. Her name was Kadie.'

There, I've done it. I've said the word.

'How long has it been?'

'A year.'

Despite my best intentions, the tears roll down my cheeks. Stan rummages in his pocket and hands me a handkerchief. It's white and neatly ironed. 'Go on,' he urges. 'Take it.'

Gratefully I dab my eyes and turn away, trying to compose myself. I hate anyone seeing me like this, wearing the eternal mourner's garb.

'Sometimes I'm afraid to sleep,' I tell him when the pounding in my heart has lessened.

He nods understandingly. 'Because of those dreams,' he replies.

It's not until we walk back to the track — Stan to his ute and me to the rusted bicycle — that I ask the question that's been gnawing at me but I've been too afraid to broach. 'You haven't told me, Stan. Who's buried in the graves?'

'I thought you knew.'

'No.'

'Jenna's buried there,' he replies, throwing the shovels in the back before opening the door and clambering behind the wheel. 'Jenna and her daughter, Kathryn.'

CHAPTER 26

Ngayla's baby was born the following spring. He was brown and sturdy like his father, and she named him Jinbi which means 'star'. In the early months, she carried him about the house in a sling she wore around her chest, or he slept in his basket in the kitchen.

In unguarded moments Jenna touched her hand to his soft cheek, or watched the steady rise and fall of his chest. She, herself, had not been so lucky. The months had come and gone and still her own belly lay flat. The need for Adam's child had become a dull ache inside her. Katie should have brothers and sisters, lots of them, and most of the bedrooms in the house lay reproachfully empty. It was such a large house to fill.

There was a comfortable familiarity between her and Adam these days. She didn't love him and knew she never would, but she respected and admired him, and he adored Katie. She knew his likes and dislikes, anticipated his moods and prepared his favourite meals. At night, after Katie had gone to bed and supper things had been cleared away, they played cards or read, or Jenna picked out a few notes on the piano. Even the silences between them were relaxed these days and she felt no awkwardness in them, no need to fill them with words.

Many new families had arrived in the local area, taking up land and setting down roots. There was now a weekly mail service, instead of monthly. Hawkers passed by regularly, their wagons loaded with produce. Life was changing, moving on around her, yet some days Jenna felt as though she was standing still.

Earlier that same year, Adam organised the construction of a horse track near the homestead and over two hundred locals had arrived for the St Patrick's Day races. Aleyne and Lalla, wearing white aprons and bibs over their usual dresses, had been kept busy organising food and drink.

Adam enjoyed himself immensely. Jenna watched from the sidelines as he greeted guests and made them feel welcome. He cheered when one of his horses won a race, and he invited everyone back to celebrate the following year. He pulled her forwards, introducing her to new-made friends. While she felt part of them, caught up in the fun of the day, in some ways she had never felt so alone.

'It'll be an annual event,' Adam declared magnanimously as the wagons started rolling homewards on dusk, their occupants weary and windswept. 'St Patrick's Day at the O'Loughlins'.'

For that one day he was proud of his Irish heritage. He was also king of his domain, and his domain was Diamantina Downs.

Later, as he undressed in their bedroom, pulling his shirt over his head, she was struck by the odd sensation of having been in that same scene before, a feeling of déjà vu. She was back in Mary's house, in the early days of her relationship with Conor. And it was Conor she now remembered, pulling a similar shirt over his head; she recalled seeing the sprinkling of fair hairs on his chest and the tanned muscular skin of his forearms.

Sun and moon: fair and dark — as always, she couldn't help comparing them.

But time had lessened the pain of Conor's death, and her memory of him was less distinct, softened around the edges. Sometimes in her mind the two brothers blurred and became one. She could imagine for a moment that it was Conor now nuzzling her breast, or running his fingers lightly but insistently along her inner thigh.

She parted her legs at his touch, drew him inside her. Felt the force of him, the emotion. She raised her mouth to his, her hips. Her senses soared, sang.

'Jenna!' he cried as he climaxed, and she was surprised — shocked, even — to realise the voice was not Conor's at all.

Meanwhile, the usual rains hadn't arrived. The countryside lay browning under a relentless sun and one by one the water holes dried. The pelican population dwindled. Jenna watched at sunset as great flocks of them lumbered off into the golden dusk, in search of other rivers. It was like a desertion, of sorts. Come back, she wanted to call out to them. Don't leave.

Mobs of dingoes came in from further west. She could hear them at night, that mournful wailing. Invariably there'd be several lambs mauled the following morning. Adam spent hours out in the paddocks, setting poisoned baits.

As summer progressed, dust storms became a weekly occurrence. She learned to recognise the warning signs — trees thrashing about in sudden squalls and a rapidly approaching line of pink on the western horizon — and went about the house methodically closing the windows and doors, despite the fact that the heat inside became even more oven-like.

Later, when the storm passed, she'd stand and survey the damage: tree branches lying smashed on the ground and sand piled up in great drifts on the verandahs. She could imagine it, all those layers of red soil being lifted up and deposited hundreds of miles away, the interior of the country eroding away to nothing.

Katie was a constant delight. She was almost three years old, a squat solid child with a ready smile and sunny disposition. Her long hair, lovingly teased into ringlets each morning by Aleyne, was dark like Jenna's. Her favourite game was hide-and-seek and, at the sound of Adam's horse approaching each afternoon, she would run and take cover somewhere in the house.

It became a ritual, Adam pulling off his boots at the front door and calling loudly: 'Alright. Where's my girl?'

There would be no reply.

'Katie?' he'd call, louder now as he came through the front door, kissing his wife on the mouth.

'Little Miss Katie's gone to town,' Jenna would tell him in mock seriousness. 'She saddled up a horse all by herself and rode off.'

'Oh, really?' Adam would say in a loud voice, going from room to room and randomly flinging open cupboards. 'All the way to town by herself? She must be a very smart girl.'

'Oh, our Katie *is* a very smart girl,' Jenna acknowledged, following him, suppressing a smile. 'She tied her own shoelaces this morning.'

Eventually, pretending surprise, he'd find her hiding behind some curtain or under a bed. (Once she squeezed into the wardrobe in the room Jenna and Adam shared, and only a loud sneeze had given her away.) Laughing, she'd run into his arms, calling, 'Daddy, silly Daddy. Of course I didn't ride into town. I wouldn't know the way.'

'I know that, precious,' he'd say, hugging her fiercely to his chest. 'As if I'd let you go by yourself!'

Then he'd carry her off for her bath, washing away the day's dirt and grime.

It was like that between them these days, that easy banter, Katie drawing them together, making them laugh. Adam ordered a bracelet for her third birthday. It was rose gold with a name plate on one side. Adam had it engraved with her initials. 'K O'L' it said, in scrawly lettering. The little girl wore it constantly, refusing to remove it at bath time, no matter how much Jenna cajoled.

'Let her be,' Adam shrugged. 'It's not important.'

The months dragged by, hot and dry. Summer slid into autumn and suddenly there were frosts on the ground each morning. From Adam's tower room above the house, there was no sign of green winter grass. Daily Jenna heard the sounds of gunshots ring out, echoing back to her from the dry riverbeds and gorges as Adam put the starving sheep from their misery. At night, seen from the window of the tower room, the sky was clear and filled with stars.

Right from the very first day, Jenna suspected she was pregnant. Excited, she bit back the urge to tell Adam, waiting until several months had come and gone, wanting to be certain. The drought was worsening and he wore a perpetual worried frown these days. The good news, she knew, would cheer him.

She was resting on her bed, mid-afternoon, when Adam came in early, shaking the dust from his clothes. 'Goodness, it's freezing out there. The wind goes right through you like a knife.'

'Have a bath then and warm yourself up,' she suggested, snuggling further under the blanket.

'Where's Katie?' he asked as she opened one lazy eye. These days she felt so tired.

'She's having a nap. I just looked in on her.'

The Aboriginal women had gone back to their camp for the afternoon and wouldn't return until it was time to prepare the evening meal. The house was quiet, the silence broken only by the sounds of ticking clocks. 'A bath sounds like a splendid idea,' agreed Adam. 'Then I might just join you in there.'

Later, when he slid into the bed beside her, she told him the news she knew he'd been waiting to hear. 'There's going to be another baby.'

He drew back, regarding her, his mouth curving into a smile. 'Are you sure?'

'A woman knows these things.'

'When, do you think?'

'Five months, maybe. Before Christmas.'

He trailed a finger lightly across her belly and she imagined it round and solid with his child. 'I'd like lots of children,' he said suddenly.

'How many?' She licked her tongue teasingly across his ear.

'Half a dozen at least.'

'Only six? I thought perhaps eight.'

'Well, eight, then. I don't mind. This house is so big and empty. Sometimes I think it echoes when we talk.'

She thought about that — the noisy babble of children they might one day have filling the empty corridors and rooms — and smiled.

If anyone had asked, Adam wouldn't have known how to describe his feelings at that precise moment when Jenna had told him about the baby. Surprised, certainly: he'd long since ceased to think he'd ever become a father. Pleased. No, not *pleased* — that word didn't carry enough weight — but delighted, elated, energised.

Those words ran through his mind later, each one bearing its own importance. He felt as though some current was surging through his body, rejuvenating

422

him. The past year had been wearing, both mentally and physically.

The rains still hadn't come and the Diamantina Downs landscape lay brown and bare. Desperately he scanned the sky for signs of rain, but the only things visible on the horizon were the storms that brought clouds of choking red dust.

Despite his intention, there had been no annual St Patrick's Day races that year. The local farmers were too busy tending to their rapidly dwindling stock to bother. Adam, helped by Wongaree and Pigeon, herded his own diminishing flocks of sheep from one rancid water hole to the next, trying to keep them alive. The animals were skeletal, their fleeces ragged. As Adam watched them totter and fall, he could easily have wept. Not in his wildest dreams could he have imagined all this.

Jenna was often confined to bed during those middle months of her pregnancy. Aleyne prepared herbal drinks to quell the nausea while Lalla shoed Katie from the bedroom. 'Shh,' she whispered, drawing the curtains. 'Mumma's sick. You have to be quiet.'

Sometimes Adam took Katie into the paddocks with him, to allow Jenna some rest. At other times he let her accompany him to the stables or down to the largest of the water holes while he checked on the sheep. She followed him like a puppy, asking questions. He made her stay in the buggy and cover her ears with her hands when he held the gun to the head of some stray ewe. When Jenna asked if he thought she should be exposed to such scenes he replied, 'Why not? She's a country girl.'

'Why did you kill the sheep?' Katie asked.

'Because it was dying anyway.'

'Why?'

'There's no water or stockfeed.'

'Why isn't there?'

'Well, it hasn't rained in a long while.'

'Why doesn't it rain?'

'Because there's a drought.'

'What's drought?'

'When it doesn't rain.'

On and on they went, the endless questions, and he loved it.

He treasured the warm solidity of her, the way she snuggled onto his lap and laid her head against his chest. He cherished the kisses she rained along his cheek, and the way her head bobbed up and down earnestly when he tried to explain the workings of the land. He tried to imagine life without her, the daughter of his brother whom he had come to love like his own, and failed miserably. She completed him, made him whole.

Meanwhile, he worried about Jenna constantly. Was she warm enough on those chill winter's days? Was she eating properly? Perhaps she should see a doctor, confirm that everything was alright.

He skirted around her, wary, trying not to seem too anxious. She hated that. 'I'm not ill,' she'd say, awarding him a wry smile. 'I'm just having a baby. It's the most natural thing in the world.'

Of one thing Adam was certain: this child wouldn't be born in the bush. He'd take Jenna to town before the birth with plenty of time to spare.

There was no way he'd risk his wife's life again, or that of his unborn child.

By the time spring arrived, she'd begun wearing loose-fitting shifts to hide the swell of her belly. Already, so early in the season, the days were hot and still. Often, around midday, dark clouds appeared teasingly on the horizon, not coming any closer. Sometimes thunder rumbled and a few wet drops fell with a plop, making small craters in the dust. Then, as soon as it had come, the rain — or the promise of it — was gone, leaving the smell of gidgee in the air and a mass of unspent energy. Down at the camp, Yapunya and Pigeon sang songs and beat stones together to drive away the drought spirit. Adam could hear them most nights, that mournful clunk-clunking drifting across the paddocks.

He was at a loss what to do. There was little of his own money left — the profits of the last few good seasons had been wiped out with the paying of recent bills — and Jenna's money had long since been spent on the building of the house and the furnishings. Carefully he eked out the precious remaining pounds. At night he laboured over his desk, tallying and calculating and predicting. Glancing in a mirror as he passed, he noted the perpetual frown that wrinkled his brow.

One night Jenna pulled him close and placed his hand against her belly. He felt a slow ripple, like the concentric circles on the surface of a pond after a stone has been thrown, as the baby moved.

'Can you feel that?' she asked.

And he nodded his head in the dark, too overcome to speak.

It was a lengthy nightly ritual, Jenna tucking Katie into bed. First there was a bedtime story to be read, then prayers to be said. 'I've left the lamp on,' said Jenna, walking out onto the verandah after she'd kissed her daughter goodnight. 'You know she hates the dark.'

Adam stood, his hands gripping the timber railing as she watched him from the doorway. His shirt sleeves were turned upwards over his tanned forearms. He was staring out into the dark.

The thought struck her then, sudden and insistent, about how everything was finally coming right in their lives — except for the lack of rain. Katie. A new baby. The sorrows of the past — Conor, her mother, Michael — had faded. She had moved on and accepted the inevitable. The future, as long as the rains came soon, promised happiness.

Stars twinkled in a cloudless sky above. A faint breeze rustled through the pepper trees and she smelled the sudden sharp tang of the leaves. From the blacks' camp drifted the endless rainmaking sounds. She liked this time of day best, when the women had gone back to their own homes and it was just the three of them left in the house.

'If the rains don't come soon, I don't know what we'll do,' said Adam, breaking her train of thought.

His words floated away from her into the darkness, and she stared at the nape of his neck, at the place where his hair and the tanned skin met. A frisson of desire curled through her. Tomorrow I must cut it, she thought, thinking she might put her mouth there, against the warm skin. She imagined how he would turn to her, how she'd meet his mouth with hers.

'We'll manage somehow,' she replied, forcing her attention to his words.

'The money's almost gone. There's no stockfeed. And at this rate the water holes will all be dry within a month.'

She tilted her head towards the nearby camp. 'Maybe they have the answer.'

He laughed, a short, sharp sound. 'Sometimes it seems odd hearing heathens offering up prayers.'

'They have their gods,' she replied softly.

'Gods, yes. But hardly Christian ones.'

'They're as real to them as your God is to you.'

'Maybe.'

'Sometimes,' said Jenna pensively, 'I wonder about your God. *Our* God. Don't you think it's better to live your life according to morals and values, and a sense of what's good and true, rather than by Godly ideals?'

'Perhaps they're the same thing?'

Jenna walked behind him, wrapped her arms around his chest and laid her head against his back. Through the fabric of his shirt she could feel the muscular solidity of him. 'Why is it I can never win an argument with you?'

His voice sounded surprised. 'We're arguing?'

'Perhaps.' She laughed, dislodging her arms.

'Never. Just a difference of opinions, which is one of the things I love about you. You're not some namby-pamby wife who can't hold her own view, and you're never afraid to voice what you feel. Besides, I love you too much to *argue* with you, and you know what they say?'

'*They?*'

'You can never win an argument with a woman.'

He was smiling down at her. She saw his mouth curve in the lamplight, saw the love in his eyes. He gathered her against his chest, the child a not-unwelcome barrier between them. Pressing his mouth against her hair, he brought his hand down until it cupped the underside of the mound. The baby wriggled and he laughed, a gentle sound. 'Jenna?'

'Yes,' she replied, drawing slightly away and taking his hand.

'I think it's time for bed, don't you?'

Wordlessly she led him inside, down the hallway towards the room they shared.

CHAPTER 27

Later I sit at the kitchen table, staring blankly at the diaries and station journals spread before me. My mind is a confused muddle. I think about the old house — the cold air inside the rooms and the sense that I wasn't alone, the scream I was certain I'd heard.

But there had been no one there. Had there?

Was I going mad?

My thoughts slide sideways, seeking comfort from Stan's words.

It's as though the O'Loughlins are still around ...

Stan doesn't seem the sort of person to exaggerate or make things up. He's a black and white man, I suspect, with no varying shades of grey in between. A straight thinker. Had he really seen the ghost of a child in the house, or were his old eyes playing tricks on him? Was it Katie that he believed he'd seen, Jenna's daughter, the same little girl of my dreams? For I was certain now that it was she who had been running through my subconscious, wearing those old-fashioned clothes and stout boots.

The scream, I think again, wrapping my arms around myself, shivering involuntarily. A child's cry. High-pitched. Terrified. It had seemed so real, so immediate, and so damn scared. What if I hadn't imagined it? At the time my first thought had turned to Kadie but now, after speaking with Stan, I'm considering other options.

It's as though the O'Loughlins are still around ...

I let the words settle, examine them, reflect on the possibilities. Is it feasible that something of us remains in a place long after we're gone? In years to come, will some essence of Brad and me linger in this house on the Diamantina we have called home for the past four weeks? Is it possible that the spirit of Kathryn — Jenna and Conor's daughter — still inhabits the old house?

Stan seems to think so.

I shake my head, not knowing. So many questions, I think, and so few answers, so I turn my attention to the journals and diaries.

Adam's station journals, I've discovered, are dry but informative. The entries contain technical information about the running of Diamantina Downs, the weather and rainfall, the cost of supplies. *Temperature 118°,* he wrote on one scorching summer's day. Then: *No rain, and no sign of it either. Began sheep muster today. Flour and sugar low. Cost of goods up. They blame it on the drought.*

These records provide a background, a skeletal frame. But sadly they don't give me much insight into the man himself.

It's through the diaries that I've come to know Adam and Jenna. Despite my initial reluctance, I feel a sense of right in reading them. I'm enjoying the transcribing, taking unexpected pleasure in trying to decipher the words and worrying over their meaning. Sometimes the hours fly by, unnoticed, while I work.

The words are a link between their time and mine, dissolving the intervening years. It's making me feel part of this place. It gives me an understanding of the kind of life Adam and Jenna led, how it was back in those early pioneering days. There are times when the two of them are as existent to me as Brad or Ella or Stan. No longer are they simply names in a history book or unsmiling faces in a photograph. They're real people, with likes and dislikes, fears, and the ability to love. I see their foibles, and their strengths. I almost believe I can reach out and touch them.

But it's not all pleasantries. There are days when the diaries make me look at myself, at what I've become. It's two worlds colliding, over a century later, and all my old hurts are rising to the surface again, raw and unwilling. It's making me analyse the way I feel, or don't know how I feel, about Brad.

How have I degenerated from that happy carefree person, during those first heady days of romance and lust and love, to this pathetic indecisive woman I am now? There must have been steps, a gradual progression. But I've been so caught up in myself that I've failed to notice.

Brad and I scarcely seem to be talking to each other these days. We argue constantly. We can never agree on anything. Each morning sees us go our separate ways — me to the diaries and Brad to the 4WD and distant water holes. Breakfast is eaten on the run and dinner is usually a silent affair, with my husband scraping his chair back as soon as he's finished his meal. He heads towards the clearing away of dishes, the washing up: it's our tacit agreement. It's also been several weeks since we've made love. Sex seems to be the least important thing on our minds these days.

How weird, I think, closing the diary with a snap, unwilling to read further. An insistent question has been niggling at me for days now and I must give it proper consideration.

Why has Jenna come into my life at this time? Or, alternatively, why have I come into hers?

If you asked Brad, he'd say it was karma, fate, or whatever. He'd go on about how things are meant to be, in their own good time. *Things are where things are.* He believes that. Truly.

'You were meant to see those diaries,' he'd told me days earlier.

'How do you figure that?'

'Well, we could have come here a month later and Betty might have already given them to the historical society in town. Then you wouldn't have known they existed. Or someone could have thrown them out years ago. It's like they've been sitting there, waiting patiently all this time for you.'

But I'm less sure. The whole thing could be mere coincidence. Maybe they would have been better off in someone else's hands. Perhaps I'm not doing these memoirs justice. That familiar sense of self-doubt creeps in again.

All I know for certain is that I have trouble tearing

myself away from these old books. They've become compulsive, and I sit at the table from morning until night, copying and rewriting until the words become dark dancing blurs on the pages.

'Come to bed,' Brad inevitably says. We don't spend time together anymore and I can tell he's beginning to get annoyed, wishing maybe that I'd never seen these books.

'Just a few minutes more,' I mumble, dog-tired yet unable, or unwilling, to let go.

I'm washing up the lunch dishes when Brad comes in, late afternoon. I hear the slam of the front screen door and the thump of his boots through the house. He's whistling, and immediately I feel an anger bubbling up inside me.

'Hi,' he says, depositing several specimen jars and a pile of data sheets on the kitchen bench. 'Good day?'

'I've just cleaned there,' I say tersely, waving the dishcloth in the direction of his equipment. 'Can you move them?'

'Oh, and it's nice to see you too,' he says casually, in a tone that's meant to jolly me out of whatever mood I've found myself in.

I sink my hands back into the soapy water, searching for the plate and knife that I know are in there, eluding me. 'Don't patronise me. Please.'

'Okay. Okay.' He steps back and raises his hands in a gesture of defeat. 'I give in. You'd better tell me what's wrong, to save me guessing.'

I throw the plate and knife onto the dish drainer and yank out the plug. The water makes a loud gurgling sound as it rushes down the drain. 'How dare you say anything to Stan!'

'Stan?' Brad looks puzzled. 'What are you talking about?'

'I went out to the old homestead today. Stan was there. You told him about Kadie.'

'I did?' He shrugs. 'Perhaps. I can't remember. I often talk about Kadie.'

'So you just lay all our private life bare to people we hardly know?'

'It's hardly private. Lots of people know about our daughter. She's not a secret. We can't lock the memory of her away. She existed, she was real. You mightn't like to talk about her, but it doesn't mean I can't.'

'Well, the least you could have done was warn me!'

'Why, so you could have steered clear of Stan, avoided getting into a conversation with him? You can't shun people forever, just because of what they might say to you.'

'Maybe not. But at least it'd be my choice.'

'Sometimes there are no choices, Jess. Life just happens around us and we're powerless to stop it.' He stares at me, thoughtfully, his gaze intent. 'Why is it we can see things happening to other people yet we're blind to them ourselves?'

'What do you mean? What things?'

'Us,' says Brad firmly, emphasising the word. 'What's happened to us: Jess and Brad? Two people who used to be so much in love that we couldn't keep our eyes, our hands, off each other.' He crosses his arms. Frowns. 'It's been weeks since we even kissed each other, let alone made love.'

'I didn't think you'd noticed.'

He ignores my comment. 'Sometimes I think you're avoiding me.'

'Let's not get into this now,' I say, a little too quickly. 'In a week or so we'll be heading back to the city. Everything will be different then. Things will settle down, be back to normal.'

'Will they?'

I am holding my breath, not daring to move. What is he about to say? I shake my head, not trusting myself to speak.

'I can't live like this anymore. Being around you is like walking on eggshells,' he goes on. 'I have to analyse everything I say before I speak, just in case I upset you.'

The past wasn't all terrible, and the good times far outweigh the bad. Why can't I remember those? He takes one step away from me, then another. It's almost like a physical thing, this pulling apart, and there's a sinking feeling in the pit of my stomach. Has this all gone too far?

He leans over the bench and sweeps the specimen jars and field notes into his arms. 'I'll just get rid of these,' he says as he turns and walks from the room.

Sometime during the night I wake. I lie there, listening to my husband's deep and regular breathing. He's rolled over to the far side of the bed. As far away from me as possible?

There was a time when we were never apart, even when we slept. Legs tangled. Fingers entwined. One arm slung casually over the other's chest. But not now.

Now it's strained silences and physical avoidance. Sleeping on the furthest edge of the mattress. Skirting around each other. Going to bed at separate times. Sliding inconspicuously between the sheets, trying not to disturb the other.

The not touching becomes an effort in itself. It's difficult in confined spaces, in this place called the Diamantina, where there's only the two of us. No friends or family to escape to, though I now know Brad's been confiding in Stan. We circle each other warily, in bed and out of it. I feel uptight and guarded, waiting for one of us to explode, although Brad, I know, hates the confrontations as much as I do.

I think about tonight's argument, which was about Kadie, as usual. Kadie. Always Kadie. It seems we're too frayed, too exhausted, to fight about anything else.

Some days I think I can't take any more. I want to crawl into a small space, curl up and sleep until the pain has passed and I can function properly again. There are times when I wish everyone would leave me alone and stop trying to rate the progress of my so-called recovery, stop imposing their views.

But now a fear has begun building inside me, and I must face the awful truth. Here, in this unfamiliar place where there's nothing to remind me, the memories of Kadie are fading. There are days when whole stretches of time pass without me thinking of my daughter. Then, when I do, I feel guilty. It's at least a week since I've had the dream — and even then I woke not knowing if it was my own daughter or Katie O'Loughlin who flitted through my subconscious. Why is that? I wonder. Is it because I've been so involved with the diaries and journals that they've taken over my dreams as well as my waking hours?

I try to picture Kadie in my mind, how she was on that last day. Brad clicking her into her car seat. The first drops of rain plopping onto the driveway. Kadie smiling; me waving. *Blow Mummy a kiss.*

A glimmer of panic shudders its way through me. I try to remember Kadie's face, her features, but there's nothing in my memory. She's a blank canvas, no mouth or eyes or nose. Simply pale skin.

Frantically I push away the sheets and struggle from the bed. Brad groans and rolls over but doesn't wake. I run to the kitchen, stubbing my toe on the corner of a chair as I go. *Shit! Shit! Shit!* I hop, wincing with the pain. But the hurt seems incidental to the terror that's building inside me.

Where's my wallet?

I flick on the light. Momentarily blinded, I rummage through the contents of the handbag lying on the bench. Keys. Sunglasses case. Half-empty packet of peppermints. My hands are shaking. I'm breathing hard, as though I've been running. I close my eyes, trying to regain my composure. Slow down, Jess. Get a grip on yourself.

Where's my bloody wallet?

At last my fingers close over it. I yank it out and flick it open, feeling the soft flood of remembrance. A sense of relief washes over me as I run my finger over the chubby face, blue, blue eyes and dimpled chin. Kadie's familiar well-loved features stare back at me.

'Oh, my God!'

I've voiced the words, although I haven't meant to. They echo dully around the room, bouncing back at me from odd angles. Night surrounds me. I can see it through the windows, hot and heavy, a dark mass that lies further out. My own image is reflected in the window glass. Hair awry. Pale face. Chest heaving.

I pull the photo from the wallet, press its coolness against my cheek. If I close my eyes I can imagine her there, smelling of soap and talcum, her chubby body snuggling against mine. I can almost imagine the weight of her.

'Jess?'

Guiltily, like a schoolboy caught doing something naughty, I shove the photo back in my purse. Brad's standing in the doorway, blinking against the light. His hair is tousled and he's rubbing his eyes. 'I thought I heard something. What are you doing up?'

I can't speak. The words lodge in my throat, jagged like broken glass. Instead I go to him, laying my head against his chest as the tears come, sudden and hot. 'Don't let me forget,' I say between sobs.

'I've decided to go into town,' says Brad the next morning. 'I'd like to catch up with one of the chaps at the EPA office. He's been doing some similar research to me and we want to compare notes. Want to come?'

'To help you compare notes? You don't have to babysit me.'

I'm still smarting from the argument the night before and can't seem to keep the sarcasm from my voice.

'Come on, Jess. Lighten up. It'll be fun, and good to get away for a day.'

'So what am I supposed to do while you talk shop?'

'You can do your own thing,' he explains patiently, refusing to be ruffled. 'Betty says there's a half-decent local museum. That'd be interesting.'

I think about the diaries. I'm fully absorbed in them right now and don't want to tear myself away, especially since we only have a week left here. Do I really want to take a day off? Or, more importantly, do I really want to spend the day with my husband?

But he's looking at me with a pleading puppy-dog expression on his face.

'Oh, what the heck. Alright.'

Town is a two-hour drive away, so it's mid-morning by the time we arrive. Betty has asked Brad to pick up some supplies from the stockfeed place, so we go there first and load them into the back of the ute. In the city we wouldn't dream of doing that — they'd be stolen. But here, it seems, there's no such concern. In one of the general stores I buy a fresh supply of writing paper and bread, a few groceries. Then we head off to the local EPA office.

Aiden, the man Brad wants to exchange notes with, invites us for lunch at the pub. 'Not for me,' I say with a laugh. 'I'm going to poke around the museum. I'll leave you two to it.'

The town is a historic one, with a mixture of old and modern buildings lining the main street. It's a popular tourist destination for those wanting to experience 'Waltzing Matilda' country. A few hundred miles up the road is Dagworth Station where Banjo Paterson wrote the words to the popular poem.

It's in the middle of what's called 'the channel country' or the Mitchell grasslands, and is a stopping-off place on the main route north. An array of dust-caked 4WDs, mostly with caravans in tow, are pulled up outside the tourist centre where a board proclaims the high-tech displays and light-and-sound show that starts every hour, on the hour. There are a couple of pubs, a chemist and menswear store, bank, Chinese takeaway, and a gift shop with a selection of opals — plus the usual souvenirs — in the display window.

I browse inside, thinking I'd like to buy some memento of our visit. Then I grab a quick sandwich at the café and slide behind the wheel of the ute. Aiden has given me general directions to the museum on the outskirts of town.

Like many country towns, the streets are wide and laid out at right angles to each other, and they bear the names of early explorers and land leases. The footpaths are lined with coolibah trees. Houses are mostly old and in need of a lick of paint, but tidy. Lawns are patches of green.

I park in the shade of a tree. There's a closed sign on the museum door; it's only open a few hours each day. Damn! Another half hour to wait. So I cool my heels by walking along the street, studying the houses and gardens.

The local historian is in her sixties, with wispy grey hair and a booming voice. I'm the only person waiting when she opens the door, fifteen minutes after the appointed time. 'Oh, sorry,' she says, fanning her face with her hand. 'Went home for lunch and fell asleep in the chair. Awful hot day, isn't it? Thank goodness it's air conditioned inside.'

She's interested when I tell her where Brad and I have been staying. 'Diamantina Downs! The old O'Loughlin place!' she exclaims in a loud voice.

I nod and tell her about the diaries and station journals, how I've been transcribing them. 'Betty says she's going to bring them in to you when I finish. The writing is a bit hard to make out, so it's been taking a while. I can let you have a copy of my notes when I finish, if you like.'

'That'd be good. Adam O'Loughlin and his brother Conor were some of the early white men to take up land around here. Conor was killed by the Aborigines. The tribe wasn't a local one, though, but from somewhere down south. That was back in ...' She stops and taps her forehead as though willing the year to come. 'Oh, about '73, I think, but there's no official record of his death. Apparently there is a surviving grave though.'

I've only seen two graves on Diamantina Downs and they belong, according to Stan, to Jenna and Katie. 'I didn't know that.'

'It's out in the bush somewhere. You'd need someone to show you where it is. Stan — you've met Stan? He knows, I'm sure.'

'I was wondering if you have any more information on the O'Loughlins?'

The woman — she's introduced herself by now as Doris — shakes her head. 'There's not much here. A few old newspaper clippings, copies of the original lease documents, that sort of thing. The O'Loughlins didn't stay in the area for very long. Some sort of tragedy happened out there, I think. They went back to the city and the property was vacant for a long time after that. Apparently the old homestead is still standing. I must get out there and take some photos before it falls down.'

I spend several hours browsing through local history books and a surprisingly good collection of photographs. There's not one of Adam, though, so I make a mental note to forward a copy of the one Ella's given me.

It's late when I finish and, as I step outside, a blast of hot air hits my face. Brad's waiting in the car, reading. He's walked from the pub, he tells me.

He nods towards the museum. 'Find anything interesting?'

'Not really. Thanks to the diaries and journals, I have heaps more info than Doris.'

'Doris?'

I laugh. 'Don't ask. Actually I've been killing time for a while. You should have come inside and told me you were waiting.'

'I haven't been here long. Ten minutes max.'

'How was lunch?'

'Great. Aiden's done a heap of research.'

It was almost like old times, Brad and me chatting about our day and what we'd done. I let him ramble on, only half listening. The local historian's words kept spearing back at me. 'Some sort of tragedy happened out there, I think. They went back to the city and the property was vacant for a long time after that.'

What tragedy had happened on Diamantina Downs?

Doris obviously hadn't been referring to Conor's death — she'd already mentioned that separately. But Stan had told me that the graves at the back of the old homestead belonged to Jenna and her daughter. Had there been an accident of some kind? Did they die together or separately? I'm almost at the end of the last diary and journal, so I'm certain that all will be revealed soon. And while part of me is curious, desperate even, for the knowledge, another part of me is reluctant to know.

After a few minutes I glance at my watch, noting the lengthening shadows on the ground. 'I guess we'd better get going then.'

'Well, I had an idea. How would you like to see a movie?'

'There's a cinema here?'

'Not like we're used to,' he laughs. 'It's open air, and the lady who runs it says to bring a can of mozzie repellent. They show nostalgia movies through the week. Tonight's Cary Grant. I thought we might have a meal in the pub first.'

Suddenly I'm ravenous. All I've eaten today is one sandwich. 'Sounds good.'

Over dinner — a surprisingly good rump steak — Brad tells me more about his meeting with Aiden. Later, at the theatre, he puts his arm around my shoulder, pulling me close. We could be young lovers, hiding there in the dark on the canvas seats.

The movie is one I've never seen, and I laugh and cry at the appropriate moments. Afterwards we grab a cappuccino at the café, and by the time we make our way back to Diamantina Downs, it's late.

Lightning zigzags along the western horizon and there's the occasional rumble of thunder. Brad's worried that it might rain, and I can see his frown of concentration in the reflection from the dashboard lights as he navigates the potholed road. We've a two-hour drive in front of us and these black dirt roads are treacherous in the wet, even with a 4WD.

After a while I'm aware of lights behind us. 'Someone following?' I ask.

Brad adjusts the rear-vision mirror to night mode, angling it downwards so the reflection isn't as bright. 'They've been there for a while. Wish they'd overtake. The headlights are annoying.'

It's quiet in the car. The radio's off and the engine noise is muted. I'm keeping an eye out for kangaroos. The lights — there appear to be two of them — stay behind us. Brad speeds up, hoping to put some distance between us and them, and the lights speed up as well.

'Odd,' he says. 'I'll try slowing down, then they might pass.'

He slows and I wait for the vehicle to overtake, but in the side mirror I can see the lights have come no closer. Ahead there's a dip in the road. When we come out of it, onto flat ground again, one of the lights has gone.

It's beginning to feel creepy. I fold my arms across my chest and repress a shiver. 'Do you think it's some weirdo playing silly games?' I ask. 'I wouldn't like to get into trouble out here.'

'It's okay,' Brad replies, tapping impatiently against the steering wheel. 'We've got the satellite phone.'

I pick up the phone receiver, testing the connection. The reception is awful. There's nothing but a loud crackle of static coming down the line. We go down another dip in the road and when we come up the other side, Brad swings the car to a standstill at the side of the road.

I'm terrified. My heart is pounding and when I speak my voice comes out as a sort of shrill croak. 'What are you doing?'

'There's something strange going on back there. I want to find out what it is.'

There's a resolute, set expression to his mouth and I know better than to argue. Instead I take a deep breath then exhale slowly, willing my heart to slow. We wait. I lean forward, expecting to see the approaching light in the side mirror.

'Is it coming?'

But there's nothing. Just eternal dark.

Brad turns the ignition off. He dims the lights, leaving the parkers on. Minutes pass, or are they merely seconds? Time seems to be both standing still and racing hysterically forward. We look at each other, faces green in the reflection of the dashboard lights. There's still no sign of any approaching vehicle.

'Bloody hell!' Brad yells at last, flinging open his door.

Bright light floods the cabin and I blink. Brad gets out and walks to the rear of the car.

'Where are you going?'

He doesn't reply so I open my own door and step out into the night. There's no sound except for the ticking of the car engine as it cools. The breeze is warm after the air conditioning inside. I strain my eyes in the dark, looking back in the direction from which we've come. Searching for something, anything.

Suddenly there's a thumping noise, the sound of running. I scream. A blurred shape hurtles towards us, eyes reflecting the car's parking lights. It brushes so close to us that I can almost hear its breath. Then, as suddenly as it appears, it's gone, merging back into the night. My heart feels as though it's going to burst through my chest.

'What was that?'

'It's okay. Just a 'roo.'

Brad takes a deep breath and I can tell that for just one moment he's been consumed by fear too. 'Come on,' I urge. 'Let's get back into the car.'

'Shh. Wait!'

He cocks his head, as though he's listening. There's no moon, and not a star to be seen. A low rumble of thunder echoes towards us and a flash of lightning makes the landscape momentarily bright, like daylight.

'You don't think we imagined those lights?' My voice is a hoarse whisper.

'No!'

'Then what —?'

The words die, unsaid, in my throat. There is a loud whooshing sound and two lights spear over the rise towards us. Automatically I reach for the door handle. But before I can seek the relative safety of the car, the lights veer away. Across the paddock they go, skimming the tree tops. Then they vanish and we're left there in the dark, staring after them.

I can't breathe. The air seems lodged in my throat, a tight ball. My heart is pounding madly. Brad wrenches at my door, opens it and pushes me inside. Then he runs to the other side and pours himself in. 'Lock your door!' he yells.

Fumbling, hands shaking, I slam my hand against the door button. Then I turn towards Brad. I can see his eyes, large and unblinking, staring back. 'Hell!' I gasp. 'What was that?'

He's silent for a moment. I can see his throat working and the knuckles on his hands, as he grips the steering wheel, are white. 'I think,' he says at last, slowly, teasing each word reluctantly from his mouth. 'I think maybe Stan would call that the min-min light.'

CHAPTER 28

It's six o'clock in the evening, the night before the funeral. We've all gathered at the place where they're holding Kadie's body. Brad and me. My parents. My sister Carys.

We sit on chairs in the waiting room. Brad rubs his arm, the broken one, massaging above the top of the cast. No one's talking. We don't know what to say to each other anyway; the words are no longer there. Carys keeps turning her head away, wiping furtively at her eyes. Does she think that by her twisting her head we don't see?

By this late stage, the arrangements have already been made. The music has been selected, the speakers decided upon. Not for our daughter the anonymity of a celebrant. It'll be us — Brad and me, our family and friends — who'll speak on Kadie's behalf: the people who knew her best.

I feel numb, as though this is all happening to someone else, not me. My eyes are raw from crying. My voice is hoarse. Aided by the tablets Brad's been making me swallow, the days since the accident have all blurred together. Now I'm not certain what day of the week it is, or even how many days have passed. All I know is that tomorrow I'll have to face the ordeal of the funeral.

Despite Brad's misgivings, I need to be here. I haven't seen my daughter since the day of the accident, when she'd waved goodbye to me from the car. Brad thinks it'd be better to keep that as my last memory of her. So do my parents. I know because they've told me, tried to dissuade me from coming here tonight. But I need to reassure myself, to see for myself that she really is gone.

I remember seeing a documentary on television, years ago, about a woman who gave birth to a stillborn baby. She took the child home for a few days, placed it in her bed while she slept, bathed the child, let her older children hold it. At the time I was horrified. It all seemed so macabre, so morbid. Why prolong the misery? I'd thought. I was certain I could never do that.

But since I've become a mother myself, I understand. It's that reluctance to let go immediately, a need to keep that person as part of your family, if just for a short time. Now it seems natural, not odd at all.

The funeral director comes to the door, clears his throat. 'You can come in now,' he says, not looking directly at anyone.

Brad takes my arm as we rise, as though protecting me. 'You don't have to do this,' he whispers. His voice is so choked with emotion he can barely speak.

I wrench away from his grasp. Already we're at odds with each other. Kadie's death has become a barrier between us, a hurdle too high to jump. 'I need to,' I tell him angrily. 'Alright?'

Carys looks sharply at me, then glances away. It seems we can no longer meet each other's gaze. The others walk towards the door.

Kadie is lying on a trolley. It's high, several feet off the ground, and my first instinct is that she should be on something lower, in case she falls. But commonsense, and the way she lies there, all white and limp and still, tells me otherwise.

She looks so small and vulnerable, her tiny frame swamped by the size of the trolley. Someone has combed her hair back; it doesn't flop across her forehead like it used to. Instead it falls back against the sheet, blonde and lacklustre. She's wearing her favourite dress. I'd chosen it from her wardrobe and Brad had brought it in the previous day. I stare at the colour — pale blue — and a pain rises up inside me, so sudden, so acute, that I have to stop myself from crying out.

Carys and my mother are crying openly now, not making any attempt to hide their tears. Carys strokes Kadie's limp hand. I see her pink finger moving against Kadie's white ones. Up and down it goes, moving in the same pattern, the same configuration, and I'm mesmerised by the sight.

'I think it's time to go,' says Brad.

My parents and Carys walk solemnly towards the door. Carys opens it and they step through. Now it's just Brad and me in the room. I wonder how I can bear to tear myself away. I need to spend more time here, create memories that will have to carry me through a lifetime.

I turn to Brad. 'I just want to stay a little longer,' I say.

He glances at me, looking worried. 'Okay,' he says, closing the door behind the others.

'By myself,' I say firmly. 'I want to stay by myself.'

'Jess, no!'

I shake my head firmly. 'Please go, Brad. I want to be alone with Kadie.'

He hesitates. His mouth opens, as though he's planning to speak.

'Just go,' I say, leaving no room for argument.

It's quiet in the room after he leaves. I walk over to the trolley, standing there for what seems like an eternity. Then I bend and gather my daughter into my arms. Her weight is insubstantial; she feels as light as a bird. As I sit in one of the chairs that line the side of the room, I know the heaviness is all in my heart.

She's cold, so cold. My first thought is that I must warm her and awkwardly I tug at my coat, fold it so that it partly covers her too. She lies there, limply, as dozens of thoughts and memories race through my mind, each one vying for recognition.

Kadie: newborn, her mouth working furiously at my breast.

Kadie: toddling around the garden, picking off the heads of flowers and placing them in my waiting hands.

Kadie: climbing onto my lap and wrapping her arms around my neck. 'I love you, Mummy.'

'How much do you love me, baby girl?' Why do I need to hear the words?

She spreads her arms wide. 'This much, Mummy.'

Now, remembering, I stroke her hair, then her face. I trace the outlines of eyes and nose, her perfectly formed mouth. My finger follows the length of her neck, finally stopping at the small hollow at the base of her throat. The thought occurs to me, bizarre and silly: if I tickle her, will she wake up?

I've been dreading this moment, and the holding brings unbearable heartache. I rock backwards and forwards. It's a natural thing, habitual. I hum the tune of a song we used to sing together at bedtime. But now it sounds simply sad, like a dirge. But this is the last chance I'll ever have to hold my daughter, sing for her, and the pain is all encompassing.

Time passes, though I've lost track of it. From the angle I'm sitting, I can't see my watch. I think of Mum and Dad, Carys and Brad waiting outside, but still I can't bear to rise, leave my daughter.

There's a tentative knock on the door. 'Jess?'

I ignore it, thinking stupidly that whoever it is might go away.

After a minute or so, the door opens. It's my father. He stands there for a moment, looking at me. I can see, even from this distance, his eyes are brimming with tears.

'Jess, love,' he says, 'it's time to go.'

I shake my head. 'It can't be. I'm not ready.'

'You'll never be ready. Death isn't like a test. It isn't something you can prepare yourself for.'

He's right, I know he is. He walks towards me. Gently he lifts Kadie from my arms and places her back on the trolley. My skin is cold where her body has lain and I wrap my arms around myself. I walk out the door, not looking back.

I've returned to the loving arms of my family. 'Jess,' they say, taking my arm, my hands, holding me close. But I am frozen beyond tears. My mind is a conflicting mass of emotions. I want everyone to go away, leave me alone. Yet some part of me craves their warmth, their sympathy.

I know now that death is not relative to size. The loss of a young child is never a lesser loss — it's huge, monstrous, bigger than anything I've ever experienced before. And already, after only a few days, I'm not the person I was. I've been made smaller by my loss, lonelier, more isolated. And I know that what lies ahead, however painful it might be, will be my own private journey.

It's only six o'clock on the Diamantina and the morning is stifling already. I sit on the verandah hoping to catch a stray breeze. Jenna's diaries, the station journals and my note pad are spread out before me on the table.

I've taken certain liberties when transcribing the diaries. Jenna's writing is precise and meticulous. Sometimes it's very personal. At other times she skirts certain issues, taking a neutral stance. So I use my sense of them, my intuitive knowing, to fill in the gaps in Jenna's stories, to flesh them out. I imagine conversations, actions and reactions. I see Jenna as she was then, dark-haired and fiery, not afraid to stand up for herself and her beliefs. I see Adam, solid and dependable, the 'rock' on whom Jenna can rely, and imagine the way he loved Katie, his tiny niece, as though he, himself, was the child's father. And, in a sense, he was.

Sometimes it's like they're all sitting next to me as I write, butting in, adding scenes and dialogue to my work. *No, it was like this,* I can almost hear Adam say. *We did it this way.*

I've woken early to an idea. 'I'm going to write Jenna's story. What do you think?' I ask Brad when I tell him my plan over a cup of coffee.

'I think it's a bad idea.' He shakes his head, looking concerned.

'Why?'

'Well,' he begins, looking doubtful, 'in hindsight, I think what these diaries are doing is revisiting old wounds. You've had a tough year, Jess, and getting involved in some sad story over a century old —'

I hate that, when he jumps to conclusions, forms opinions before he knows the full details. 'How do you know it's a sad story? It might be uplifting and inspiring.'

'Because Stan told me about the graves. You don't need to be a rocket scientist to figure out that the story's going to end badly. I wish you'd never seen the diaries now.'

'Ah.'

'So you don't know how the story ends? Stan hasn't told you?'

'I didn't ask.'

Brad awards me an odd look. Why do I feel the need to explain?

'I want to find out for myself, if you must know. This whole thing is like a journey, and knowing what happened, out of context, would be like arriving at your destination having missed the last part of the trip. When I get to the end of Adam and Jenna's story, I want to know why things happened, not simply that they did happen.'

'That's a bit rich, coming from someone who always flips to the end of the novel when they're only halfway through just to see how the story finishes.'

'That's different.'

'How?'

Why can't he see? 'For Christ's sake, Brad, novels are made-up, imaginary. But this is real! It happened!'

'Well, don't say I didn't warn you.'

I stare at him for what seems a very long time. I'm feeling a bit rocky from the night before. After our strange experience on the roadside, we'd driven home in silence, neither of us feeling the need to speak. My sleep had been peppered with dreams of strange lights and kangaroos thumping towards me in the dark. Several times I'd woken to a racing heart and a dry mouth.

Now, nothing moves in the room. A shaft of sunlight remains stationary on the floor. The air feels stifling about my face. I blink, closing my eyes to the sight of his earnest face, his concern. Always his *bloody* concern.

We seem to be travelling in different directions, my husband and me. He's trying to protect me, I know, steering me away from unpleasant outcomes. But I have to go on, finish the story. I need to know what happened to these two people, this man and woman who had circled each other for so long, and who had come to realise that there was strength in their union. Jenna had moved on and accepted her life. Perhaps, in time, I could too.

Would Brad understand, if I tried to explain, how Jenna's story is helping me see my own life differently? How, I can't yet explain. It's more an intuition, a hunch, than anything tangible. Jenna's losses are putting my own into perspective. In number, hers were more than mine. But out of that she soldiered on, turned adversity into new strength. Wasn't she expecting Adam's child?

'I'm too involved to stop now,' I tell him flatly.

'Suit yourself,' he says. 'I'll be here to pick up the pieces.'

I turn my back on him, resume my transcribing.

Half an hour later, a station wagon pulls up at the front gate in a swirl of dust. Betty and Ella heave themselves out and proceed up the path towards the house. Resignedly I close the diary I'm working on.

'We've come to take you sightseeing,' says Betty.

I look helplessly towards Brad who's lacing his boots, preparing for a day further along the river banks. In his box next to the front door there's an assortment of water-testing metres and secchi dishes.

'Go,' he says, straightening into an upright position and shooing me towards them. 'It'll do you good to get out for the day.' He turns to Betty and Ella. 'That's practically all she's done for days: sitting there, nosing in those diaries. I don't think she'd stop to sleep if she didn't have to.'

I flash everyone a weak apologetic grin. Brad and I only have less than a week left on the Diamantina, and although I'm making good progress with the diaries I'm desperate to finish my task. However, with these two woman standing waiting, and Brad's vocal approval, I have no choice but to go. They have obviously arranged the outing especially for me, and I can tell by the expectant smiles on their faces they think I'll be delighted by the prospect.

'Where are we going?'

'Conor O'Loughlin's grave. It's about a two-hour drive. And there's plenty of countryside to see on the way.'

'What will I bring?' I ask, stalling for time. Why, I'm not sure. These women are about as obstinate as a bulldozer. They're not about to change their minds.

'Nothing,' replies Betty over her shoulder as she heads back out to the car. 'I've packed a picnic and drinks. We'll be gone most of the day.'

I grab my camera on the way out. Betty ushers me through the front passenger door while Ella climbs into the back seat.

It seems Ella is the navigator, directing us this way and that. She leans through the division between the two front seats, pointing out various landmarks along the way. 'The old Abo bush instinct,' she offers with a smile when I ask her how she remembers the way. 'An Abo never gets lost in the bush.'

'Never?'

She thinks for a moment. 'Well, hardly ever. Though Stan reckons I'm not much chop at navigating.'

'We'll be the judge of that,' says Betty briskly as we arrive at a fork in the road. 'Now, which way? Left or right?'

'Left,' says Ella without blinking.

'This is all very coincidental,' I tell the women as we drive along. 'It was only yesterday that Doris at the museum mentioned Conor's grave, and here we are, a day later, on our way there.'

'It was Doris who reminded me,' answers Betty, beaming triumphantly as the car lurches over what seems like the gazillionth pothole. 'She phoned last night to say she wanted to come out and take some photos of the old homestead. We got to talking about the diaries and journals, and Conor's grave. The historical society thinks we should do something special there, something commemorative. Anyway, I rang Ella and — well, here we are.'

We drive for over an hour, navigating gullies and washaways and overgrown dirt tracks. Small bushes scrape the duco as we pass. Betty grips the wheel, a frown of concentration on her face. She doesn't have much time for talk, so Ella and I fill the silences between us as the old beast of a car struggles like an arthritic dinosaur up dry riverbeds. The chassis creaks and groans in protest, and there are moments when I fear it'll split in two.

We come at last to an open plain. Clumps of yellow wildflowers make a vivid carpet, stretching almost as far as I can see among the tufts of Mitchell grass.

'Almost there,' says Ella, pointing to a distant line of trees that obviously denote a riverbed.

I take a deep breath. I'm curious, yet apprehensive, about seeing Conor's grave. And I wonder momentarily why I'm here to see the burial place of a man who died over a hundred years earlier, yet I've never been to my daughter's.

I make myself a pledge, right then and there. When I get back to the city I'll go to the cemetery, take the time to sit by Kadie's grave. I'll talk to her, tell her about the past year and how difficult and sad and unbearable it's been. Perhaps I'll take a teddy bear or doll from the shrine-like room that was once Kadie's and place it on the grave. Then I'll tell her about the dreams, and a little girl called Kathryn O'Loughlin who's buried on a place called Diamantina Downs, miles from anywhere.

'Just down here,' says Ella, breaking my train of thought.

We climb out of the car and manoeuvre down a rocky ledge to the highest bank of the river. The grave, fenced off by sturdy mesh, is under the leafy branches of a river red gum. Above, a crow sits in the branches sending out a disjointed squawk. There's a white cross bearing the words *Conor O'Loughlin* and the dates *1851–1873*. Tufts of grass grow over the mound and through the mesh fence.

'Jack and Stan put a proper fence around it a few years back,' says Betty. 'There was an old wooden one but it had rotted and mostly fallen over.'

It's hot here. No breeze comes along the riverbed and a trickle of sweat runs down my back. Betty is fanning herself with a folded newspaper she's taken from the car. Ella has hitched her dress up to her knees and is wading through ankle-deep water. 'You should try this, Jess,' she says.

'Looks inviting.'

'They call this place Murdering Creek,' Ella adds, and I remember that day, weeks earlier, when I'd pointed it out to Brad on the map. 'And over there —' she indicates a nearby jagged peak that rises out of the trees — 'is Mount Misery. It was on the river, just below, that Ngayla's tribe members were murdered. There's no official record of the slaughter, though. According to the government bureaucrats it never happened.'

'But it did!' I interject. 'It's all in one of the station journals. I can even give you an exact date.'

Ella smiles sadly. 'Doesn't matter, anyhow,' she says. 'Knowing the date won't change anything. Dead is dead! The important thing is that we all know. The story's been passed down through Stan's family: how Ngayla's mother and sister were killed, and Adam finding her, bringing her back to Diamantina Downs.'

We're quiet for a few minutes, thinking about what Ella has said. Then I take a few photos from different angles — one of the grave by itself, and several others with Ella and Betty standing by the mesh. It's a quiet place, solemn. There's a hushed sense of peace here. For some reason we talk in whispers.

We eat lunch on the river bank. Betty has prepared a feast, none of which I feel like eating in this heat. I take a sandwich, nibble it. When she isn't looking I throw it into a clump of nearby bushes. The ants will be grateful, I think.

I lie on my back in the grass and stare upwards at the rocky crag that towers over us. It was there that the men from Ngayla's tribe had hidden on that long-ago night, injured and desperate, before they'd raided Conor's camp. I try to replay the scene in my mind, but my imagination keeps jamming at the place where the men crept towards Conor and the fire. Somehow I can't bring myself to think about the spear and the surprised frightened look on Conor's face, or the thud of wood against flesh.

After we've finished eating, the clouds slink in and blot out the sun, though it seems no cooler. We clamber back into the car. On the way home we stop at the ruins of an old homestead.

The building, unlike Adam and Jenna's, was made of stone. It's rather dilapidated now. Most of the roof is missing and the skeletal remains of the rafters are dark against the sky. The stone walls, now exposed to the weather, are crumbling. Sheets of corrugated iron have been nailed across the windows.

We get out of the car and walk around. Betty and Ella are talking about the family who used to live there but I'm not interested. There doesn't seem to be room in my mind for anyone other than the O'Loughlins. Instead I wander away, kicking at the ground. Brad says you can sometimes find interesting things in the dirt around these old places. Like bottles, for instance, or old coins.

Small puffs of dust rise as I scuff at the ground with the toe of my shoe. There's something there, old and rusty, one end protruding. I bend down, pick it up. It's a horseshoe.

'That's a good find,' says Ella, coming up behind me.

'It is?'

'Well, horseshoes are generally regarded as lucky. But it's even better if you find one, rather than one being given to you.' She takes it from me, holds it in a 'U' shape. 'You must hang it like this, though. If you hang it the other way, all your luck will run out.'

I look back towards the 4WD. Betty is pouring tea from a thermos, using the fold-down back door as a table. Even from this distance I can see steam rising from the mugs.

'You know, Jess,' Ella says slowly, deliberately. 'I'm not trying to pry, and you can tell me to mind my own business, but sometimes it helps to talk about your problems.'

Unwillingly my mind draws itself back. Pushing Kadie on a swing, hearing her high-pitched peal of laughter. Reading her a story at bedtime, seeing her eyelids fluttering as I read. Pink cheeks. Smell of talcum and Pears soap. Blonde hair falling about her face.

I close my eyes and purposely push the memory away. Kadie isn't part of my life anymore and the emptiness there, the hole that her leaving has left, is too big to ever be filled.

'Problems? Who says I have any?' I shrug, try to act nonchalant, but my voice comes out all wrong. It's risen an octave, and there's a timbre to it that's tense.

Ella shrugs. 'Like I said, it's none of my business. It was just a feeling I had, but perhaps I was mistaken.'

She turns to walk away and suddenly I'm struck by how much I want — no, *need* — to talk to this woman. 'No, you weren't,' I say abruptly. 'You weren't mistaken at all.'

Ella walks back to me and lays one hand on my arm. I feel the warmth of her, the caring, and my eyes fill with tears. Angrily I brush them away. 'I feel like I've lost control.'

'You haven't, you know.'

I stare at her in disbelief. 'Look at me! It's been over a year, and nothing's changed. I'm a mess. My daughter's dead but I'd give anything to be able to take it all back, be as we were. You don't think I ever wanted any of this to happen, do you? Of course I've lost control!'

'It's up to you how you handle what life throws at you, how you react to it. That's the ultimate form of control.'

I stare resignedly at her through tear-smudged eyes. 'I'm not handling life very well, am I?'

'I'm not being critical, Jess. And it's easy to be opinionated about things you've never experienced. I can't even imagine the pain you've gone through. What I am saying, though, is that you do have choices. You can give in to what's happened, admit defeat and get bitter about it. Lose your marriage, maybe, as a result. Or you can accept what's happened and move on.'

'You're telling me to forget about my daughter?'

Ella sighs and places a hand on each of my shoulders. 'I would never do that! Never! What you're going through is a normal process of grieving.

First you're upset, then angry. Then you accept. That's the natural order.'

'I know all about that. People have given me books.'

'Did you read them?'

'Not really.' I shake my head. At the time I couldn't bear to read more than a few pages, enough to get the basic idea. I felt like my grief was different somehow. More intense, more personal. How could words in a book explain how I felt?

'Ah, Jess, who always knows best!' She's being brutal and blunt, but she gives me a watery smile, which softens her words. 'You can't go through the rest of your life being stuck on "angry". There's a point when you have to stop, to move to the next stage, or you'll let your daughter's death destroy everything else good left in your life.'

'Good? I don't think there's much good in my life!'

'It's easy to discount the positives when you're upset. What about Brad? Your marriage? What about the people who love you? Don't you think they're angry too? But they're not stuck on that one emotion.'

I give a bitter laugh. 'You make it sound so simple, so easy.'

She gathers me in an embrace, holding me close. I need to feel that, the closeness of another person, the reassurance. I sag against her. The strength, the fight, has gone out of me. There's nothing left inside me but quiet submission.

'You can do it, Jess,' she whispers forcefully in my ear. 'I'm not saying it's going to be easy, because it's not. You already know that. But if you accept that in many ways you *are* still in control, then you can do it.'

We're all fairly quiet during the ride home. I've elected to sit in the back; I don't feel like talking. My eyes sting. Every muscle in my body aches. I wish I could sleep, put the day far from my mind. But there are two hours of body-jarring before we arrive home.

Back at Diamantina Downs, I ask Betty to drop me at the main gate. I want to walk across the paddock to the house, delay my arrival. Brad's car isn't there and I know no one's home. The thought of walking into an empty house is suddenly unsettling.

Betty lurches away in the car, in the direction of Ella's place, leaving me to close the gate. Part way across the paddock I stop and lean against a tree. Only now I'm alone do I allow myself the luxury of dissecting Ella's words.

There are several sentences that keep niggling away at me, the words demanding attention. I see Ella's face, so firm and unwavering. I hear the controlled tone of her voice. There had been no cajoling, no persuasion on Ella's part. And no treating me like a wayward child. Simply calm reassurance and the belief that somewhere inside me I can find the strength to deal with all the heartache in my life.

You can't go through the rest of your life being stuck on 'angry'.

It's up to you how you handle what life throws at you, how you react to it.

You can do it, Jess.

It's then that I feel a glimmer of hope. Ella has given me back my confidence, the sense that some day I'll be able to let go of the grief. It won't happen today, or tomorrow. But maybe during the following months I'll find that anger dissolving, slipping away.

Trust Ella, I think as I open the front door and walk inside, to come right out and say what she thinks, not skirting around the issue like everyone else.

But, I realise with a smile, Ella isn't like everyone else.

PART SIX

Sliding Away

CHAPTER 29

The shearing of the few stock that remained was done. Three days: that was all it had taken, when only two years earlier the shearers had stayed on Diamantina Downs for several weeks. Jenna had taken Katie down to the shearing shed each day, bearing trays of scones and small cakes for smoko. She'd watched as the men bent over the sheep, blades flashing. There was a smell of sweat and lanolin there, a musty fusty odour that stayed long after the men and beasts were gone.

After they'd been shorn, the pitiful animals, bones now prominent because their fleece was gone, ran down the chutes on spindly legs out into the sunshine. The bales of wool — and there were only a few this year — were pressed and packed, then bound with iron bands. They were, Jenna knew, destined eventually for the London mills, a fact that seemed to annoy Adam.

'Bloody English,' he'd muttered, glaring at the miserable result of a year's hard work. 'The profit will only just cover the shearers' wages. There'll be nothing left.'

'Surely it'll rain soon,' she'd murmured.

'What if it doesn't? I don't know what we'll do then.'

For several days now the blacks had been holding a corroboree for rain down at the camp. Adam and Jenna had been invited along one night. It was an honour, Wongaree had told them, never usually extended to white people. Jenna had watched, fascinated, by the light of several brushwood fires. Adorned with feathers and kangaroo tails, Wongaree had led the men. They'd moved slowly, then quickly, stamping their feet, suddenly looking like a flock of birds settling as they threw themselves down in a crouching position. The women had circled the men, beating sticks in unison.

Jenna sighed, remembering, then she turned her attention back to the present. There was a crowd at the dining table for breakfast that last morning: their own small family, shearers, jackaroos and station hands. Jenna heard the babble of their voices as though from far away. Instead she pressed her hand hard against the shape of the child as it twisted and turned inside her. The shearing was ended; her focus was the future now. Katie. This new baby.

Later she stood on the verandah with her daughter and waved as the last of the wagons passed, loaded with men and supplies, bound for the next station further south.

It seemed she couldn't settle that morning. The house seemed abnormally quiet after the men had gone. Katie was out in the back yard with Aleyne who was hanging out the morning's washing. Adam had gone out into the paddocks, rifle under his arm. From the kitchen came the sound of singing. Ngayla was there with Jinbi, kneading the bread dough.

Jinbi was a year old now, a brown sturdy boy who tottered around after his mother on unsteady legs. At other times she carried him while she worked, his mouth often latched permanently to her breast. Jenna had tried to persuade Ngayla to wean him, but the young girl had refused. 'No, Missy,' she'd said, shaking her head, 'Jinbi good boy. Even Mista Adam say so. One day he get big enough go help other men. Need lotsa good milk, make him strong.'

Now Jenna smiled wearily, hearing the young girl's sing-song voice. Already her back ached. She walked to the window in the dining room and leaned on the sill, taking the pressure off her spine.

Across the distant paddocks, the heat shimmered. Closer in, she could see a mob of emus, dark gangly dots outlined against the mauve hazy ridges, zigzagging through the grass. Grey-green coolibahs moved in the hot wind, a slow dance. The sky was so blue it made her eyes ache.

There was a hushed expectancy to the air, a restlessness that magnified itself in her unborn child. He — she was convinced this time that it was a boy — rolled and kicked out at her. 'Ouch!' she murmured, idly massaging the spot with the flattened palm of her hand. A flock of corellas rose up, close in, and flew screeching towards the river. It was one of those unpredictable days, she thought, where the weather might suddenly change. Already there was a tell-tale pinkish tinge on the western horizon.

Dust storm. The first of the season.

Jenna sighed and leaned her head against the cool glass of the window, remembering the previous summer. She and Aleyne had spent almost a whole day shovelling the great drifts of sand from the verandahs and gardens after one particular storm. Surely today wouldn't be the same. She had no energy for it now. It was mere weeks until the babe was due and it was as much as she could do to walk around the house. Lord knows how she'd survive the trip to town for the birth, as Adam was insisting.

After lunch she put Katie to bed for her usual afternoon nap. Several minutes later she looked in on her daughter. The little girl was already asleep, her dark hair damp against her skin. How she could sleep amazed Jenna: the air in the room was stifling.

Exhausted, Jenna went to the bedroom she shared with Adam. He'd insisted, right from the start of her pregnancy, that she had an afternoon nap while Katie was asleep.

'I'm not sick!' she'd protested at first, laughing.

'No, but you'll need all your strength for when the baby comes.'

But today she was certain she'd never sleep. The room was no cooler than her daughter's and a fly buzzed annoyingly against the window. The baby kicked mercilessly. A brief painless spasm hardened her belly to surprising tightness.

She slipped off her dress and lay on the bed cover, staring at the ceiling. From the kitchen came the muted voices of Aleyne and Ngayla. Once the clearing up of the lunch dishes was completed, they'd go back to the camp for the remainder of the afternoon, not returning until later to prepare supper. The air was oppressive, hushed, as though gathering force for some later onslaught.

Purposefully she took a deep breath and closed her eyes, willing sleep to come.

Adam lifted the rifle and fired, watching as another sheep jerked into lifelessness. Squinting in the sunlight, he saw another mob further across the paddock lying under the shade of a coolibah. At the sound of the gun, several of them had tried to struggle to their feet, and failed. Resignedly he mounted his horse and rode towards them.

This wasn't how he'd imagined his life on the Diamantina. All these years he'd held some sort of conviction in his head of how things should be. Slowly building up the property. Making improvements as he could afford them. He'd budgeted and waited, unlike Jenna, saving his money for the proverbial rainy day. However it wasn't rain that was now ruining his careful plans, but rather the lack of it.

Jenna's money was all but gone, spent on the house and furnishings. It had been hers to use as she liked, and he'd wanted none of it. He supposed it had made her happy, and their lives had certainly been made more comfortable because of it. God's truth, he begrudged her nothing. Bush life was hard enough. So what if his wife and child — and he, too, by default — lived in comparative luxury while around them the property was falling into ruin? Drought was a product of nature, and money couldn't buy rain.

He shaded his eyes with his hand and stared hard into the distance. There, on the horizon, the sky was pink, a thin band that ran and merged with the rocky outcrops that rose up randomly from the flat land.

Dust storm.

He supposed they'd be even more regular this summer. As the grasses died, there was nothing left to hold the soil together. The wind currents picked it up and drove it skywards, sweeping it along, depositing it sometimes hundreds of miles away.

From across the paddock, a gust of hot wind swept towards him, pulling small burry bushes in its wake. He had an hour, at the most, he estimated, before the storm arrived.

Resolutely he disposed of the few remaining sheep and turned his horse towards home. He had no inclination to be out here, miles from the homestead, in the blinding choking dust.

Jenna woke to a darkened room. The storm had hit and she heard the clatter of dirt against the glass. A film of perspiration dampened her top lip and her skin felt clammy. Her hair, where her head had rested against the pillow, was damp. From the way the curtains hung limply she knew that someone — Ngayla perhaps? — had closed the windows while she slept.

She stretched like a cat, rolling onto her side to peer at the clock on her bedside table. What time was it? Goodness. After four, though it seemed like night, the light was so poor. She'd been asleep over two hours. Slowly she heaved herself from the bed and picked up her dress from the floor where she had dropped it earlier.

On bare feet she padded along the hallway to her daughter's room, pushing open the door. 'Katie? Katie, darling?'

But the bed was empty.

The window in this room was open, the wind whipping the curtains about. Jenna leaned out. Sand stung her eyes. She could scarcely see a dozen feet in front of her. Grabbing the catch on the window, she slammed it shut.

She stared for a moment at the rumpled bed, realisation dawning. Katie would be in the kitchen. Aleyne would have come back from the camp by now and they'd be in there together, making biscuits or a pastry for tonight's supper.

But the kitchen was also empty, the fire almost out.

Jenna slung another piece of wood on the coals. She went through to the dining room and parlour, the music room, study. No Katie. Back along the hallway she went, flinging open the doors of the other unused bedrooms, calling her daughter's name. 'Katie? Where are you? Come on out!'

Katie loved to hide and it had become a daily game, the little girl running to some cupboard or other when she heard Adam's voice as he came in from the paddocks. But today the game was wrong. It was too early. Adam wasn't here. *No one*, it seemed, was here.

A bubble of disquiet rose in her chest and she shivered, trying to dispel it. Adam would say she was being silly, worrying unnecessarily. But she'd grown to be like that over the years. Life and death was so unexpected. Take Michael, for instance. And her mother. Conor. But Katie wasn't like them, she reasoned. Any moment now she'd find her daughter. A few stern words later and they'd be heading off towards the kitchen to start preparations for supper.

The house was quiet, unnervingly so, except for the sound of her own footfalls. She threw open the last bedroom door. 'Where are you?' she screamed, surprised to hear her own voice jangling back at her, shrill and fearful.

Down on all fours she went, awkwardly because of the baby, pulling back the cover and peering under the bed. But there was no sound of suppressed laughter, no darting flurry.

The front door slammed. *Katie!* she thought, levering herself to her feet again and running towards the foyer.

But it was only Adam there, pulling his boots from his feet. 'Thank God I'm home. That wind is so strong —'

'Have you seen Katie?' she cut across his words.

He stared at her, looking puzzled. 'No. Should I?'

'I can't find her. She was gone when I woke up.'

'She'll be hiding.' He went to the nearest cupboard, opened it. 'Katie! Come out this instant! Your mother's getting worried.'

There was no reply.

'*Katie!*' He strode through the house, flinging open doors as Jenna had done minutes earlier. 'She can't be gone. Where would she go?'

Jenna came to an abrupt halt behind him as the memory speared back.

Little Miss Katie's gone to town. She saddled up a horse all by herself and rode off.

Shocked, she brought her hands to her mouth as though stifling a cry. Her voice was scarcely louder than a whisper. 'You don't think ... She wouldn't ... try and take herself into town?'

Together they ran to the front door and out onto the verandah. In the space where Katie's boots usually sat, there was nothing but a few scattered grains of sand.

'She's gone!' screamed Jenna.

Frantically her eyes scanned the swirling dust for some sign, some clue. But the haze was so thick that, apart from a few pepper trees, their branches bending and thrashing under the force of the storm, nothing could be seen.

'We should check the stables.'

Why hadn't she thought of that? Faint hope surfaced, making Jenna light-headed. 'The stables, of course. That's where she'd go.'

Together they ran towards the building, struggling against the wind, dirt stinging faces and eyes. Adam wrenched open the door and they almost fell inside. 'Katie,' he yelled over the rattle of the storm.

Frantically they ran down the wide centre aisle, peering over the gates into the stalls. The horses were uneasy, snorting and stamping their feet. Jenna was aware of the smell of chaff and molasses, and her own mounting dismay as they came to the last of the stalls. The horses were all there but there was no sign of Katie.

Everything seemed to be spinning, revolving around Adam's face which swam in and out of focus. She thought she might faint. Adam reached out, as though sensing her shakiness, and took hold of her shoulders. 'Think!' he commanded. 'Where else could she be? What if Aleyne saw the storm coming and took her down to the camp, knowing she'd be scared if she woke up and you were still asleep?'

Jenna shook her head. Why were they standing here, discussing possibilities, wasting time? They should be out there, searching. 'She's never done that before. Why now?'

Adam led her back to the verandah and forced her into a sitting position on the bench seat. 'I'll go down to the camp,' he said tersely, 'and see if she's there. If not, I'll bring some of the men back with me and we'll form a search party.' He took one step backwards and nodded towards the thrashing trees. 'Promise me you'll not do anything silly. I don't want to be having to search out there for you too.'

He refused to go until she gave her word. Precious minutes were ticking away, and goodness knows how long Katie had already been gone. 'You've got ten minutes,' she agreed unwillingly. 'Then if you're not back I'm going after her.'

The minutes passed, long and drawn out, or so it seemed to Jenna as she waited on the verandah. Dust stung her eyes until they watered. She covered her nose with a handkerchief, trying not to breathe in too much of it. She tried to see into the thick swirling mass. But there was nothing.

Adam returned from the camp with Aleyne and the men. Wordlessly he shook his head at her. Even in that eerie pink half-light, his face was white with worry.

He showed Wongaree the place where Katie's boots had been. Wongaree walked down the steps and into the yard, head bent low, inspecting the ground. 'Wind takes tracks away. Nothin' left to follow,' he muttered, sweeping his arm dismissively towards the sky. 'Footprints belong'm Miss Katie all gone now.'

Jenna gave a choking sob. 'Please, Wongaree. We have to find her.' A ball of nausea had formed in her belly. Unable to contain it, she ran to the end of the verandah, vomiting into the bushes there.

'Are you alright?' Adam asked, coming up behind her.

'It's nothing,' she said. 'I'll be fine. We have to go and look for her now.'

She ran towards the steps that led down into the yard but Adam grabbed her arm, forcing her to a halt. 'Where are you going?'

She swung away from him, jerking her arm from his grasp. 'God, Adam! I'm going to find her.'

'You're in no condition to go anywhere. Think of the baby.'

'I'm thinking of my daughter. She'll be terrified out there. It'll be night in a few hours. You know how she hates the dark.'

'Jenna,' he said patiently, cupping his hands around her cheeks, forcing her to look directly at him. 'You're to stay here. No arguments. What if Katie finds her way back home and you're not here?'

What indeed? She hadn't thought of that, the possibility that her daughter might simply emerge safely from the storm with no help from any of them.

Adam pushed her back, gently, towards Aleyne. The black woman took a firm grasp of her arm. 'Come inside, Missy. Aleyne make cuppa tea. You feel better then.'

'Do you think she might ...?' Jenna began, hope see-sawing inside her chest.

But Adam was already striding away from her, taking the front steps two at a time, the other men at his heels. Seconds later they were swallowed by the choking dust.

She paced up and down the verandah, eyes stinging. From time to time, Aleyne offered to make a pot of tea, tried to lead her back inside the house, but Jenna shrugged her away.

Adam came in at dusk. The storm was still blowing but it was in its last ragged phase. 'There's no sign of her,' he said as she sagged against his chest. 'I'm sorry, Jenna, but we can't see a thing out there. She could be merely yards away and we'd walk right by her. We'll have to wait until this dies down.'

She could barely walk inside, thinking with each footfall that she would slide to the ground. Adam held a hand under her arm, guiding her to the table where Aleyne, at the sound of Adam's arrival, had served a hastily prepared supper.

'Eat up, Missy,' the black woman instructed, but it was all Jenna could do to push the food around on the plate with her fork. If she ate a mouthful she knew she'd be sick again.

She tried to keep busy, clearing away the dishes and helping Aleyne to wash up, but she felt the rising threat of panic. All she could think of was Katie wandering aimlessly through the bush, hungry and thirsty and scared.

About nine o'clock the storm ended. The clouds skimmed away and the moon shone high in the sky, cold and silver. In its light, Jenna could see sand piled against the front fence in great drifts, where before there had been none.

Adam took a lantern and Jenna watched it bobbing across the paddock as he went with the trackers. Debil-debil light, she thought, remembering Aleyne's prophecy: anyone who followed the light and caught it would never return to tell the tale.

After dark had fallen, had Katie seen that mysterious light that wavered and dipped across the paddocks? Had she followed it through the storm, thinking it might lead her home? What if she'd found the light, seen it up close?

The questions rose in her mind, requiring answers. Desperately she fought them back, thinking: *Any minute Adam will walk in out of the dark with my daughter safely in his arms. Then it'll all be over.*

She sent Aleyne back to the camp. 'I'll be fine, I promise,' she told the older woman. 'Besides, there's nothing you can do here. Go home, get some sleep.'

She sat on the seat on the verandah, her mind flip-flopping with tiredness. From time to time she heard Adam call, 'Katie!' The word floated back to her across the paddocks, vague and misshapen.

There was no answering reply.

From the direction of the blacks' camp came the distant thwang and thump of the bullroarers. The steady repetitive sounds led her back into the past and muddled images speared back at her. Michael's death. Her mother's. That first day when she'd come to Diamantina Downs and Adam had told her that Conor was dead.

Suddenly her heart was beating very fast. *Oh, Lord!* she thought, burying her face in her hands and taking great gulps of air. *Katie has to be alright. I can't go through this again. I can't!*

Raising her face at last, she thought she saw a shadow move in the darkness beyond. Hope surged wildly. 'Katie,' she whispered, scrambling from the chair. She placed her hands against the verandah railing and stared hard into the night. But it was only a kangaroo hopping along the fence line, trying to get to the greener grass inside.

She went back to the seat and curled on its surface. She was tired, so tired. Her eyes drooped, fell closed. She dreamed of her daughter — hard disjointed images that blurred and ran into each other. Katie running through the bush on booted feet, sliding over rocks and burrs. Katie crying, sobbing, hands held out in front as the dust ran in circles around her.

She woke to a thumping heart and stared stupidly around for a moment, wondering where she was, why she was there. Then she remembered and the knowledge was like the blow of a hammer slamming against her chest.

Katie, she thought. *Katie's gone.*

She shivered and ran a hand over her body. Arms. Breasts. Belly huge with the child. Adam's baby. Her hand lingered there and, as though on cue, it moved inside, a long drawn-out shudder. Hopefully she peered out into the dark. She couldn't hear the men. *I mustn't sleep again*, she told herself. *I must stay awake, keep vigilant. Keep watch for Katie.*

It was late when Adam returned. Exhaustion had smudged his eyes bruised-black and she went to him, wrapping her arms around his shoulders. 'What time is it?'

'Midnight.'

'Is there any ...?'

She couldn't go on, couldn't say the words.

Hope flared then died as Adam shook his head. 'I'm sorry, Jenna. There's no sign. Maybe in the morning when there's more light ...'

And she collapsed, weeping, into his arms.

CHAPTER 30

Jenna slept little that night. Exhausted, Adam climbed into bed, hoping for a few hours' sleep before beginning the search again. 'Come with me,' he said, holding her close for a moment. 'You're not doing the baby any good. You need your rest.'

But she shook her head and sat on the verandah instead, waiting, watching as the moon slid across the sky. Perhaps she dozed — she wasn't sure. Her mind seemed frozen, caught in some place other than here. She tried not to consider the unthinkable. Katie would be found. She *had* to be. They'd lit every available lamp and placed them on the verandahs. If Katie wandered close she'd be able to see them, find her way home.

The men were off again before dawn. Jenna watched as they made their way into the gloom, lamps swinging. Again she begged to be allowed to go with them but Adam pushed her firmly back. 'Don't even consider it. Do you know what the temperature is going to be out there today?'

Of course she knew! But Katie was out there.

She tried to keep busy throughout the day. The usual chores dragged, became unbearable. The *waiting* was intolerable. Seconds, minutes, then hours clicked over on the clocks in the kitchen, the parlour, the bedroom. Wherever she went there were clocks ticking, marking time, counting off the minutes since Katie's disappearance. Out there, in these temperatures, without water, the little girl would never survive. If they didn't find her soon ...

The heat came at Jenna in waves, making her feel nauseous. She kept going to the front door and looking out. The horizon was a waving mirage of cool water and the gums danced in its shimmering wetness.

From time to time she climbed the staircase to Adam's tower room, her eyes searching the landscape for some sign of life. But there was nothing, except for the occasional emu or kangaroo resting in the shade. Even Adam and the men were gone from her view.

One by one the women came up from the camp, offering her hope.

'Boss come back soon, bring Missy Katie.'

'Mebbe she be sittin' longa big water hole, waitin' to be found.'

'Doan you worry about those debil-debil lights. Missy not silly enough follow them.'

Debil-debil lights: how could she not worry?

The afternoon grew late and shadows lengthened on the grass. The sky darkened to indigo. A red slice of departing sun over the western horizon promised another scorching day as Jenna scanned the sky. There was no sign of clouds or cool welcoming rain. A breeze ruffled the grass. Birds made one final dash for home before nightfall. Away in the east came the first glimmer of the evening star. She stared at it for what seemed like an extraordinarily long time, remembering. What had her mother, Mary, said in one of her more lucid moments?

Make a wish on the evening star and it'll come true.

Jenna blinked and looked away.

Silly nonsense, she thought. Adam would be the one to find her daughter, bring her home. Any minute they'd walk in the door.

Adam had spent a sleepless night, trying to anticipate in which direction Katie might have wandered the previous day. But it was desolate country out there and luck was definitely against them. The dust storm had wiped any trace of the little girl from the ground, possible footprints swirled high into the air by the hot wind. Day-time temperatures were searingly high. The only water in the river channels, if Katie had wandered in that direction, was stagnant and foul-smelling.

The men set off again on horseback when the sky was still dark. As it became lighter, flocks of corellas rose shrieking from the trees as they passed. Plovers ran before them through the grass, wings raised in alarm, protecting their nests with their harsh shrill cry. Kangaroos paused, glancing up, while a mob of emus darted away on spindly legs.

'Katie!' Adam called from time to time, waiting expectantly for an answering cry.

But there was none.

After the sun came up they dismounted from their horses and spread out, combing the ground for possible remaining clues, still calling her name. The black men examined bushes as they passed, to see if twigs had been recently broken off or if Katie's dress had caught on one and had torn the fabric, leaving a shred behind as evidence. Hope rose strong in Adam's chest. Hopefully today there would be some sign, some indication. She was only small and surely couldn't have gotten far. They had horses but Katie was on foot. They had to catch up with her soon.

Then came the niggling possibility. North, south, east or west: she could have gone towards any point on the compass. What if they were looking in the wrong direction?

After several hours of fruitless searching the men separated into two groups, Adam and Wongaree agreeing to scour further along the riverbeds while Pigeon and Wandi headed west into the higher spinifex country.

Through the exhausting heat of the day, Adam and Wongaree rode through tangles of lignum bushes in dry riverbeds, under creek wilga and river red gum, the horses' hooves kicking up puffs of dust behind them. They searched gullies and washaways, and scoured the sour muddy banks of water holes. The black man led Adam through dozens of caves that overhung the river, where the air was cool and musty, and the rock walls were painted with pictures of emus and snakes. There were deep niches in the rocks where, Wongaree told him, in times past Aboriginal girls had put their babies to sleep.

But of Katie there was no sign.

Outside the last cave, he closed his eyes and listened. There were the usual bush sounds — crickets chirping, crows cawing. Even in the dappled shade of the overhanging trees, the sun felt hot on his face. He opened his mouth. '*KATIE!*' he yelled, as loud as his voice would allow, and the word came back at him a dozen times, echoing dully from the rocks walls that hung overhead.

As the day wore on, the apprehension grew in his gut. It festered away, roiling and churning like a bucking horse. He had to find Katie, he *had* to. She'd been gone almost a day and time was running out. He couldn't bear to return home to the look of disappointment in Jenna's eyes.

But what if she was already dead?

He'd been suppressing the thought for hours but now, tired and hungry, he allowed it to slide unchecked into his mind.

No! He closed his mind off to that possibility, refusing to let it take hold. He couldn't give in, not yet. He'd search for another few hours at least. Until dark. Then he'd have to reassess the situation.

'Come on, Wongaree,' he said, pointing to a nearby ridge. 'Let's try along there.'

By nightfall he knew there was scant hope. Without water there was no way Katie could still be alive. If it was winter she might have stood a chance, but not in this unrelenting heat. Adam drew his horse to a halt, wiped his hand across his forehead and shook his head at the black man. Their own water supply was low and they should return home.

Another day passed and dusk slid into night. Back at the homestead, the noise from the blacks' camp reverberated through the dark. It had been going on for days now but tonight it seemed louder, more intense, as it slid through the suffocating heat towards Jenna. She heard the clunk of the ceremonial stones being struck together, the thumping of sticks. Whoompah, whoompah, whoomp went the dull whirr of the bullroarers.

The vibrations flew at her through the still air, battering her already fragile senses. They leapt along the hardened backbones of the sandy ridges. At unexpected times they swung along the water holes and played among the leaves of the coolibahs. Frantically they bounced off the walls of the house and slid past her, along the hallway, sidling into every room. There was no escape.

She imagined them — those eerie noises that went on and on, relentlessly, until she wondered if she might go mad with it — as living, breathing entities. They existed, were real. If she reached out she might touch them, as one would touch a table or chair, or another's hand. Sometimes she put her hands over her ears, but somehow the sounds still crept into her head.

Clunk.

Whoompah, whoomp.

'Wha! Wha! Wha!'

Whether the blacks were praying for rain or Katie — or both — Jenna was uncertain.

There was a sound behind her, more immediate, and she turned, her mind already forming the word: Katie. However it wasn't her daughter standing there, but Adam, his face blurred by layers of dust. The question died on her lips, unasked. She already knew the answer by the resolute set to his mouth. He shook his head.

'Tomorrow,' she said, trying to muster optimism. 'Tomorrow you'll find her. I know it.'

He reached out and took her hands in his. Then he said the hated words. 'We have to face the truth. Katie couldn't possibly have survived out there.'

Her own voice was a whisper. 'She has to. She's my daughter.'

'It's been too long. Over two days —'

'*Adam!*' Her voice cut through his words.

How dare he voice such doubts when her own heart was so full of hope. Any minute now one of the other men would walk through the door with Katie in his arms. She'd be scared, hot and thirsty, but nonetheless unscarred from her ordeal. So she, Jenna, wouldn't — *couldn't* — let any doubts creep in. To do so would jeopardise the chances of Katie's discovery. She had to remain positive, certain they'd find her.

'Jenna, be reasonable.'

'Nothing's happened to Katie! I'm her mother! I'd know, I'd feel it in here, if she was gone.'

She raised her hands and beat her fists against Adam's chest, each blow thudding uselessly against his breastbone. He stood, taking the brunt of her attack, at first not attempting to fend her off. After a few seconds he grabbed her wrists and held them. She stared at him, scarcely registering the exhaustion in his own eyes. 'Just go,' she cried. 'Go back out there and find my daughter.'

He released her and she stepped out onto the verandah. The air was no cooler there, but the sounds from the camp were louder. Her hands were shaking and she put them under her armpits, willing them still. Discordant thoughts raced through her mind. *Katie's dead! No, she's alive! Adam's wrong. He* has *to be.*

Frantically she paced back and forth, to and fro, each time trying to avoid stepping on the loose board that gave a loud creak. Through the open windows she could hear Adam inside, talking to Aleyne, who had stayed back to keep her company. She heard the occasional word.

'Baby.'

'Worried.'

'No use.'

Were they talking about her?

Shortly, Aleyne came to the door and asked her if she wanted something to eat. Jenna waved her away. She didn't want to be distracted. If she kept on thinking about Katie, if she focused on the fact that her daughter would be found alive and well, then soon this terrible nightmare would be over and they'd be together again as a family. The alternative was untenable.

'You must eat, Missy,' Aleyne admonished. 'Think of the baby.'

'I'm thinking about Katie!' Jenna rounded on her. 'She's the one who's important now.'

Later, when the house lay quiet, she stood in the doorway to Katie's room. It was all darkness and shadows in there. The sheer curtain billowed inwards and the lamp's flame swayed in the sudden gust of wind, sending the shadows scurrying back into the corners.

The room seemed expectant, waiting. Just as Katie had left it that day when she'd slipped from her bed and walked out into the storm. The cover on the bed was turned back, the sheets slightly wrinkled. Above the bed, her dolls sat on a shelf, their frozen faces turned towards her. Through her tears, Jenna saw that one had a garish smile on its face, a pink slash where its mouth should be.

She placed the lamp on the dresser and walked slowly to the bed. Katie's pillow still held the indent of her head. Slowly Jenna picked it up and pressed it to her face, trying to capture the last scent of her. When she brought it away, the fabric was wet with her tears.

She moved to the window and stared out through the open curtains. In the moonlight, nothing moved. She could see the shape of the pepper trees standing sentinel at the front fence near the gate. Savagely she pulled the curtains across then walked backwards until she came up hard against the wall.

She felt the strength leave her legs. They were shaking, refusing to support her. Slowly she let herself slide down the wall until she was sitting on the floor, the child a hard wedge under her ribs. The tears came then, hard and furious.

On and on she sobbed, until she could cry no more.

CHAPTER 31

During the days that followed, Jenna began to blame herself. The thoughts, the reasons, all followed the same convoluted path, leading back to her own stupidity. If only she hadn't fallen asleep that afternoon. If only she'd found that Katie was missing earlier. If she hadn't been pregnant then maybe she wouldn't have been so tired.

If, if, if . . .

The idea occurred to her that perhaps she was being punished. For having sex with Conor before they were married. For not loving Adam as a wife should. For allowing Katie to wander away and become lost in that seemingly endless array of channels and dry creek beds.

She felt constantly nauseous and fragmented, as if parts of her were peeling away like the layers of an onion. Soon all that would be left would be the raw inner core of her.

'I can't believe she's dead,' she told Adam. 'I don't *want* to believe it, because if she is then life is all so pointless and —'

Adam clasped his hands around hers and said, 'Jenna, *please*,' in a tone of such anguish that it brought tears to her eyes, just when she'd thought she could cry no more.

'Katie was just a little girl. She never hurt anyone.'

'You can't keep blaming yourself. It wasn't your fault!'

'It was! I know it was! Michael, and now Katie. If I hadn't been sleeping, if I'd kept better watch over her ...'

'Some things are meant to be, have you ever thought of that? God —'

She threw her hands up in a motion of defeat. 'What sort of a *God* would do this?'

Aleyne, Lalla and Ngayla came to the house with a mixture of gypsum and mud paste smeared on their faces. It was, she knew, a native custom when in mourning. Jenna promptly ordered them to scrub it off.

'But this *our* way!' Aleyne protested.

'My daughter isn't dead, so how dare you wear that on your face!'

'Jenna, you're tired and upset,' said Adam, trying to calm her as he steered her away from the kitchen. 'They mean well. Let it go.'

Adam kept searching, long after he knew there was no way they'd find Katie alive. He tried to anticipate where she might have gone, in which direction, but always his mind came back to the dust storm — she'd have lost her way whatever route she'd taken. Besides, there was no knowing what sort of a start